"I need to apologize, Jacob..."

Hannah glanced up at Jacob, and then away <del>yesterday, and I'm very sorry. I know better than to speak let alone to someone who is being kind to us."</del>

"It's my fault. I stuck my nose where it didn't belong."

Now she laughed outright. "Perhaps you did, but it was probably something I needed to hear."

"Apology accepted."

"*Danki.*"

"*Gem gschene.*" The age-old words felt curiously intimate, shared there on the bench with the sun slanting through golden trees.

"It's a fine line," Hannah said. "Giving him the extra attention and care his condition requires, but not being overly protective. I'm afraid I'm still learning."

"You're doing a *wunderbar* job."

Which caused her to smile again, and then suddenly the tension that had been between them was gone.

He realized that what Hannah was offering with her apology was a precious thing—her friendship.

For now, he needed to be satisfied with that.

VANNETTA CHAPMAN
& JO ANN BROWN

Amish Beginnings

Previously published as *A Widow's Hope* and *His Amish Sweetheart*

LOVE INSPIRED
INSPIRATIONAL ROMANCE

LOVE INSPIRED®
INSPIRATIONAL ROMANCE

Recycling programs
for this product may
not exist in your area.

ISBN-13: 978-1-335-98486-9

Amish Beginnings

Copyright © 2020 by Harlequin Books S.A.

A Widow's Hope
First published in 2018. This edition published in 2020.
Copyright © 2018 by Vannetta Chapman

His Amish Sweetheart
First published in 2016. This edition published in 2020.
Copyright © 2016 by Jo Ann Ferguson

This edition published by arrangement with Harlequin Books S.A.

For questions and comments about the quality of this book, please contact us at CustomerService@Harlequin.com.

Love Inspired
22 Adelaide St. West, 40th Floor
Toronto, Ontario M5H 4E3, Canada
www.Harlequin.com

Printed in U.S.A.

CONTENTS

A WIDOW'S HOPE

Vannetta Chapman

This book is dedicated to JoAnn King,
who has recently become an avid reader. JoAnn, you're a constant
source of encouragement and joy. Thank you for your friendship.

Acknowledgments

I would like to thank Melissa Endlich for inviting me
to join the wonderful group of authors at Harlequin/Love Inspired.
I'd also like to thank my fellow LI authors who have willingly
answered questions, explained procedures and offered guidance.
Thank you to Steve Laube for overseeing my career.

And a big thanks of gratitude to my husband, Bob,
for getting up at first-bark and taking care of pets, laundry,
grocery shopping, cooking and the countless other things
that I neglect because I'm squirreled away in my office.

And finally, "Giving thanks always for all things unto God and the
Father in the name of our Lord Jesus Christ" (*Ephesians* 5:20).

And we know that all things work together
for good to them that love God.
—*Romans* 8:28

The Lord hath heard my supplication;
the Lord will receive my prayer.
—*Psalms* 6:9

Chapter One

Monday mornings were never easy. Though Hannah King heard her four-year-old son calling, she longed to bury her head under the covers and let her mother take care of him. She'd had a dream about David. It had been so real—David kissing her on their wedding day, David standing beside her as she cradled their newborn son, David moving about the room quietly as he prepared for work.

But he wasn't in the room with her, and he never would be again. A late-summer breeze stirred the window shade. In the distance she could hear the clip-clop of horses on the two-lane, a rooster's crow, the low of a cow. Summer would be over soon. Here in northern Indiana, where she'd grown up, September was met with a full schedule of fall festivals and pumpkin trails and harvest celebrations. She dreaded it all—had no desire to walk through the bright leaves, or decorate with pumpkins or bake apple pies. Fall had been David's favorite time of year. Matthew was born in September. The accident? It had occurred the last week of August. That terrible anniversary was one week away.

This year, the thought of autumn overwhelmed her. Her entire life left her feeling tired and unable to cope. She was happy to be home with her parents, but she hadn't realized the extent of their financial troubles until she'd already moved in. Their church in Wisconsin had used money from the benevolence fund to pay for Matthew's surgeries, but her parents had paid for all of his rehab from their savings. Now they were operating month-to-month, and the stress was beginning to show. She needed to find a job, to help them with the bills, but how could she work when her primary responsibility was to care for Matthew?

She should at least make an attempt to find employment, but she wanted and needed to be home with her son. If she were honest with herself, she dreaded the thought of interacting with other people on a daily basis. She hadn't enough energy for that.

Hannah pushed off the bedcovers, slipped her feet into a pair of worn house shoes and hurried to the room next door as her mother stepped into the hall.

"I can take care of him if you like."

"*Nein.* I'm awake."

She should have said more, should have thanked her mother, but the memory of David was too heavy on her heart, her emotions too raw. So instead she quickly glanced away and opened the door to Matthew's room.

Though her son was four years old, soon to be five, he still slept in a bed with rails along the side. This was mainly to keep him from falling out.

The thinnest sliver of morning light shone through the gap between the window and the shade, fell across the room and landed on little Matthew. He was lying on his back, his legs splayed out in front of him. Matthew smiled and raised his arms to her, but instead of picking him up, Hannah lowered the wooden rail that her *dat* had fastened to the bed and sat beside him. Matthew struggled to a sitting position and pulled himself into her lap. For a four-year-old, his arms were incredibly strong, probably to make up for the fact that his legs were useless.

"*Gudemariye, Mamm.*" The Pennsylvania Dutch rolled off his tongue, thick with sleep.

"Good morning to you, Matthew."

He reached up and touched her face, patted her cheek, then snuggled in closer.

She gave him a few minutes. Long ago, she'd learned that Matthew needed time to wake up, to adjust to the world. When he was ready, he said, "Potty?"

"Sure thing, Matt."

But before she could pick him up, her father was standing in the doorway. No doubt he'd been awake for hours, and he carried into the room the familiar smells of the barn— hay, horses and even a little manure. It was an earthy smell that Hannah never tired of.

"I thought I heard young Matthew awake."

"*Daddi!*" Matthew squirmed out of her lap and launched himself at her father, who caught him with a smile and carried him into the bathroom across the hall. She could hear them there, laughing and talking about the upcoming day.

Hannah slipped back into her room, changed into a plain gray dress, black apron and white *kapp*. Once dressed, she hurried to the kitchen. If she'd thought she could help her mother make breakfast, she was sadly mistaken.

Steam rose from the platter of fresh biscuits on the table. Another dish held crisp bacon, and her mother was scooping scrambled eggs into a large bowl. Hannah fetched the butter and jam, set them in the middle of the table and then gladly accepted the mug of coffee her mother pushed into her hands.

"Did you sleep well?"

Hannah shrugged, not wanting to talk about it. Then she remembered her bishop's admonition to speak of her feelings more, to resist the urge to let them bottle up inside. Easy enough for him to say. His spouse was still alive and his children did not struggle with a disability. It was an uncharitable thought and added to her guilt.

She sipped the coffee and said, "I fall asleep easily enough, but then I wake after a few hours and can't seem to go back to sleep, no matter how tired I am."

"Normal enough for a woman in mourning."

"It's been nearly a year."

"Grieving takes a different amount of time for different people, Hannah."

"I suppose."

Her mother sat down beside her, reached for her hands.

"Did you have the dream again?"

"*Ya.*" Hannah blinked away hot tears. She would not cry before breakfast. She would not. "How did you know?"

Instead of answering, her mother planted a kiss on her forehead, making her feel six instead of twenty-six. Then she popped up and walked back across the kitchen, checking that she hadn't forgotten anything they might need for breakfast. Holding up the coffeepot, she asked Hannah's father and son, "Coffee for both of you?"

"*Mammi.* I drink milk."

Matthew's laughter lightened the mood. Her father's steadiness calmed her nerves. Her mother's presence was always a balm to her soul.

The first week she was home, her dad had insisted on learning how to care for Matthew, how to help him into his wheelchair. Now Hannah turned to see her father and son, her father standing in the doorway to the kitchen, his hands on the back of Matthew's wheelchair. Both looked quite pleased with themselves and ready to tackle whatever the day might bring.

Jacob Schrock didn't need to hire a driver for the day's job. Though the Beiler home was technically in a different church district, in reality they were only a few miles apart. That's the way things were in Goshen, Indiana. There were so many Amish that his own district had recently divided again because they had too many families to fit into one home or barn for church.

Theirs was a good, healthy community. A growing community.

Which was one of the reasons that Jacob had plenty of work.

The night before, he'd loaded the tools he would need into the cargo box fastened on the back of his buggy. The lumber would be delivered to the job site before lunch.

Bo stood stamping his foot and tossing his head as if to ask what was taking so long. Jacob hitched the black gelding to the buggy, glanced back at his house and workshop and then set off down the road. As he directed the horse down Goshen's busy two-lane road, his mind raked back over the letter he'd received from the IRS. How was he going to deal with the upcoming audit and complete the jobs he had contracted at the same time? The accountant he'd contacted had named a quite high hourly rate. The man had also said he'd need a thousand-dollar retainer in order to start the job. Jacob had given serious thought to hiring the accounting firm in spite of their high fees, but in truth he didn't make enough money to afford that.

Jacob had asked around his church, but no one who was

qualified had been interested in accounting work. The one young girl who had expressed an interest had quit the first day, and who could blame her? Jacob's idea of filing consisted of giant plastic bins where he tossed receipts.

Jacob loved working for himself, by himself. He'd rather not have anyone in his small office. The bulk of his income came from residential jobs and a few small business contracts, but his heart and soul were invested in building playhouses for children with disabilities. He needed to juggle both, and now, on top of that, he needed to prepare for the audit.

Twenty minutes later he pulled into the Beilers' drive. It wasn't a home he'd ever been to before; that much he was sure of.

Jacob parked the buggy, patted Bo and assured him, "Back in a minute to put you in the field. Be patient." Bo was a fine buggy horse, if a little spirited. Jacob had purchased him six months before. The horse was strong and good-tempered. Unfortunately he was not patient. He'd been known to chew his lead rope, eat anything in sight and paw holes into the ground. He did not handle boredom well.

Grabbing his tool belt and folder with design plans, Jacob hesitated before heading to the front door. This was always the hardest part for him—initially meeting someone. His left hand automatically went to his face, traced the web of scar tissue that stretched from his temple to his chin. He wasn't a prideful man, but neither did he wish to scare anyone.

There was nothing he could do about his appearance, though, so he pulled in a deep breath, said a final word to the horse and hurried to the front door. He knocked, waited and then stood there staring when a young, beautiful woman opened the door. She stood about five and a half feet tall. Chestnut-colored hair peeked out from her *kapp*. It

matched her warm brown eyes and the sprinkling of freckles on her cheeks.

There was something familiar about her. He nearly
smacked himself on the forehead. Of course she looked familiar, though it had been years since he'd seen her.

"Hannah? Hannah Beiler?"

"Hannah King." She quickly scanned him head to toe. Her
gaze darted to the left side of his face and then refocused on
his eyes. She frowned and said, "I'm Hannah King."

"But…isn't this the Beiler home?"

"*Ya.* Wait. Aren't you Jacob? Jacob Schrock?"

He nearly laughed at the expression of puzzlement on
her face.

"The same, and I'm looking for the Beiler place."

"*Ya,* this is my parents' home, but why are you here?"

"To work." He stared down at the work order as if he
could make sense of seeing the first girl he'd ever kissed
standing on the doorstep of the place he was supposed to
be working.

"I don't understand," he said.

"Neither do I. Who are you looking for?"

"Alton Beiler."

"But that's my father. Why—"

At that point Mr. Beiler joined them, telling Hannah he
would take care of their visitor and shaking Jacob's hand.
Surely he noticed the scar on Jacob's face, but he didn't dwell
on it. "You're at the right house, Jacob. Please, come inside."

"Why would he come inside?" Hannah had crossed her
arms and was frowning at him now.

He'd never have guessed when he put on his suspenders
that morning that he would be seeing Hannah Beiler before
the sun was properly up. The same Hannah Beiler he had
once kissed behind the playground and several years later

asked out for a buggy ride and dinner. It had been a disastrous date for sure, but still he remembered it with fondness. The question was, what was she doing here?

But then he peered more closely at Alton. Yes, it was Hannah's father for sure and certain. Older, grayer and with wrinkles lining his face, but still her father.

"I haven't seen you in years," Jacob said to Alton.

"Do we know each other?"

"Barely." Jacob chuckled, though Hannah continued to glare at him. "Hannah and I went on a date many years ago."

"It was hardly a date," Hannah chimed in.

"I took you in my buggy."

"Which hadn't been properly cleaned, and your horse was lame."

"I should have checked the horse more carefully."

"We never even made it to dinner."

"I'm surprised you remember."

"And I had to walk home."

"I offered to walk with you."

Hannah rolled her eyes, shook her head and headed back into the house.

"She hasn't changed much," Jacob said in a lower voice.

"Oh, but she has." Alton opened the door wider so that Jacob would come in. "I'm sorry I didn't recognize you."

"It has been ten years."

They passed through a living room that appeared to be sparsely but comfortably furnished. Jacob could smell bacon and biscuits. His stomach grumbled and he instantly regretted that he hadn't taken the time to eat a proper breakfast.

"So your dating Hannah must have been when we were at the other place, on the east side of the district."

"Indeed."

"Obviously we've moved since then." Alton stopped before entering the kitchen, seemed about to say something and then rubbed at the back of his neck and ushered Jacob into the room.

"Claire, maybe you remember Jacob Schrock. Apparently he took our Hannah on a buggy ride once."

Jacob heard them, but his attention was on the young boy sitting at the table. He was young—probably not school-age yet. Brown hair flopped into his eyes and he had the same smattering of freckles as his mother. He sat in a regular kitchen chair, which was slightly higher than the wheelchair parked behind him. No doubt moving back and forth was cumbersome. If he had a small ramp, the chair could be rolled up and locked into place. He should talk to Alton about that. It would be easy enough to create from scrap lumber.

Hannah was helping the child with his breakfast, or perhaps she was merely avoiding Jacob's gaze.

The boy, though, had no problem with staring. He cocked his head to the side, as if trying to puzzle through what he saw of Jacob. Then a smile won out over any questions, and he said, *"Gudemariye."*

"And to you," Jacob replied.

Hannah's mother, Claire, motioned him toward a seat. "Of course I remember you, Jacob. Though you've grown since then."

"Ya, I was a bit of a skinny lad." This was the awkward part. He never knew if he should share the cause of his scars or wait for someone to ask. With the child in the room, perhaps it would be better to wait.

Hannah continued to ignore him, but now the boy was watching him closely, curiously.

"You're taller too, if I remember right. You were definitely not as tall as Alton when you were a *youngie*. Now you're a good six feet, I'd guess."

"Six feet and two inches. My *mamm* used to say I had growth spurts up until I turned twenty." Jacob accepted a mug of coffee and sat down across the table from the boy.

"Who are you?" he asked.

"I'm Jacob. What's your name?"

"Matthew. This is *Mamm*, and that's *Mammi* and *Daddi*. We're a family now." Matthew grinned as if he'd said the most clever thing.

Hannah met Jacob's gaze and blushed, but this time she didn't look away.

"It's really nice to meet you, Matthew. I'm going to be working here for a few days."

"Working on what?"

Jacob glanced at Alton, who nodded once. "I'm going to build you a playhouse."

Hannah heard the conversation going on around her, but she felt as if she'd fallen into the creek and her ears were clogged with water. She heard it all from a distance. Then Matthew smiled that smile that changed the shape of his eyes. It caused his cheeks to dimple. It was a simple thing that never failed to reach all the way into her heart.

And suddenly Hannah's hearing worked just fine.

"A playhouse? For me?"

"For sure and certain."

"How come?"

Jacob shrugged and waited for Alton to answer the child.

"Some nice people want you to have one."

"Oh. Cool."

"*Dat*, we can't…"

"We most certainly can, Hannah. The charity foundation contacted me last week to make sure it was all right, and I said yes. I think it would be a fine thing for Matthew to have."

"Will I be able to move around in a playhouse? Like, with my wheelchair?"

"You most certainly will," Jacob assured him.

"You're sure?"

"I'm positive."

"Because it don't always fit good. Not in cars or on merry-go-rounds. Sometimes not even in buggies and we have to tie it on the back."

"Your chair will fit in your playhouse. I can promise you that."

Matthew laughed and stabbed his biscuit with his fork, dipped it in a puddle of syrup he'd poured on his plate and stuffed the gooey mess into his mouth.

Hannah's head was spinning. Surely it was a good and gracious thing that someone had commissioned a playhouse for Matthew, but would it be safe for him to play in one? What if he fell out of his chair? What if he rolled out of the playhouse?

How could her father agree to such a thing?

And why was it being built by Jacob Schrock? She hadn't thought about him in years, certainly hadn't expected to see him again. Why today of all days, when her heart was sore from dreaming of David? Why this morning?

"Can I help?" Matthew asked.

"Oh, no." Hannah abandoned her future worries and focused on the problems at hand. "You'll leave that to Jacob."

"But *Mamm*…"

"We can't risk your getting hurt."

"I'll be super careful…"

"And you'd only be in Jacob's way."

Matthew stabbed another piece of biscuit and swirled it into the syrup, but he didn't plop it in his mouth. Instead he stared at the food, worried his bottom lip and hunched up his shoulders. Her son's bullheadedness had been quite useful during his initial recovery. When the doctors had said he probably couldn't do a thing, Matthew had buckled down, concentrated and found a way. There were days, though, when she wondered why *Gotte* had given her such a strong-willed child.

Jacob had drunk half his coffee and accepted a plate of eggs and bacon, which he'd consumed rather quickly. Now he sat rubbing his hand up and down his jaw, his clean-shaven jaw. The right side—the unscarred side. Was the injury the reason he'd never married? Was he embarrassed about the scar? Did women avoid him? Not that it was her business, and she'd certainly never ask.

"I just wanted to help," Matthew muttered.

"Now that you mention it, I could use an apprentice."

"I could be a *'rentice*." Matthew nodded his head so hard his hair flopped forward into his eyes, reminding Hannah that she would need to cut it again soon.

"It's hard work," Jacob cautioned.

"I can work hard."

"You sure?"

"Tell him, *Mamm*. Tell him how hard I work at the center."

"You'd have to hand me nails, tools, that sort of thing."

"I can do that!" Matthew was rocking in his chair now, and Hannah was wise enough to know the battle was lost.

"Only if your *mamm* agrees, of course."

She skewered him with a look. Certainly he knew that he'd backed her into an impossible corner. Instead of arguing, she smiled sweetly and said, "If your *daddi* thinks it's okay."

Hannah's father readily agreed and then Jacob was pulling out sheets of drawings that showed a playhouse in the shape of a train, with extra-wide doors—doors wide enough for

Matthew's chair, room to pivot the chair, room to play. How could she not want such a thing for her child? The penciled playhouse looked like the stuff of fairy tales.

When she glanced up at Jacob, he smiled and said in a low voice, "We'll be extra careful."

"I should hope so."

And then she stood and began to clear off the dishes. The last thing she needed to do was stand around staring into Jacob Schrock's deep blue eyes. A better use of her time would be to go to town and pick up the Monday paper so she could study the Help Wanted ads. It looked like that wasn't going to happen. There was no way she was leaving Matthew outside, working as an apprentice to a man who had no children of his own. She'd come home to find he'd nailed his thumb to a piece of wood, or cut himself sawing a piece of lumber, or fallen and cracked something open. Secondary infections were no laughing matter for a child who was a paraplegic.

She'd be spending the morning watching Matthew watch Jacob. As soon as he left for the day, she'd head to town because one way or another, she needed to find a job.

Chapter Two

Hannah pushed aside her unsettled feelings and worked her way through the morning. She managed to complete the washing and hang it up on the line, and she helped her mother to put lunch on the table, all the while keeping a close eye on what was happening in the backyard.

When it was time for lunch, Matthew came in proclaiming he was an "official 'rentice now," and Jacob followed behind him with a sheepish look on his face.

Her father joined them for the noon meal. Earlier, he had stayed around long enough to confirm where the playhouse would be built and then he'd headed off to the fields. It worried her sometimes, her father being fifty-two and still working behind a team of horses, but her mother only scoffed at that. "What is he supposed to do? Sit in a rocking chair? Your father is as healthy as the bull in the north pasture, and if it's *Gotte's wille*, he'll stay that way for many more years."

The meal had passed pleasantly enough, though Hannah

didn't like how enamored Matthew was with Jacob Schrock. They laughed and described their morning's work and talked of trains as if they'd been on one.

"There's a place in town called Tender Jim's." Jacob reached for another helping of potato salad. "Have you heard of it, Matthew?"

Matthew stuffed a potato chip into his mouth and shook his head.

"Down on Danbury Drive. Isn't it?" Her father sat back, holding his glass of tea with one hand and pulling on his beard with the other. "Nice *Englisch* fellow."

"And what were you doing in Tender Jim's?" Claire asked.

"Curious, mostly. I'd taken Dolly to the farrier and had to wait a bit longer than I thought I would. Wandered down and talked to the fellow."

"Did he have trains?" Matthew asked.

"Oh, *ya*. Certainly, he did. Small ones and large ones."

"As large as my playhouse?"

"*Nein*. They were toys."

"Perhaps we could go by and see them sometime," Jacob said.

Hannah jumped up as if she'd been stung by a bee. "Matthew has a full week planned with his physical therapy appointments and all, but *danki* for the offer."

This was exactly why she didn't want a man like Jacob around—or any man for that matter. They'd raise her son's hopes, promise him things they wouldn't deliver and then disappear one day when they realized that Matthew was never going to walk, never going to be normal.

She pretended to be occupied with putting things up in the refrigerator as Jacob, her father and Matthew went out to look at the "job site." Her job was to protect Matthew— from strangers who would pretend to be friends, and from upheaval in his life. Which reminded her that she still hadn't been to town to purchase a newspaper.

She needed to stop worrying, which was easier said than done. Jacob would be finished with the playhouse in a day or two and then Matthew wouldn't see him anymore. Didn't Jacob mention that he was part of a different church district? She hadn't been home long enough to sort the districts out, but she did know there were a lot of Amish in the area. It would explain why she hadn't seen him at church.

Hannah and her mother cleared away the lunch dishes and put together a casserole for dinner and then her mother sat at the table. Hannah continued to peer out the window. What were they doing out there? How could Matthew possibly be helping? Why would Jacob want him to?

"Come sit down a minute, Hannah."

"But—"

"Come on, now. You've been on your feet all morning."

Hannah peeked out the window one last time, then walked to the table and sank into one of the chairs. *Mamm* was putting the finishing touches on a baby quilt for a new mother in their congregation.

Hannah had to force her eyes away from the pastel fabric and the Sunbonnet Sue and Overall Sam pattern. Her mother had given her a similar quilt when Matthew was born. When Hannah had first wrapped her son in that quilt, she'd trusted that only good things would happen in their future. She'd hoped that one day she would wrap her daughter in the same quilt. Now such beliefs didn't come so easily.

"I know you wanted today's paper, but last week's is still next to your father's chair in the sitting room."

"How did you know I wanted a paper?"

"Matthew told me you mentioned it."

Had she told Matthew?

Abandoning any attempt to figure out how her mother knew things, Hannah fetched a highlighter from a kitchen drawer and the newspaper from the sitting room, folded it open to the Help Wanted section and sat down with a sigh.

"I wish you wouldn't worry about that."

"But we need the money."

"*Gotte* will provide, Hannah."

"Maybe He's providing through one of these ads."

The next twenty minutes passed in silence as Hannah's mood plummeted even lower. The part-time positions paid too little and the full-time positions would require her to be away from home from sunup to sundown, if she could even get one of the positions, which was doubtful since she had no experience. She could always be a waitress at one of the Amish restaurants, but those positions were usually filled by younger girls—girls who hadn't yet married, who had no children.

"He's nice. Don't you think?"

"Who?"

"You know who."

"I don't know who."

"We sound like the owl in the barn."

Hannah smiled at her mother and slapped the newspaper shut. "Okay. I probably know who."

"I guess you were surprised to see him at the door."

"Indeed I was." Hannah should have kept her mouth shut, but she couldn't resist asking, "Do you know what happened to him? To his face?"

"A fire, no doubt." Her mother rocked the needle back and forth, tracing the outline of a Sunbonnet Sue. "We've had several homes destroyed over the years, and always there are injuries. Once or twice the fire was a result of carelessness. I think there was even one caused by lightning."

"A shame," Hannah whispered.

"That he had to endure such pain—yes. I'll agree with that. It doesn't change who he is, though, or his value as a person."

"I never said—"

"You, more than anyone else, should realize that."

"Of course I do."

"You wouldn't want anyone looking at Matthew and seeing a child with a disability. That's not who he is. That's just evidence of something he's endured."

"There's no need to lecture me, *Mamm*."

"Of course there isn't." She rotated the quilt and continued outlining the appliqué. "I can see that Jacob is self-conscious about his scars, though. I hate to think that anyone has been unkind to him."

"His scars don't seem to be affecting Matthew's opinion. He looks at Jacob as if he had raised a barn single-handedly."

"*Gotte* has a funny way of putting people in our life right when we need them."

"I'm not sure this was *Gotte*'s work."

"I know you don't mean that. I raised you to have more faith, Hannah. The last year has been hard, *ya*, I know, but never doubt that *Gotte* is still guiding your life."

Instead of arguing, Hannah opted to pursue a lighter subject. "So *Gotte* sent Jacob to build my son a playhouse?"

"Maybe."

She nearly laughed. Her mother's optimism grated on her nerves at times, but Hannah appreciated and loved her more than she could ever say. *Mamm* had been her port in the storm. Or perhaps *Gotte* had been, and *Mamm* had simply nudged her in the correct direction.

"You have to admit he's easy on the eyes."

"Is that how you older women describe a handsome man?"

"So you think he's *gut*-looking?"

"That's not what I said, *Mamm*."

Claire tied off her thread, popped it through the back of the quilt and then rethreaded her needle. "Tell me about this first date you two had, because I can hardly remember it."

"Small wonder. I was only sixteen."

"*Ya?* Already out of school, then."

"I was. In fact, I was working at the deli counter in town."

"I remember that job. You always brought home the left-over sandwiches."

"Jacob and I attended the same school, in the old district when we lived on Jackspur Lane. He's two years older than me."

"I'm surprised I don't remember your stepping out with him."

"Our house was quite busy then." Hannah was the youngest of three girls. She'd always expected her life to follow their fairy-tale existence. "Beth had just announced her plans to marry Carl, and Sharon was working with the midwife."

"I do remember that summer. I thought things would get easier when you three were out of school, but suddenly I had trouble keeping up with everyone."

"The date with Jacob, it was only my second or third, and I was still expecting something like I read in the romance books."

Her mother tsked.

"They were Christian romance, *Mamm*."

"I'm guessing your date with Jacob didn't match with what you'd been reading."

"Hardly. First of all, he showed up with mud splattered all over the buggy, and the inside of it was filled with pieces of hay and fast-food wrappers and even a pair of dirty socks."

"Didn't he have older brothers?"

"He had one."

"So I guess they shared the buggy."

Hannah shrugged. "We'd barely made it a quarter mile down the road when we both noticed his horse was limping."

"Oh my."

"It was no big thing. He jumped out of the buggy and began to clean out her hooves with a pick."

"While you waited."

"At first. Then I decided to help, which he told me in no short fashion not to do."

"There are times when it's hard for a man, especially a young man, to accept a woman's help."

"I waited about ten minutes and finally said I was heading home."

"Changed your mind before you were even out of sight of the house."

"Maybe. What I knew for sure was that I didn't want to stand on the side of the road while Jacob Schrock took care of his horse—something he should have done before picking me up."

"Could have been his brother's doing."

"I suppose."

"I hope you didn't judge him harshly because of a dirty buggy and a lame horse."

"Actually, I don't think I judged him at all. I simply realized that I didn't want to spend the evening with him."

"Well, he seems to have turned into a fine young man."

Hannah refolded the newspaper and pointed her highlighter at her mother. "Tell me you are not matchmaking."

"Why would I do such a thing?"

"Exactly."

"Though I did help both of your sisters find their husbands."

"I need a job, *Mamm*. I don't need a husband. I have a son, I have a family and I have a home. I'm fine without Jacob

Schrock or any other man." Before her mother could see how rattled she was, Hannah jumped up, stepped over to the window and stared out at Jacob and Matthew.

"At least you parted friends…or so it seems."

Hannah suddenly remembered Jacob kissing her behind the swing set at school. It had been her first kiss, and a bit of a mess. He'd leaned in, a bee had buzzed past her and she'd darted to the right at the last minute. The result was a kiss on the left side of her *kapp*. She'd been mortified, though Jacob had laughed good-naturedly, then reached for her hand and walked her back into the school building. It was three years later when he'd asked her out on the buggy ride.

Remembering the kiss, Hannah felt the heat crawl up her neck. Before her mother could interrogate her further, she busied herself pulling two glasses from the cabinet and said, "Perhaps I should take both of the workers something to drink."

She filled the glasses with lemonade, snagged half a dozen of her mother's oatmeal cookies, put it all on a tray and carried it outside.

After setting it down on the picnic table under the tall maple tree, she turned to watch Jacob and Matthew. In spite of her resolution to maintain a safe distance from Jacob Schrock, her heart tripped a beat at the sight of him.

Which made no sense, because Jacob Schrock was not her type.

He was eight inches taller than she was, whereas David had been her height exactly.

He was blond. David had been dark haired.

His eyes were blue, and David's had been a lovely brown.

Nothing about the man standing near her son appealed to her, least of all the suggestion that he knew what was good for Matthew.

She couldn't help noticing, though…

The sleeves of his blue shirt were rolled up past the elbow, revealing his muscular, tanned arms.

Sweat gleamed on his forehead and caused his blond hair to curl slightly.

As she watched, he handed one end of a tape measure to Matthew, stepped off what was apparently the length of the project and pushed a stake into the ground.

When he was done, Jacob glanced up, noticed her waiting and smiled. Now, why did his smile cause her heart to race even faster? Perhaps she needed to see a doctor. Maybe the depression that had pressed down on her like a dark cloud for so long had finally taken its toll on her heart. Or maybe she was experiencing a normal reaction to a nice-looking man doing a kind deed.

Of course, he was getting paid for it.

But he didn't have to allow Matthew to tag along.

He certainly didn't have to smile at her every time she was near.

Jacob stored the tape measure they were using in a tool belt and said something to Matthew. When her son twisted in his wheelchair to look at her, she had to press her fingers to her lips. Yes, he still sat in his chair, but he looked like a completely different boy. He had rolled up his sleeves, sweat had plastered his hair to his head and a smear of dirt marked his cheek. When he caught her watching, he beamed at her as if it were Christmas Day.

In short, he looked like a normal child having a great time building a playhouse.

Jacob glanced back at Hannah in time to catch her staring at Matthew, the fingers of her right hand pressed against her lips. Jacob considered himself open to beauty. Maybe because of his own disfigurement, he found contentment in noticing *Gotte*'s handiwork elsewhere.

He'd often stood and watched the sunset, thinking that *Gotte* had done a wonderful thing by providing them such splendor. He'd helped his brother when it was time for birthing in the spring: goats, horses, cows, and once when a terrible storm came through and they couldn't get to the hospital—a son. Jacob didn't mind that such things brought him to tears, that he often had to pause and catch his breath, that he was sensitive to the joys of this world.

But when he looked up and saw Hannah, an unfamiliar emotion brushed against the inside of his heart. It couldn't be attraction, as he'd never asked a woman out on a date because of how she looked—not before the fire and not since. He hadn't asked a woman out in years, and he wouldn't be starting today. As for her personality, well, if he were to be honest with himself, she was pushy, obviously overprotective of her son and taciturn to the point of being rude.

She was beautiful, though, and more than that, her obvious love for her son was moving. Her vulnerability in that moment reached deep into his soul and affected him in a way he didn't realize he could be touched.

So he stooped down and said to Matthew, "Best take a break. Your *mamm* has brought us a snack."

He walked beside the boy as they made their way toward the picnic table.

"*Mamm*, I'm helping." Matthew reached for a cookie, broke it in half and stuffed the larger piece into his mouth.

"It appears you worked up an appetite."

Matthew nodded, and Jacob said, "We both did."

Hannah motioned for him to help himself. He popped a whole cookie into his mouth and said, "Wow," before he'd finished chewing. Which caused Matthew to dissolve in a fit of laughter.

"What–id I–ooh?" Jacob asked, exaggerating each syllable.

"You have to chew first," Matthew explained. "And swallow!"

Jacob did as instructed, took a big sip of the lemonade and then said, "*Danki*, Hannah. Hit the spot."

"Looks as if actual construction on this playhouse is slow getting started."

"Measure twice, cut once," Matthew explained.

"We've managed to mark off the dimensions and unload my tools."

"You brought all that lumber in your buggy?"

"*Nein*. The store in town delivered it. I guess you didn't hear the truck."

"I guess I didn't."

"It was this big," Matthew said, holding his arms out wide.

"The playhouse will go up quickly," Jacob assured her. "I'll begin the base of the structure today. The walls will go up tomorrow, and the roof and final details the third day."

"Kind of amazing that a child's toy takes so long to build." Hannah held up a hand and shook her head at the same time. "I did not mean that the way it sounded. It's only that when you consider we can build a barn in one day, it seems funny that a playhouse takes three."

"Sure, *ya*. But this isn't a barn, and, as you can see, young Matthew and I are the only workers."

"I'm going to help," Matthew exclaimed, reaching for another cookie.

Hannah's son was rambling on now, explaining that he could mark the wood before Jacob made the cut and hand him nails as he hammered.

"Wait a minute, Matt. We have therapy tomorrow."

"But—"

"*Nein.* Do not argue with me."

"*Ya*, but this is kind of therapy."

"What time is Matthew's appointment?" Jacob asked, recognizing the escalating disagreement for what it was. Hadn't he argued in the same way when he was a young lad? Maybe not over physical therapy appointments, but there was always something to pull him away from what he'd wanted to do—fishing, searching for frogs, climbing trees.

"Matthew is scheduled for therapy three afternoons a week—Tuesday, Wednesday and Friday."

"That's perfect, because I need help tomorrow morning."

Matthew and Hannah both swiveled to look at him.

"In the afternoon, I'll be doing other stuff that an apprentice isn't allowed to do. But the morning?" Jacob rubbed his hand up and down his jawline as if he needed to carefully consider what he was about to say. Finally he grinned and said, "Mornings will be perfect."

"Yes!" Matthew raised a hand for Jacob to high-five. "I gotta go inside and tell *Mammi*."

Without another word, he reversed the direction of his chair and wheeled toward the house.

"That was kind of you," Hannah said.

"Actually, he is a big help to me."

Instead of arguing, she again pressed her fingers to her lips. Was it so she could keep her emotions inside? Stop her words? Protect her feelings?

"It's only a little thing, Hannah. I'm happy to do it. It's plain to see that Matthew is a special young man."

She picked up the plate of cookies and stared down at it. "He never eats more than one cookie. In fact, he often passes on snacks and desserts. Today he ate two and drank a full glass of lemonade."

"Is that a problem?"

He thought she wouldn't answer. She glanced at him and then her gaze darted out over the area where construction had not yet begun. "The doctors said that the steroids might suppress his appetite, but that it was best to encourage him to eat more."

"And what purpose do the steroids serve?"

"They're supposed to decrease swelling around the spinal cord." She placed the plate on the tray and transferred the empty lemonade glasses to it, as well. "I'm sorry. I didn't mean to bore you with the details."

"Do I look bored?"

She sat on the picnic bench then, staring back toward the house, seemingly lost in her worries over Matthew. "The last thing we needed is him losing weight. Then there are the other complications…"

"Such as?"

"Children with spinal cord injuries often struggle with pneumonia and other breathing disorders. Secondary infections are always a worry—it's why I was afraid for him to help you. If he were to get a cut or take a nasty fall, it could spiral into something worse."

"It must be a lot for you to monitor."

"Matthew needs all his strength, even when it comes in the form of oatmeal cookies."

"I'd like to ask what happened, but I know from personal experience that sometimes you feel like sharing and sometimes you don't."

Hannah jerked her head up. She seemed to study his scars for a moment and then she nodded once. "It's true. Sometimes I want to talk about it, *need* to talk about it, but then other times…"

"I'm listening, if today is one of those days you want to talk."

She pulled in a deep breath and blew it out. "There's not

really that much to tell. David and I bought a farm in Wisconsin, after we were married. Life was difficult but *gut*. Matthew came along—a healthy baby boy. My husband was out harvesting, and Matthew was riding up on the bench seat with him. This was a year ago...one year next week."

"What happened?"

"There was a snake coiled in the grass. The work horse nearly stepped on it. He reared up, throwing both David and Matthew. David was killed instantly when the harvester rolled over him. I suppose because he was smaller, Matthew was thrown farther. Otherwise he would have been killed, as well."

"Instead he was injured."

"He suffered a complete spinal cord break."

"I'm so sorry."

Jacob allowed silence to fill the hurting places between them. Finally he asked, "Surgeries?"

"*Ya*—two. The first was for the initial diagnosis, to evaluate and stabilize the fractured backbone. The second was a follow-up to the first."

"And you had to handle it all alone."

"Of course I didn't." Now her chin came up and when she glanced at him, Jacob saw the old stubbornness in her eyes. "My church helped me, my sister came to stay awhile and then...then my parents suggested I move home."

"Family is *gut*."

"*Ya*, it is, except that our being here is a drain on them."

Jacob was unsure how to answer that. He didn't know Claire or Alton Beiler well, but he was certain they didn't consider Hannah and Matthew to be a drain. It was plain from the way they interacted that they wanted their daughter and grandson at home with them.

"I'm happy to have Matthew working with me, Hannah,

but only if it's okay with you. I promise to be very careful around him."

She didn't answer. Instead she nodded once, gathered up the tray and followed her son into the house.

Leaving Jacob standing in the afternoon sunshine, wondering what else he could do to lighten the burden she carried, wondering why it suddenly seemed so important for him to do so.

He needed to stay focused on his business, on making enough money to pay an accountant before the audit was due, on the other playhouses he would build after this. But instead, as he went back to work, he found himself thinking of a young boy with dirt smeared across his nose and a beautiful mother who was determined to keep others at arm's length.

Chapter Three

Hannah was grateful that she was busy the next morning.
Maybe it would take her mind off of finding a job, which
was becoming all she thought about. She'd spent an hour
before breakfast going over the Help Wanted ads once again,
but nothing new had appeared. There wasn't a single listing
that she felt qualified to do, and she doubted seriously that
anything new had been listed in the last few days. So instead
of obsessing over what she couldn't change, she focused on
helping her mother.

Tuesday was baking day. They mixed bread, kneaded
dough, baked cookies and prepared two cakes. The kitchen
was hot and steamy by the time they were finished. Her
mother sank into a chair and said, "You're a big help, Hannah. I wouldn't want to do all of this alone."

Of course, she wouldn't need so much if they weren't there.

And Hannah knew that her mother rarely baked alone.
Most weeks her niece Naomi came over to help. Still, the

compliment lightened her heart as she called to Matthew. She'd helped him change into clean clothes after lunch, and he had promised not to get dirty. Now he was sitting in his chair, watching out the window as Jacob raised the walls of his playhouse.

"Looks like a real train, huh?" her mother asked.

Hannah cocked her head left and then right. "Can't say as it does."

"To me it's plain as day."

"Which is all that matters." She reached out and mussed her son's hair. "We should get going so we won't be late."

They made it to the PT center in downtown Goshen twenty minutes before their appointment. For the next two hours, Hannah sat in the waiting room and crocheted, or attempted to. Her mind kept wandering and she'd find that she'd dropped a stitch and then she would have to pull out the row and start over. After an hour, she'd made very little progress on the blue shawl, so she decided to put it away and flip through some of the magazines.

The center served both Amish and *Englisch*, so the magazine selection was varied. There were copies of the *Budget*, but there were also copies of *National Geographic*, *Home & Garden* and even *People* magazine.

She reached for *Home & Garden*.

On the cover was a picture of a sprawling country home, with flowers blooming along the brick pavement that bordered the front of the house. Orange, yellow and maroon mums filled containers on the porch. Pink begonias hung from planters on either side of the door.

"It would be nice if life were like those pictures." Sally Lapp sat down beside her with a *harrumph* and a sigh. Sally was plump, gray and kind.

"How's Leroy?"

"*Gut.* I suppose. Ornery, if I were to be honest."

Sally reached into her bag and pulled out a giant ball of purple yarn and two knitting needles. She'd shared the previous week that she was expecting her forty-second grandchild, and they were all sure it would be a girl. If by some strange twist of fate it was a boy, she'd save the blanket for an auction and knit another in an appropriate shade of green or blue.

"Is Leroy able to get around any better?" Hannah asked.

"Old coot tried to move from the living room to the bedroom by himself, without his walker. I was outside harvesting some of the garden vegetables when he fell." She glanced over her cheater glasses at Hannah, but never slowed in her knitting. "Fell, bruised his hip and scared a year of life off of me."

"I'm so sorry."

"Not your fault, child. How's young Matthew?"

"*Gut.*" Hannah flipped through the magazine, too quickly to actually see anything on the pages.

"There's more you're not saying, which is fine. Some things we need to keep private, but take it from me—it's best to share when something is bothering you. Share with someone you can trust not to shout it to the nearest *Budget* scribe."

Hannah considered that for a moment. Maybe it would help to share her worries, especially with someone outside the family, and she could trust Sally to keep anything she said confidential.

"The Sunshine Foundation purchased supplies for a playhouse for Matthew—a special one, you know. It will have handicap rails and all."

"What a *wunderbaar* thing."

"And the National Spinal Cord Injury Association hired someone to build it."

"Even better. I know your father is very busy with his crops."

"Jacob Schrock showed up yesterday—to build the playhouse, which is in the shape of a train. I'm afraid that Matthew is fairly smitten with him."

Sally glanced at her once, but she didn't offer an opinion. She continued knitting, as if she were waiting for Hannah to say more. But Hannah didn't know what else to say. She didn't know why it bothered her so much that Matthew liked Jacob.

"I suppose I'm worried is all. I know Jacob will be done in a few days and then…most likely… Matthew won't see him anymore. I've tried to explain this, but Matthew doesn't listen. He prattles on about how he's Jacob's apprentice."

"It's natural for young boys Matthew's age to look up to their elders—your father, your brothers-in-law, the men in church."

"*Ya*. I know it is. But those are all people who are a constant presence in his life."

"Soon he will be in school," Sally continued. "I'm sure you realize that some teachers stay a long time, but others only last a year."

"I hadn't thought of that."

"Some people are in our lives permanently. Others? *Gotte* brings them to us for a short time."

Instead of answering, Hannah sighed.

Sally turned the baby blanket and began a row of purl stitches. They flowed seamlessly together with the knit stitches. The result was a pattern that looked as if it had been produced in an *Englisch* factory.

"Jacob Schrock, he's a *gut* man."

"Is he in your district?"

"He was, but we had to split recently. So many families. So many *grandkinner*."

"I went to school with him, but that was years ago."

"Before his accident, then."

"Ya." Hannah pulled the shawl she was supposed to be working on back out of her bag, but she didn't bother with hunting for the crochet needle.

"Terrible thing. Both of his parents were killed. The fire chief said the blaze was caused by a lightning strike. Jacob was out in the buggy when it happened. I heard that he saw the blaze from the road, ran into the burning house, and pulled out his *mamm* and his *dat*, but it was too late."

Hannah's hand went to her left cheek. "That's how he got the scars?"

"For sure and certain. He was in the hospital for a long time. The doctors wanted to do more surgeries…graft skin onto his face. They said that he would look as *gut* as new."

"So why didn't they?"

Sally shrugged. "He would still be a man who had lost his parents in a fire, who had endured unfathomable pain. Removing the scars from his face wouldn't have removed the scars from his heart."

"Yes, but—"

"Jacob decided not to have the additional surgeries. Our bishop would have allowed it, but Jacob said no. He said the money that had been donated should go to someone else."

"Kind of him."

"Ya, he is a kind man. He was also very depressed for…" Sally stared across the room, as if she were trying to count the years, to tally them into something that made sense. "For two, maybe three years. Rarely came to church. Kind of hid inside his house."

"What changed?" Hannah asked. "When did he start making playhouses?"

"I suppose the playhouse building started a few years ago. As to what changed, you'd have to ask Jacob."

"He seems happy enough now."

"Trouble finds us all from time to time. Now Jacob is dealing with this tax audit."

"Tax audit?"

"They're not saying he did anything wrong, mind you. Only that he'll have to produce ledgers and receipts."

"Can he?"

Sally grimaced as she again turned the blanket and began a new row of knit stitches. "My granddaughter tried to work for him. She lasted less than a day. Said that he'd apparently been paying his taxes based on some system he kept scribbled on random sheets of paper. Said she couldn't make any sense of it at all."

"Oh my."

"And the receipts? Thrown into bins with the year taped on the outside. A giant mess according to Abigail. Said she'd rather keep waitressing than deal with that. Fortunately, she was able to get her old job back."

"But what about Jacob?"

"He's still looking for someone." Sally's needles stopped suddenly, clicking together as she dropped them in her lap. "Seems I remember you being very *gut* in math."

"That was years ago."

"It's an ability, though, not something you forget."

"I wouldn't—"

"And didn't you mention last week that you were worried about your parents' finances?"

"Well, yes, but… I'm looking for a job that pays well, something in town perhaps."

"Any success?"

"Not yet."

Sally picked up her needles again, and Hannah hoped the subject was dropped. She could not work for Jacob Schrock. He would be out of her life by the end of the week. The last thing she needed was to be in constant contact with him, working with him on a daily basis. The way he looked at her? Such a mixture of pity and compassion. She didn't need to face that every day, and how could she leave Matthew?

Always her mind circled back to that final question. How could she leave her son eight, maybe even nine hours a day? Could she expect her mother to pick up the slack? How was *Mamm* supposed to cope with one more thing on top of all she had to do?

Matthew wheeled through the doorway and into the waiting room, a smiley sticker on the back of his hand, and Hannah began gathering up her things. It was as she turned to go that Sally said, "Think about it, Hannah. It could be that you would be a real blessing to Jacob, and maybe…maybe it would solve your problems in the process."

She'd have to ask Jacob about the job.

Only of course, she wouldn't. It was all none of her business. Soon he'd be done with the playhouse and she wouldn't see him again, which would suit her just fine. Dolly clip-clopped down the road, more content with the day than Hannah was.

She would be content, if she had a job. If they didn't have financial problems. If she wasn't so worried about Matthew.

It would be crazy to consider working for Jacob.

He might be a kind, talented man, but he was also damaged. He'd suffered a terrible loss, which might explain why he pushed his nose into other people's business. Just the day before, he'd looked at her as if she was crazy when she'd tried to put a sweater on Matthew. True, it was eighty degrees, but Matthew had been known to catch a cold in warmer weather than that.

Nope. Jacob Schrock didn't belong in her life.

Matthew peeled the sticker off his hand and stuck it on to the buggy.

"Your therapists said you did a *gut* job today."

"Uh-huh."

"They also said you did everything fast, that you seemed to be in a rush to be done."

"Are we almost home?"

"A few more miles."

"Faster, please."

"You want me to hurry this old buggy mare?"

"*Daddi*'s horse is faster."

"Indeed." Her father had ordered a second buggy horse when she'd come home to live. Hannah had protested it wasn't necessary, but he'd insisted. Come to think of it, maybe he'd insisted because Dolly was getting older and they'd have to replace her soon, which didn't bear thinking about. Dolly was the first buggy horse that Hannah had learned to drive.

While Matthew stared out the window, he pinched his bottom lip in between his thumb and forefinger, pulling it out like a pout and then letting it go. It was a habit that she saw only when he was anxious about something.

And she didn't doubt for a minute that the source of his anxiety was right now hammering two-by-fours into the shape of a train.

They were about to pass the parking area for the Pumpkinvine Trail. Hannah pulled on the right rein and called out to Dolly, who docilely turned off the road.

"Why are we stopping?" Matthew frowned out at the trail, a place he usually enjoyed visiting.

"We need to talk."

Now he stared up at her, eyes wide. "Am I in trouble?"

"No, Matt. Not at all."

"Then what?"

Instead of answering, she studied him a minute. Already he had such a unique personality—with his own likes, dislikes and ideas. Admittedly, she felt more protective of him than most mothers might feel of a nearly five-year-old child, but she understood that this concern wasn't only about his disability. It was also about his not having a father, about his missing the presence of a dad in his life.

"You like Jacob a lot. Don't you?"

"Yes!"

"But you remember that he's only at our house because some people paid him to be there."

"Uh-huh."

"He's doing a job."

"And I'm his 'rentice."

Hannah sighed, closed her eyes, and prayed for patience and wisdom. When she opened her eyes, Matt reached out and patted her hand. "Don't worry, *Mamm*. He's a *gut* guy. Even *Daddi* said so."

"Oh, *ya*, I'm sure he is."

"So what's wrong?"

"Nothing's wrong, really. But you do understand that Jacob is only going to be at our house for a few days, right? Then he'll have another job, building another playhouse for someone else."

Matt frowned and pulled on his bottom lip. "Another kid like me?"

"I don't know."

"Okay."

"Okay?" Hannah reached out and brushed the hair out of his eyes.

"Uh-huh."

"What do you mean, okay?"

"It's okay that Jacob won't be at our house because he'll be at somebody else's house making them happy."

Since she didn't have an answer for that, she called out to Dolly, who backed up and then trotted out of the parking area, back onto the two-lane.

She was willing to admit that possibly her son saw things more clearly than she did. Didn't the Bible tell them they were to become like little children? Hannah wasn't sure she'd be able to do that—her worries weighed too heavily on her heart, but maybe in this situation she could follow Matt's lead. At least for a few more days.

And she would double her efforts looking for a job because she most certainly was not going to ask Jacob about what kind of help he needed.

Jacob had always enjoyed working on playhouses. He liked building things with an eye for small children. Some people might say it was because his own father had built him a similar type of playhouse. But his father had also taught him to play baseball and he had no urge to coach the *youngies*. His father had taught him how to sow seed and harvest it, but he had no desire to be a farmer.

He was grateful for his father, for both of his parents, and he still missed them terribly. But learning to build wooden playthings for children had been a gift from *Gotte*, a real blessing at the lowest point in his life. Today he was able to share part of that blessing with young Matthew, and he wanted every piece of it to be as good as he could make it.

So he measured everything twice—the main doorway into the train, the back door which ended on a small porch and the entryways between the cars. Wheelchairs required extra room and Matthew would probably require a larger chair as he grew. Though he was nearly five now, children as old as ten or even twelve often played on the structures that Jacob made. As Matthew grew, no doubt his chair would become a bit bigger. Jacob wanted the playhouse to be as accessible to him as his home.

He sanded the floor smoothly so that the wheels of the chair wouldn't hang up on an uneven board.

He added a little extra height so that Matthew's friends who would be standing and walking and running could play along beside him.

And when he heard the clatter of a buggy, he put down his tools and ambled over to meet Hannah and Matthew.

"Hi, Jacob. I can help now."

"You already helped me this morning. Remember?"

"*Ya*, but—"

"Actually I'm about to call it a day."

"Oh."

"There is one thing I need…won't take but a minute."

"Sure! Anything. What is it?"

"I need you to come and do an early inspection."

"You do?"

"Yup. I need my apprentice's opinion before I move forward."

"Cool!"

Hannah had parked the buggy, set the brake and jogged around to help Matthew out.

Jacob stepped forward as if to help, but a frown from Hannah and a short shake of her head convinced him not to try. She was obviously used to doing things on her own. So instead he stood there, feeling like an idiot because a woman weighing roughly the same as a hundred pound sack of feed struggled with simply helping her son out of a buggy.

As he watched, she removed the straps that secured the wheelchair to the back of the buggy, then set it on the ground, opened it, secured something along the back. Finally she opened the buggy's door wide so that Matthew's legs wouldn't bang against anything.

"Ready?" she asked.

"Ready." He threw his arms around her neck and she stepped back as she took the full weight of him, then settled him into the chair.

How would she do this when he was seven or ten or twelve? How would Hannah handle the logistics of a fully grown disabled son? Was there any possibility that he would ever regain the use of his legs? Jacob had a dozen questions, and he didn't ask any of them because it wasn't really his business.

He reached into the buggy, snagged Matt's straw hat and placed it on his head. The boy gave him a thumbs-up, and adjusted himself in the chair as easily as Jacob straightened his suspenders in the morning.

"Let's go," Matthew said.

"Whoa. Hang on a minute. We need to see to your *mamm*'s horse first."

"I can take care of Dolly," Hannah insisted.

"Nonsense." He stepped closer to Hannah and lowered his voice. "What kind of neighbor would I be if I let you do that?"

"You're our neighbor now?"

"In a sense."

"So you want to take care of my horse?"

"*Ya*. I do."

"Fine. I'll just go inside and have a cup of tea."

"But I thought you might go with us and…" His words slid away as she walked toward the house, waving without turning around.

"Come on, Jacob. Let's do this."

Matthew wheeled alongside him as he led the mare into the barn.

"Her name's Dolly," Matthew said when they stopped inside the barn.

The horse lowered her head so that she was even with the boy. Matthew sat in front of her and stroked from her forehead to her muzzle.

"Good Dolly," Matthew said.

Jacob unhitched the buggy, took off the harness and placed it on the peg on the wall, and then led Dolly through the barn to the pasture.

"Now?" Matt asked.

"Now."

Matt had to move slowly over the parts of uneven ground that led to where the playhouse was being constructed. It was definitely the best place for the structure, as Alton had noted. But the going was a little rough, and it occurred to Jacob that a wooden walk would make things much easier. He had enough lumber scraps at home to do it. An extra day, maybe two, and he could have a nice smooth path from the driveway to the playhouse.

"That is way cool," Matt exclaimed, sounding exactly like an *Englisch* boy Jacob had built a playhouse for the week before. Kids were kids, and *cool* was a pretty standard response to something they liked.

"Let's show you the inside."

Jacob let Matthew go first and watched as he maneuvered his way up the small ramp and into the main cabin of the train. The engine room was to his left and the passenger car was to his right. Beyond that was a small back porch. On an actual train, this would be the end of the observation car, and the area would resemble a roofed porch. Now that he thought about it, a roof wasn't a bad idea. He could add it easily enough.

Matthew made his way to the front of the train. Jacob had created a space where he could pull up his wheelchair and pretend he was in the conductor's seat. To his right Jacob had fastened a wooden bench and in front of him there were knobs and such for him to pull and pretend to direct the train.

"Wow," he said.

"We're not finished yet, buddy. We still need to put on the roof, and...other stuff."

"Can I help?"

"I'm counting on it. I'll be here early tomorrow morning."

They were standing right next to each other, or rather, Jacob was standing next to Matthew. Before Jacob realized what was happening, Matt had pivoted in his seat and thrown his arms around his legs.

"*Danki,*" the boy said in a low voice.

"*Ger gschehne.*" Jacob found that his voice was tight, but the words of their ancestors passed between them as easily as water down a riverbed.

Jacob pushed Matthew's chair the length of the car. They moved slowly, studying every detail, until Hannah's *mamm* came outside and rang the dinner bell.

Jacob did not intend to stay and eat, but it seemed that Claire expected it. She'd already set an extra place at the table. It would have been rude to refuse, or so he told himself.

The meal was satisfying and the conversation interesting. He realized that too often he ate alone, that he actually missed the back-and-forth between family members. There was no reason for it either. His brother lived next door, and he had a standing offer to eat with them.

Why had he pulled away?

Had it been so painful to see what he would never have?

There was no such awkwardness with Hannah's family. Claire spoke of the painted bunting she'd spied on the bird-bath. Alton updated them on the crops. Hannah described how well Matthew had done at physical therapy.

As for Matthew, he was practically nodding off in his seat by the time they'd finished eating.

Hannah excused herself, transferred him from the dinner chair to the wheelchair and pushed him down the hall.

"She's pretty amazing, your daughter." He hadn't meant to say the words. They'd slipped from his heart to his lips without consulting his brain.

If Alton and Claire were surprised, they hid it well. Claire stood and began clearing the table. Alton offered to see him out. They'd stepped outside when Jacob shared his ideas for a wooden walk to the playhouse as well as a small platform for the dinner table.

"Must be hard on Hannah, on her back I mean—moving him from one chair to the other so often."

"And I have to be fast to beat her to it. Your ideas sound *gut*, but I'm afraid the grant doesn't cover that, and I don't have any extra money at the moment."

Jacob waved away his concerns. "I have leftover lumber. It won't cost me anything but time."

"Which is precious for every man."

"It's okay. I don't have to start the next job until Monday." He didn't mention the orders he had at his shop. He could put in a few hours each night and stay ahead on that.

"Then I accept, and I thank you."

"You can tell me it's none of my business, but Hannah seemed particularly preoccupied tonight. Is something wrong? Something else?"

Alton stuck his thumbs under his suspenders. "Money is a bit tight."

"How tight?"

"Missed a few payments on the place."

"What did your banker say about that?"

"Said they could extend me another thirty days, but then they'll have to start the foreclosure process."

"I'm sorry, Alton. I had no idea. Have you spoken to your bishop?"

Alton waved that idea away. "My family has received plenty of help from the benevolence fund in the last year. We'll find a way through this on our own."

"And Hannah?"

"Hannah is determined to find a job."

The entire drive home he thought of Alton's words, of the family's financial problems and of the help he needed in order to prepare him for the IRS audit. He could ask Hannah. It wasn't a completely crazy idea. He remembered that she was good at sums, and it wasn't as if she needed to understand algebra. It only required someone more organized than he was.

She was stubborn and willful and curt at times, but he wasn't going to be dating her. He was going to hire her.

Or was he?

It wasn't until he was home and cleaning up for bed that he realized the error of his thinking. He caught sight of his reflection in the small bathroom mirror and stared for a moment at his scars. His fingers traced the tissue that was puckered and discolored. He'd been so fortunate that his eye wasn't permanently damaged, and in truth he'd become used to the sight of his charred, disfigured flesh.

Others, though, they often found his face harder to look at. They would turn away, or blush bright red and hurry off. Sometimes children cried when they first saw him.

Had he forgotten about those reactions?

Did he really think that his appearance wouldn't matter to a woman, to an employee? Hannah had been polite, sure, but that didn't mean that she wasn't horrified by the sight of his scars.

As for the thought of her working with him, she probably wouldn't want to spend her days in the company of a disfigured man. Possibly he even reminded her of the accident that had killed her husband. He would be a constant reminder of her misfortune.

He'd been around her for two days, and he was already creating sandcastles in the sky. Probably because he'd felt an instant connection to her and that was okay and proper. As a friend. As a brother. But what about as an employer?

He hadn't spent much time around women in the last few years. It was simply easier not to. Sure, he knew what he was missing out on, but it wasn't as if he had a chance with any of the single girls in their district. Even the widows could do better than him. He might have grown comfortable with his disfigurement, but he wouldn't ask that of a woman.

But he wasn't thinking about courting. He was thinking about a business arrangement, which was crazy. He'd seen the look of relief pass over her features when he'd promised her he would be done this week. She was already looking forward to having him out of their lives. Why would he offer her a job?

On top of which, she'd had enough tragedy in her life. He wouldn't be adding to that burden with his own problems. No, she'd be better off working in town, working for an *Englisch* shop owner. He'd do best to keep his distance. As for the audit, perhaps he could scrape up enough money for the accounting firm. He'd need to do something and do it quick, because the clock was ticking down to his deadline. Not that he remembered it exactly, but it was within the next month. That much he knew for certain.

Four weeks, maybe a little less.

By then, he needed to have found a solution.

Chapter Four

Hannah had scoured the paper on both Wednesday and Thursday looking for a job. What she found was discouraging. The Amish restaurant in town wanted her to work the four-to-nine shift. She wouldn't be home to share the evening meal or put Matthew to bed. The thought caused her stomach to twist into a knot.

Amish Acres in Nappanee needed someone in the gift shop, and they understood that Amish employees didn't work on Sundays. They even provided a bus that picked up workers in downtown Goshen for the twenty-minute ride. But she would be required to work on Saturday. In an Amish household, Saturday was a day spent preparing for Sunday— cooking meals, cleaning the house, making sure clothes were cleaned and pressed. She wouldn't be able to do any of that if she worked at Amish Acres.

And with any of the jobs she considered, the same questions lingered in the back of her mind. Who would take Matthew to his physical therapy appointments during the week? Could she really expect her mother to add one more thing to her already full schedule? Could her mother handle the physical demands of lifting Matthew in and out of the buggy?

She studied the local paper once more Friday morning, in between helping her mother with the meals and taking care of Matthew. After lunch, she again donned a fresh apron and set off to take Matthew to his appointment. She had an interview for a job late that afternoon, and her father had offered to meet them in town.

"You didn't have to do this," she said as she helped Matthew into the other buggy.

"I like riding with *Daddi*," Matthew piped up. "He drives faster than you do."

"I could have…"

"What? Taken him with you? *Nein*. It's not a problem. My order had come in at the feed store, and young Matthew can help check off items as they load them in the back of my buggy. Besides, I know this interview is important to you."

"Yes, but it's not for another hour. I could have brought him home."

"Go and order yourself a nice cup of tea at that bakery." Her father had clumsily patted her arm and then turned his attention to Matthew.

"Ready, Matt?"

"More than ready. Is Jacob done with the playhouse yet? Is he still there? Because I made him a drawing. I need to give it to him."

Hannah didn't hear the rest of the conversation as they pulled away. She didn't have to hear it to know what Matthew was saying. He'd been talking about the playhouse and Jacob all week.

She, on the other hand, had specifically avoided Jacob that

morning. The more she thought about the job opening he had, the more irritated she grew. He definitely knew that her family was in a tough financial situation. She'd heard her father talking to him about it. Why hadn't he offered her the job?

Did he think she wasn't smart enough to handle a column of numbers?

Did he worry that she wouldn't be a good employee?

Or maybe—and this was the thing that pricked her heart—maybe he would be happy to be free of her and Matthew. Building a playhouse for a week was one thing. Involving yourself in someone's life, especially when that someone had special needs, was another thing completely.

Hannah's interview was at the new craft store in town. The ad said they were looking for an experienced quilter. That was one thing Hannah was quite good at, but then wasn't every Amish woman? Still, if it was the job she was meant to have, *Gotte* would provide a way.

She arrived early and carefully filled out the employment questionnaire, balancing the piece of paper on her lap with only a magazine under it for support. When she had finished, the cashier had taken it from her and told her to wait. The young girl had returned twenty minutes later and led her into a back office.

The owner of the shop was in her forties, stylishly dressed, sporting short black hair, dangly earrings and bright red fingernails.

She stared at the questionnaire for a moment and then she asked, "Do you wear your bonnet every day?"

"Excuse me?"

"Your..." The woman touched the top of her head.

"It's a prayer *kapp*, and *ya* we always wear it when we are out in public."

"Oh, good. I think the customers will like that, and your clothing—it's so quaint, so authentic. Wouldn't want you showing up in jeans and a T-shirt."

"I don't own any jeans."

"It would also be helpful if you'd park your buggy out front so that tourists can see it."

"There's no shade out front, and I wouldn't want Dolly to stand on the concrete pavement all day."

"I see." The woman pursed her too-red lips and steepled her fingers. "I'm sure we can work something out. Also, we'd like you to speak as much German…"

"Pennsylvania Dutch," Hannah corrected her softly.

"Excuse me?"

"We speak Pennsylvania Dutch and *Englisch*, of course."

"Yes, but that's the thing. I'd rather you speak your language." The woman sat back and rocked slightly in her leather office chair. "I know you people aren't particularly business savvy, but this is a big venture for my executive board. We have stores in Ohio and Pennsylvania, but this is our first in Indiana. I intend for it to be the best."

"Which means what, exactly?"

"Tourists come here to catch a glimpse into a different life, to experience in some small way what it means to be different."

"I'm different?"

"We don't want to minimize that—we want to showcase it. We'll be selling the experience of meeting an Amish person as much as we're selling fabric."

"Selling?"

"And didn't you mention on your form that your son…"

"Matthew."

"Isn't he disabled? If you could bring him in with you, just now and then when he'd be in town anyway, I think that would be a real plus."

"Bring Matthew in for *Englischers* to gawk at?"

But the woman wasn't listening. She'd already opened a file and was flipping through sheets of paper. "How would you feel about appearing on the flyers that we're going to place around town? You're young enough, and if we added just a touch of makeup I think you'd photograph well."

The muscles in Hannah's right arm began to quiver and a terrible heat flushed through her body. She hadn't been this angry since…well, ever. Knowing she was about to say something unkind, Hannah gathered up her purse, politely thanked the woman and rushed from the store.

Once she made it back outside, she stood beside Dolly, running her hand down the horse's neck and breathing in the scent of her. Slowly the tide of anger receded, and she was left shaking her head in amazement. How could a person be so insensitive? How could she think that such tactics were acceptable? Hannah would not allow herself or her son to be put on display. What was the woman thinking? Only of her business, of making a profit, of selling the Amish experience.

Hannah understood that tourism was a big part of the Goshen economy. It benefited both *Englisch* and Amish, and there were many places that treated Plain folks with respect. Meeting people from other states was fun for both parties, and the added income was often a big help to families. But she would not be wearing makeup or putting her son and horse on display for anyone.

She would not be working for the new craft shop in town.

Jacob looked up as Hannah pulled into the drive. He'd been watching for her. He'd actually finished the job a few hours ago, and now he was looking for things to do until she came home. Since they didn't attend the same church, it would be his last time to see her unless they happened to run into one another in town or at a wedding or funeral.

Hannah practically jumped out of the buggy and didn't so much as glance his way.

Was it possible that she was unhappy with what he'd done?

Jacob turned and surveyed the play area. The train playhouse was complete, and if he allowed himself to think about it, the finished structure looked better than he'd imagined. The boardwalk leading to it was smooth and wide enough for Matthew's wheelchair.

But the crowning jewel of the project wasn't the structure itself but the boy he'd built it for. Matthew was sitting in the front engine room, a train conductor's hat perched jauntily on his head as he tooted the horn and spoke to his imaginary passengers and crew. The young boy had quite an imagination, and he was enthusiastically happy with the new playhouse. Jacob closed his eyes, prayed that *Gotte* would bless young Matthew, and his family—his grandparents, his aunts and uncles, and of course his mother.

He'd no sooner thought of Hannah than she appeared before him, clutching an envelope in her hand.

"Hire me to work in your office."

"Excuse me?"

"Sally Lapp says you're looking for someone."

"*Ya*, I am."

"So why haven't you offered the job to me?" She took a step closer and Jacob took a step back.

"I didn't think—"

"Didn't think I could handle it?"

"Of course you can, but—"

"I beat your class at math drills even though you were two years older."

"I remember."

"And I have experience in accounting. I did some before Matthew was born."

"That's *gut*, but—"

She waved the envelope in front of his face so that he had to step back again or risk being swiped by it.

"Do you know what this is? A notice from the bank. *Dat* has less than a month to come up with his back payments. If he doesn't, they'll begin the foreclosure process."

"I'm sorry to hear that."

"While you were out here building a playhouse my parents stand to lose their farm."

"The playhouse didn't—"

"Didn't cost them anything? *Ya*, I know. But we do. Matthew and I do. There's the extra food and the clothing and Matthew's medical expenses…" Her eyes shone brightly with tears, and she quickly pivoted away.

He gave her a moment—counted to three and then did so again. Finally he stepped forward and said, "I'd be pleased to have you work in my office. I didn't ask because I wasn't sure you'd want such a challenge."

He couldn't bring himself to admit that he didn't think she'd want to be around him, that his scars might repulse her or even remind her of Matthew's accident.

"You don't think I'm up to it, do you?" The fire was back—softer, simmering this time.

"I don't doubt your bookkeeping skills, Hannah. However, I'm not sure you realize how terrible I am at filing and record keeping."

Hannah waved that away. "I know all about that. I even know you had one girl quit after only a day."

"And I didn't blame her."

"So what did you plan to do?"

"About?"

"About the IRS audit." Hannah squinted up at him quizzically, waiting to hear what his plan was. Only Jacob didn't have a plan.

"I still have almost three weeks. I figured…well, I figured it would work itself out somehow."

"That's not a plan."

"You've got me there."

"Is this a permanent position?"

"I haven't really thought about it."

"Why am I not surprised?"

"It could be, I guess. Don't know how much work there would be once the records are straightened out. I guess we could get past the audit and then decide."

Hannah crossed her arms and studied the playhouse, really saw it for maybe the first time since he'd begun construction. "It's a *gut* playhouse."

"*Ya*, it is."

"Matthew loves it."

"He's a great kid."

"*Danki.*"

"*Ger gschehne.*" And there it was, a tangible bond between them—the ways of their parents and grandparents, the river of their past that set them apart and also drew them together.

"I'll start Monday," she said and then she named what she expected to make per hour.

Jacob almost laughed. He would readily pay more if she was able to get him out of the paperwork jam he'd created, but instead of offering more he simply nodded. Perhaps he could give her a bonus once the audit was complete.

Hannah's eyebrows rose in surprise that he'd agreed, but she was holding something back. She was chewing on her thumbnail, a habit they'd all teased her about in school. The memory blossomed in Jacob's mind with the force of a winter wind—Hannah standing at the board, worrying her thumbnail as she worked out some impossibly difficult math problem. At least it had seemed impossible to him.

"What is it?" he asked, the question coming out more gruffly than he'd intended. "What's worrying you?"

She stood straighter, glanced at her son and then looked back at Jacob. "I'll need to take off during Matthew's appointments."

"Of course."

"So you wouldn't...you wouldn't mind?"

"*Nein.* Your son's therapy is important. I would be a fool not to understand that."

She nodded once, and then she stuck the offending envelope from the bank in her apron pocket and went to her son. She climbed the steps and sat beside him in the engine room, leaving Jacob to enjoy the sight of them and the sound of their laughter as Matthew set his conductor cap on her head.

"We were hoping Jacob would stay for dinner."

Hannah's mother set the large pot of chicken and dumplings in the middle of the table. Beside it was a loaf of fresh bread, butter and a large bowl with a salad that Hannah had managed to throw together.

"He told me he has a mess at home to clean up." Matthew slathered butter on top of his piece of bread and took a large bite. When he caught Hannah staring at him, he smiled broadly.

Her father spoke of the rain forecast for the next week. Her mother had been to visit a neighbor and her infant girl. She described how the baby cooed, how rosy her cheeks were, even how she smelled.

Finally Hannah broke into the conversation. "I have a job."

Everyone stopped eating and stared at her.

"With Jacob. I have a job with Jacob." She felt the blush creep up her neck. "I'm going to be helping him with his accounting. It might not be permanent."

"That's *gut*," her father said, reaching for another helping of dumplings. "You always excelled with numbers."

Her mother nodded in agreement. "And you have a real knack for organizing things. Since you've been here you've straightened up every closet and cabinet, even my spices."

"They were a mess."

"Well, now they're in alphabetical order."

"Which makes them easier to find."

"I think it's *wunderbaar*, dear."

It was Matthew who was the most excited about her news. He'd begun tapping his spoon against his plate. "So I will get to see him. You told me that I might not see him anymore, that he'd be helping other kids. But if you're working for him, I'll get to see him. Right? He even said he'd teach me to whistle."

And that was when Hannah knew she'd made a big mistake. Possibly she'd found a way to help her parents, but in the process she had delayed the inevitable. She could tell by the sparkle in her son's eyes that he didn't realize Jacob was not a part of their family, not even really their friend except in the most broad sense of the word.

The elation she'd felt at landing the job slipped away. She would need to be very careful, not with her own emotions—which weren't an issue at all since she was not attracted to Jacob Schrock—but with Matthew's.

She would protect her son.

Whether from financial hardship that might push him out of his home or emotional attachments that couldn't possibly last.

Chapter Five

Jacob spent Saturday catching up on projects that he'd let slide in order to complete Matthew's boardwalk. There was a dresser that he'd promised to redo for Evelyn Yutzy. Her granddaughter had recently arrived in town, moved from Maine back to Indiana, and they'd converted the back porch into a bedroom. It was insulated, so the girl wouldn't freeze, but she needed somewhere to put her clothes.

He had only half-finished the crib for Grace Miller, and her baby was due in two weeks. He couldn't put it off any longer. Then there was the workbench that he'd agreed to make for Paul Fisher. It was good that business was…well, busy. But Jacob's heart was with the playhouses, something that he charged as little as possible for. In order to make a living he had to take care of the individual work orders as well as the business projects that he had lined up.

Speaking of which, he was supposed to begin a cabinetry project on a new house the following week. He'd written the details down somewhere, but where? He wasted the next hour looking for the small sheet of paper, which he eventually found in his lunch pail.

Normally once he started a project he had no problem focusing on it, but he found himself lagging further and further behind as the day progressed. He stopped for lunch and went into his house, but even there he couldn't help looking around him and seeing the place through Hannah's eyes. It was pitiful really, and he didn't know how it had happened.

Dishes were stacked in the sink, where he usually ate standing and staring out the window. Copies of the *Budget* covered every surface in the sitting room, along with woodworking magazines that the library gave him when they were too far out-of-date to display. That seemed ridiculous to Jacob—woodworking wasn't something that changed from one season to the next. Still, he enjoyed receiving the old copies and looking through the magazines. He occasionally found new ideas to try.

When his childhood home had burned down, he'd purchased a prefab house and had it delivered to the property. The building was small, around six hundred square feet, but more than what he needed. The workshop had been left intact. As for the fields, his brother Micah farmed them in addition to his own, which was adjacent to the old homestead.

The workshop was larger than his home. The vast majority of it was filled with supplies, workbenches and projects in various stages of completion. The office was a cornered-off ten-by-ten space. On one side of the room, windows looked out over the fields. On the other, windows allowed him to see into the workshop. As far as mess, it was in worse shape than the house. Jacob's heart was in the projects, not the filing systems, or lack thereof, and that showed. He was attempting to move around stacks of paperwork in the office when his brother Micah tapped on the open door.

"Am I interrupting?"

"*Ya*. Can't you see? I'm making progress on my backed-up carpentry orders."

"Huh. Looks to me like you're tossing papers from one shelf to another." Micah crossed the room, stopped in front of one of the plastic bins and raised the lid. "What is all this stuff?"

"Receipts, I guess."

"What's your system?" Micah pulled out a Subway sandwich receipt, stared at it and then turned it over and stared at the writing on the back.

Jacob snatched it out of his hand and tossed it back into the bin. "If it was something that I felt like I needed to keep, I threw it in a bin. The next year I'd buy another from the discount store and begin tossing things in it. There's one for the past...six years."

Micah let out a long whistle. "No wonder the IRS is interested in you, *bruder*. They must have heard about your filing system."

"The last thing I want to talk about is the IRS."

"*Gut*. Because it's not why I came by."

Jacob grunted as he picked up a bin from the floor and dropped it on the desk. Deciding it looked worse, looked even more disorganized there, he put it back where it was.

"Why did you come by?"

"To invite you to dinner, and don't tell me you have plans."

"I do have plans. I should be out there working." He shifted his gaze and stared through the window into the workshop. He could just make out the corner of Grace Miller's crib. It would probably take him another two hours to finish it.

"Then why aren't you?"

"Why aren't I what?"

"Out there working."

"Because Hannah's coming on Monday, and if she sees this place like it is, she'll probably turn tail and run."

When his brother grinned and dropped into a chair, Jacob realized that the news was already out about his new bookkeeper. No doubt Micah was here to tease him, and the dinner invitation was just a handy excuse.

"Heard young Matthew likes his caboose train."

"*Ya*, he does. Young kids like him, kids who don't lead normal lives, the little things seem to make a big difference."

"And what about Hannah?"

"What about her?"

"Still as pretty as when she was in school?"

"Seriously? That's what we're going to talk about?"

"Why not? It's the first woman you've shown interest in since your accident."

"I'm not interested in her." Jacob reached up and scratched at his scar. "I'm hiring her to bring some order to this chaos."

"So you don't find her attractive?"

"I didn't say that."

"You do find her attractive, then."

"This is the problem with you."

"Problem with me?"

His brother smiled as if he'd just told the funniest joke. It made Jacob want to chuck the bin of papers he was holding right at his head.

"You always think you know what's best for me, but you don't."

"And you always think that your scars preclude you from dating, but they don't."

"What would you know about scars?"

Micah stood, raised his hands, palms out, and shook his head. "I don't know why we do this every time."

"I know why. You insist on sticking your nose in my business."

"We worry about you. Emily and I both do."

"Would you please stop? Would you just trust me to live my own life the way it's meant to be lived?"

"Alone? Moping over what happened?"

"You weren't there, Micah. Don't pretend that you know what happened. Don't pretend you can understand. I'm the one who pulled their bodies from the fire. I'm the one who didn't get there fast enough."

Micah strode to the door, but he stopped dead in his tracks, the afternoon sunlight that was streaming through the open workshop door spilling over his shoulders. Because his back was to Jacob, his words were muffled, softer, but they hit him just as hard as if they'd been standing face-to-face. "You say that you trust *Gotte*, and yet you won't let anyone into your life. You say that you pray, but you don't believe."

And with that, he trudged back outside, across the field and to his own home—leaving Jacob to wonder why everyone thought they had to fix him. They didn't live in his skin. They didn't look at his scars every morning, and they knew nothing of his guilt and loneliness.

Jacob understood his scars for what they were—the penance that he deserved for not saving his parents from the fire that took their lives.

Hannah had been living back in Goshen long enough that Matthew no longer drew obvious stares when they met for church. She was grateful for that, thankful that their neighbors were learning to accept him.

She looked forward to their church services. Loved the familiar faces she'd grown up seeing and the sound of her bishop's voice—the same man who had baptized her. Other than the loneliness that occasionally plagued her and the constant worry over Matthew's health, she was happy, living again with her family.

Church was held every other Sunday and always at a member's home. This week they were at the Yutzy place, which was on the northwest side of town. A portion of their property bordered the Elkhart River. It was a beautiful, peaceful spot, and Hannah could feel its calming power even as she made her way into the barn where they would have church. The large main room had been cleaned out, the doors and windows flung open, and benches arranged on two sides of a makeshift aisle.

At the back of the benches a few tables had been set up with cups of water and plates of cookies for the youngest children. It was sometimes difficult for them to make it all the way through a three-to four-hour meeting without a small snack.

The service was exactly what she needed to quiet her soul. She'd spent too much time since Friday worrying about the job at Jacob's. She knew she could do the work, but would Matthew be okay without her? Was she doing the right thing? Could the small amount of money she was making help her parents' financial situation?

The questions had spun round and round in her head, but that all stopped when they stood to sing the *Loblied*. The words of the hymn reminded her of the good things in her life, the things that *Gotte* had given her. She forgot for a moment the tragedy of losing her husband and the trials of having a special needs son.

Once the service was over and she'd finished helping in the serving line, she went to find her sisters. Both Beth and Sharon were in the last trimester of their pregnancies. In fact, their babies were due only a few weeks apart. They'd tried to help in the serving line and had been shooed away.

"Finally we get you to ourselves," Sharon said. The oldest of the three girls, it had taken her some time to become pregnant after marrying. The twins were two lovely girls full of energy and laughter and a tiny bit of mischief. Another six years had passed before Sharon had finally become pregnant again. She and her husband were hoping for a boy, just to balance things out a bit.

Beth had one daughter, ten-year-old Naomi. She'd had Naomi when she was very young, only seventeen. There had been some problems, and she thought that she couldn't have any more children, but her protruding stomach was testament to the fact that *Gotte* had other plans.

Being around them, watching them rest a hand on their baby bumps or sigh as they tried to push up out of a chair caused an ache deep in Hannah's heart. She'd imagined herself pregnant again, had thought she'd have a house full of children like most Amish women. She had been certain that she would remain married to the same man all of her life. She'd never imagined herself as a young widow.

She searched the crowd of children for her son and finally spied Matthew in his chair, pulled up to a checkerboard that had been placed over a tree stump. One of the older boys who had a foot in a cast was playing with him. As she watched, Matthew glanced occasionally at the children who were playing ball, and it seemed to Hannah that an expression of longing crossed his face.

"Tell us about your new job." Beth was the middle child and the negotiator of the family. It was Beth who had convinced Hannah to move home. Hannah hadn't wanted to be a burden to her parents, but Beth had convinced her that home was where she needed to be and that family could never truly be a burden.

"Tell us about Jacob." Sharon's eyes sparkled. She'd always been one to tease. Perhaps because of her work as a midwife, she believed in enjoying life. She saw moments of great joy every day and the occasional tragedy, as well.

"There's nothing to tell about Jacob, and as far as the job… well, I'm fortunate to find work at all." She described her attempts at finding employment in town. She even mimicked the craft shop owner's voice when she asked if Hannah could bring Matt in occasionally so the tourists could gawk at him.

"Maybe she meant well," Beth said.

Sharon rolled her eyes. "And maybe she has no filter, no sense of what is proper and what is improper. Some business owners—and I've seen it in Amish as well as *Englisch*— they become too enamored with how much money they can make. They forget their employees are people."

"Anyway. I suppose I was upset because of the interview, and I had no other ideas of where to apply." Hannah glanced around to be sure no one else was within earshot. Fortunately most of the women had moved to a circle of chairs under the trees, and the men were congregated on the porch or near the ball field. "I confronted Jacob. I walked right up to him and asked him why he hadn't offered me the job."

"Oh my." Beth placed both hands on her belly. "How did he take it?"

"He was surprised, of course. Amish women are supposed to be quiet and meek."

Both Beth and Sharon laughed at that. Sometimes the

reputation that Amish women had earned was frustrating, other times it was simply ludicrous. While they did believe that the man was the spiritual head of the house, the women Hannah knew had no trouble voicing their opinion or standing up for themselves.

"What happened then?" Sharon asked.

"He agreed. It's a temporary position until his audit is over. Then we'll see if there's enough work for me to continue."

"Oh, I'm sure there's enough work. He's probably just afraid you wouldn't want a permanent position. I still see his sister-in-law Emily because our homes are fairly close together. The dividing line for our districts is between us. Anyway, she tells me that Jacob's a real wonder with the woodworking…"

"Have you seen the playhouse he made?" Beth interrupted. "It's amazing. I stopped by yesterday and even Naomi spent an hour out in it, and she's ten. I haven't seen her in a playhouse since the summer she was six and her *dat* knocked together something from old barn lumber. Wasn't even really a lean-to, but she would drag every little friend that came over out to play there."

"What are you worried about, Hannah?" Sharon studied her sister. "You might as well share with us. Is it Matthew? Is he feeling all right?"

"Matthew's fine, I guess."

"You guess?" Now Beth was on alert. "Tell us. What's happened?"

"Nothing has happened." Hannah blew out a sigh of exasperation. "I'm starting a new job that I know nothing about."

"Which you asked for—" Beth reminded her.

"I'm leaving Matthew with *Mamm*, and she has enough to do."

"I've already spoken to her about that. She's welcome to bring Matthew by anytime—"

"You're seven months pregnant, Sharon, and you're still delivering babies. The last thing you need is—"

"My nephew? Actually I do need to spend time with him and so do my girls. He's family, Hannah. We want him around."

"Naomi asks me every day if Matthew can come over." Beth rubbed the side of her stomach. "We'll help *Mamm*. Don't worry about that."

Which effectively shut down her doubts about leaving Matthew during the day.

"I'm not sure it will be enough money," she admitted. "The amount they owe? I was surprised. I knew they'd helped me and Matt, but I didn't know... I didn't know they'd sacrificed so much."

"It's what families do, Hannah." Sharon took on her older sister tone. "You've forgotten because you moved away. You and David moved, what was it..."

"Three months. We moved three months after we were wed."

"Right, and I understand how you'd want to try the community in Wisconsin, but while you were there maybe you learned to be independent, maybe too independent."

"Now you're with family, and we take care of one another," Beth chimed in.

Hannah didn't need a lecture about family. Yes, she appreciated her parents and sisters and brothers-in-law, but they didn't understand just how much of a burden Matthew's disability could be. They hadn't experienced an emergency run to the hospital because of a minor cold that had quickly morphed into pneumonia.

"Back to the money..." she said.

"Simon has some saved, which he has offered to *Dat*." Sharon's husband worked at the RV factory in Shipshewana two days a week. The rest of the time he farmed their land.

"Carl does too." Beth raised her foot and stared at her swollen ankle. "*Dat* told me he doesn't want to take it unless he's sure it will cover the balance. He doesn't want to drain our savings for a place he might lose anyway."

And there it was—the real fear of losing their childhood home. It was common for Amish to up and move for a variety of reasons—a disagreement with the way the church district was being run, a rumor that land was more plentiful and less expensive in another state, even a vague restlessness to see somewhere different.

But this wasn't that.

This was being forced from your home, and to Hannah that made it a much graver thing.

"How much will you make?" Sharon asked.

Hannah told them the hourly wage she'd asked for and how many hours she thought she could work. "Not a full forty," she explained. "I told him that I still want to take Matthew to his appointments."

"We could do that for you."

"I know you could, Sharon. I know you both would, and *danki* for offering." She smoothed her apron out over her lap, then ran her hand across it again before looking up to meet her sisters' gazes. "This is something I'd like to continue to do, if I can."

Both sisters nodded as if they understood, and maybe they did.

Sharon scrounged around in her purse for a receipt and a pen. On the back of the receipt she added up what Simon had saved, what Carl had pulled together and what Hannah would make in the next month minus any taxes she would have to pay.

"You saw the letter." Sharon chewed on the end of the pen. "How much did it say they owed?"

When Hannah quoted the amount, Beth leaned closer to the paper. "We're a little short."

"But we still have thirty days."

"Twenty-eight." Hannah glanced over at her mother, who was sitting with the other women and watching the *youngies* play ball. "Twenty-eight days. Between now and then, we need to find a way to come up with the difference."

Chapter Six

Hannah tried on all three of her dresses Monday morning. The gray one made her look like a grandmother. The green was a bit snug. Had she actually gained weight since moving home? She could thank her mother's cooking for that. The dark blue was her oldest, but it was all that was left other than what she wore to Sunday services, and she wouldn't dare wear that to Jacob's workshop.

Frustrated that she cared about how she looked, she donned the dark blue dress, a fresh apron and her *kapp*. One last shrug at her reflection in the window, and she walked down the hall to Matthew's room. She didn't enter, though. Instead she paused at the door. She heard her son moving around, and yet he hadn't called out to her. That was a good sign. It meant he'd slept well.

She turned the knob and walked into the room.

The sky had barely begun to lighten outside, but she pulled

up the shades and then sat on his bed. He smiled up at her, curling over on his side.

"You look *gut*—pretty."

"Danki."

"Are you excited?"

"About my job?"

"Ya." He reached out for her apron strings, ran them through his fingers. "I would be excited, if I was going to spend all day with Jacob. Why can't I go? Please…"

He drew out the last word, and Hannah almost laughed. It sounded so normal, so everyday, that she actually didn't mind the whining.

"We've been over this. I will be working with numbers all day—"

"I can write my numbers."

"Yes, but I'm afraid it's a bit more complicated than that."

"And Jacob will be working."

"He will."

"On a playhouse?"

"I don't know."

Matthew considered that for a moment, and then he said what must have been on his mind all along. "I'd like to see some of his playhouses. They're not all trains—I know that because he described a few. I'd like to see what the others look like."

"Would you now?"

"Do you think that maybe…maybe we could?"

Hannah hesitated. She didn't want to encourage this infatuation that her son had for her boss. At the same time, as Sally had pointed out, it was natural for Matthew to look up to men in their community. "If they're in the area, and he tells me where they are…well, I don't see why we couldn't drive by when we're out on errands."

Matthew's smile was all the answer she needed. How could such a small thing bring him such joy? How was it that he managed to accept his condition so easily without bitterness? He pushed himself into an upright position and raised his arms for Hannah's father to pick him up.

"I didn't hear you come in," Hannah said.

"Because I'm as quiet as a cat and as quick as a panther." Her father winked at her as he carried Matthew out of the room.

"Have you ever seen a panther, *Daddi*?"

Matthew had slept well, woke up with no signs of a cold or infection and was showing a real interest in the things going on around him. It was a good day for certain, so why was a part of Hannah still worried?

She walked back into the room to fetch Matthew's clothes for the day.

"He'll be fine." Her father paused to kiss the top of her head, which made her feel like a small child again. It also made her feel loved and cared for. "And I appreciate your taking the job. I hope you know you don't have to."

"I know, *Dat*, but I want to help."

"Your *mamm* and I appreciate that."

"It's important—to be able to stay in this place, to raise Matthew surrounded by familiar things and people."

"Familiar to you, but not so much to Matt." Her father glanced across the hall into the bathroom to be sure that Matthew was fine without him. With a nod to indicate that the boy was all right, he sat down beside her on the bed. "You know, Hannah, it could be that *Gotte* has other plans for us, that we're not meant to stay in this house or even in this community."

"But you would want to…if you could. Right?"

"Things turn out best for the people who make the best of the way things turns out."

"Really, *Dat*? Your answer is a proverb?"

His smile eased the anxiousness in her heart and reminded her of Matthew. The two were more alike than she had realized.

"If you enjoy the job and if you can help Jacob, then you have my blessing. Listen to me closely though, Hannah. If you find it's too much pressure, I want you to remember that your priority is your son, not how much money you can make."

"*Ya, Dat,* but it's something I want to do."

He nodded as if he understood, and maybe he did.

Hannah barely ate any breakfast, though she did help to clean up the kitchen. After going over the morning instructions one last time with her mother, the entire family shooed her out of the house.

She hurried toward Dolly, who her father had already hitched to the buggy, turning back to call out, "I left Jacob's phone number on the sheet."

"We have it, but we won't need it."

"And I'm sorry I can't go to the store for you."

"Stop worrying. Matt and I will take care of it."

"I'll try. See you around four thirty."

Her mother had actually packed her a lunch. She should have done that herself.

Clucking to Dolly, she set off down the road.

When was the last time that she'd gone somewhere without her son? When was the last time she'd been alone? She found herself enjoying the drive, smiling at the other drivers on the road—both Amish and *Englisch*—and noting how well the flower gardens had bloomed. Every home she passed had some spot of color brightening their lawn, or bordering their vegetable rows or in pots on the front porch. Goshen was a tourist destination, nearly as popular as Shipshewana, and the houses and businesses made every effort to present a clean, colorful picture.

It took her less than twenty minutes to reach Jacob's place, and she was embarrassed to find herself there a full thirty minutes early.

"He'll think I'm overeager." She shook her head as she pulled down the lane. So what if she was? What did it matter? She was impatient to finally be of some help instead of a burden, and if she were honest, a little bit of her was looking forward to the quiet and challenge of a column of numbers.

Jacob was sitting on the front porch of the workshop when Hannah pulled down the lane. He shouldn't have been surprised that she was early. She seemed like the kind of person that would be.

By the time she set the brake on the buggy, he was standing there beside her. He took the reins and slipped them around the waist-high tie bar situated a few feet from the front of the shop.

"I can't believe that I've never been here."

She seemed a bit out of breath and flushed and beautiful. He shook the thought out of his mind and tried to pay attention to what she was saying.

"Not even when we were kids?"

"Maybe for church. I can't remember."

"The place looked different then."

He pointed to the area where his parents' home had been. "Micah and I cleared off the site after the fire and extended my mother's garden to cover the old homestead. We thought it would be a nice way to remember them."

"It's lovely, and I'm so very sorry about your parents."

"Every life is complete." He said the words without thinking about them. It was what they believed, what they always said during such times. It was only during those terrible nights when he relived the destruction of the fire in his nightmares that he struggled with the concept. In the light of day, with Hannah smiling at him, it was easy enough to believe that *Gotte* had a plan and purpose for each of their lives and that sometimes that plan was beyond their understanding.

"And you live over there?"

He glanced back at the twenty-foot prefab. It looked rather pitiful and shabby in the morning light. He'd done nothing to spruce it up—no porch or rocking chairs or flowers. It wasn't really a home, and he knew that. "*Ya*. It's temporary."

"How long have you lived there?"

"Six years."

Hannah looked directly at him for the first time since arriving, a look of surprise coloring her features. When he started laughing, she did too. He didn't mind her seeing the humor in the situation, mainly because she was laughing with him instead of at him.

Finally Hannah said, "I suppose it's enough for a bachelor."

"It is. Let me show you the workshop."

He took her through the main room, explaining the various stages that each project went through from commission to design, cutting, assembling, sanding and finishing.

"There's a lot to it," Hannah said.

"*Ya*." He was proud of his workshop. Every tool had a place. He cleaned each item after he used it and placed it on a peg on the wall. Sawdust was swept up each evening. Small projects were kept in large cubbies under one window that ran almost the entire length of the room. Bigger projects were lined up along the other wall. Design plans for playhouses were rolled and stored in smaller bins behind his worktable. A potbelly stove, rocking chair, hand-hooked rug made by his sister-in-law and small refrigerator adorned one corner.

The room looked better than where he lived.

"Bathroom's back in that corner."

"Place smells nice—like a lumberyard."

"The office is over here." He pointed to the room in the opposite corner.

Hannah raised an eyebrow and motioned for him to lead the way.

When they walked into the room, Jacob experienced a flash of panic. Who would want to work in this cramped little space all day? He'd made a feeble attempt to clean it up, but there was no hiding the fact that it had been neglected for years.

"This was my father's office. As you can see, I haven't used it much." He walked to the shelves and glanced at the items that had been there since the day his father had died. He hadn't wanted to move a thing, hadn't felt like he should. Fortunately, Hannah wouldn't need shelves, as there was a large desk.

Hannah stood there, frozen, letting her gaze drift from left to right and then back again. He waited for her to say something, but for once she seemed speechless.

"These tubs are full of receipts, and as you can see, each is labeled with the year."

"*Ya?*"

"I also put in the deposit slips each year, so you should be able to figure out what I earned versus what I spent. I tried to keep up with what people paid me by noting it on slips of paper, and you'll find a few of those."

"Slips of paper…"

"I'm afraid that after I figured my taxes each year, I probably tossed the worksheets, though I did keep a copy of the returns and they're in the box, as well."

Hannah raised the lid off one of the tubs, stared inside for a moment and then quickly closed the lid. "Well. I see I have my work cut out for me."

"I cleared off the desk."

"Danki."

"And there's a ledger, which I've never used."

"Obviously."

Jacob wondered if she would tell him that it was too big a job, that he was crazy to have been so lax with his record keeping, that he deserved whatever penalties the IRS threw at him. Instead she set her purse and lunch bag on the desk.

"You can write down your hours on that pad, and I'll pay you on Monday for the previous week's work if that's okay."

"That will be fine." Hannah touched the desk chair, which looked as if it might fall over.

How long had he had that thing? His dad had purchased it in some garage sale years and years ago.

"I'll go and look after Dolly."

"Oh, I can do that. I just wanted to make sure you hadn't changed your mind first."

He gave her an odd look, shook his head and said, "I'll be back in a minute."

And then he turned and left, because if he stood looking at Hannah King one more minute, wearing her pretty blue dress with the morning light shining through on her freshly laundered *kapp* and lightly freckled face...he'd start daydreaming again, and that was the very last thing that he needed to do.

★ ★ ★

Once Jacob left the office, Hannah glanced over at the bins in horror.

She stepped closer to the window and stared out at the fall day, watching as Jacob moved Dolly into the shade and fetched her a bucket of water. A man who cared properly for animals was a good man. Why hadn't Jacob ever married? Why did he live in a tiny trailer on this large piece of land? Surely he could afford better.

At least it looked as if business was booming.

She was good at math, and she had helped her husband with his business records in Wisconsin, but she'd never seen a mess like this before.

She stepped closer to one of the bins, opened the lid and peered inside. She pawed through the stack of paper—all sizes of paper, from a receipt from a cash register, to a bill that looked as if it had been scribbled on across the back, to a Publishers Clearing House flyer.

Looking closer, she sent up a silent thanks that at least she could read his handwriting.

Jacob walked back into the room, and she slammed the lid shut again.

"Problem?"

"Why would you say that?"

"I don't know. You look as if you've seen a runaway buggy."

She tried to smile. "Nope. No buggies. Just lots of receipts."

Jacob's smile vanished. "I know it's a lot of work, Hannah, but at least I kept the receipts separated by year."

"*Ya*, I see that."

"Six years. Six bins. That helps. Right?"

"I'm sure it will."

He stepped closer and reached out to put his hand on her arm.

"Hannah, I need to tell you something."

She didn't move, didn't breathe.

"I appreciate what you're doing, more than you could know."

She tried to listen to his words, but her heart had taken off at a galloping pulse, and she was staring at his hand on her arm. His fingers against her skin stirred something inside of Hannah, something she didn't realize she still possessed. Mixed with hope, and sprinkled with a dash of optimism— all things she hadn't felt in quite some time.

Jacob seemed to notice her discomfort. He dropped his hand to his side, then fiddled with the sleeve he'd rolled up to his elbows. "You're a real godsend."

"I haven't done anything yet." She laughed nervously and moved around the desk, running her fingers across the wood.

"I guess I'm headed out for the day. Just...make a list of any questions, and we'll go over them this afternoon or first thing tomorrow morning."

"Jacob—"

He seemed to brace himself against what she was about to say.

"I should thank you—for the job."

"Thank me?"

"The way I asked, *nein*, demanded, you to give it to me— that wasn't proper."

"You were right, though."

"I was?"

"This place is a mess. Even I can see it."

"There's a lot here for one person to take care of. You

probably should have hired help earlier. I hope I can rise to the challenge."

"I remember how you were with numbers in school."

"That was a long time ago."

He'd stuck his thumbs under his suspenders and walked to the door, but now he turned back toward her. "I did know about your father's difficulties. I just wasn't sure you'd want to leave Matthew."

"And I don't, but my parents and my sisters...everyone is going to pitch in and help. That's what family does, *ya*?"

Instead of answering, Jacob fetched his hat from a hook on the wall and rammed it on his head. "If anyone calls, please write down a message."

"Oh, you're leaving?"

"*Ya*. I just said I was headed out."

"I thought you meant...to the fields or something."

"My *bruder* works the fields on this place. I work here in the workshop or out on jobs."

"So that's where you're going? To a job?"

"One of the local builders has me putting in cabinets this week, in the new homes on the north side of town."

"Oh..."

"Some weeks I work here in the workshop."

"I see."

"I prefer to work on the playhouses whenever it's possible, but the cabinetry work—"

"It pays the bills."

"*Ya*. That it does." He looked out the office window.

Hannah wondered if he was stalling, though she couldn't imagine why. He seemed quite uncomfortable with her there and no doubt couldn't wait to be gone.

"I'll just get to work on these receipts, then. Most current year first?"

"I suppose."

"Okay…"

"I guess I'll see you this afternoon."

Hannah pushed her *kapp* strings back. "I planned to leave around four thirty."

"Weren't you taking Matthew to therapy today?"

"*Nein*, that's tomorrow and, well… I thought we'd wait and see how much work there actually is for me to do, and whether it's going to be a problem getting everything in order before your audit."

She wanted to say something more, to somehow put him at ease, but she had no idea how. Then she remembered the reason she was there.

"The IRS letter, you still have it?"

"Oh, *ya*. It's in the top right drawer. I guess you need to look it over."

"And you're sure you wouldn't rather take this all to an accountant?"

"I did go and see one, but the price they quoted was quite high."

"I'll try, Jacob."

"Which is all I can ask. The letter seems pretty straight-forward as far as what they want to see, which is why I need you."

"They don't take boxes full of receipts?"

"Apparently not." He pulled his hat off, turned it round and round in his hands. "If there are any other supplies you need, there's petty cash in the bottom drawer."

Jacob left so abruptly that Hannah stood staring after him for a moment. She'd spent much of the night worrying about how she'd be able to work with him in such close proximity. Apparently that wouldn't be a problem. He wouldn't even be on the property. Hannah waited until she saw his buggy drive past the workshop and down the lane before returning inside to the small office.

Though he'd apparently made an effort to clean the mess off the top of the desk, dust lay thick across its surface.

A clean desktop is the sign of a cluttered desk drawer. The proverb popped into her mind unbidden. Walking around to the other side of the desk, she spied what she'd known was somewhere close by...a box stuffed with everything that had been on top of it.

The window was smeared with dirt, and the floor hadn't been swept in ages.

He wasn't paying her to clean the office. On the other hand, who could work in these conditions? Would the IRS agent want to receive books covered in dust and grime? Not to mention what this room would do to her clean apron.

She tsked as she walked back through the main room in search of cleaning supplies. Finally she found them in a corner on the far side of the building—a broom, mop bucket, rags and even furniture polish. She carted it all back to the office and set to work.

Two hours later the place was sparkling. Opening the window had allowed a fresh, clean breeze to blow through. The desk was made from a beautiful dark cherry wood, and it shone from the furniture polish she'd used. She ran her palm across the surface and wondered if Jacob had built it. The chair was a real hazard, so she walked back into the main room and found a stool that was at least sturdy.

The box beside the desk held a tape dispenser, some pens, a stapler and rubber bands that had long ago aged to the point that they snapped when she tried to put one around a bundle of receipts. She dug through the supplies and found a box of pencils (though there was no sharpener that she could see), and a pad of paper.

As she ate her lunch, she began making a list of supplies, then found the petty cash box and placed both next to her purse. She'd stop by the general store while Matthew was at therapy the next day.

Finally she pulled the most recent bin over to the desk.

An hour later she had a list of questions for Jacob.

She couldn't begin entering things in the ledger until she spoke with him, and apparently that wouldn't be until the next morning. She could tape up receipts, but even the tape was yellowed and old, which left her quite a few hours to kill before she had to leave. Glancing around the small office, she decided one thing she could do was clear a bigger workspace.

She walked into the main room of the workshop and snooped around until she found two empty boxes. Taking them back into the office, she cleared off the items on the shelves. Dusty canning jars filled with an odd variety of nails and screws and even buttons. A broken pipe. A spool of thread. Some very old *Farmers' Almanac* editions dating back forty years.

She couldn't fathom why he was keeping most of the items, and she was tempted to scrape all of it into the trash bin. The basket by her desk wasn't large enough. Plus, it wasn't her place to decide what was and wasn't trash.

It was her place to put his financial records in order, and to do that she needed more space.

It took a little pushing and grunting, but she'd managed to move the desk closer to the shelves.

Now she'd be able to easily move between both, and she could also look out the window instead of having it at her back. She poured another mug of coffee from her thermos, snagged a cookie from the lunch her mother had packed and moved to the front porch. Sitting there she looked out over Jacob's land.

It was *gut* land. She could tell that, though she was only a farmer's daughter, not a farmer herself. It looked well cared for, so Jacob's brother must spend a fair amount of time working there. But the place that Jacob lived? She stared at it a minute before shaking her head in disbelief and going back into the office. There was no understanding the ways of men, especially confirmed bachelors.

Having no way to put off the inevitable, she once again pulled over the most recent bin containing the previous year's receipts and began pulling out scraps of paper. Perhaps she could stack them together by what appeared to be type— supplies, income notations, even hours spent on a job that were scribbled on a flyer about their annual school auction.

The rest of the afternoon flew by and the list of questions grew and grew until they filled up two sheets of paper. She was surprised to look up and see the hands on the clock had passed four. She was thinking of gathering her things to leave when she heard the clatter of a buggy. She wasn't too surprised when she glanced out the window and saw it was Jacob. Perhaps he had finished his day's work early.

She was standing in the doorway looking around in satisfaction when he walked up behind her.

Jacob had been a little afraid he'd arrive home to find that Hannah had left. The last girl had put a note on the desk and told him he didn't owe her for the morning's work. She'd also suggested he hire an accountant. It seemed that Hannah was made of tougher stuff. Perhaps if she'd survived the first day, it meant that she'd see the project through to the end. It wasn't so much that he wanted her around, but he was a man who could admit that he needed help. As far as accounting and the IRS went, Jacob needed all the help he could possibly find.

He walked up behind Hannah. Her tiny frame blocked the doorway, but he could see over her head into the office. Something looked different, but he couldn't put his finger on what it was.

"Did you have a *gut* day?"

"*Ya.*" She smiled back at him and stepped aside so he could see. "I think I accomplished a lot."

He stared at the office, or at least he thought it was his office, but it looked nothing like the room he'd left earlier that morning. He reached out for the door frame to keep from stumbling backward.

"What did you do?"

"What did I do?"

"What..." He walked into the office, strode across to the shelves that had held the precious mementos from his father. "Where did you put my father's things?"

"Do you mean the broken pipe and the jar full of mismatched doodads?"

Jacob bit back the first retort that came to mind. He closed his eyes—determined to count to ten—and made it to three. "*Ya,* those things. Where are they?"

"I didn't throw them away, Jacob. I put them in boxes and stored them in the utility closet."

"Why would you do such a thing?"

"Because I needed more space than the top of that desk."

"I could have built you a workbench."

"But the shelves were right there, and you weren't here to build me a workbench. What was I supposed to do all day?"

"Who moved the desk?"

"I did."

"By yourself?"

"Yes, by myself. It wasn't that hard. I got behind it and—"

"Pushed. You pushed it across the floor."

He squatted, ran his hand over a scratch in the wooden floor.

"Did I do that? I'm... I'm sorry, but this is a barn. Am I right? It's not like it's your living room."

No, his living room was part of a prefab house that held no meaning at all in his life, no memories of his parents. All he had that remained of his childhood was this old barn, the office, the garden that his mother had loved.

He clenched his jaw, determined not to speak harsh words. What was the old proverb? Think before you speak, but don't speak all you think.

Walking to the window, he stared out at his mother's garden. At least Hannah hadn't pulled up any of the plants in her compulsion to reorganize things. Suddenly he noticed how clean the windows were, and the floor, even the walls looked as if they'd been dusted.

"Did you do any of the work you were supposed to do today?"

"Excuse me?"

"I'm not paying you to clean windows or dust shelves."

"As I think I explained, I need those shelves, and I also need more light in this room if I'm to stare at your receipts all day."

"So you did at least look at them."

"Which was all I could do since I have no idea what your scribbling means."

"My scribbling?"

"When you actually took the time to label what you'd written onto some scrap of paper."

Hannah stomped toward the desk and yanked the bottom drawer open.

"You cleaned out the drawers too?"

For her answer she pulled out her purse and slammed the drawer shut. "I'll be going now."

"Going?"

"And if you expect me to work in this small, stuffy, poorly lit office, then I suggest you get used to the changes."

"Oh, is that so?"

"And don't bother offering to hitch up Dolly. I'm quite capable of doing it myself."

Chapter Seven

Hannah was so angry her ears felt hot.

No doubt they had been bright red as she stormed out of the office. What did she care if Jacob Schrock knew how aggravated she was?

Hitching up Dolly helped to burn up some of her anger. By the time she'd pulled out onto the two-lane road, she was composing her resignation letter in her head.

But as she drove the short distance to her parents' farm, she realized that she couldn't quit, not yet. She needed a job, and she was good at accounting. She could even bring order out of Jacob's chaos, if he'd let her.

Glancing out at the countryside, it struck her what day it was—the anniversary of the accident. Had her emotions recognized that all along? Was that why she was so emotional?

It wasn't until she was pulling into the lane, arching her neck forward to look for Matthew, that she realized the other source of her anxiety. It was true that Jacob's office had been a mess, and she had needed a better workspace, but it was also true that she was nervous about being away from Matthew all day. She was his mother. She should be there.

Her father met her at the door to the barn. "I'll take care of Dolly. How was your first day?"

"Fine," she lied. "Matthew?"

"In his playhouse. He's had a *gut* day."

Those words eased the worry that threatened to choke the breath out of her.

Had she become a helicopter parent? She knew practically nothing about helicopters. She'd seen one a few times, but she'd never ridden in one. She didn't know how that term could relate to her parenting abilities, but she'd seen the article in a magazine's headlines. Helicopter Parents' Horrendous Kids.

She'd actually paged through it as she waited for the woman in front of her to check out at the supermarket.

According to the article there were ten ways that she'd managed to mess up Matthew's life, and he wasn't even five years old. Among other things, she needed to start letting him work out his social issues, involve herself less in his day-to-day life and in general stop fussing over him. She'd shaken her head in mock despair and placed the magazine back on the rack.

But it wasn't mock despair she was feeling now.

Maybe she really had messed up his life.

She'd been gone less than eight hours, but it felt like she hadn't seen him in a week. The truth was that she couldn't stand to have him out of her sight.

He might need her.

And she was afraid to let him fail.

Hadn't he had enough disappointment in life?

She envisioned outlandish things happening to him.

Just that morning she'd worried that he might fall out of the buggy if her mother didn't make sure the door was shut. Her mother had been driving a buggy longer than Hannah had been alive.

Was it so wrong to worry though? Matthew was disabled. He was special, and he had special needs.

She pulled in a deep breath, put the parenting article out of her mind and headed for the train.

The next thirty minutes she spent listening to Matthew tell her about his day, as he pretended they were passengers headed to Alaska, and trying not to laugh as he wheeled himself back and forth across the train with the conductor hat on his head.

Her mood had improved dramatically by the time they went inside to help with dinner.

After they'd eaten and were clearing the dishes from the table, her temper had cooled enough that she'd begun to feel ashamed of herself. Her father had taken Matthew to the barn to help settle the horses for the evening. She peeked out the window, didn't see them and refocused on the plate she was drying.

"Problem, dear?"

"Why do you say that?"

"Because you just put a clean plate in the oven."

"I did?"

"Why don't you sit at the table and start shelling the purple hull peas? You can tell me about your day."

So she did. She told her mother about being overwhelmed by the task of preparing Jacob's files for a tax audit, of cleaning up his office with complete disregard to his preferences and of worrying Matthew might fall out of the buggy.

To her surprise, her mother started laughing and then couldn't stop.

"I don't see what's so funny."

Pulling off her reader glasses, her mother swiped at her eyes.

"I can't even tell if you're laughing or crying."

"I'm laughing."

"But why?"

Instead of answering, her mother put the kettle on to boil and dropped two bags of decaf raspberry tea into two mugs. She set a plate of oatmeal cookies between them and smiled at Hannah.

"You've always been an organizer."

"I have?"

"One day when you were little, I found you sorting through your father's socks, lining them up from most stained to least stained."

"I don't remember that."

The kettle on the stove whistled, and soon Hannah found herself holding a steaming cup of raspberry tea. She inhaled deeply and smiled over the rim at her mother.

"I remember organizing your button jar. It was one of my favorite things to do."

"One time I found them by color."

"And one time by size."

The memory touched a tender spot in Hannah's heart. It reminded her of a time before life had become so complicated. She reached for an oatmeal cookie. It was sweet, crunchy around the edges and full of raisins. It was bliss after a long, trying day.

"I suppose I might have been a bit hasty in scooping everything into the box."

"Perhaps those items had some sentimental meaning to Jacob."

"I don't see how."

"What were they?"

"An old pipe, some glass jars, old copies of *Farmers' Al-manac*..."

"Sounds like things that could have belonged to his father."

"But there was nothing valuable there."

"The office used to be his father's?"

"I suppose. That would also explain why he was upset that I moved the desk."

"You moved it?"

Hannah waved away her concern. "Wasn't so heavy when I pushed. I needed to move it to have better light, but perhaps I should have asked first."

"Perhaps..." Her mother reached for a cookie, chewed it thoughtfully and finally said, "You and Jacob are alike."

"No, we're not."

"Hear me out."

Hannah rolled her eyes and immediately felt twelve instead of twenty-six.

"You've both been dealt quite a blow."

"I suppose."

"You've both learned to live with that, and to keep going regardless of the strange and terrible turns that life can take."

Hannah shrugged.

"And you've both kept yourself apart from others."

"We're supposed to do that. We're Amish." She drew out the last word, as if her mother were hard of hearing.

"*Ya*, I'm aware, but you know very well that's not what I mean."

Hannah motioned for her to go on. Somehow it was easier to accept her mother's advice, her insights, when she was eating one of her favorite desserts.

"Neither of you are used to dealing with other people on a regular basis."

"We both have family."

"True."

"We go to the store."

"*Ya.*"

"See people at church."

"You know what I mean, Hannah King, so don't act like you don't."

Hannah popped the remainder of the second cookie in her mouth. She'd regret eating all of it later, but for now it made her feel marginally better.

"You're saying that because we don't date. Well, I don't. As far as I know, Jacob takes a different girl out in his buggy every night."

"Doubtful."

"I suppose."

"I'm only saying that you're both used to doing things your own way and not asking others their opinion."

"So I've lost my social skills?"

"Pretty much."

"Great."

"But the good news is you have another chance to improve those skills tomorrow."

Hannah groaned and pushed herself up from the table. "Any suggestions for how I should do that?"

"You could start with an apology."

Apologizing was the last thing that she wanted to do. She patted her mother on the shoulder and went in search of her son. After she'd helped Matthew with his bath, tucked him in, read a bedtime story and listened to his prayers, she knew what she needed to do. So she went to her room, spent a few minutes in prayer and finally opened her well-worn

Bible. It didn't take long to find the verse that was weighing on her heart. She thumbed through the pages until she found the book of Matthew, the fifth chapter, beginning in the twenty-third verse.

Therefore if thou bring thy gift to the altar, and there rememberest that thy brother hath ought against thee; leave thy gift before the altar, and go thy way; first be reconciled to thy brother, and then come and offer thy gift.

There didn't seem to be much wiggle room in Christ's words. Obviously she had offended Jacob. After speaking with her mother, she understood that clearly. Now all she had to do was work up the courage to admit that she'd been wrong, she'd acted hastily, and she was sorry to have raised her voice and left so abruptly. It shouldn't be that hard of a thing to get through, and even if it was, she was pretty sure apologizing would be the first item on her list at work the next day.

Relief washed over Jacob when he heard Hannah's buggy approaching. He'd convinced himself that he'd blown it and that she wasn't coming back.

He pretended to be busy working on a coffee table when she walked inside.

"I thought you'd be at your job site already."

"I thought you might not come."

Their eyes locked for what seemed like a lifetime, and finally Hannah smiled ruefully, walked toward him and sat down across from his workbench.

"I did consider resigning…"

"You wouldn't be the first."

"But then I realized that I need this job."

"Hannah, we both know you can find a better job—one that pays more and doesn't require you to mop the floor."

He glanced up at her and then stared back down at the coffee table. Had he been sanding or staining it?

"Maybe I could find another job, but I didn't like what was out there."

"Apparently you didn't like what was in here, either."

"Jacob, I am sorry for raising my voice at you yesterday and for disregarding your father's things."

Jacob's head snapped up, and he found Hannah staring at him, a look of regret on her face.

"I should have asked first."

He smiled for the first time that day as the knot in his stomach slowly unwound. "*Dat* would have told me to clean the office long ago. He always said he was going to, but then he'd get distracted by something else."

"Still, those items were special to you, and if you want them on the shelves I'll put them back."

"No need to do that."

"I'm not sorry for cleaning or moving the furniture, but if you don't want to pay me for those hours, I understand."

"You're so *gut* at cleaning, maybe you could tackle my house." When she straightened up in alarm, he said, "I'm kidding. What I mean is that I've probably grown used to things being a bit messy."

Hannah ran a finger across the top of his workbench and held it up. "Your workshop is clean enough. See? No dust."

No dust. That meant he had been staining the piece he was working on, not sanding it, which also explained the rag in his hand. Honestly, what was wrong with his train of thought these days?

"*Ya,* having a clean workspace is important when I'm staining wood, and it helps to keep my tools in good condition." He sighed and grimaced, knowing what he needed to say next. "I'm sure having a clean and functional work area is important for your work too. I'm sorry I overreacted."

"So we're *gut*?"

"We are."

"Great." She hopped off the bench. "Oh, one more thing, though. I would like to leave early on days that Matt has therapy appointments. So today I'll work through lunch and leave at one."

"That isn't a problem."

"You're sure?"

"I thought we had already agreed on that. You'll be taking off early on therapy days—Tuesday, Wednesday and Friday. Right?"

"Right. It's possible I could take some of the work with me and do it in the office waiting room."

"Only if you want to."

She walked across to the office and then pivoted to face him. "Why aren't you at the job site today?"

"The builder didn't get all the supplies in on time, but he was expecting a shipment later today. I guess I'll head back over tomorrow."

"Okay. Do you have time to answer some questions?"

"I can try."

"You might want to bring a mug of coffee."

"For myself or both of us?"

Her smile broadened, and Jacob realized she was one of the prettiest women he knew. The fact that she had called him on the wreck of an office he'd wanted her to work in? He could see now that he'd deserved that.

"Bring a cup for both of us. I have a lot of questions."

Hannah told herself she needed to get over her nerves if she was going to work in close proximity with Jacob every day.

She felt like a schoolgirl with a crush. What was she thinking? She did not have romantic feelings for Jacob Schrock. She was a grown woman with a young child and a job. She was way beyond crushes.

Jacob pulled the old office chair back into the office. "Don't look at me that way. It's not for you to sit on. I brought it for myself."

"*Gut.* What I mean is, I was afraid it would collapse under me."

Jacob's grin widened as he handed her a mug of coffee. "Sorry I don't have anything sweet to go with this. I'm not actually a baker."

Hannah popped up, retrieved her quilted lunch bag and pulled out a Tupperware container filled with snickerdoodle squares. "Apparently my *mamm* thinks this job is going to require massive amounts of sugar."

The food and coffee helped to ease what tension remained between them.

Hannah pulled out the notes she'd made the day before and began firing questions at him.

"What does the notation *R* mean?"

"Money I received for a job."

"And *P* means…"

"Something I paid for."

"Okay. I'd sort of figured those out, but what in the world is *Q*?"

"Means I had a question. Wasn't sure if the receipt was important or not."

"Give me an example."

"Buggy repairs."

"Excuse me?"

"*Englischers* take off car repairs…"

"*Nein.* They take off mileage, and they're allowed so much

per mile for traveling to and from locations that are job related."

"So can I take off mileage?"

She tapped her pen against the pad of paper and made a notation.

"What did you write down?"

"A note to call your accountant and ask him or her."

"I don't have an accountant. That's why I'm in this mess."

"You're in this mess because you are ignorant…"

Jacob choked on his coffee.

"By that I mean you're uneducated in the ways of *Englisch* laws. There are going to be questions I can't answer, Jacob. We need to ask a professional."

"*Gut* point."

"I'll make a list and you can call whomever you trust."

Jacob pulled the pad toward him and wrote the name of a Goshen accounting firm across the top of the page, then added the name of the person she should contact.

"You call them. I'm making accountant questions officially a part of your job."

"I imagine they'll bill you for the time."

"It'll still be much less than having them tape up receipts." He leaned back in his chair, causing it to let out an alarming groan, and laced his fingers behind his head. "Do you know how to use the phone?"

"*Ya.* I've used one a few times." She tried not to stare at the muscles bulging in his arms. Who would have thought that a woodworker would be in such good shape?

"So no phone lessons are required."

"I'm a little surprised you have one here in the shop."

"The bishop allows it, and truthfully my mother wanted one. She was always worried one of us would injure ourselves with a table saw. The woman had quite an imagination. Anyway, when the bishop started allowing them for businesses, she ordered one."

"So she could call 911?"

"*Ya.*"

"Did she ever have to?"

"Only when my *dat* was bit by a snake. He wanted to drive himself to the hospital, but she had an ambulance on the way before he could hobble to the horse stall."

"Was it poisonous?"

"Probably not. The critter crawled away, and he didn't have a chance to identify it. The doctors treated him all the same, and *Mamm* was forever saying that she'd saved his life by having the phone installed."

"They sound like very special people."

"They were." Jacob swallowed hard, but he didn't look away from her. "I suppose that sometimes I forget the good memories...you know, trying not to dwell on the bad."

"I can understand that." Hannah thought of what her mother had said, that they'd both been dealt a blow.

Jacob cleared his throat and sat forward, arms crossed on the desk. "How do you know so much about accounting and IRS reports?"

"I first worked doing some accounting here in town, down at the furniture factory when I was a *youngie.*"

"I didn't know that."

"You and I didn't stay in touch after our failed attempt at dating, not really."

"Maybe we should have."

"Why?"

She half hoped that he would answer, but he seemed suddenly interested in the snickerdoodle in his hand, so she let it slide.

"Okay, let's see what else I have here."

They went down her list of questions until she felt like she had a fair understanding of his system—which wasn't much of a system, but at least it was consistent.

Finally she said, "This isn't going to be as complicated as I feared. You only have a few categories that your deductions will fall under. I am curious, though—how did you even pay your taxes without knowing exactly what you'd made and what you'd spent?"

"I tried to fill out the IRS worksheets, but mostly that was a guessing game. Mainly I looked at my balance in my bank account and paid based on that."

"But you must have spent money that wasn't business related."

"Look around, Hannah. Does it look like I've spent much on the place?"

"I see your point."

"No big vacations, no major purchases, it seemed pretty straightforward to me."

"Everyone has to file taxes—even Amish."

"Not if we make under a certain amount, and believe me, if I made over that amount, it wasn't by much."

"That's true for individuals, but businesses must file whether they have a profit or loss."

"Which I did."

"And yet you're being audited. Perhaps you didn't include all the forms you were required to include."

When he looked at her skeptically, she explained, "After I married, I did my husband's taxes for the farm. We even had a nice Mennonite woman come to the local library and help us."

"*Wunderbaar.* Then you know what you're doing."

"Let's hope so." She tapped her pen against the pad.

"What?"

"You might have some money coming back to you. There are a lot of deductions that wouldn't have shown up as an extra expense. Like, say, the use of this part of the barn."

Jacob glanced left and right and then leaned forward. "You mean this room? I've heard it's small and stuffy and poorly lit."

She crossed her arms in defense, but she couldn't help smiling. "*Ya.* I think you're right. Still, it's deductible because it's the place you do business, as is the part out there where you work on your projects."

"You're *gut* at this, Hannah."

"Better wait until we're through the audit to decide that. Speaking of the audit…"

This time it was Jacob that groaned instead of the chair.

"We only have ten days, Jacob."

"Are you sure?"

"According to the letter they sent, an agent will be here to examine your files on September 10."

"Oh."

"Today is August 28."

"Can we ask for an extension?"

"We can, but…the Mennonite woman in Wisconsin, she had a college degree in accounting and worked for a local accountant. She said that the IRS will grant an extension, but they'll look at things more closely because of it. Also, any penalties you have would be greater because more time will have passed since you owed the taxes."

"I just want to build playhouses."

"*Ya*, most business owners love what they do, but they're not prepared for the amount of paperwork that comes with it."

"Can you have it ready? By the tenth?"

"Maybe, if I take it home with me, work on it a little each

night and put in as many hours here as possible." Even as she uttered those words, Hannah wondered what in the world she was doing. She wanted to spend time with Matthew. She wanted to work in the garden. She didn't want to spend every free minute taping up Jacob's receipts.

"You would do that?"

"I guess, but is there anyone else who could help? Anyone who could at least tape these receipts onto sheets of paper for me? That would save a lot of time."

"I have five nephews who live next door. They're always bugging me to come see them."

"You don't go next door to see your nephews?"

"I've been busy is all." Jacob began gathering up their cups and putting the lid back on the empty Tupperware.

"How old are they?"

"Oldest is eleven, no...twelve."

"That's certainly old enough to help with this project, and my niece Naomi was looking for a way to earn a little Christmas money."

"Let's tell the *kinder* that I'll pay them two bucks an hour. Wait, will I be in trouble with the child labor laws?"

"I don't think taping receipts for an hour each night falls into that category."

"Gut." He stood, holding the cups in his left hand and tapping on the table with his right. "I'll load up one of the bins later today in your buggy for you to take to your niece."

"Load two. I'll work on one and Naomi can work on the other."

"And I'll take two over to my nephews."

"We need to get the past five years in order. Can you do the last one?"

Jacob shook his head in disbelief. "You're pushy, you know that?"

But the way he smiled at Hannah sent a river of good feelings through her.

Jacob turned to go back into the main room. As she worked she could hear him in there—humming and sanding, and occasionally using some sort of battery-powered tool. She felt a new optimism that maybe they could be ready in time. It would take a tremendous effort, but she'd never minded hard work.

And with the extra overtime hours, she might just be able to help save her parents' farm.

As for Jacob, it wasn't as if they were friends, but it felt good to have an employer she could talk to. It helped to know that he'd forgiven her for her behavior the day before.

Despite the silly schoolgirl feelings she sometimes had around Jacob, she also understood that she was a mother and her sole focus was her child. She wasn't interested in dating or expanding her social circle. Still, they could learn to enjoy working with one another—as long as they kept things on a professional basis, she saw no harm in it.

To be professional one needed to extend certain courtesies, so perhaps her mother was right. Maybe they both needed to work on their social skills.

Chapter Eight

Jacob had fallen into a comfortable routine by Thursday afternoon. On days that Hannah left early to take Matthew to therapy, he would putter around in his workshop until she arrived. Then they'd spend thirty minutes talking about what progress they'd made on the accounting reconstruction, whether she had any questions and if he'd thought of any other items she needed to know about his business.

His excuses for being there were relatively lame—needing to put a final coat of sealant on a birdhouse, giving his gelding Bo time in the pasture, not wanting to get caught in early-morning traffic.

On the days when she didn't leave early, he was gone before she arrived. He did this so he could be at the job site early, finish his work well before four and come home in time to spend the last hour or so with Hannah. They didn't work together. He was usually in the workshop, and she was in the tiny office. But just knowing someone else was there seemed to give the old barn new life.

His schedule was set, and he was pretty happy with it.

He left for work late on therapy days—Tuesday, Wednesday, and Friday. He left for home early on Monday and Thursday. He always had an answer ready in case anyone asked, as if he needed to justify his irregular hours.

He didn't share his excuses with Hannah. Instead he recited them to himself over and over in his mind.

He should be there in case she had questions.

He needed to catch up on his small jobs.

She might need something moved in the office.

But with each day that passed, he understood that those were just excuses. *You might be able to fool someone else part of the time, but you can rarely fool yourself.* The memory of his father's words brought a smile as he made his way home early Thursday afternoon.

Deep inside, beneath all the layers of why it wouldn't work and how foolish he was being, Jacob understood that he was falling for Hannah.

It was hard to believe that she had been working in his office for less than a week. It seemed like she belonged there.

Thursday he arrived home around two o'clock. His days on the job site were getting shorter and shorter, but the boss was happy with what he'd been able to accomplish, and that was what mattered.

He'd opened the large doors of the barn to let in the fall air and was working on a front entry bench for one of his *Englisch* neighbors when Hannah plopped into a chair next to his workbench.

"Problem with the receipts? Let me guess, you can't tell my threes from my eights."

"*Nein.* It's not about the numbers."

"What is it? Is Matthew okay?" He clutched the piece of sandpaper he'd been using in both hands. Surely she would have told him if Matthew wasn't well.

"He's fine. It's only that he's turning five in a couple of weeks."

"When is his birthday?"

"September 25."

"We should have a party."

Hannah crossed her arms, as if to ward off more unwelcome ideas. "Matthew prefers to have small, private celebrations."

Matthew did? Or Hannah? He was about to ask when common sense saved him and he closed his mouth. It wasn't his business how she raised her child, or at least it shouldn't be. Should it?

"But that's not what I came to tell you. I'm going to need to leave early today, even though it's not a therapy day."

Jacob pushed away the disappointment that welled up inside him. "That's not a problem."

"You're sure?"

"*Ya.* I know you're doing extra work at home. From the stack of pages on your desk it would seem the great taping project of the year is nearly done."

"Speaking of taping...how's your bin coming along?"

Instead of admitting that he hadn't actually started, he asked, "Why do they have to be taped up anyway? A receipt is a receipt."

Hannah's eyes widened and she looked at him as if he were wearing two pairs of suspenders. "Because the IRS doesn't deal in scraps of paper, and when I enter them in the ledger, I do so by date."

"You have to sort them by date?"

Hannah shook her head in mock despair, or maybe it was

real despair. "Stick to your woodwork, Jacob Schrock. Leave the office work to me."

He liked the sound of that. He liked the idea that she planned to stick around longer than the next two weeks.

Hannah went back into the office, ignoring the way that Jacob was looking at her. Maybe she was imagining it, but he seemed happy when she was around, almost as happy as he had been when he was working on Matthew's playhouse.

She plopped down in front of the desk. She was helping him out of a jam. Of course he was happy. Why wouldn't he be happy? Things weren't that clear-cut, though. She understood all too well that he was helping her out of a jam at the same time.

She'd taken the most recent year of receipts herself, and she'd stayed up well past her normal bedtime—sitting at the kitchen table, taping receipts and sorting them by month. Now, back in Jacob's office, she opened the journal and began entering them under the proper category headings. She immersed herself in the work, and thirty minutes later was surprised to hear the clatter of buggy wheels outside.

Looking up, she saw that it was her brother-in-law and began tidying up the desk. She'd brought a quilted bag from home, and she carefully placed the next two months of receipts in it, along with the ledger, a few extra pencils and the battery-operated sharpener she'd purchased at the store.

By the time she'd made it out into the larger room, Jacob was wiping his hands off on a cloth and frowning at the buggy that had parked in front of the workshop.

"Your ride?" he asked.

"*Ya.*"

He nodded once, curtly, and turned back toward his workbench.

"I'm taking some work with me, to make up for the time I'm missing." When he didn't answer she added, "Thanks again, Jacob."

He bobbed his head but was suddenly completely focused on cleaning some of his tools. It all seemed like rather odd behavior. Usually Jacob was the friendly, outgoing sort.

Shrugging, she said, "See you tomorrow, I guess."

Still no answer, so she gave up on making conversation and walked outside.

Her brother-in-law had just pulled up to the hitching post and jumped out of the buggy.

"Carl, *danki* for picking me up."

"No problem."

"When *Dat* dropped me off, he thought he'd be able to come back and get me."

"*Ya*, he told me as much, but his errands in town took longer than he thought. It's really no problem, Hannah."

He put his arm around her shoulders and gave her a clumsy hug. Carl was the big brother she'd never had. He'd been in the family over a dozen years, and Hannah thought the world of him. It helped that he was so good with Matthew, who happened to be sitting in the back seat practically bouncing up and down, if a boy with a spinal cord injury could bounce.

Hannah stuck her head inside. "What are you doing here?"

"Carl said I could come."

"And why would you want to do that?"

"I told you, *Mamm*. I want to see where you work. Is Jacob here? Can I come inside?"

"Oh, I don't think we have time for that."

"Sure we do," Carl said. "I even brought his chair."

Hannah resisted the urge to ask why in the world he would do that. Carl was just trying to help, and Matthew's fascination with Jacob hadn't lessened one bit in the last few days.

She didn't think this was a good idea, but Carl was already removing Matthew's wheelchair from where it was strapped on the back of the buggy.

"All right," she said with a sigh. "Let's get this over with."

Jacob had immediately gone to the window when Hannah walked out of the room. He knew he shouldn't be aggravated with her. He couldn't expect her to work all of the time, and of course she had a social life. Why wouldn't she? Hannah was a smart, beautiful, young woman. She'd been a widow for over a year now. Of course she was lonely and ready to step out again. He was surprised she didn't have beaus dropping her off and picking her up every day.

When the man jumped out of the buggy and gave her a hug, Jacob understood the full depth of his misery. Not only had he fallen for a woman who could never possibly care for an ogre like himself, but she was already being courted. He could have asked around. He could have saved himself the embarrassment.

He thought to sneak out the back and over to his house or the garden or anywhere that he wouldn't have to watch the two of them when the man walked around to the back of the buggy. He reappeared with Matthew's wheelchair. She had trusted Matthew with this fellow? They must be even closer than he feared.

Now he was torn, but that feeling didn't last long because the man had plopped Matthew into the chair as if he weighed no more than a sack of potatoes. Matthew was grinning up at his mother, and Hannah was pointing at the workshop. There was no way he was going to sneak out of this. He wasn't beneath slipping away and being borderline rude to an Amish man, but he couldn't find it in his heart to ignore young Matthew.

So he pulled in a deep breath, straightened his suspenders and walked out into the fall afternoon.

Matthew let out a squeal the minute he saw him.

"Jacob! Carl brought me over to see where you work."

Hannah reached forward and straightened Matthew's shirt. "I thought he came to pick me up."

"That too." Carl stepped forward and offered his hand to Jacob. "It's been a while."

A while?

"We were in the same church district, before we grew too big and had to split."

He did look familiar.

The man laughed good-naturedly. "Carl Yoder. I'm married to Hannah's sister, Beth."

The flood of relief that swept through Jacob confirmed what he had already figured out—he'd developed feelings for Hannah King, and he was in much too far to back out now.

He spent the next twenty minutes walking Carl and Matthew through the workshop, showing them the types of things he made and answering Matthew's endless supply of questions.

"I want to see your playhouses, Jacob."

"You have one of my playhouses, buddy."

"But I want to see the other ones. The ones that you made for other people. Are they all for disabled kids like me?"

"Yes, they are, but different kids have different special needs."

"I don't know what that means."

"Some disabilities you can see on the outside, but others, they're inside—so those playhouses might not have grab bars. Maybe the person can't see well, so the playhouse is flat on the ground—no steps and no ramps."

"How's that a playhouse, then?"

Jacob laughed and ruffled the hair on the top of Matthew's head.

"Say, isn't there one over by me?" Carl asked. "Built like a ship. That has to be your work."

"*Ya*. Made it last year for a young boy with cancer."

"Can I see it?" Matthew began tugging on his hand. "Can we go there? Would he let me play with him?"

"I'm not sure how Jasper is doing now. We'd need to check with his parents."

"Will you? Will you call them?"

"That's enough, Matthew." Hannah had moved behind Matthew's chair and had pivoted it toward the barn door. "Jacob has lots to do. He can't be ferrying you around to playgrounds because you're curious."

"I could take you both on Saturday."

Matthew squealed in delight and raised his hand for a fist bump. Jacob obliged and then he noticed the frown on Hannah's face.

"Oh. Unless you had something else you needed to do on Saturday."

"I had planned on working on your receipts."

"We could go without you. I don't mind taking him."

"You need to work on receipts too."

"Well, we could do that in the morning and go to see the playhouse in the afternoon."

"Come on, *Mamm*. Please…" Matthew drew the word out in a well-practiced whine, but he added a smile, which caused his mother to sigh heavily.

"Okay, but only for an hour."

"Jacob could come for lunch and then we could—"

"Let's not strain your *mamm*'s patience. She has things planned for her Saturday."

Carl had been studying a row of birdhouses. He picked one up and asked, "How much?"

"Ten."

"Costs you more than that to build it."

"*Nein*. I use old barn wood. Costs practically nothing to build it."

Carl grinned. "I'll take two, then. Beth will love them."

Matthew offered to hold the birdhouses, and Carl once again shook Jacob's hand. "This has been great, but I need to get back before Beth thinks I've taken off for the auction in Shipshe without her."

"I didn't know you were going," Hannah said.

"She wants goats, if you can believe that. As if she doesn't have enough to take care of, and the new baby on the way…" Carl shook his head as if he couldn't fathom the ways of women and offered to wheel Matthew back to the buggy.

Hannah hung back, and Jacob had the feeling that it wasn't to say *thank you*.

"I'm sorry he pressured you into that."

"It's not a problem."

"A four-year-old can be quite persistent once they've made up their mind, and Matthew doubly so. He's been pestering me about coming to see you since I started on Monday."

"I really don't mind."

"The thing is…" Hannah hesitated and then pushed on. "Matthew gets attached to people and then they move on to other…phases of their lives. He doesn't handle that very well."

"Where would I move on to?"

"He gets too attached, if you know what I mean."

"I don't." He waited, wondering what she did mean and trying not to be stung by her suggestion that he was going to somehow let Matthew down.

"It's up to me to protect him."

"From what? *Freinden?*"

"You're not his *freind*, Jacob."

"Of course I am."

"*Nein*. You're my boss."

He stared out the window for a moment, watched Carl lift Matthew out of his wheelchair and place him in the buggy. He wondered how hard it was for Hannah to depend on other people, especially after losing her husband. "Let me take you both out on Saturday, show him a couple of playhouses. We'll keep it to an hour so it doesn't disrupt your whole day."

"Okay, fine. I guess."

"I know the owners, and they wouldn't mind Matthew playing on them. Most are for children his age."

"Playdates don't always go well with Matthew."

"What do you mean?"

"Other children can't possibly understand his limitations, why he needs to be careful..."

"I've worked with several disabled kids. They seem pretty intuitive about such things."

"And I've seen children point and ask cruel questions, or, worse yet, ignore him completely."

"Is that what you're worried about? Or is it that you're afraid I'll somehow let Matthew down? Because I can assure you right now that isn't going to happen."

"He's too taken with you."

"Excuse me?"

"He doesn't understand that you were simply hired to do a job, and that now I'm hired to do a job. He thinks...well, he thinks that there's something more to it."

"Hannah, what you're saying is true, or was true. I was hired for a job, and now I've hired you for a job." He wondered if he should just shut up, but ignored that idea. "I think, though, that Matthew is also right. We're part of a community. We belong to the same church."

"Different districts."

"We are neighbors and *freinden*."

She nodded once, curtly, and turned. He walked beside her as she made her way back outside. Carl had climbed into the buggy and was waiting.

He'd noticed that when she was embarrassed or nervous, she liked to keep her hands busy. At the moment, she was twisting the strings to her prayer *kapp* round and round. He'd also learned that if he waited, she would eventually work through her emotions and pick up the conversation again.

"*Ya*, of course you're right. It's only that I don't want him to get the wrong idea."

"What wrong idea? That I like you? Because I do."

She cocked her had to the side, glancing up at him and allowing her gaze to linger there before flitting away. "We'll see you Saturday, two o'clock."

And then, she scurried back off to the buggy. There was simply no other word for it. She reminded him of a squirrel running back toward its safe spot in the woods.

The question was, how he was ever going to convince her that being with him was safe and that they were more than friends. Were they? Or was his imagination running wild again? He reached up to scratch at the scars on his face.

Scars.

Everyone had them, but his were hideous. He'd thought that keeping them, that refusing the cosmetic surgery, would help pay the debt he owed for not saving his parents. He'd never considered that they might push away someone that he cared about. What if Hannah simply couldn't abide looking at him from one day to the next? She'd never hinted at that, but people could hide their feelings. If she was repulsed by him, it wouldn't mean that she was shallow, only that she was human.

He walked back into his workshop and began sanding again, more aggressively this time.

He didn't know if Hannah was worried about protecting Matthew's feelings or her own, but he did know that she needed to stop shielding the boy from all of life's ups and downs. Matthew needed friends the same as everyone else, and if it meant that someone occasionally let him down... that was part of growing up.

One other thing he knew for certain. He wouldn't be the one to disappoint Matthew. Now all he had to do was find a way to convince Hannah of that.

It was risky. Putting his feelings out there would mean that he might be hurt, and he'd had his fair share of that already. But not letting her know how he felt? Not taking a chance to get to know her on a personal level? That felt like a bigger risk than he was willing to take.

Chapter Nine

Friday dawned beautiful, cool and crisp. If she'd lived closer, Hannah would have walked to work. As it was, she said goodbye to her family and drove Dolly the few miles to Jacob's place. She was still uncomfortable with the way things had ended between them the day before. Had he actually said he liked her? What did that mean?

Fortunately he wasn't there when she arrived, so she didn't have to worry about being embarrassed about the way they'd left things. She went straight to the office and was soon immersed in receipts and columns of figures and IRS categories. The morning passed quickly and her stomach began to grumble. She was about to pull over yet another box of receipts when she heard a whistle from out in the yard. She hurried to the door and saw Emily Schrock making her way toward the workshop, a basket over her arm and a smile on her face. Hannah hadn't seen Jacob's sister-in-law in years.

In fact, the last time she'd seen her they'd been in grade
school together.

"Tell me you have some cold tea or hot coffee in there."

"I have both, and scones too—fresh blueberry."

Emily was nearly as round as she was tall, and she always
had been as far back as Hannah could remember. She was the
traditional Amish woman, and probably could have starred
in one of the local Amish plays. Quick with a smile, an excellent cook and, if Hannah remembered right, she had a
whole passel of children. As Emily stepped closer, Hannah
realized she was also expecting another child, though her
baby bump wasn't yet too obvious. It seemed Hannah's lot
in life to be surrounded by pregnant women.

"Come in the office. I finally finished cleaning."

Emily let out a long whistle as she walked into the room.
"Wow. You did all of this…this week?"

Hannah allowed the woman to enfold her in a hug.

"We're so glad you're here."

"We?"

"Micah and I. We worry about Jacob, and the IRS audit…
Micah was ready to hire one of the *Englisch* accountants in
town."

"He may still need to. I haven't actually worked through
all of his receipts yet."

"And his books?"

"He doesn't have any."

"I suppose that's part of the problem. I'm sure you'll be
able to fix it, though. I remember how you were in school.
Math was your favorite subject."

"Still is," Hannah admitted. "It's what I enjoy about quilting, the measuring and calculating."

"And what I always make mistakes on. How about we go

outside? The rocking chairs looked more comfortable than the stool you have behind your desk."

Hannah readily agreed. As they walked back out into the fall sunshine, she asked, "How are you? I see you're expecting again."

"I am, and I dearly hope it's a girl, though of course we'll love whatever *Gotte* blesses us with." She opened the thermos and poured two cups of coffee.

It was much better than what Jacob made in the workshop, and Hannah sipped it with pleasure, closing her eyes and enjoying the rich taste.

"You have several boys already, right?"

"Five. Samuel is twelve. He's our oldest. The twins—Timothy and Thomas—are ten. Eli's nine, and Joseph is six."

"I'll never remember all those names." Hannah laughed and plucked one of the scones from the basket.

"You know how it is with Amish families—big and loud and messy." As if suddenly remembering Hannah's situation, she set down the scone she'd been eating and brushed off her fingertips on her apron. "I was so sorry to hear about Matthew's accident, and your husband...a real tragedy."

"Danki." The word was barely a whisper.

"I should have come to see you."

"Nein. Why would you? You have your hands full with your own children and husband to care for, your home to maintain and—"

"Why would I?" Emily looked truly shocked at the question. "Because we're *freinden.* Because we take care of each other, like family."

Nearly the same words that Jacob had said to Hannah earlier.

Emily picked up her scone and finished it off with the last of her coffee. "I know we're not technically in the same district, but that doesn't matter. We're still one community. Maybe you could bring Matthew to meet my boys."

"Oh, I don't know—"

"They're rambunctious but they're *gut* boys."

"Where are they at this morning?"

"With my parents, who live on the other side of us. They'll all be in school this year. My youngest is only a year older than Matthew. He's four, right?"

"Nearly five."

"And Joseph is barely six. They could be *gut frienden*."

Hannah didn't answer that. She thought it unlikely that a healthy six-year-old would want to be friends with a disabled five-year-old. The thought stung her, stirred the old ache, and she pushed it away.

"Tell me about Jacob," she said, more to change the subject than anything else.

"Oh, *ya*, sure. There's not a lot to tell. You know about the fire."

"My mother told me about it."

"Happened six years ago, but he still hasn't healed from that night, in my opinion."

"He was here when it happened?"

"*Nein.* He was downtown, courting a young girl from the next district. He came back late and the home was already ablaze."

"Lightning is what *Mamm* said."

"So the firefighters told us. Jacob blames himself, I think."

"For a lightning strike?"

"More because he wasn't here. He didn't get to them in time, or he might have saved them—at least that's what he said when they were transporting him to the hospital. Maybe he blames Micah too. Our place is next door but over the hill. We didn't realize what had happened until we heard the fire trucks."

"Jacob ran into it…into the fire?"

"He did." Emily began tidying up, offered Hannah another scone, then repacked the picnic basket. "His scars—the ones on the inside—they are far worse than the ones on his face."

"It must be hard—being disfigured."

Emily shook her head so hard that her *kapp* strings swung back and forth. "No one even notices anymore. What they see is what he is—a *gut* man who is hurting."

Hannah realized Emily was right; she hadn't really thought of his scars in a long time. She certainly didn't notice them anymore. "And yet it's hard to be different."

"Not if we're humble, it isn't."

Hannah bit back the retort that came too quickly to her lips. *What would you know of being different?* It was often easy for those not suffering from a thing to tell you how to handle it. She didn't utter either of those thoughts aloud, however. Emily obviously cared for Jacob and only wanted what was best for him.

Hannah set her chair to rocking, determined not to butt into the other family's affairs. Emily, however, wasn't done yet, perhaps because she had no other woman in her household to share her worries and concerns with.

"I know several *gut* women who would be happy to court Jacob, but he can't see past his own scars. It worries me, for sure and certain it does."

"You care about him."

"All I know to do is keep trying, because if you ask me, Jacob needs a family. He needs to get his attention off himself and onto someone else. He needs to learn to love again."

★ ★ ★

Friday didn't work out the way Jacob had hoped. He had to be at the job early, before sunrise, so that he could finish the cabinetry work in time for the job superintendent to approve what he'd done. He could have pushed some of the work off until Saturday, but he had plans with Hannah and Matthew the next day. That thought had him whistling through his breakfast of oatmeal and coffee.

He finished the cabinetry job well before lunch. He told himself that he didn't work quickly so that he could at least say hello to Hannah before she left for Matthew's appointment, but in truth he wanted a glimpse of her. Somehow seeing her each day improved his mood, even if it was only to have her shove a scrap of paper into his hands and say, "Can you explain this one to me?"

The job site manager grinned as he checked off the boxes on his approval form. "Hot date, Jacob? I've never seen you work so fast."

"Some orders are backed up in my shop is all."

Which was a true statement, if not completely honest. Or was it completely honest? There was no real reason to be at the shop with Hannah. She seemed to be doing fine on her own.

"Uh-huh, well, as usual you've done an excellent job. Sign here." The man thrust a clipboard toward him. "Your payment should be processed early next week."

"*Danki.*"

"Thank you, and I'll be needing you for that job in Shipshewana mid-September, if that still sounds good to you."

"Sounds great."

But the thought of riding the construction firm's bus to Shipshewana each day didn't appeal to him as it once had. The truth was that he'd rather be home.

Still, the cabinetry work allowed him to spend time on the playhouses, and he'd received another order for one the day before. He was itching to get to his workshop and work on a design plan. The little girl had cerebral palsy. Her form said that she loved anything pink, sparkly or related to Princess Belle. He'd had to ask a coworker what that last one meant.

"*Beauty and the Beast?* Surely you've seen it."

When Jacob shook his head, the man had said, "Come to my house. My littlest watches it at least once a day."

So instead of going straight home at noon on Friday, he stopped by the library and used the computers to find a short description of the movie. Pulling out a scrap of paper from his pocket he'd written:

bright, beautiful, young woman.

beast lives in castle.

he has a good heart and she loves to read.

Not a lot to go on, but those three lines were enough. Suddenly he knew what he wanted to build. A castle with bookcases and one of those giggle mirrors that was both safe and fun. He'd seen them on a school playground he'd helped build. In fact, if he remembered correctly, the construction manager had ordered it from the local hardware store.

He walked from the library to the store, ordered the mirror and set off toward home. It was only a little after noon, so he should get there before Hannah left for the day. He'd hardly spent any time with her, but he had peeked into the office each evening. It smelled and looked better, and he had to admit that her changes to the room made a lot of sense. She seemed to be making progress, based on the stacks of taped receipts and notations in the spiral notebook she'd bought. She'd even begun to write in the accounting book he'd purchased.

He arrived a few minutes after noon to find Hannah and

Emily sitting in the rockers underneath the porch of the workshop.

"Any scones left for me?" he asked, dropping down onto the porch floor.

Emily peered into the basket. "Looks empty."

"I know you are teasing me, Emily." Jacob pulled the basket out of her hands, dug around inside the dish towels and came away with a giant oatmeal cookie. "This will do."

"You're in an awfully *gut* mood."

"Why wouldn't I be? Finished my job early. The check is in the mail, and I get to work on a new playhouse this afternoon."

"Who is this one for?" Hannah asked.

"Young girl here in town actually. She has cerebral palsy. It's a disease that—"

"I know what it is," Hannah said softly. "CP affects muscle tone, posture, even eyesight."

"The poor thing." Emily poured Jacob a mug of coffee from her thermos and handed it to him. "Any idea what kind of playhouse you're going to build?"

"Apparently she likes some *Englisch* movie called *Beauty and the Beast*, so I'm thinking it should be in the shape of a castle, complete with turrets, bookcases and a funny mirror. That's my initial plan, anyway."

"It will be *wunderbaar*, Jacob." Emily began storing items back into her basket. "I better get home. The boys went to town with Micah, but they'll be back soon."

"I hope my *bruder* and my nephews appreciate you and your cooking abilities." Jacob finished the cookie and snagged the thermos of coffee before she tucked it away. "Sure there aren't more cookies in there? I'm still hungry."

"Because you need to eat real food, not just sweets. Speaking of hungry…don't forget brunch on Sunday."

"Oh, I..."

"Jacob Schrock, you will not be working on Sunday, and since there's no church, I expect you to be at our house by ten thirty in the morning."

Jacob glanced at Hannah, a smile tugging at his lips. "My sister-in-law can be quite bossy, if you haven't noticed."

"You should listen to her."

"I should?"

"Sure. She's a *gut* cook and your nephews apparently don't see you very much."

"Now, that makes me think you two have been talking about me."

Emily stopped what she was doing and studied Hannah, her head cocked. "You should come too."

"Me?"

"Bring Matthew. He can meet the boys."

"Oh, I don't think—"

"And your parents. I haven't seen Claire and Alton in ages."

"I'm sure they have other plans."

Emily ran a hand over her stomach, then placed the basket over her arm and smiled at Hannah. "Just ask them. We'd love to have you."

With a small wave, she set off across the property to her house.

"You two do this every day?"

"I've only been here a week. This is actually the first time Emily has stopped by."

"It's *gut* she did. Emily doesn't get enough girl time according to Micah. I suppose living with a house full of males could try anyone's patience."

But Hannah wasn't listening. She'd dumped the contents of her coffee mug onto a nearby plant, repositioned the rocking chairs and headed back inside without another word.

Jacob followed her, suspecting something was wrong but clueless as to what it might be.

"It would be great if you and Matthew could come Sunday…and your parents too, of course. Emily usually has a small-sized group—enough to get up a game of ball, but not so many that the buggies are crowded together."

Hannah definitely wasn't listening. She'd practically run into the office, and now she was perched on her stool pulling yet another stack of receipts toward her.

"Hannah? What's wrong?"

"We won't be coming on Sunday."

"Oh. I just thought Matthew might enjoy—"

"You don't know anything about what Matthew might or might not enjoy." Two bright red spots appeared on her cheeks, but her gaze remained on the receipts, which she was now pulling out haphazardly. "Meeting new people is very hard for him."

"For him…or for you?"

"That's not fair."

"Oh, really?"

"Yes, really." She jumped off the stool, nearly toppling it over in the process. Hands on her hips, she said, "It's easy enough for you to boss me around, but when was the last time you were at your *bruder's* house?"

"That's not the point."

"Isn't it? You're telling me that it's *gut* to be together, but apparently you stay here in your workshop whenever possible, hiding away."

"I'm not hiding." His temper was rising, and he fought to keep his voice down. "It's true I've been busy, but I don't avoid seeing them, and you shouldn't avoid introducing Matthew to new people."

"Why would you say that?" All color had drained from

her face. "Why would you pretend to know what I should or shouldn't do?"

"I worked with Matthew on the playhouse. I know he's lonely."

"You know nothing! You haven't seen him on Sundays, longing to do what the other children do, but confined to his chair."

"I'm sure that must be difficult for you."

"You don't hear him cry when he has a terrible dream or when he's wet his bed because he can't get up by himself."

"I wasn't saying—"

"You know nothing of our life, Jacob Schrock, and I'd thank you to stay out of it."

With those words, she pushed past him, hurried across the main room of the workshop and dashed into the bathroom, slamming the door shut behind her.

Hannah managed to avoid Jacob for the next hour. When it was time for her to leave, she would have walked through the main workroom without speaking, but Jacob called out to her before she reached the door.

"If you'd like to cancel tomorrow, if you'd rather not take Matthew to see the playhouses, I understand."

She was mortified that she'd actually hollered at him. He'd been nothing but kind to both her and Jacob, and she'd responded with accusations and bitter words. So instead of jumping on his offer, she murmured, "*Nein*. We'll see you at two o'clock."

She was feeling so miserable about the entire situation that she found herself confessing to Sally Lapp as she waited for Matthew to finish his PT appointment.

"I shouldn't have said those things, but he made me so angry."

"Which is understandable, dear."

"What does he know of raising a child like Matthew?"

"Some people are like buttons, popping off at the wrong time!"

"Now I don't know if you mean me or Jacob."

"Perhaps both."

"Plus we're spending an hour tomorrow with him. Did I tell you about our plan to go and see his playhouses?"

"*Ya.* Sounds like a nice afternoon out."

"But seeing him both days of the weekend? It seems a little much…"

Hannah had brought a stack of the receipts with her and was beginning to enter them in the ledger. She looked down at what she'd done. Her handwriting was a tight, precise cursive and her numbers lined up perfectly, but seeing the progress she'd made on Jacob's accounts didn't ease the guilt she felt.

"I'll need to apologize to him."

"We often feel better after we do."

"And I will, even though he's wrong. Matthew does not need to be thrown into new situations."

"Mothers often know best."

"He's barely had time to settle in from the move, get to know his cousins and *aentis* and *onkels*, not to mention his new church family…"

"And yet children are ever so much more resilient than adults." Sally had finished the blanket she'd been working on the week before. Her yarn was now variegated autumn colors. It reminded Hannah of cool nights and shorter days.

"So you think we should go to Emily's on Sunday?"

"Oh, it's not important what *I* think. What is your heart telling you to do?"

Hannah stared down at the column of numbers, embarrassed that tears had sprung to her eyes. Why was she so emotional? Why did she feel the need to run from Jacob Schrock? And what was she so intent on protecting her son from when he was thriving?

"Sometimes I'm not sure," she admitted.

"Pray on it. Make a decision when you're rested, not in the middle or at the end of a long, hard day. Maybe talk to your parents."

The door to the waiting room opened, and a nurse pushed Matthew's wheelchair through.

"*Gut* day?" Hannah asked.

"Awesome day."

He pestered her about Jacob all the way home—wanting to know if she'd seen him, what he was working on, what he'd said about their plans to visit a couple of his playhouses the next day. Hannah realized as they pulled into the short lane leading to her parents' home that it wasn't only Matthew she was trying to protect. She was also trying to protect herself.

Raising any child was difficult, but raising a special needs child presented issues she'd never imagined. She constantly felt on guard for his feelings as well as his personal safety. She didn't think she could handle Matthew's look of disappointment when the other children ran off to play, or the whispered comments when no one thought she was listening or the looks of pity as she pulled his wheelchair from the buggy.

Life was difficult.

The one thing that made it easier was being home, alone, where the eyes of the world couldn't pry. She only guessed that it made things easier for Matthew, but she was certain that it made things easier for herself.

Hannah needn't have worried about making a decision as to whether they should join Jacob's family for Sunday dinner. Emily had spoken with Hannah's mother when they saw each other at the grocer in town. Plans had already been set in motion.

She had no valid objections, so she didn't bother to argue, but the entire thing made her tired and cranky. She had hardly slept Friday night after her argument with Jacob, and Saturday she worked twice as hard around the house—trying to make up for being gone all week. By the time they'd set lunch out on the table, she was tempted to beg off, say she had a headache, stay home and take a nap.

One look at Matthew told her that wouldn't be possible. He was wiggling in his chair and tapping his fingers against the table.

During the meal Matthew peppered her with questions about the playhouses, and when she'd said *I don't know* to over a dozen questions, he moved on to asking her about Jacob's family.

"Do they have animals?"

"I'm sure they do."

"Sheep?"

"Why would they have sheep?"

"Camels?"

Hannah began to laugh in exasperation, but her father combed his fingers through his beard as if he were in deep thought. Finally he leaned toward Matthew and lowered his voice as if to share a secret. "Only Amish man I know in this area with camels is Simon Eberly over in Middlebury. I'm sure I would have heard if Jacob's family had any—so no, probably not."

Which only slowed Matthew down for a moment. He proceeded to fire off questions about camels and declare that he'd love to have one. When Hannah thought her patience was going to snap, her father took Matthew outside to see to the horses.

"He'll be fine, you know." Her mother started washing the dishes, which meant it was Hannah's turn to dry.

"Why do you say that?"

"It's plain as day you worry about him."

"Of course I worry."

"He'll be in school this time next year."

"Unless I hold him back a year. With his birthday being in September, we could decide to wait…"

"He's such a bright young boy. Already he's better with his letters and numbers than you girls were at that age. Why would you want to hold him back?"

"I don't know, *Mamm*." Hannah was tired, and she wasn't yet halfway through the day.

The time inched closer to two o'clock, and finally her mother suggested she might want to freshen up a bit.

Hannah waited until she'd left the room to roll her eyes. Freshen up? It wasn't a date. They were driving around to look at playhouses. She'd switch out of her cleaning dress, but she was not donning a fresh *kapp*. She certainly didn't want Jacob to get the wrong idea.

Then she remembered her conversation with Sally Lapp about the way she had treated Jacob. She'd made up her mind then, and she wasn't going to change it now. She needed to apologize to Jacob, and the sooner the better. Suddenly what she wore seemed much less important.

Jacob made sure he arrived exactly at two o'clock.

He'd apparently pushed a little too hard the day before. He hadn't even known that he was pushing, but the way Hannah had melted down told him that he'd touched on a very sensitive subject. He wanted today to be fun and relaxing, not stressful. So he was careful not to arrive early or late.

Which meant that he had to pull over on the side of the road and wait a few minutes before turning down the dirt lane that led to her father's house.

He needn't have worried about being early. Matthew and Hannah were waiting on the front porch. The sight of them—her standing behind his wheelchair, and Matthew shading his eyes as he watched down the lane—caused Jacob's thoughts to scatter, and for a moment he couldn't remember why he was there. Then he glanced over and saw Matthew's playhouse. "You're getting old, Jacob. Or daft. You could be growing daft."

Ten minutes later they were off.

The first stop was Jasper's house. The boy wasn't Amish, but he was sick. For three years now he had been valiantly fighting the cancer that threatened to consume his small body. Though nearly nine years old, he was approximately the same size as Matthew.

"Wanna see my boat?"

"*Ya.* I have a train."

"Did Jacob make it?"

"He did."

"He's *gut* at building things."

Jasper's mom explained that she needed to stay inside with the baby, who was sleeping. "But make yourself at home. I was so glad to hear from you, Jacob, and Hannah, thank you for bringing Matthew. Jasper doesn't have a lot of visitors."

After walking her around the playhouse, which was built in the shape of a sailboat, Jacob pointed to a bench a few feet away. "Care to sit?"

"*Ya.* We cleaned all morning, so I'm tired."

"I heard you're working on a big accounting job during the week."

She laughed, then pressed her fingers to her lips.

"It's okay to laugh, Hannah. You're allowed."

"Oh, am I, now?" She tucked her chin and gave him a pointed look. He raised his hands in mock surrender, and she shook her head, then sighed.

"Do I exasperate you?" he asked.

"*Nein*. It's only that I need to do something I don't enjoy doing."

"Now?"

"*Ya*."

"I'm intrigued."

"I need to apologize, Jacob." She glanced up at him and then away—toward the sailboat, where Jasper was showing Matthew how to hoist a miniature sail. "I was rude to you yesterday, and I'm very sorry. I know better than to speak harshly to someone, let alone someone who is being kind to us."

"It's my fault. I stuck my nose where it didn't belong."

Now she laughed outright, causing the boys to look over at them and wave.

"Perhaps you did, but it was probably something I needed to hear."

"Apology accepted."

"*Danki*."

"*Gem gschene*."

The moment felt curiously intimate, shared there on the bench with the sun slanting through golden trees. Jacob cleared his throat and tried to think of something else to say, but for the second time that day, his mind was completely blank.

"It's a fine line," Hannah said. "Giving him the extra attention and care his condition requires, but not being overly protective. I'm afraid I'm still learning."

"You're doing a *wunderbaar* job. Don't let any fool neighbor or cranky boss tell you different."

Which caused her to smile again, and suddenly the tension that had been between them was gone. He was tempted to reach for her hand or touch her shoulder, but he realized that what Hannah was offering with her apology was a precious thing—her friendship. For now, he needed to be satisfied with that.

Hannah felt herself softening toward Jacob. How could she resist? He was patient with Matthew, kind toward her and it was plain that he was a good man. They stopped at three different playhouses—Jasper's sailboat, a precious miniature cottage built for a young blind girl named Veronica, and a tiny-sized barn made for an Amish boy named John.

"I spoke with John's parents. They said we could come by and look, but that they wouldn't be here."

"Is he sick too?" Matthew asked.

"Not really sick, no, but he needed a special playground nonetheless."

"What's wrong with him?"

"John was born with only one leg. His left leg stops at the knee. It's a bit hard for him to get around at times."

"He uses crutches?"

"He does, and he wears a prosthetic."

"Prophetic?"

"*Nein.* A…" He glanced at Hannah, obviously hoping for help.

"It's a plastic leg, Matthew. Remember the older gentleman you see at physical therapy sometimes? He has one."

"But his is metal. I know because he let me touch it. Looks like a robot. He laughed when I told him so."

"John's is plastic, but I've seen the metal ones." Jacob resettled his hat on his head. "It bothers him sometimes, and he likes to take it off when he gets home. The challenge for me was to make him a playhouse where it was safe to do that."

"This was a fun trip, Jacob. You're a *gut* builder."

"Thanks, Matt."

Jacob's use of a nickname that only her father and her husband had used melted another piece of Hannah's heart.

After they'd visited the small barn, Jacob drove them to town, bought ice cream for everyone and laughed with Matthew as they chased swirls of pink down their cones. It was all Hannah could do to remind herself as they drove home that this was an outing for Matthew, that it had nothing to do with her and Jacob, and that he was not interested in dating her.

Who would want a widow with a disabled child?

She knew how precious Matthew was, but she also understood firsthand the trials, the terrible nights, the emergency hospital visits, the mountain of bills. No, it would be wrong to consider letting anyone share such a burden. A preposterous thought, anyway. Jacob had been nothing but friendly toward her. Yes, he had said *I like you*, but that could be said of the neighbor's buggy.

Raising Matthew was a road that she was meant to travel alone.

When they reached the house, she went to transfer Matthew from the buggy to the chair, but Jacob was there to do it for her. His hand brushed against hers and then his brown eyes were staring into hers, searching her face, causing her hands to sweat and her heart to race.

As they thanked Jacob for the afternoon and she pushed

a very tired young boy into the house, she paused to glance back over her shoulder. Jacob Schrock was a good man, and there was no doubt in her mind that *Gotte* had a plan for him, a plan that more than likely included a wife and family.

A whole family.

One that wasn't carrying the weight of her baggage.

Chapter Ten

Sunday morning dawned crisper and cooler than the day before. Jacob owned two Sunday shirts—they were identical in size, color and fabric. So why did he try on the first, discard it, try on the second and then switch back to the first?

He studied his face in the mirror. If he turned right the reflection was of a normal man—not particularly good-looking, strong jawline, dark brown eyes, eyebrows that tended toward being bushy. If he turned right, he saw his father staring back at him.

But if he turned left, he saw in his scars the detour his life had taken—the pain and the anger and the regret. He saw what might have been.

It had taken him some time to learn to shave over the scars. Their Plain custom was for unmarried men to be clean shaven, so he worked the razor carefully over the damaged tissue, using his fingers more than his eyes to guide the blade.

Finishing, he tugged the towel from the rack and patted

his face dry. He could lie to himself while he was sanding a piece of oak or shellacking a section of maple wood, but for those few moments each day when he faced his own reflection in the mirror, he saw and recognized the truth.

He was lonely.

He longed to have a wife.

He dreamed of a family and a real home.

There was a small kernel of hope buried deep in his heart that those things were possible.

The moment passed as it always did, and he finished preparing for the visit next door to see his brother's family.

He chose to walk and wasn't too surprised when the only one to meet him was his brother's dog, Skipper. No one had been able to figure out exactly what kind of mutt Skipper was, though there was definitely some Beagle, Labrador and Boxer mixed in his background somewhere. Jacob bent down to scratch the old dog behind the ears and then together they climbed the steps to the front porch. Skipper curled up in a slat of sunlight, and Jacob let himself in.

His brother's voice let him know the family was still having their devotional in the sitting room.

"'Therefore I am troubled at his presence; when I consider I am afraid of Him. For God maketh my heart soft, and the Almighty troubleth me.'"

"That doesn't make any sense." Samuel, the oldest of his nephews, sat on the far end of the sofa. Next to him were the twins, Tim and Thomas, then Eli, who was younger by eleven months, and finally Joseph, the baby of the group at six. All five nephews were lined up like stair steps.

"Why do you say that?" Micah asked, nodding at Jacob, who pulled a chair from the kitchen and took a seat.

"*Gotte* loves us." Samuel craned his neck and stared up at

the corner of the ceiling as if he might find answers there. "The Bible says so. Remember? We read it just last week."

"*Ya*, that's true," Emily said.

"But Job is…what did you read?"

"He's afraid of *Gotte*," Eli piped up.

"Maybe Job did something wrong," Tim said.

"*Ya*, like when we get in trouble, and we know what we did was wrong and we're afraid of you finding out." Thomas pulled at the collar of his dress shirt. "Like last week when I put that big worm in the teacher's desk. It was awfully funny, but I knew even when I did it that I'd pay for it later."

"Sometimes we're afraid because we know we've sinned," Micah agreed. "But think back to the beginning of our reading this morning."

Micah thumbed through the pages of the old Bible—one of the few things they'd been able to recover from the fire. The cover was cracked and singed in places. The pages retained a slightly smoky odor, but it still held the wisdom they needed. Perhaps that Bible was like Jacob. It had been through a lot, but *Gotte* was still able to use it. *Gotte* was still able to use him.

"'There was a man in the land of Uz, whose name was Job,'" Micah read. "'And that man was perfect and upright, and one that feared *Gotte*.'"

Samuel shook his head. "Still doesn't make sense."

"Maybe your *onkel* Jacob can explain it better than I can."

Jacob met his brother's gaze, then turned his attention to the boys lined up on the couch. The five of them were so young to be learning the hard truths of life, and yet it was his and Micah's and Emily's jobs as adults, as elders in the faith and as the boys' family, to prepare them for such things.

Jacob understood what his brother was asking.

He thought of that morning, of the reflection in the mirror of two different men—only there weren't two different men. His scarred self didn't exist in isolation from the whole. He was one person, and if he believed the truth in the Good Book his brother was holding, then he needed to accept the person *Gotte* had created him to be.

Clearing his throat he sat forward, elbows propped on his knees, fingers interlaced. "Job loved *Gotte*, as we do, *ya*?"

All five boys nodded in unison.

"But his experiences had taught him that *Gotte's* plan for his life might be painful, might be hard to understand at times. Those plans had him scarred and hurting, and so he was afraid."

No one spoke, and Jacob knew that they were waiting, that his family had been waiting for him to reach this point a long time—for six years, to be exact.

"It's a hard thing to know that bad things can happen to us, like the fire that took *Daddi* and *Mammi*."

"They're in heaven now." Joseph swung his foot back and forth, bumping the bottom of the couch.

"*Ya*, they are."

"But you're still scarred." Eli touched the left side of Jacob's face.

"I am scarred," he admitted. "And I have to accept that somehow *Gotte* still has a plan for me, that what happened— that it wasn't a mistake. After all, *Gotte* could have sent a rainstorm and put out that fire…right?"

"*Ya*." Thomas, the practical one, crossed his arms. "I don't get it."

Jacob's laughter surprised everyone, including himself. "I'm not sure that we have to *get it*, but we do need to keep the faith, whether we understand or not."

They joined hands then, heads bowed in silent prayer, until Micah spoke aloud and asked the Lord to bless their day. The moment he said *amen*, the twins were headed out the door, Eli pulled a book out of his pocket and began to read it, and Micah asked for Samuel's help with setting things up for the luncheon. Joseph muttered something about a pet frog and hurried toward the mudroom.

It was Emily who held back. Standing on tiptoe, she planted a kiss on the left side of Jacob's face. Her stomach was rounded with her sixth child, and she had to lean forward to kiss his cheek. For a moment, Jacob thought he felt the life inside of her press up against him.

"What's that for?" Though he was embarrassed, he couldn't stop the smile that was spreading across his face.

"Just glad to see you is all." But the tears shining in her eyes told him it was more.

He patted her on the shoulder. Even he knew that pregnant women were emotional. He didn't want to be the cause of starting the waterworks before everyone arrived.

He needn't have worried, though. She was humming a tune as she waddled into the kitchen. It was only as he was left standing in the sitting room alone that he realized the song she was humming was "Amazing Grace."

By the time Hannah and Claire were done with the breakfast dishes, Hannah's father and Matthew were in the sitting room, waiting. Their devotional was from Christ's Sermon on the Mount.

Her father patiently answered Matthew's questions and then they all prayed for a few minutes. The devotional time reminded Hannah of her childhood, of sitting with her sisters, squirming on the couch much as Matthew was now squirming in his chair.

It took another hour to pack up the dishes they were taking for the luncheon, along with any special items Matthew might need. The weather was warm for the first weekend of September, and there was no chance of rain, which made it a perfect day for a Sunday social. They had to drive past Jacob's place to reach Emily's.

Matthew pointed out the workshop to his grandparents. "That's where *Mamm* works. I saw it, and Jacob took me around to look at his projects."

He rode in the back seat with Hannah and had his nose pressed to the buggy window. "Why can't we go there?"

"Because lunch is at Emily's," Hannah explained for the third time.

"And Emily is Jacob's *schweschder*."

"*Ya*. She married Jacob's brother, Micah. That makes them *bruder* and *schweschder*."

Matthew had more questions, but they were pulling into Emily and Micah's drive, and their buggy was suddenly surrounded by boys as well as an old gray dog.

Before Hannah had a chance to protest, her father had loaded Matthew into his wheelchair and Emily's boys had taken off with him across the yard.

"Maybe I should go…"

"He'll be fine," Emily assured her. "Come and have a glass of lemonade. It's warm out today, *ya*?"

She introduced Hannah to her parents and two more couples who were neighbors. They spent the next twenty minutes drinking lemonade and talking about crops and school and the general state of things in Goshen. Hannah was pretending to pay attention, but trying to catch sight of Matthew. Emily's boys had whisked him away, and she hadn't even had a chance to explain how to set the brake on the chair or what to do if he stopped breathing.

That last thought was ridiculous.

Why would he stop breathing?

But he might, and she hadn't explained what to do.

She excused herself from the group of adults and made her way over to the trampoline where Emily's twins were practicing flips. No sign of Matthew there. Hurrying toward the barn she spied the two oldest boys throwing horseshoes. Matthew wasn't watching that either. Which left the youngest boy—Joseph. Her son's life was in the hands of a six-year-old.

Her heart thumped and her palms began to sweat as she hurried toward the barn. Two thin lines in the dirt assured her that Matthew's chair had been pushed in this direction. She practically ran into the barn and slammed straight into Jacob.

"Whoa, there. Something wrong?"

"It's Matthew…" She glanced up at him, remembered his fingers brushing her arm the day before and glanced away. "I've been looking for him. I was worried that—"

"Just breathe, Hannah. Matthew is fine."

"Are you sure?"

"*Ya.* Come with me. I'll show you."

Jacob led her through the main room of the barn and toward the area where Micah kept his horses.

He reached the last stall and stopped, motioning for her to tiptoe toward him. They both peered around the corner.

Joseph was picking up a newborn kitten and setting it in Matthew's lap.

"I can hold him?"

"Sure."

"But what if I—"

"You won't."

"Are you sure I won't hurt him?"

"Look, he likes you."

The cat's cries subsided as Matthew bent over the small furry bundle in his lap.

"He's purring," Matthew said.

"*Ya.* He's happy."

"And the momma cat doesn't mind?"

"Probably not, for a minute or so at least."

They proceeded to discuss the merits of the different kittens—stripes over solids, large over small, loud over quiet. Jacob tugged on Hannah's arm and pulled her away from the stall. They walked out the side door of the barn into a day that was more summer than fall. Perhaps because he'd been in the barn the colors seemed brighter, the breeze sweeter. Or maybe that was due to the woman standing beside him.

He stepped to her left so that the right side of his face would be facing her. Then he realized what he'd done and felt like an idiot, as if he could impress her with half of his face. He hadn't been particularly good-looking before the fire.

They walked away from the barn, and he steered Hannah toward Emily's garden. The vegetables had all been harvested, but the flowers were a sight to behold.

"When Emily first married Micah, she couldn't keep a tomato plant alive. She'd spend time with *Mamm* in the garden every afternoon, and I guess some of *Mamm*'s gardening skills rubbed off on her."

"This is beautiful."

They walked up and down the rows and finally stopped at a bench.

"*Danki,*" Hannah said.

"For?"

"For taking me to him."

"You were worried."

"For inviting us here."

"That was really Emily's doing."

"For being our friend."

"Of course I'm your friend, Hannah."

Instead of answering, she became preoccupied with her *kapp* strings, running them through her fingers again and again.

Finally he said, "Tell me about David."

Her eyebrows arched up in surprise. "My husband?"

"*Ya.*"

"You mean how he died."

"I heard about that, and I'm sorry."

She glanced away, but she seemed more surprised than offended so he pushed on.

"I meant more what was he like? I know he was from the Shipshe district, but I only met him once or twice, both times at the auction."

"He was a *gut* man."

"I'm sure he was."

"I miss him."

"Of course you do."

Hannah smiled and chuckled softly. "He wasn't perfect, though. He thought Wisconsin was the promised land. We moved there only a few months after we married."

"And was it? The promised land?"

"In truth it was remote, and the Plain community there was different. I won't say it was worse, but it took some getting used to. One half allowed for gas appliances, even solar energy. The other? They were more Old Order, at least in practice."

"I've heard about the ice fishing there."

"*Ach.* The winters were incredibly difficult. We had more than forty inches of snow each of the winters I was there."

"That much?"

"*Ya.* It was very different from here."

"Were you happy—living in this promised land?"

"We were."

"That's *gut*."

"I haven't spoken of him, for a while. You know how it is in a Plain community."

"We believe his life was complete."

"Yes." Her voice grew softer so that he had to lean toward her more to make out her words. "I want Matthew to know about his father. He might not be old enough to have his own memories, but I want to share mine."

"You're a *gut mamm*."

She shrugged her shoulders. "Some days I wonder about that."

There was a racket across from them and then Matthew and Joseph tumbled out of the barn, Joseph pushing as fast as he could and then jumping on the back of the wheelchair as if it were a bicycle. Matthew's laughter carried across to them.

"I should go and see if he needs anything."

"Does it look like he needs anything?"

She laughed then. "I suppose you're right."

"I want to show you something."

He led her down the path to the other end of the garden.

"Why have you never married?" Her hand flew to her mouth and her eyes widened. "That was rude of me. I shouldn't have asked."

"It's nothing my family doesn't ask me every chance they get."

"They worry about you."

"I suppose. Emily and Micah, they think because they're happy that everyone should be married with a houseful of *kinder*."

"And you don't want that?"

"I don't know. It would take a special person to be able to put up with me."

"Because of your scars?"

"Partly."

"But they're only…scars."

Jacob glanced at her and then away. "I don't really see them anymore. Sometimes I forget and look in the mirror and I'm surprised. Or a child sees me, say an *Englischer* in town or a new family in our community, and they point or ask questions…"

"Curious, I suppose."

"Yes, but it reminds me that my face is frightening to some people."

"Surely it's not as bad as all that."

Jacob didn't argue the point. She couldn't know what it was like to live his life, to see the looks of revulsion on people's faces.

"This is what I wanted to show you." He led her under an arbor with a thick vine covering it. A path wound through clumps of butterfly weeds with bright orange flowers sitting atop three-foot stems. Back among the taller blooms on a piece of board taken from an old barn, someone had painted the names of his parents and placed it into the ground like a street sign.

"It's how we remember them."

"You have a garden at your house too."

"*Ya.* Not as well tended as Emily's, but we both make an effort to spend time in them. It's our way of being sure my parents' memory stays with the children."

"It's nice here. I like it."

"*Mamm* loved her garden. She sometimes needed time away from two rambunctious boys. *Dat* would tell us to clean up the dishes, and he'd head out to the garden with a cup of hot tea for her. I'd find them there sometimes, hold-ing hands, their heads together like two *youngies*."

"That's a special memory, Jacob."

"It is."

"Thank you for sharing it with me—for showing me this."

"You're welcome. I'm glad you and Matthew were able to come today."

And then he did something he wouldn't have believed that he had the courage to do. He stepped forward, touched Han-nah's face until she looked up at him and softly kissed her lips.

She froze, like a deer caught in a buggy's headlights.

Blushing a bright red, she stepped away, stared at the ground, looked back at him and finally said, "I really should see if he needs me."

Jacob nodded as if he understood, but as she was hurry-ing back over to the picnic tables, it seemed to him that she wasn't actually running toward Matthew. It was more as if she was running away from him, and could he really blame her? What had possessed him to think that she would enjoy a stroll through the garden with him?

What had prompted him to kiss her? Perhaps that had been a mistake. It wasn't something he could take back, though, so he straightened his suspenders and headed over to where the boys were playing horseshoes.

Hannah didn't breathe freely until she was sitting among the women, listening to them discuss the best fall recipes. She wasn't thinking about pumpkin-spice bread or butter-nut squash casserole, though. She was thinking about her son holding a kitten, about the fact that he had a new friend, about the garden and about Jacob.

She was thinking about that kiss.

When he'd spoken about his scars, she'd had an urge to

reach out and touch them, to assure him that they all had scars.

She'd wanted to tell him that she had scars too.

Her heart probably looked worse than his face…it was only that people couldn't see those scars. She kept them hidden. She smiled and pretended everything was fine.

She pretended through the meal as she made sure that Matthew ate.

She pretended as she watched Matthew go off again, this time with Emily's entire clan of boys.

She pretended while the women circled up and spoke of the upcoming school auction.

"I'm growing old and forgetful," her mother said. "I meant to clean out my casserole dish before the leftover potatoes become as hard as concrete."

"I'll get it, *Mamm*."

"Oh, I didn't mean for you to do that."

"It's not a problem." She was actually relieved to be away from the group of women, though she'd run toward them before the meal. Still, an hour spent in their presence and her cheeks hurt from trying to smile. She was happy for an excuse to spend a few minutes alone.

She retrieved the dish from the table, took it into Emily's kitchen and rinsed it out.

As she scrubbed away at the residual cheese, her thoughts returned to Jacob—to doubts and questions and scars and hurts.

She was thinking of that, of how some hurts showed physically while others remained concealed when she stepped outside and practically collided with Elizabeth Byler.

"Hannah. Could you help me with this?"

Hannah made a practice of avoiding Elizabeth, who she remembered from her youth. Elizabeth was a negative person with a nasty habit of gossiping, but the woman was holding a large tray filled with used coffee mugs.

It would be rude to run away.

"Of course. Let me hold the door."

"Emily was going to leave this out in the sun, covered with flies. Best to get them in and cleaned."

"Oh…"

"If you'll wash, I'll dry."

Hannah smiled her answer, since there seemed to be no way to avoid spending twenty minutes in the kitchen with the woman.

She'd barely run soapy water into the sink when Elizabeth started in on what was obviously her agenda.

"Saw you walking off with Jacob."

"*Ya*, he wanted to show me the garden."

"You're not the first."

"First?"

"Probably won't be the last."

"The last to what?"

"Set your *kapp* on Jacob Schrock, which is why I thought it my job to warn you."

"Warn me?" Hannah stared at the woman in disbelief.

"That road goes nowhere. You're wasting your time with that one."

Hannah felt her temper rise. She tried to focus on the mug she was filling with soapy water, but the buzzing in her ears was a sure sign that she was about to say something she'd regret.

"Give it a month, at the most two, and you'll be crying on someone's shoulder about how your heart is broken. Best to listen to sense. No disrespect to Micah, but his *bruder* Jacob is spoiled goods."

Hannah's hands froze on the mug she was washing. "Surely you don't mean that."

"Don't look at me that way, Hannah. You know better than anyone what it's like to live with a person who has been damaged. Would you want Matthew married to someone?"

"Excuse me?" Hannah dropped the mug into the water, causing suds to splash up and onto her sleeves.

"Don't get me wrong. *Gotte* has a plan for every life."

"Nice of you to admit that."

"Jacob's tried dating a few times, but it didn't work out. He has quite the chip on his shoulder. I will admit that financially he's certainly a catch since he inherited that farm from his parents."

"So now he's a catch?"

"Some women think so."

"Elizabeth, I don't know what to say."

"You could thank me for speaking the truth. I'm only trying to help you see straight."

"That's very kind of you."

"Wisdom, Hannah. It comes with age. You'll see. Think about it. What woman would want to wake up to a disfigured husband every morning?"

"That's uncharitable, Elizabeth."

"Not to mention that Jacob feels sorry for himself, as if he's the only one who has troubles."

Hannah gave up on washing the mug, dropped it into the sudsy water and carefully dried her hands on a dishrag. She attempted to count to ten but only made it to three.

"I think I'm needed outside."

"It won't be the first time I'm left to do dishes by myself."

"Maybe that's because you're a bitter, unpleasant person."

Beth's mouth opened into a perfect *O*, but no sound came out.

"I'm sorry. I know your life has been hard too, with Jared's drinking problem and all..."

"I do not want to talk about Jared."

"But your personal trials don't give you a reason to speak ill of Jacob—"

"I did not."

"Also, I'd appreciate it if you'd refrain from determining the course of my son's life when he is but four years old." And with that, Hannah turned and walked back out into the afternoon sunshine, feeling better than she had in a very long time.

It wasn't until she was on her way home in the buggy that she allowed her mind to comb back over Elizabeth's harsh words. Her parents were speaking quietly in the front, and Matthew had fallen asleep with his head in her lap. She was brushing the hair out of his eyes, thinking of what a beautiful and kind child he was, when Elizabeth's words came back to her as clearly as if the woman were sitting beside her in the buggy.

You're not the first.

Probably won't be the last.

Financially he's certainly a catch.

There were women in their district interested in Jacob? Well, of course there were. That shouldn't surprise her one bit, and it certainly wasn't any of her business.

She had no plans of dating the man, despite the kiss. That had been an impulsive thing for him to do. Somewhere deep inside she'd known he was going to. She should have kept her distance. What had she been thinking?

She worked for him. She wanted to help her parents and to provide for Matthew. She didn't need to step out with anyone. She had no intention of doing such a thing. If Elizabeth thought so, that was her misunderstanding.

Jacob was a friend, a neighbor of sorts and her employer. He was nothing more, and though she might defend him to nosy interfering women, she had no intention of falling in love with the man. Her heart had suffered enough damage, or so she told herself as the sun began to set across the Indiana fields.

Chapter Eleven

The next week passed quickly. Jacob managed to finish the bin of receipts that he'd been assigned, as had his nephews and Hannah's niece. If he managed to survive this audit, it would be because they'd worked together.

He peeked into the office as often as he dared, and slowly Hannah managed to create order out of his chaos. She'd asked him to find a filing cabinet, and earlier in the week he'd spied one that had been set out in the trash by a local Realtor. After checking to be sure it was free, he strapped it to the back of his buggy, brought it home, cleaned it inside and out, and oiled the tracks the drawers ran on.

"Could use a new paint job, but I suppose it will do."

"It's perfect." Hannah had already purchased a box of folders and the next day she transferred the taped-up receipts to the file drawers—chronological, three years per drawer, orderly and neat.

He hoped the IRS agent would be impressed. He certainly was. The bins were stacked in the corner of the room and when they were all empty, he carried them to the stall he used as a storage place.

Hannah beamed as if she'd baked the perfect apple pie. She was proud of her work, as she should be. He thought again of the bonus he meant to give her, almost said something, but decided to wait. If he owed money to the government, he would need to meet that obligation first. It would be wrong to suggest she might receive extra money for her labor and then disappoint her.

But he wanted to raise her hopes, to ease the worry he saw in her eyes. How much money had her sisters and parents been able to raise? He spoke to her again about approaching her bishop and asking for help, but she only shook her head and said something about *humility* and *Gotte's wille* and *stubborn men*.

Every time he saw her, he thought of the kiss they'd shared.

Hannah, on the other hand, seemed completely focused on the audit. It was after lunch on Friday when she finally admitted, "I think we're ready."

The office barely resembled the place it had been before Hannah came to work there. A bright yellow basket of mums sat next to a pot of aloe vera. The afternoon light splashed through the sparkling panes of glass. Hannah's sweater was draped across the back of the new office chair he'd purchased and the shelf held her quilted lunch bag. She opened the bottom drawer of the desk and pulled out her purse.

"So you're headed home?"

"*Ya*. Matthew has therapy today."

"Of course. How's he doing?"

"*Gut*. Getting stronger, I think. It helps that he's able to have the same therapist every time he goes."

She stood there, waiting, as Jacob's mind jumped back and forth looking for something else to say. He wasn't ready for her to leave, but he realized he looked like a fool, standing there silently and twirling his hat in his hands. He crammed it back on his head and said perhaps too gruffly, "*Danki* for your help."

"Of course. It's what you hired me for."

"*Ya*, but we both know you've gone above and beyond. I don't know if we'll pass the audit or not, but if we do, it's because of you."

"And your nephews and my niece."

"*Ya*." The same thought he'd had earlier. It was almost as if she understood his thoughts.

She blushed prettily then, and he nearly asked her out to eat or to go for a buggy ride or perhaps hire a driver to take them to Shipshe. But she was already gathering her things together, talking about a cousin from Pennsylvania who was coming into town and how she needed to help her *mamm* prepare.

It seemed her weekend was full of plans, so he wished her a good afternoon and pretended there was a rocker he needed to finish working on.

There was a rocker he needed to work on—and a dresser, a coffee table, as well as plans for a playhouse later in the month. He tried working on each one, but he couldn't seem to find the right sandpaper, or varnish or idea. Finally he gave up, harnessed Bo to the buggy and headed toward town.

Jacob was standing in line at the library and thought the woman in line ahead of him was Hannah. He made a fool of himself calling out to her only to have the stranger look at him oddly and hurry off.

His gelding, Bo, seemed full of energy, so Jacob decided to head north of town and scout the area where he'd be building a playhouse for a child with Down syndrome. He thought he passed Hannah on the road and his heart rate accelerated and he waved his hand out the window, but it wasn't Hannah. Of course it wasn't. Matthew's therapy appointment was in the middle of town, not on a country road headed north, plus the horse he'd just waved at was a nice roan and Hannah's horse was chestnut.

He even convinced himself that it was her buggy parked in front of his brother's house. When he pulled in, with the excuse that he'd promised his nephews he'd come by and pick up one of the kittens, he found it was one of the older women from the next district who'd stopped by to drop off two bags of clothes for the boys. Too late—he either had to admit he'd made up the excuse or go to the barn and pick out a kitten.

The boys gave him the black one with white patches around its eyes.

"Don't forget to feed it." Tim looked concerned.

"Of course I'll feed it."

"Do you even have cat food?" Thomas asked.

"No. I don't have a cat."

"You do now." Samuel reached forward and scratched the kitten between the ears. "We'll loan you some until you get to the store."

Joseph ran off to fetch a container.

Jacob tried to stifle the groan, but without much success.

"Didn't know you were in the market for a cat, *bruder.*" Micah stood grinning at him, as if he too could read his mind.

"I've been wrestled into this."

"*Ya,* my *kinder* are quite convincing."

"And don't leave him in the barn alone, Jacob." Eli looked at him with the seriousness only a nine-year-old could muster. "Are you sure you don't want two?"

"I'm not sure I want one."

"Then put him in your mudroom. He needs to be able to hear you so he won't be scared."

His trailer didn't have a mudroom, but Jacob decided not to point that out. Perhaps he could make a place for the kitten next to his washing machine, or in the office. Wouldn't that be a nice surprise for Hannah? The IRS agent might not appreciate it, so perhaps he'd wait until the end of the audit. In the meantime, he'd try to find out whether she even liked animals.

He whistled as he drove back toward his house, realizing that he'd made it through Friday. Two more days to stumble through and then Hannah would be back at her desk.

"It's *gut* when family comes to visit, *ya*?" Hannah's mom slipped a cup of coffee in front of her.

Matthew was in bed.

Her father was checking things in the barn.

And the weekend was finally over.

"*Ya*, it is."

"Only...?"

"I wasn't about to add anything else."

Her mother sipped her coffee, studying her over the rim of the cup.

"I suppose I was thinking about the audit tomorrow," Hannah said.

"Are you ready?"

"I've done my best."

"Then you're ready." Her mother reached forward and patted the back of her hand.

When Hannah looked down and saw that, her mother's hand on top of hers, something stirred in her chest. Too often she took her parents for granted, took her life for granted.

What would Jacob give for just one more hour of sipping coffee with his parents?

"And now I've upset you."

"*Nein.* It's only, I was thinking of Jacob and how awful it would be to lose your parents."

Her *mamm* sat back, reached for a peanut butter bar, broke it in half and pushed a portion of it toward Hannah. "No one lives forever."

"I know that."

"Not that I'm in a hurry to die."

"I should hope not."

"You're thinking of this all wrong."

"I am?"

"It's true that Jacob is lonely, and that he's looking for his way in life."

"He's lonely?"

"But as for his parents? Don't mourn them, Hannah. They are resting in the arms of *Gotte*, dancing around his throne. What we see dimly they see clearly now."

Hannah couldn't help laughing. "I guess when you put it that way…"

"Now tell me about Jacob."

"About him?"

"Has he kissed you yet?"

"Mamm!"

"You don't have to share if you don't want to."

Hannah changed the subject. They sat there for another half hour, speaking of relatives, the coming fall and Matthew's birthday. What they didn't discuss sat between them. Though Hannah wanted to ask about the amount they owed the bank and how they were progressing toward meeting that debt, she didn't want to ruin this moment on a Sunday night, sitting in the house she'd grown up in. She didn't want to think about where they might be in a month or a year. She wanted to close her eyes and pretend, just for a moment, that everything would be fine.

Hannah and Jacob stood shoulder to shoulder, staring out the window as the small green car pulled down the lane. It stopped well shy of the parking area.

"What's she doing?" Hannah stepped closer, practically rubbing her nose against the glass.

If anything, she seemed more keyed up than Jacob felt.

He attempted to ease her nerves by putting a hand on her shoulder, but she jumped as if he'd stuck her with a hot poker.

"It's going to be fine," he said.

"*Ya*, but what's she doing? Who stops in the middle of a lane?"

"Looks like she's on her phone."

"Maybe she thinks she can't use it in here."

"Or maybe she has an important call. Maybe there's an emergency audit that she needs to leave for."

Hannah bumped her shoulder against his. "Don't joke that way. We need this to be over."

"She's moving again."

The car stopped next to the hitching post.

"How can an *Englisch* vehicle be that quiet?"

"My guess would be that it's electric and expensive."

"Electric? So she has to...plug it in?"

"*Ya*, they have a large battery that holds a significant charge. You have to plug them in at night."

"What if you run out of..." Hannah twirled her finger round and round.

"Juice? There's a backup fuel supply like other *Englisch* cars use."

"How do you know all this?"

Jacob shrugged. They might be Amish, but they didn't live on the moon. Most men, Amish or *Englisch*, were interested when a new type of vehicle came out. He'd read a few articles on electric cars. He considered explaining that to Hannah, but she was already moving toward the door of the barn, so he squared his shoulders and followed her.

The *Englisch* woman looked to be in her early twenties. She had pale skin, spiky black hair and multiple piercings in both ears. Roughly Hannah's height, she looked more like a girl than a woman. She was dressed in a sweater-type dress that settled two inches above her knees and high-heeled leather boots. Jacob wouldn't have guessed her weight to be more than a hundred pounds.

She'd made it out of the car, but now she stood halfway between it and them, staring down at her phone, her thumbs flying over the mobile device. There was a swish sound and then she dropped it into her leather handbag and looked up at them.

"I'm Piper Jenkins, your IRS auditor. You must be Jacob."

"*Ya*, Jacob Schrock. Good to meet you."

She turned to Hannah, but then a buzz came from her purse. She reached into it and scooped out her phone. Rolling her eyes, she dropped it back into the bag.

"I'm Hannah King. I've been helping Jacob with his accounts." Hannah clasped her hands in front of her. She'd admitted earlier that morning that she was worried the auditor would question her credentials.

Jacob almost laughed at the look of relief on her face when Piper said, "Oh, good. I'm glad to hear that he has help. Many of the Amish men I've audited try to take care of accounting on their own, and that doesn't usually end well."

"It's certainly not something I excel at," Jacob said. "If

you'd like to come inside, we've set up a place for you to work in the office."

Hannah had arrived a half hour early that morning, all in a frenzy because they hadn't thought to set up a work area for the woman. In short order, Jacob had dragged in a desk that he was working on for a client, Hannah had popped her chair next to the desk and he'd retrieved the stool that she had originally used.

"Are you sure you wouldn't rather have your old office chair?" He'd put it in the corner of his workroom and used it to stack items on. The new kitten, Blackie, had taken it over and turned it into her daytime napping spot.

"That old thing? I'm surprised it holds the cat. No thank you. I'll take the stool."

They'd pushed the desks so that the two women would be facing each other. It was crowded, but it worked.

Now Piper walked into the room, paused a moment and then nodded in approval. "Let's see what you've got for me."

It occurred to Jacob that he should be tense, but honestly he believed that he'd done right by the US Treasury Department. Perhaps he hadn't filed the correct forms, but he'd paid his fair share of taxes. He wasn't worried about the outcome, especially with Hannah at the helm.

She had saved him, in more ways than one.

He no longer rose each morning wondering what the point was, or went to sleep worried that the days stretched out endlessly in front of him. She'd done more than straighten up his accounting—she'd added hope and optimism to his life.

That thought was foremost on his mind as the two women began pulling out files and pencils and calculators and highlighters and rulers. He'd never been so happy to walk into the other room and pick up a piece of sandpaper in his life. He did not want to be anywhere near what was going on between those two, but he'd stay close just in case they needed him.

His fervent prayer was that they wouldn't.

"It's you and me, Blackie." The cat wound around his legs, purring and leaving a trail of black hair. Arching her back, she stretched, then flopped in a ray of sunlight.

"Uh-huh. Well, the rest of us have work to do."

Three days later, the audit was over.

"We're not allowed to recommend businesses to help with audits." Piper stole one last glance at her cell phone, typed something in with a flurry of her thumbs, then dropped it into her purse. She finished putting her pens, highlighters, computer and notepad into her matching designer backpack. Finally she glanced up at Hannah and seemed surprised to find her still there. "I'm sorry, what was I saying?"

"That you're not allowed to recommend businesses."

"Right. But there is a place on the Goshen Chamber of Commerce website to list your services, and I recommend that you do so. I see a lot of businesses, especially Amish businesses, that could use your organizational skills."

Hannah glanced up at Jacob, who was trying to hide a smile.

"Danki," she said. She didn't add that she wouldn't be listing her services. She had a job with Jacob, and she liked the work. Plus, he needed her. Left to his own devices he'd be stacking up bins of receipts again in no time.

A small buzz permeated the silence. Piper snatched the phone back out of her bag, typed again, smiled to herself, and dropped it back in before turning her attention to Jacob. "I hope you appreciate her."

"Oh, I do." He glanced at Hannah and wiggled his eyebrows.

She gave him her most stern look.

How could he play around with an IRS auditor standing in the office?

"You'll receive a letter within ten days stating that the audit has been closed." She glanced at Hannah, smiled and leveled a piercing gaze at Jacob. "You passed with flying colors, and the refund that you're owed will be applied to this year's bill, per your instructions."

She headed toward the door, then stopped and turned back toward them. "I want to thank you both for the work you do for children with disabilities. It's a very good thing, and I'm sure it brings much joy into their lives."

And then she was gone.

Hannah finally let out the breath that it seemed she'd been holding since Monday morning. "I wonder what she does on that phone."

"Same as writing a letter—at least that's what the *youngies* say."

"Who has that many letters to write?"

"Indeed."

"Makes me glad we don't have them."

"Oh? You don't want an *Englisch* cell phone?"

"I do not." She knew he was teasing and realized she shouldn't rise to the bait, but she couldn't help herself. "I'm the one who spent the last few days with Piper Jenkins."

"I was hiding in the workshop."

"I noticed."

"Can you blame me?"

"The woman couldn't finish a sentence without checking the screen of her cell phone at least once. Seems a complete waste of time to me." She sounded old, sounded like one of their elders who insisted that all change was dangerous. She didn't believe that, but she didn't know how to explain to Jacob what she was feeling and why.

So instead she turned her attention to pulling out her work for the day—the receipts Jacob had given her from the previous week. She knew he was still standing there, still watching her and it made her heart beat wildly and her palms sweat. Finally she looked up, met his gaze and tried not to return the smile.

She pretended to glance back down at her work. She was finding it harder and harder to maintain the distance she had sworn that she would put between her and Jacob. He'd somehow found a way to worm into her heart, slide beneath her defenses and scale the wall she'd built with such determination.

He reached into his jacket and pulled out an envelope. "This is the missing check you couldn't find."

"Oh."

"I wrote it a week ago."

"You did?"

"And I've been holding it for the right moment."

She glanced up now, and when she looked at Jacob she felt like she was leaping into a giant pool of water. Though she'd been terrified when he'd kissed her, today it seemed like the fear that had permeated her decisions and her emotions since the accident was gone. "Now is the right moment?"

"It is."

She took the envelope and stared down at her name in his familiar handwriting.

"It's for me?"

"*Ya*, it's for you, Hannah, because of how much help you've been."

"But you pay me a salary to be helpful."

"You've gone above and beyond. Believe me, I know that I

couldn't have passed that audit without you. I'd have needed to hire one of the *Englisch* accountants, and that would have cost me much more than the amount of the check you're holding."

"Jacob…"

"Open it."

She turned it over, slipped her nail beneath the flap and opened the envelope. When she pulled out the check, when she saw the amount written there, she tried to thrust it back into his hands.

"I can't take this."

"Of course you can."

"It's too much."

"*Nein.* It's the right amount, and it was the right amount whether we passed the audit or not." He walked around, took the envelope and check from her, and set them on the desk. Then he reached for her hands. "I know you've been taking work home, working longer hours than you've been reporting."

"I wanted to be ready." She tried to still the trembling in her arms and resist the urge to look up into his eyes. She knew if she did, if she allowed herself to see the goodness and kindness there, that there would be no turning back.

Jacob's voice was soft, and he rubbed his thumbs over the backs of her hands. "And I appreciate that. The amount of the check, even with what I've been paying you, it's nowhere near what the accountant in town was going to charge me."

"But—"

"I want you to have it, Hannah. I want you to use it to help your father."

And those were the magic words that convinced her to pull her hands away from his, pick up the check and tuck it into her purse.

Her heart was hammering, and she was trying to remember what she was about to do before he'd offered her the envelope.

Jacob walked back to the door and had stepped into the main room, but he pivoted back toward her, still smiling. "I forgot to tell you that your *dat* called. He's going to be later than he thought and asked if I could take you home."

"You don't have to do that."

"It's a long way to walk."

He laughed and she realized what a handsome man Jacob was. She'd not really thought about it. Oh, she'd spent many hours thinking about how she felt around him, but not about his appearance. She understood as she studied him with the afternoon sun slanting across the floor that when she looked at Jacob she didn't see his scars anymore. They weren't who he was, they were simply a reminder of something that had happened to him and of how precious life really was.

"I need to go by the Troyer home. It's on the way to your place. Do you mind?"

"*Nein.*"

"Leave in an hour?"

"*Ya.* An hour will be fine." She couldn't look at him any longer, couldn't meet those eyes that made her feel like she was falling. Instead she stared down at the receipts in her hand until she heard him walk away.

Then she collapsed into her chair and covered her face with her hands.

The audit was over.

They'd passed.

And hopefully she'd made enough money to help save her father's farm.

Chapter Twelve

Jacob tried to focus on the bedside table he was working on finishing. It was a simple piece made from walnut wood, and he should have been done with it already. He opened the drawer, confirming that it slid smoothly along the grooves. Then he stood it up on his workbench and began cleaning it one final time. Some furniture makers used fancy cleansers, but Jacob preferred doing things the old way—a little dish soap in warm water worked fine.

Using a soft cloth, he went over the table's surface three times. He wanted to remove all dust particles before putting on the final coat. Thirty minutes passed, and he found he was still cleaning the piece. In fact, he'd been rubbing the cloth over the same side for several minutes.

Once he was sure it was completely dry, he would apply a final coat of beeswax on the piece, but what was he to do with the next twenty minutes while Hannah finished up in the office? The memory of how she'd smiled at him, of the look of gratitude on her face when she'd accepted the check, made his thoughts scurry in a dozen directions—directions his thoughts had no business going.

Because it wasn't possible that Hannah King was interested in him romantically.

But what if she was?

She hadn't exactly run away when he'd kissed her at his brother's. Okay, she *had* run away, but maybe because she was embarrassed or confused. It didn't necessarily mean she didn't like it.

He dropped the rag in disgust and walked outside.

Maybe fresh air would help to clear his head.

But the problem wasn't the stuffiness in the workshop or the table he'd been working on. The problem was admitting what he felt for Hannah.

He walked across to the garden, wandered down the path and stopped at a bench. Sitting down, he glanced around him, then hopped right back up. He needed to keep moving. He needed to settle the restless feeling that made his heart gallop like Bo running across a field. That was normal behavior for a horse, but he was a man and he should have better control of his thoughts and his feelings.

A butterfly landed on a white aster bush in full bloom and then a red bird hopped onto the path in front of him. He stood there, frozen, watching it. Red birds were his mother's favorite bird. Her voice came back to him in that moment—gentle, full of wisdom, full of love.

A cardinal can be a special sign from your loved one in heaven.

When he closed his eyes he saw both his mother and father sitting on the front porch, talking and shelling peas between them, when the cardinal alighted on the porch rail. He had walked up and laughed at them, told them they looked like two old folks sitting around rocking and gossiping. His father had smiled knowingly, but his mother had pointed out the red bird.

Jacob missed them more than he would have thought possible, even after all these years. They'd been good people and what had happened to them, it didn't make any sense to him.

It wasn't that he doubted *Gotte's wille* for their lives; it was only that he didn't understand why it had to cause such pain...why their lives had to be complete at that moment, why they couldn't have stayed and grown old together and met all of their grandchildren.

Walking on through the garden, he circled back toward the workshop and saw the silhouette of Hannah working in the office. What would his mother think of her? Of Matthew? He knew the answer to both questions, and the knowledge of that caused him to laugh out loud. He'd turned twenty when his mother had begun to tease him about settling down and marrying.

A plump wife and a big barn never did any man harm.

An industrious wife is the best savings account.

Marriage may be made in heaven, but man is responsible for the upkeep.

They had never doubted that he would one day marry, that having a family was the life *Gotte* had chosen for him just as it was for his brother.

Yes, his mother would like Hannah and Matthew.

She would approve of the feelings that Jacob was struggling with.

Both his mother and his father would want him to continue on with his life, and in that moment he knew that it was all right for him to want a family, to want Hannah and Matthew. It was all right for him to move on from mourning his parents, and to finally let go of the guilt that he carried. He might not understand the path his life had taken, the scars and battles and fears that had consumed the last few years, but he understood where he was at this moment.

And he understood that it was time to step out in faith.

Hannah was quiet as they made their way down the road. She knew she should make conversation, but she didn't know what to say, and her mind kept going back to the bonus check.

Had she thanked him properly?

Should she try to do so now?

But Jacob was talking about the weather and seeing a red bird, and the school auction and picnic coming up on Saturday.

"Well?" he asked.

"Well, what?"

"Your thoughts were drifting."

"*Ya*, I suppose they were."

"I was asking if I could take you to the picnic...you and Matthew."

There were a dozen reasons she should say no, but she heard herself say, "*Ya*, Jacob. That would be nice."

He looked as surprised as she felt.

Grinning he resettled his hat on his head. "*Gut*. I'll be by at eleven on Saturday."

Had she just agreed to go on a date with Jacob? What would she wear? What was she thinking? Was it a date if Matthew was going along? How would she explain to her son that they were just friends? How was she ever going to make it through the workday tomorrow without dying of embarrassment each time he walked into the office?

She couldn't date her boss!

He directed the mare to turn down a lane, toward a house that Hannah had never been to before. It was technically in Jacob's district, and it was newer so it hadn't been there when they were children, when the two districts were one.

"Judith and Tom moved here a few years ago. Their daughter's name is Rachel."

"She's the little girl with cerebral palsy?"

"Right. She's eight, loves to read and is fascinated with any story about princesses."

They found Judith Troyer in the garden behind the house, pulling the last of the produce from her garden. She wore a drab gray dress and a black apron. Her hair was pulled back so tightly that it puckered the skin at the edge of her *kapp*.

Jacob introduced her to Hannah and then said, "The giggle mirror arrived. I was hoping I could install it, if you don't mind."

"Of course I don't mind. *Danki* for bringing it over."

Which was when Hannah noticed the small figure in a wheelchair sitting in what looked like a castle's turret, though it was actually only a couple of feet off the ground. Hannah longed to go and look at the playhouse, to see what Jacob had done, but she felt rude leaving Judith, who had returned to harvesting the few remaining carrots, snap peas and tomatoes.

"May I help?"

Judith looked her up and down and finally shrugged. "Suit yourself."

The house wasn't poor exactly. Hannah picked up a basket from the gardening supplies and moved up and down the rows of vegetables. She kept glancing at the single-story home, the garden, the yard. She tried to put her finger on what was missing.

She pulled off a large bell pepper, a lovely deep red with a rich green stem, and glanced back at the house. That was it. There was no color. No flowers in pots or beds or the garden.

Everything was utilitarian.

No toys scattered around the yard. In fact, the only color came from the playhouse. Jacob had somehow found pink and purple roof tiles which he'd fastened to the top of the turret along with a small flag that waved and crackled in the slight breeze.

"Jacob told me about your son," Judith said.

"Oh. Matthew. *Ya,* Jacob built him a playhouse too. It's how we met—how we met again. We attended school together many years ago, but now my family lives in the next district."

"If you ask me, the playhouses are foolishness."

"Excuse me?"

"A waste of *Englisch* money. I would have told the foundation no, but Tom…" She waved a hand toward the barn. "Tom thinks it will help her, as if a playhouse could do such a thing."

"I'm sorry…about Rachel's condition."

"Not your fault." Judith dropped to her knees and began digging up potatoes. Each time she'd find one, she'd shake it vigorously, as if the dirt clinging to its roots offended her, and then place it in her basket with a *tsk* of disapproval.

"Matthew has enjoyed his playhouse. He can spend hours out there, pretending and reading and enjoying the sunshine." She hadn't realized what a blessing the playhouse was until that moment, until she felt a need to defend it to this woman.

"And what good does that do?"

"Pretending?"

"That and playing…"

"Surely children need to play."

"Acting as if all is well when it isn't and it never will be again."

"So our children shouldn't enjoy life? Because their futures are…" She almost said *bleak,* but she didn't believe that. She thought of Matthew's smile, his quick wit, his loving personality. She thought of his legs, withered and useless. Like Jacob's scars, they weren't who he was; they were only representative of what he had been through.

"They have no future." Judith yanked especially hard on a potato, again spraying dirt over her apron. "No real future at all."

"Of course they do. It might be limited. I know that Matthew will never work in a field or build a barn, but that doesn't mean his life is useless. *Gotte* still has a purpose for his being born, for his being among us."

"Your child is what…four?"

"Nearly five."

"My Rachel is eight. Come back in three years and let's see if you're still so optimistic."

Hannah would have offered a hand of comfort to the woman, because her words seemed to come from a place of deep pain, but Judith was back on her feet moving toward the okra plants at the end of the row. "You can leave the basket by the tools when you're done."

Jacob pushed Rachel's wheelchair as they gave Hannah a tour of the playhouse.

Hannah seemed quite taken with the child. She would repeatedly squat by the chair and ask Rachel questions about what books she liked, who her favorite princess was, whether she enjoyed school.

"I don't always go," the young girl admitted.

Her speech was distorted by the disease, but it was easy enough to make out what she was saying if you listened. Her wheelchair had a special head pad, because she sometimes jerked back and forth. Based on what Tom, the child's father, had explained to Jacob, Rachel was better off than many of the children with CP. She could speak, could feed herself, although it required a special spoon strapped to her hand, and her intelligence was on the normal scale.

Jacob thought she was a beautiful child with a very special smile.

"School prepares people to work," Rachel continued. It was obvious she was repeating what she'd been told by someone, probably her mother. "I won't ever hold a job, so I don't have to go if I don't want to."

"I'm sure you go when you can," Hannah said.

"*Ya*, but *Mamm* says that it doesn't matter much and that if I'd rather stay home…" Rachel's right hand jerked to the side, hitting the padded rail that covered every part of the playhouse. "She says that I don't have to go. I like school, though, and *Dat* says that the teacher misses me when I'm not there."

"I'm sure she does."

Rachel grinned up at both Hannah and Jacob.

"I woke up feeling *narrisch*, but after I lay around all morning *Mamm* finally said I could come out here. I always feel better when I'm in my castle."

"Let's see this funny mirror that Jacob installed."

"It's the best."

They spent the next five minutes giggling and making silly faces in the mirror which pulled and distorted their images like taffy. Finally they wheeled Rachel back to the front porch, and Judith came out and retrieved her without a word. Rachel waved as they walked away, and Jacob assured her he'd be back the following week to see if any updates needed to be made to the playhouse.

Once they were back in the buggy, he noticed that Hannah was uncharacteristically quiet.

"Something wrong?"

"*Nein.*"

"Hmmm…because you were laughing with Rachel, but now you seem quite serious."

Hannah stared down at her hands. "It's only that I spoke with her *mamm*, and it left me feeling…uncertain of things."

Jacob sighed. "I should have warned you about Judith. She has *gut* days and bad ones. I take it today was a bad one."

"She's so bitter and angry."

"Tom thinks it's depression. He finally talked her into a seeing a doctor who did prescribe some medication, but many days she doesn't take it…or so Tom says."

"Can't she see how beautiful Rachel is? What a blessing she is? She's that little girl's mother. She should be able to look past the child's disability."

"I agree with you. All we can do is pray that she'll have a change of heart, that the medicine will work. We'll support them however we can."

"It makes me angry," Hannah admitted.

"Because you have a big heart. You care about children."

"I'm sure Judith cares about Rachel. It's only that…" Tears clogged her voice.

"Don't cry…"

They were nearly to her house. He reached over and squeezed her hand, directed the gelding down the lane, and parked the buggy a discreet distance from the front porch. "What's this about? Why the tears?"

"Because…because…" She swallowed, scrubbed both palms against her cheeks and finally spoke the words that tore at her heart. "Because I was like that."

"You weren't."

"I was, Jacob. You don't know…my thoughts, my anger at *Gotte*, even at other people…people with normal families."

"You're being too hard on yourself." He put a hand on

each of her shoulders and turned her toward him. "Listen to me, Hannah. You're a kind, *gut* person, and you're a *wunderbaar* mother. But you're not perfect. No one expects you to be. I'm sure you have spent plenty of nights consumed by anger...same as me."

He waited until she met his gaze. "Same as me, same as probably everyone who has endured a tragedy."

He caressed her arms, clasped her hands in his, reached forward and kissed her softly. "But you came out the other side of that anger. Your faith and your family and your friends saw you through. Judith will find her way too. It's only taking a little longer."

Hannah nodded her head as if what he said made sense, but she quickly gathered her purse and lunch box from the floor of the buggy, whispered, "*Danki* for the ride," and fled into the house.

Hannah waited until Jacob had driven away, then she pulled in a deep breath, scrubbed at her cheeks again and squared her shoulders. She honestly didn't know why meeting Judith had affected her so. The woman was bitter and angry and hurting, but Judith's life wasn't her life.

She walked into the kitchen, surprised no one was there. Pulling the envelope with the bonus check out of her bag, she set it in the middle of the table.

Where was everyone?

She peered out the window at the backyard, garden and playhouse, but no one was there either.

Where was her mother?

Where was Matthew?

Then she heard the sound that she spent nights waiting for, the sound that she often heard in her nightmares—a wet, deep, shuddering cough that meant her son was in trouble.

She ran to his room.

Matthew was in his bed, curled on his side, facing toward her with his eyes shut.

Her mother sat beside him in a chair, and on the nightstand next to her was a basin and a cloth that she was wringing out.

"Hannah, it's *gut* you're home. Matthew isn't feeling so well."

She hurried to the bed, dropped beside it and reached to feel her son's brow. He had at least a low-grade fever, maybe more, but what sent a river of fear tumbling through her heart was the cough. He began hacking again, seemed to lose his breath and finally recovered. Opening his eyes, he smiled briefly at her and reached for her hand.

"My chest hurts," he said in a gravelly voice.

His breath came in short, shallow gasps.

"I know it does, sweetie. We're going to get you some help. You'll feel better soon. Deep breaths, okay?"

Matthew nodded and closed his eyes.

He'd fallen asleep early the night before. She should have noticed. She should have paid closer attention, but her mind had been on the audit.

"We need to get him to the hospital," Hannah said.

"It's only a cough…"

"If you'll go and get the buggy, I'll pull together his things."

She'd left early with her father that morning, left before breakfast. She'd checked on Matthew, but only for a moment and even then she'd been distracted.

Her mother still hadn't moved, though she'd set the cloth down by the basin. "It started this morning, and by this afternoon he seemed a little worse so I put him to bed. The fever is only ninety-nine."

"*Mamm*, listen to me." She turned to look at her mother and saw the fear and confusion there, so she knelt down in front of her and clasped her hands. "You did nothing wrong, but we need to take him to the hospital. We need to go now."

Her mother nodded, though she still seemed confused, dazed almost.

Hannah jumped up and began digging through Matthew's dresser for a change of clothes, the favorite blanket that he kept near him when he was sick and the book they'd been reading.

Her mother moved to her side and said, "Tell me what's happening." She reached out and covered Hannah's hands with her own. "Hannah, look at me and explain to me what is happening."

Hannah took a deep breath, tried to push down the anger and fear. "Because of the injury, Matthew's lungs don't work the same. A small cold can change into pneumonia very quickly."

"Since this morning?"

"*Ya*, since this morning."

Her mother pressed her fingers to her lips and then nodded once, decisively. "Are you sure I should hitch the buggy? Wouldn't it be quicker to call for an ambulance?"

"*Ya*, you're right. That's a better idea."

"I'll go to the phone shack right now."

She heard her mother running through the house, heard the front screen door open and then slam shut.

Hannah stopped digging through the bureau drawer and sank to the floor next to Matthew's bed. "It'll be okay, Matthew. It'll be okay, darling."

He tried to smile at her, but fell into a fit of coughing again, and then he began to shake. "I'm so c...co...cold."

"You'll feel better soon. I promise." She pulled the covers up to his chin and pushed the favorite blanket into his hands.

It seemed only a moment before her mother returned and went into Hannah's room to pull together an overnight bag. "Stay with him. I'll get you a change of clothes. Will we ride with the ambulance?"

"I will, but you'll need to bring the buggy."

Hannah was watching out the window, praying the ambulance would hurry, when her mother walked up beside her and pulled her into her embrace. "I called the bishop too. He's praying, Hannah. Soon our whole congregation will be praying for Matthew. He's going to be all right."

Hannah blinked back hot tears and tried to smile. She needed to be strong now—needed to be strong for Matthew and for her family. They hadn't experienced this type of emergency before, and it could be upsetting—the ambulance and the doctors and the hospital. *Englisch* ways could sometimes be overwhelming and disorienting, and she couldn't begin to guess what the financial cost would be. Her mind darted away from that. There would be time enough to worry over money once Matthew was well, and he would get well.

Her father arrived as the paramedics were loading Matthew into the ambulance. He left the horse untied, still hitched to the buggy and ran toward them.

"*Mamm* will explain. I have to go." Hannah kissed him on the cheek and hopped up into the back of the ambulance.

The siren began to blare as the paramedic slammed the doors shut and then they were speeding down the road.

Chapter Thirteen

Jacob stopped by his brother's place around dinnertime. He wanted to tell his brother about the good news with the IRS audit, and it might have been in the back of his mind that a home-cooked meal would be nice for a change. Emily could work wonders in the kitchen, especially given the fact that she did so with five boys wandering in and out of the room.

But he knew the moment that he arrived that something was wrong.

"Jacob, I was about to send Samuel over."

Samuel stood at the back door, his straw hat pushed down on his head so far that it almost touched his eyes—which would have been comical except for the somber look on his face.

"What's wrong?"

"It's Matthew."

"Hannah's Matthew?"

"He's in the hospital."

"That's not possible." He plopped down onto a kitchen chair. "I was just there, only...only an hour ago."

"It happened fast according to Sally Lapp, who heard it from the bishop."

"But—"

"Sally said it's probably pneumonia." Emily placed a glass of water in front of him and sat down in the adjacent chair. "He's at the hospital. Hannah's parents are there with her. So is our bishop and hers. Sally was planning on going up as soon as she could get there. Apparently she and Hannah have become quite close."

"I need to go. I need to be with her."

"*Ya*, you do." Emily reached out and covered his hand with hers, and that simple touch almost unnerved him.

He'd taken his family for granted for too long.

He could see that now.

"I'll... I'll go straightaway."

"I want to go too." Joseph had been sitting at the end of the table reading a book from school. When Jacob looked over at him, he put a homemade bookmark in the book, shut the cover and stood up. "He's my friend. I should be there."

Samuel tried to talk his younger brother into going outside with him, but Joseph would have none of it. He crossed his arms and declared, "I'm going."

Even Emily couldn't dissuade him.

Finally Jacob said, "I'll take him and send him home with someone else if I decide to stay."

"Of course you'll stay, Jacob. Hannah needs you. Bishop Amos can bring him back. He won't mind."

"*Gut* idea."

"I would go, but..."

"Stay here, with your family. Hannah will understand."

His nephew peppered him with questions all the way to the hospital.

"How did Matthew get sick so quickly? We were just playing together last week. Was it because of something we did?" Joseph took a breath, then kept on going.

"I pushed him fast in the chair, *Onkle* Jacob. Did that cause it?"

And the most pressing question, the one that Jacob couldn't answer.

"When will he come home?"

They'd traveled for a few moments in silence when Joseph said, still staring out the window, "Matthew is like David."

"What's that?"

"Like David…in the Bible." He made the motion of winding up and letting go a slingshot. "He's a warrior just like David, only he battles what's wrong with his body."

The hospital's lights broke through the night like a beacon, spilling out into the darkness.

Being situated in the middle of Goshen, where roughly half the population was Amish, there was plenty of buggy parking. Jacob tied Bo to the rail, assured the gelding he'd be back soon. Then he and Joseph practically sprinted into the building, through the automatic doors to the visitor information desk, then down a hall, up an elevator and down another hall.

He heard the murmur of voices before they turned the corner, and he really shouldn't have been surprised, and yet he was. The room was filled with Amish. Hannah's parents, the bishop from both her district and Jacob's, both of Hannah's sisters and their husbands and their children. Sally Lapp and her husband—Sally seemed to be knitting. Leroy was discussing crops with Tobias Hochstetler, who was Claire and Alton's neighbor. So many people, waiting on word of a very special boy.

He thought Joseph would join the other boys playing checkers, but instead he slipped his hand into Jacob's and walked with him over to Hannah's parents.

"Any word?"

"No, Jacob. Sit down. We're all still waiting to hear from the doctor." Hannah's father tossed a newspaper onto the coffee table. "Sit. You look as if you've been rushing around."

"*Ya*, I suppose I have."

It was Joseph who stepped in front of Hannah's *mamm*, eyes wide, his small hat in his hands. "Is Matthew going to be okay?"

"Yes, Joseph. I believe he is going to be fine."

"But right now he's sick."

"Yes, he is."

"So, I can't see him."

"*Nein*. Only his *mamm* can be with him now, but I think Matthew would be very happy to know that you're here."

Joseph pulled in his bottom lip, blinking rapidly. Finally he said, "Okay. I'll just wait—over there," and he walked slowly to where the other boys were. Jacob noticed that he sat beside them, watching the game of checkers, but he didn't join in. Instead his eyes kept going to the hall, the clock, Jacob and then back to the board, as if he was afraid he might miss something.

Someone had brought a basket of baked goods, and there was coffee in the vending machines. After an hour of waiting, Jacob wandered down the hall to purchase a cup. He must have stood there for five or ten minutes, staring at the options of black, cream, cream and sugar, vanilla cream and sugar. The possibilities seemed endless, but it made no difference how he had his coffee, only that the caffeine worked to push back the fatigue. He needed to be awake and alert when Hannah called for him, and he knew that she would.

"Pretty nasty stuff," Hannah's father said, coming up beside him and staring at the machine.

"*Ya*, I remember."

"They let you drink it when you were in the hospital?"

"Not really, but occasionally I'd sneak out of my room and purchase a cup. The nurses, they don't like patients drinking caffeine after dinner. They insisted it wasn't good for us. Probably they were right, but I also think they didn't want us restless when things should be quieting down."

"How long were you in the hospital?"

"The first time…four weeks. I went back for three other procedures. Those other stays were shorter—three to five days most of the time."

"Must have been difficult."

"*Ya*. Being here, under the fluorescent lights with the constant whir and beeping of *Englisch* machines, it grated on me after a while. I think the worst part was being away from everything that was a part of my life—the farm and workshop and family." He blinked away the tears and punched the button for black coffee.

"I meant the surgeries must have been hard, the pain of the injuries."

"*Ya*, that too."

"I'm sorry we weren't there for you, son."

Jacob jerked at the use of the word *son*, or perhaps it was the touch of Alton's hand on his shoulder that surprised him.

"I barely knew you then, Alton."

"And yet you were a part of our community."

"It was after we'd divided into two districts."

"Still, we are connected through our history, through being one community before. We aren't so big that we can't still care for one another." Alton cleared his throat and chose a coffee with cream and sugar. When he turned to study Jacob, a smile pulled at the corners of his mouth. "Claire and I believe that *Gotte* brought you into Hannah's life for a reason...into all our lives. You've been a *gut* friend to her and maybe something more, *ya*?"

"I have feelings for your *doschder*, if that's what you're asking, but I'm not sure...that is, I don't know if Hannah..."

"Have you asked her?"

"About how she felt? *Nein*. It took all of my courage to ask her to Saturday's picnic."

Hannah's father laughed and steered them back toward the waiting room. "Young love presents its own challenges. You and Hannah, you will find your way."

Is that what he felt for Hannah?

Love?

Something pushed against his ribs, and he thought of the cardinal in the garden he'd seen just that afternoon, of Hannah smiling as she agreed to go to the picnic with him, of the way that Judith had brought such sadness to her, of Matthew smiling as he donned his conductor's hat and asked to be pushed out to the playhouse.

Ya, he did love her. He loved them both, and as soon as he had a chance he planned to make sure she knew.

Hannah had only moved from Matthew's side to use the restroom. She was aware that her parents were in the waiting room, but she didn't want to go to them until she had some answers. Matthew was still sleeping fitfully, waking every few minutes to attempt to cough the congestion up from his lungs.

A woman in a white coat walked into the room carrying a computer tablet and wearing a stethoscope. "I'm Dr. Hardin. You must be Matthew's mother." She looked awfully young to be a doctor. Her hair was cut in a short red shag, and she wore large owlish glasses.

"*Ya*, I'm Matthew's *mamm*. Is he all right? Did we get here in time?"

"You did the right thing bringing him in so quickly. Often parents wait, hoping the situation will improve on its own. In this case, your quick decisiveness probably saved Matthew a potentially long stay in the hospital."

Hannah had to sit then. Actually she fell into the chair behind her. She hadn't realized how heavy the weight of her guilt was until it was lifted from her. She felt so light that she might simply fly away.

"They explained to me when Matthew was first hurt that it was something we must watch for…" Tears clogged her voice, and she found she couldn't finish the sentence.

Dr. Hardin patted her shoulder, then moved to Matthew's side. She listened to his chest, checked his pulse, placed a hand against his forehead. Hannah knew well enough that the nurse had already done these things, and she appreciated the doctor's attention all the more for it.

She also was comforted by the fact that Dr. Hardin spoke softly to Matthew the entire time she was examining him. She seemed to understand that he was more than just a patient in a bed.

He was a young boy who was scared and hurting.

He was a young boy with a family that loved him very much.

Hannah liked this doctor and trusted her immediately.

"The chest X-rays do show pneumonia, and the CBC confirms that."

"His blood count…"

"Exactly. Since it's the bacterial form, we'll start him on some IV antibiotics, give him some breathing treatments and he should be feeling better soon." She entered data on her tablet as she spoke. Finally she glanced up and looked directly at Hannah. "I won't sugarcoat it. Children with a spinal cord injury have a harder time recovering from these events. We could be looking at a rough forty-eight hours, but if he responds to the antibiotics, Matthew will be much better within a few days."

"*Danki.*"

"You're welcome. Do you have any questions?"

"Only, did I do something wrong? Where did he…catch this?"

Dr. Hardin was shaking her head before Hannah finished her question. "You can't keep him in a bubble. Matthew could have picked it up anywhere—the store, the library, even at a church service. The important thing is that you recognized the symptoms immediately."

"Only I didn't. I wasn't home today, and my mother didn't know…"

"You got him here in plenty of time, and it helps that he's a healthy young guy. Apparently he's eating well and getting plenty of exercise."

"*Ya*, both of those things."

Dr. Hardin squeezed Matthew's hand and then walked back around the bed. She stopped beside Hannah and placed a hand on her shoulder. "If you have any questions, ask the nurses or ask them to call me. I'm here most of the time, and I'll be happy to come down and talk to you."

"What happens next?"

"A nurse will come in and start the antibiotics. He needs rest to fight the infection, so expect him to sleep a lot. We'll also continue breathing treatments, and when he's strong enough we'll get him up and around—that's very important with pneumonia patients. We'll do X-rays again tomorrow to be sure that he's improving."

Dr. Hardin had made it to the door when she turned and said, "By the way, Matthew's grandparents have been asking how he's doing. They're in the waiting room down the hall. You might want to give them a status update."

Hannah nodded, but she was suddenly completely exhausted. She wasn't sure she could drag herself down there. Still, her parents deserved to know.

A nurse, an older black man who had introduced himself as Trevor, changed out the bag attached to Matthew's IV. He hummed softly as he worked, and Hannah thought that maybe he was humming a hymn…one of the old ones that both Amish and *Englisch* sang.

I am weak, but thou art strong,
Jesus keep me from all wrong.

He glanced up at her and smiled.

"That's the antibiotics that you're adding to his IV?"

"Yes, it is. Our little man didn't even wake up, which is good. He's resting. If you'd like to step out of the room, I'm sure he will be fine."

"Okay. Perhaps for just a minute…"

"Go. Matthew's fan club is quite worried."

Hannah didn't know what he meant by fan club, but she did need to speak to her parents. She took one last look at her son, pushed through the door and trudged down the hall.

Jacob happened to look up at the exact moment Hannah appeared in the waiting room. She looked so tired, so vulnerable, that he jumped up and went to her.

She raised her eyes to his. "He's going to be okay. They think…they think we made it here in time."

The words were softly spoken, but everyone heard, perhaps because everyone had stopped what they were doing at the sight of her.

As her words sank in, there was much slapping on the back, calls of "praise *Gotte*" and nodding heads—almost as if everyone knew that would be the answer. They'd believed that *Gotte* wasn't done with young Matthew yet. His life wasn't complete.

Jacob led Hannah over to her parents, who were standing now, smiling and obviously relieved.

"Hannah, I'm so sorry that I didn't realize how sick he was. I should have...should have called you earlier. Should have rung the emergency bell or..."

Hannah pulled her mother into a hug. "You did fine. You put him into bed and were caring for him. What more could I ask?"

"So he's going to be all right?" her father asked.

"The doctor said the next forty-eight hours will be critical, but she thinks that we made it here in time."

"That's *gut*. That's such a relief," her mother said.

Her father nodded. "It is *gut*, and we'll stay with you as long as you need us. You're not alone in this."

"I know I'm not, and I appreciate the offer, but you should all go home." Hannah turned toward the group. "*Danki, danki* all of you for coming and for praying for me and for Matthew. I appreciate it more than you know. Don't feel... don't feel that you need to stay."

But no one was willing to go home just yet.

The boys were now laughing as they played checkers.

Hannah's sisters had rushed over to hear the news and now they were hugging her and asking what things they could bring up for her the next day.

Her mom shooed everyone away and insisted that she sit

and eat one of the muffins. "You have to keep your strength up, dear."

Bishop Jethro fetched her a cup of coffee.

Bishop Amos tapped his Bible and proclaimed that *Gotte* was *gut*.

Sally handed her a lap blanket that she'd finished knitting. "Hospital rooms can be quite cold. Please, take it. I didn't know who it was for when I started it, only that someone would need it. As I finished, though, these last few hours, I prayed for both you and Matthew."

It seemed that everyone wanted to offer her a word of encouragement, a touch, something to let her know that she had friends and families with her as she traveled this difficult path. But it was Jacob who stayed at her side the entire time. He didn't even consider leaving. Her pain was his pain, and her exhaustion he would try to bolster with his strength. After only a few minutes, she was ready to go back to Matthew's room.

"Can I walk you?"

"Of course."

They padded quietly down the hall, shoulder to shoulder, her hand in his.

When they finally reached Matthew's room, Hannah said, "You can come in if you like."

"Are you sure?"

"*Ya*. Matthew will ask if you've been here. He thinks of you as quite the hero."

"I'm no hero," Jacob protested.

"To that four-year-old boy lying in the bed, you are."

And what am I to you? The question was on his lips, but he bit it back. Hannah's attention was on her son, and she was no doubt exhausted, plus the next few days would be arduous. The last thing she needed was questions from him about their relationship.

He satisfied himself with saying, "You know, you didn't have to make a trip to the hospital to get out of your date with me."

Hannah smiled, and stared down at her hands and then looked back up at him. Rising on her tiptoes, she kissed him on the cheek. "Oh, you think I want out of it, do you?"

"Crossed my mind."

"I could just say I have to wash my hair."

"You could."

"I wouldn't."

"That's *gut* to know." He reached out and placed his palm against her cheek.

She closed her eyes for a moment and he wondered if she missed that…the physical touch of another. She'd been married before. She knew of the intimacies between a man and a woman. Her life had to be lonelier for the loss of it.

They walked into the room hand in hand, and when Jacob saw Matthew in the bed, his heart flipped like a fish that had landed on the bank of a river. The boy looked so impossibly small and vulnerable, and yet he had the heart of a warrior. Who had said that? His nephew, on the ride over.

And it was true.

Jacob pulled up a chair and sat there, holding Matthew's hand and praying silently for the young boy. Hannah used the time he was there to go into the restroom, freshen up and go to the nursing station. When she returned with a pillow and blanket, he jumped up to take them from her and place them in the chair.

"You're going to sleep here?"

"I doubt I will sleep, but *ya*."

"You want to be with him."

"In case he wakes up. Before...sometimes he would wake up in the hospital and not recognize where he was and be frightened."

"You'll let us know if you need anything? You can call my phone in the shop. I can sleep there in case—"

"I need you to convince those people out there to go home."

"Our *freinden*?"

Hannah smiled again, the weariness momentarily erased. "*Ya*, our *freinden*. Especially the children. They have school tomorrow."

"I'll tell them you said so."

He kissed the top of her head before he left. It seemed hardly adequate to show how he felt. He would find a better way. He would show her that he loved her and then he would tell her. He would make sure that both Matthew and Hannah knew.

Chapter Fourteen

Matthew's stay in the hospital lasted longer than anyone could have guessed. His birthday came and went. The days on the calendar slipped by, one after another, until October loomed in front of them. Matthew would improve one day only to slide back for three more. Dr. Hardin assured Hannah that this was normal, that he was fighting a particularly virulent form of bacterial pneumonia and that they were doing all of the right things.

Hannah's parents brought fresh clothes for her and would sit with Matthew to give her a few moments out of the room.

The nurses brought plates of food, even though Matthew was rarely awake enough to eat. "Then it's for you," they assured her. "You need to stay strong too."

Both bishops visited Hannah often, counseled with her and assured her that many people were praying for Matthew.

Her sisters, brothers-in-law and nieces visited every few days. They joked that someone should install a bus line to the hospital, "We'd keep it busy with folks visiting Matthew. He's a very popular guy." Sharon and Beth both had less than two months until their babies were due, and Hannah worried that the traveling back and forth wasn't healthy for them or the babies.

"I want to get out of the house," Sharon admitted. "My girls are turning seven soon, but they think they're turning thirteen. I caught one with lipstick. Now, where did she get that?"

Beth nodded in sympathy. "Naomi went through that phase too, and I suspect she'll go through it again."

She loved having her sisters and her parents and her church family there. For the first time in a long time, she realized that she wasn't alone, that others were willing and eager to lend a hand.

But it was Jacob that she longed to see each day.

He always appeared, though the time varied. If he had a job in the area, he would stop by at lunch. If he was working at home, he'd wait until the end of the day and bring her something fresh to eat from Emily for dinner.

They didn't speak of the date that had never happened or of the kiss in the buggy, but she thought of both often—especially in the middle of the night when she woke and couldn't go back to sleep.

Each time Jacob visited, he brought something for Matthew, and those items lined the windowsill—a wooden train, a book, a piece of candy for when he was well. The string of items was a testament to how long they'd been in this holding pattern, how long Matthew had been battling his illness, how faithful Jacob was.

He always stayed for at least an hour and allowed Hannah to vent her worries, to cry occasionally, to admit when she was discouraged or afraid or depressed. He never judged her and never questioned her faith, but instead he simply held her hand and assured her that he was there.

On the days when Matthew was better, was actually awake and talkative, they laughed at Jacob's stories of playhouses that he'd built, of getting stuck inside one that was supposed to resemble a baseball dugout, of forgetting to build a door in one that he'd designed to resemble a hobbit's home.

"What's a hobbit?" Matthew asked. He had to pull in a deep breath after he spoke, but his color was better and the doctor was talking about sending him home if his improvement continued.

"You haven't read him Tolkien?" Jacob's eyes widened in mock disbelief.

"We've been a little busy."

"Then perhaps I will pick it up from the library."

But instead of doing that, he'd purchased a copy at the local bookstore. After that, he'd read to Matthew for at least thirty minutes each day. Hannah had trouble understanding why that meant so much to her, why it touched her heart, but it did.

She admitted as much to her mother one day as she was walking her to the elevator.

"Why shouldn't it?" Her mother pulled Hannah away from the elevator. "Your heart is tender, Hannah. You've been through a lot in the last few years."

"That's an understatement."

"And for a time you closed off your feelings."

Hannah crossed her arms. She knew that her mother was correct, that it was an observation, not a criticism, but it was still difficult for her to think of the months following David's death and Matthew's accident.

"It's one thing to bring a gift to someone." Her mother reached out and pulled one of Hannah's *kapp* strings forward. "It's another thing entirely to spend time beside a bed, reading, simply bringing a small amount of joy into a person's life."

"I know it is." She sounded petulant to her own ears, sounded like a child.

"Jacob cares about Matthew. The quickest way to any mother's heart is to truly love her child." With those insightful words, she kissed Hannah on the cheek and pushed the button for the elevator.

After Matthew had fallen asleep that evening, Hannah turned on the small book light Jacob had given her and scanned back through the pages of *The Hobbit*. She'd read it in school, probably the same year that Jacob had. Always they'd had their reading after lunch, when the teacher or one of the older students would read aloud a chapter—sometimes two if they pleaded long enough and hard enough.

Matthew was a bit young for such a big tale, and yet he seemed to enjoy Bilbo's adventures, as well as the groups of dwarves and elves and goblins and trolls. As Hannah looked back over what Jacob had read to him a few hours earlier, she didn't hear the tale in the voice of Bilbo Baggins, though. Instead she heard Jacob's voice—clear and steady and strong.

She could admit to herself that she wanted that. She wanted Jacob in her life, but what she couldn't admit, what she couldn't begin to fathom, was why he would be interested in taking on her and Matthew.

And there it was—in the deepest part of her heart, beneath the fatigue and fear. In the place where her dreams resided, she was certain that Jacob would one day come to his senses and realize that he didn't want the challenge of a disabled son and a mother who was emotionally scarred.

★ ★ ★

Hannah woke Friday morning with the same questions circling through her mind.

How much was the hospital bill?

How could she possibly pay it?

Was her father's farm secure now?

Had they been able to raise enough money?

Where would they live if they were forced to move?

How would she break the news to Matthew?

Even as her heart rejoiced over the fact that Matthew was well enough to be discharged, Hannah's mind couldn't help rushing ahead to what was next.

"You're exhausted is all." Sharon had stopped by with fresh breakfast muffins. Now she sat in the chair by the window, knitting a baby blanket that was optimistically blue.

"Still hoping for a boy?"

"*Ya*, but if it's a girl, I'll give the blanket to Beth."

"And if she has a girl?"

"Someone in our church will have a boy." She pointed her knitting needle at Hannah. "And stop trying to change the subject."

"Which was?"

"Your exhaustion."

"Pretty lame subject."

"Tell me what's really bothering you."

Hannah bit her bottom lip, walked to the window and stared out at the beautiful fall day. It seemed as if she'd been in this hospital for months instead of weeks. "This incident with Matthew wasn't a solitary event."

"Meaning?"

Hannah glanced at her son, curled on his side, soft snores coming from him. "Meaning it's my life. This could happen again next month or next year. Or it could be something else entirely."

"You're saying that you're not a safe bet."

"Excuse me?"

"We're talking about Jacob, right? Because I know that you wouldn't change your life, your time with Matthew… even if it meant that you could have a perfect child, a healthy husband and a life without financial problems."

"*Nein*, I wouldn't."

"So you're worried about Jacob."

"I suppose." Hannah moved over and sat on the stool next to Sharon's chair. "Maybe you've hit the heart of the matter. This is my life. I am grateful to have Matthew, and somehow I will find a way to be strong for him."

"But Jacob?"

"I can't possibly ask him to shoulder the burdens of my life."

"Isn't that Jacob's decision?"

"He might care for me…"

"*Ya*, that kiss in the buggy seems to suggest he does."

"I wish I'd never told you about that."

"And stopping by every day…bringing Matthew and you small gifts. The man is smitten."

"Caring for someone is one thing."

"Indeed it is."

"Sacrificing the life you have for them, that's another thing entirely."

Sharon dropped her knitting into her bag, reached forward and put a hand under Hannah's chin. "Look at me, *schweschder*."

When Hannah finally raised her eyes, Sharon was smiling in her I-know-a-secret, older-sister way. "Perhaps for Jacob, you and Matthew aren't a sacrifice. Perhaps you're a blessing."

★ ★ ★

Jacob puttered around his workshop all of Friday morning. By lunch he'd finished all of his projects and stored them neatly on the shelf, cleaned off his workbench, stored his tools and even swept the floor. With nothing left to do, he walked into his office, Hannah's office, sat in her chair and asked himself for the thousandth time why she would want to marry someone like him.

He looked up when he heard a long whistle. His brother's boots clomped across the workshop floor. He stopped in the doorway of the office. "Someone has been cleaning house."

"How are you, Micah?"

"Gut." He plopped down into the chair across from him. "Is today the day?"

"That Matthew comes home? *Ya.* Hannah thought they would release him after lunch."

Instead of answering, Micah's right eyebrow shot up.

"Don't give me that look."

"I'm just wondering—"

"I know what you're wondering. Her parents wanted to pick them up, and…well, I thought this was a time for family."

Micah's smile grew.

"Are you laughing at me, *bruder*?"

"You remind me of a lovesick pup is all. You remind me of myself a few years ago."

"Ya?" Jacob didn't bother denying his observation. He felt lovesick—excited, worried, a little nauseous.

"Will she come back to work?"

"She wants to. She even asked me to bring over the box of receipts for her to work on at home until she's sure Matthew's strong enough to leave with her mother." Jacob pushed the box on the floor with the toe of his work boot.

"When are you going to ask her?"

"Ask her?"

"To marry you."

"What makes you think I am?"

"So you're not?"

"I didn't say that."

"So you are."

"*Ya*, only... I want to wait for the right time."

Micah sat forward, crossed his arms on the desk and studied his brother. "You're a *gut* man, Jacob. *Mamm* and *Dat*, they would be proud of who you've become."

Jacob had to look away then, because they were the words he'd needed to hear for quite some time. When had he become so emotional? He felt like he walked through each day without enough skin, as if his every feeling was displayed on the surface. Maybe that was because he'd spent so long hiding behind his scars. He wasn't sure if knowing Hannah had changed him or if time had, and he didn't want to go back, but he hadn't learned how to deal with the deluge of emotions.

He cleared his throat and said, "I thought I'd give her a few weeks to settle in. I don't want to rush her and she has to be exhausted, plus..."

"You're thinking about this all wrong."

"I am?"

Micah tapped the desk. "She wants to be here, working with you."

"You can't know that."

"She wants you in her life, Jacob."

"If I was certain—"

"Waiting will only cause her to worry that you don't want the same thing."

Jacob stared out the window and thought of his brother's

words. Hannah did seem worried, preoccupied even. She also seemed so happy to see him. Was she concerned that one day he'd simply stop coming by? Was she worried that he'd realize the awesome responsibility it would be to father Matthew? Did she think that one day he might turn tail and run?

"When did you become so wise?"

"I've been working on it."

"What if she says no?"

"She won't."

"But what if she does?"

"Better to know now. Then you can move on."

"I don't know how to do that."

"You're getting your buggy in front of your horse."

Jacob jumped up. "You're right."

"It's *wunderbaar* to hear you say that."

"I'm going over there right now, and I'm going to ask her."

"Maybe you should shave first."

"*Gut* idea."

"A haircut wouldn't hurt, either."

"I don't have time for a haircut."

"You only ask a woman to marry you once. Why not look your best?"

"Should I wash my buggy too?"

"Wouldn't hurt."

"I was kidding."

"So was I."

Jacob stopped in the doorway. "Shouldn't I take her flowers or something?"

Micah ran his fingers through his beard, tilted his head to the left and then the right. Finally he said, "*Gut* idea. In fact, Emily already thought of it."

"She did?"

"There's a basket of fresh-cut wildflowers by the door."

"For me?"

"For Hannah."

"That's what I meant."

"But you can say they're from you. Emily asked me to bring them over so you'd have something to take with you."

"How did she know I was going to see Hannah?"

Micah shrugged. "Don't bother trying to understand women, Jacob. Just be grateful that *Gotte* created them."

Hannah's mother and father arrived at the hospital before noon.

"I get to go home," Matthew declared.

"So we heard." Alton stuck both of his thumbs under his suspenders. "Didn't realize you had so much to take with you. We might need another buggy."

"Jacob made all of those things for me."

"Did he, now?"

"Were you kidding?" Matthew pulled in a big breath. He was better, but still weak from the ordeal of the past two weeks. "Do we have enough room?"

"He was kidding," Hannah's mother assured him. "I even brought a backpack to put them in."

She set the bag made from blue denim on Matthew's bed.

"I can't believe you still have that thing," Hannah said. "I haven't seen it in years."

"Why would I throw it away? I knew Matthew would need it soon."

"Was it yours, *Mamm*?"

"It was." She ran her thumb over the shoulder strap. Thinking of her school days, when she was young and innocent and naive, reminded her of how much had happened since then. The surprising thing was that she didn't feel angry like she did before. She would always miss David, and she wished that Matthew hadn't been involved in the accident, but this was the life she'd been given, and she was grateful for it.

Despite what she'd shared with her sister earlier that morning, she was grateful.

"I need to go downstairs for a few minutes. Can you two help Matthew pack up?"

"Sure thing," her mother said.

But her dad stepped out into the hall with her. "I know you've been worried about the farm."

"*Ya*, I have."

"I appreciate all you've done, Hannah. You and your *schweschders*."

"You wouldn't have needed our help if it wasn't for—"

Hannah stopped talking when her father stepped directly in front of her. He placed a hand on both sides of her face like he'd done when she was a child. His touch stopped the whirlwind of thoughts rattling through her mind.

Once he was sure that she was focused on him, he smiled and said, "We're *gut*."

"You…you had enough money?"

"We had enough. You don't have to worry about the bank loan. I stopped by the bank on the way here, and I paid all the back payments. We even had a little extra. If you don't want to keep working for Jacob, you can stay home. If that's what you want to do."

"I enjoy the work," she admitted. "There is less to do now, though. Perhaps Jacob would let me work only two days a week, the days Matthew doesn't have physical therapy."

"That's a *gut* idea."

She stood on her tiptoes and kissed him on the cheek. "I love you, *Dat*."

"And your mother and I love you."

Those words echoed in her ears as she made her way down to the business office. She hadn't wanted to bring up Matthew's hospital bill. Her parents didn't need another thing to worry about. They had enough on their plates. Still, her heart was heavy as she checked in with the receptionist and sat waiting for her name to be called. It seemed every time she solved one problem another popped up. She knew from past experience that the hospital bill would be in the thousands, maybe tens of thousands.

She'd sunk into quite a depression when they finally escorted her back to a small, neat office. The woman's name tag said Betty, and she offered Hannah coffee or water.

"*Nein*. Matthew is waiting to go home, so I should hurry."

"I understand. Have a seat and we'll go over this quickly."

Betty was matronly, probably in her sixties, and she wore her gray hair in a bun. She paused and looked at Hannah when she spoke, and her smile seemed to go all the way to her eyes.

"I'm so glad to hear that Matthew's doing well."

"*Ya, Gotte* is *gut*."

"All the time." Betty smiled broadly and then she opened the file.

"I have a copy for you of the printout listing the charges for Matthew's care." The stack she picked up was at least an inch thick and held together with a large binder clip. She slid the papers across the desk.

Hannah paged quickly through the printout to the last page and nearly gasped at the final amount. She'd known it would be high, but she hadn't expected...

"There must be a mistake," she said.

"I assure you, I went through the billing line by line. It's all correct."

"*Nein*. That's not what I meant. The...the total is wrong."

A Widow's Hope

Betty put on her reading glasses hanging from a chain and turned to the last page of her copy of the bill.

"It says we owe nothing, but I haven't... I haven't paid anything yet. So this must be wrong."

Betty pulled off her glasses and sat back. "No one told you?"

"Told me what?"

"Kosair Charities paid for Matthew's bill."

"Why would they do that?"

Betty shrugged. "It's what they do. It's part of their mission. They understand that having a child with an SCI can be a heavy financial burden, and they try to help those who need it."

"So I don't owe anything?"

"Not a penny."

Hannah brushed at the tears streaming down her face, and Betty jumped up and fetched a box of tissues.

Five minutes later, Hannah made her way back to Matthew's room, carrying the envelope in her purse that stated their bill was paid in full.

Hannah should have taken a nap like her mother suggested, but she was too tired to sleep, which made no sense.

It felt so good to be home, to see familiar things around her, to be back in the Amish world. She kept walking through the house—looking out the window, appreciating the light breeze, relishing the lack of flickering fluorescent light, drinking her *mamm*'s fresh coffee.

Matthew was asleep.

Her mother was in the kitchen, putting together a casserole for dinner.

Her father was in the barn.

Hannah walked out on the front porch, watching for... what was she watching for?

Then a buggy turned down their lane, and she realized it was Jacob and she knew that what she'd been watching for was coming toward her.

When he handed her the basket of flowers, she laughed. "Jacob Schrock, did you pick these?"

"*Nein.* Emily did."

"Well, it was very sweet of her and you."

"How's Matthew?"

"He's *gut*—asleep right now."

"Would you like to take a walk?"

The day was mild enough that she wore a light sweater, but the sun was shining, and the leaves had fallen in a riotous display of reds, greens and gold.

"I'd love that."

As they walked, their shoulders practically touching, the leaves crunching beneath their feet, Hannah felt the last of the tension inside of her unwind. She was home, and that was good. Home and family and friends were what she needed.

But what of the man walking next to her?

Was their future to be as friends, or more?

And dare she ask him now?

They stopped when they reached the pasture fence. Dolly cropped at the grass, and a red bird lighted on a nearby tree limb. Jacob saw it, glanced at Hannah and then started laughing.

"Did I miss something?"

"I think my *mamm* is telling me to get on with it."

"Your *mamm*?"

"It's a long story."

"I've always loved a *gut* story."

Hannah was aware that her heart beat faster when she was around Jacob. She didn't know what to do with her hands—

her arms felt awkward whether she crossed them or let them swing by her side. She felt like a teenager who hadn't quite grown into her limbs, and she blushed at the slightest look from him. Were those things love? Or was love the simple fact that she couldn't imagine her life without Jacob in it?

He told her about his mother and how she loved red birds and how she said they were a sort of messenger from *Gotte*.

"Did she believe that?"

"I'm not sure. She could have been teasing. On the other hand…maybe she was serious. I only know that I've been seeing red birds when I needed a nudge in the right direction lately."

"And you needed to see one now?"

They were leaning against the pasture fence, their arms crossed on the wooden beam, watching the mare. Jacob glanced sideways at her, a crooked smile pulling at his mouth. "*Ya*, I did."

Jacob knew now was the time.

He'd known it in the workshop when Micah had told him to go and see Hannah, to ask her, to face his future.

He'd known it when he'd seen Hannah waiting on the porch.

And he'd known it when the red bird had alighted on the fence beside them.

Still, it took courage to ask a girl to marry you, to spend her life with you.

His heart was hammering against his chest, and every time he glanced at Hannah his palms began to sweat. He was acting like a *youngie*, like the lovesick pup that Micah had mentioned. That image brought him to his senses. He wasn't either of those things. He was a man in love, and it was past time to find out if Hannah felt the same way.

He turned to her, clasped her hands in his own and said, "I need to ask you something."

"You do?"

"I care about you, Hannah."

"And I care about you."

"I care about you and Matthew."

"He adores you." Her voice was lower, huskier, and he thought he saw tears sparkling in her eyes. He prayed they were happy tears.

He'd lived in the past for so long that he felt as if his feet were encased in cement, his tongue was tied and his brain had stopped working completely. Somehow he needed to break free from that past.

Taking a deep breath, he squeezed Hannah's hands and plunged into his future. "Will you marry me?"

"Wow."

"Wow yes or wow no?"

"I... I wasn't expecting that."

A pretty blush worked its way up her neck. Jacob had the absurd idea that he might be dreaming this entire thing, that he might wake up and find the lovely woman standing beside him, looking up at him with those beautiful brown eyes, was a figment of his imagination.

"I'm surprised is all."

"Good surprised or bad surprised?" Before she could answer, he rushed on. "I know that I'm not a perfect man, and I would understand if you said *no* because living with me, with a man like me—"

"Do you love me?"

He'd been staring at their hands but now he jerked his head up, reached out and touched her cheek. "Yes, Hannah.

I love you, and I love Matthew, and it would be an honor to be your husband and his father."

"We love you too."

"You do?"

"*Ya.* Didn't you know?"

"I'd hoped."

He pulled her to him then, relief flooding through his soul. "You love me, Hannah?"

"Yes." She laughed and pulled back, gazed up into his eyes. "You're a *gut* man, Jacob, and a *gut* friend. I wasn't sure... wasn't sure that you'd want your life to be complicated so."

"Everyone's life is complicated, even Plain folks'."

"Matthew's crisis has passed, for now, but there will be others."

"True of any family."

"It won't be easy."

"I don't expect it to be."

"But you're sure?"

"*Ya.* Are you sure, Hannah?" He took her hand and raised it to his cheek, to his scars, held it there. "These won't bother you?"

"We all have scars. Yours are simply on the outside."

He stepped closer, kissed her softly once and then again, pulled her into his arms. They stood there, with the fall breeze dropping even more leaves around them and Jacob thought that he could feel Hannah's heart beating against his.

When she finally stepped back, still smiling, he asked, "Who do you want to tell first?"

"Matthew. Let's go and tell Matthew."

★ ★ ★ ★ ★

HIS AMISH SWEETHEART

Jo Ann Brown

For John Jakaitis
Thank you for helping us find our way home.

For if thou altogether holdest thy peace at this time,
then shall there enlargement and deliverance arise to the Jews from
another place; but thou and thy father's house shall be destroyed:
and who knoweth whether thou art come to the kingdom
for such a time as this?

—*Esther* 4:14

Chapter One

Paradise Springs
Lancaster County, Pennsylvania

Esther Stoltzfus balanced the softball bat on her shoulder. Keeping her eye on the boy getting ready to pitch the ball, she smiled. Did her scholars guess that recess, when the October weather was perfect for playing outside, was her favorite part of the day, too? The *kinder* probably couldn't imagine their teacher liked to play ball as much as they did.

This was her third year teaching on her own. Seeing understanding in a *kind*'s eyes when the scholar finally grasped an elusive concept delighted her. She loved spending time with the *kinder*.

Her family had recently begun dropping hints she should be walking out with some young man. Her older brothers didn't know that, until eight months ago, she'd been walking out—and sneaking out for some forbidden buggy racing—with Alvin Lee Peachy. Probably because none of them could have imagined their little sister having such an outrageous suitor. Alvin Lee pushed the boundaries of the *Ordnung*, and there were rumors he intended to jump the fence and join the *Englisch* world. Would she have gone with him if he'd asked? She didn't know, and she never would because when she began to worry about his racing buggies and fast life, he'd dumped her and started courting Luella Hartz. In one moment, she'd lost the man she loved and her *gut* friend.

She'd learned her lesson. A life of adventure and daring wasn't for her. From now on, she wasn't going to risk her heart unless she knew, without a doubt, it was safe. She wouldn't consider spending time with a guy who wasn't as serious and stolid as a bishop.

As she gave a practice swing and the *kinder* urged her on excitedly, she glanced at her assistant teacher, Neva Fry, who was playing first base. Neva, almost two years younger than Esther, was learning what she needed so she could take over a school of her own.

Esther grinned in anticipation of the next play. The ball came in a soft arc, and she swung the bat. Not with all her strength. Some of the outfielders were barely six years old, and she didn't want to chance them getting hurt by a line drive.

The *kinder* behind her cheered while the ones in the field shouted to each other to catch the lazy fly ball. She sped to first base, a large stone set in place by the *daeds* who had helped build the school years ago. Her black sneaker skidded as she touched the stone with one foot and turned to head toward second. Seeing one of the older boys catch the ball, she slowed and clapped her hands.

"Well done, Jay!" she called.

With a wide grin, the boy who, at fourteen, was in his final year at the school, gave her a thumbs-up.

Smiling, she knew she should be grateful Alvin Lee hadn't proposed. She wasn't ready to give up teaching. She wanted a husband and a home and *kinder* of her own, but not until she met the right man. One who didn't whoop at the idea of danger. One she would have described as predictable a few months ago. Now that safe, dependable guy sounded like a dream come true. Well, maybe not a dream, but definitely not a nightmare.

Checking to make sure her *kapp* was straight, Esther smoothed the apron over her dress, which was her favorite shade of rose. She'd selected it and a black apron in the style the *Englischers* called a pinafore when she saw the day would be perfect for playing softball. She held up her hands, and Jay threw her the ball. She caught it easily.

Before she could tell the scholars it was time to go in for afternoon lessons, several began to chant, "One more inning! One more inning!"

Esther hesitated, knowing how few sunny, warm days remained before winter. The *kinder* had worked hard during the morning, and she hadn't had to scold any of them for not paying attention. Not even Jacob Fisher.

She glanced at the small, white schoolhouse. As she expected, the eight-year-old with a cowlick that made a black exclamation point at his crown sat alone on the porch. She invited him to play each day, and each day he resisted. She wished she could find a way to break through the walls Jacob had raised, walls around himself, walls to keep pain at bay.

She closed her eyes as she recalled what she'd been told by Jacob's elderly *onkel*, who was raising him. Jacob had been with his parents, walking home from visiting a neighbor, when they were struck by a drunk driver. The boy had been thrown onto the shoulder. When he regained consciousness, he'd discovered his parents injured by the side of the road. No one, other than Jacob and God, knew if they spoke final words to him, but he'd watched them draw their last breaths. The trial for the hit-and-run driver had added to the boy's trauma, though he hadn't had to testify and the Amish community tried to shield him.

Now he was shattered, taking insult at every turn and exploding with anger. Or else he said nothing and squirmed until he couldn't sit any longer and had to wander around the room. Working with his *onkel*, Titus Fisher, she tried to make school as comfortable for Jacob as possible.

She'd used many things she hoped would help—art projects, story writing, extra assistance with his studies, though the boy was very intelligent in spite of his inability to complete many of his lessons. She'd failed at every turn to draw him out from behind those walls he'd raised around himself. She realized she must find another way to reach him because she wasn't helping him by cajoling him in front of the other *kinder*. So now, she lifted him up in prayer. Those wouldn't fail, but God worked on His own time. He must have a reason for not yet bringing healing to Jacob's young heart.

Or hers.

She chided herself. Losing a suitor didn't compare with losing one's parents, but her heart refused to stop hurting.

"All right," she said, smiling at the rest of the scholars because she didn't want anyone to know what she was thinking. She'd gotten *gut* at hiding the truth. "One more inning, but you need to work extra hard this afternoon."

Heads nodded eagerly. Bouncing the ball in her right hand, she tossed it to the pitcher and took her place in center field where she could help the other outfielders, seven-year-old Olen and Freda who was ten.

The batter swung at the first three pitches and struck out. The next batter kept hitting foul balls, which sent the *kinder* chasing them. Suddenly a loud thwack announced a boy had connected with the ball.

It headed right for Esther. She backpedaled two steps. A quick glance behind her assured she could go a little farther before she'd fall down the hill. Shouts warned her the runner was already on his way to second base.

She reached to catch the ball. Her right foot caught a slippery patch of grass, and she lost her balance. She windmilled her arms, fighting to stay on her feet, but it was impossible. She dropped backward—and hit a solid chest. Strong arms kept her from ending up on her bottom. She grasped the arms as her feet continued to slide.

The ball fell at her feet. Pulling herself out of the arms, she scooped the ball up and threw it to second base. But it was too late. The run had already scored.

Behind her, a deep laugh brushed the small hairs curling at her nape beneath her *kapp*. Heat scored Esther's face as she realized she'd tumbled into a man's arms.

Her gaze had to rise to meet his, though he stood below her on the hill. He must be more than six feet tall, like her brothers, but he wasn't one of her brothers. The *gut*-looking man was a few years older than she was. No beard softened the firm line of his jaw. Beneath his straw hat, his brown eyes crinkled with his laugh.

"You haven't changed a bit, Esther Stoltzfus!" he said with another chuckle. "Still willing to risk life and limb to get the ball."

He knew her? Who was he?

Her eyes widened. She recognized the twinkle in those dark eyes. Black hair dropped across his forehead, and he pushed it aside carelessly. Like a clap of thunder, realization came as she remembered the boy who had made that exact motion. She looked more closely and saw the small scar beneath his right eye...just like the one on the face of a boy she'd once considered her very best friend.

"Nate Zook?" she asked, not able to believe her own question.

"*Ja.*" His voice was much deeper than when she'd last heard it. "Though I go by Nathaniel now."

When she'd last seen him, he'd been...ten or eleven? She'd been eight. Before his family moved away, she and Nate, along with Micah and Daniel, her twin brothers, had spent most days together. Then, one day, the Zooks were gone. Her brothers had been astonished when they rode their scooters to Nate's house and discovered it was empty. When her *mamm* said the family had moved to Indiana in search of a better life, she wondered if it'd been as much a surprise for Nate as for her and her brothers.

She'd gone with Daniel and Micah to play at his grandparents' farm in a neighboring district when he visited the next summer, but she shouldn't have. She'd accepted a dare from a friend to hold Nate's hand. She couldn't remember which friend it'd been, but at the time she'd been excited to do something audacious. She'd embarrassed herself by following through and gripping his hand so tightly he winced and made it worse by telling him that she planned to marry him when they grew up. He hadn't come back the following summer. She'd been grateful she didn't have to face him after her silliness, and miserable because she missed him.

That was in the past. Here stood Nate—Nathaniel—Zook again, a grown man who'd arrived in time to keep her from falling down the hill.

She should say something. Several *kinder* came to stand beside her, curious about what was going on. She needed to show she wasn't that silly little girl any longer, but all that came out was, "What are you doing in Paradise Springs?"

He opened his mouth to answer. Whatever he was about to say was drowned out by a shriek from the schoolhouse.

Esther whirled and gasped when she saw two boys on the ground, fists flying. She ran to stop the fight. Finding out why Nathaniel had returned to Paradise Springs after more than a decade would have to wait. But not too long, because she was really curious why he'd come back now.

Nathaniel Zook stared after Esther as she raced across the grass, her apron flapping on her skirt. Years ago, she'd been able to outrun him and her brothers, though they were almost five years older than she was. She'd been much shorter then, and her knees, which were now properly concealed beneath her dress, had been covered with scrapes. Her bright eyes were as blue, and their steady gaze contained the same strength.

He looked past her to where two boys were rolling on the grass. Should he help? One of the boys in the fight was nearly as big as Esther was.

"Oh, Jacob Fisher! He keeps picking fights," said a girl with a sigh.

"Or dropping books on the floor or throwing papers around." A boy shook his head. "He wants attention. That's what my *mamm* says."

Nathaniel didn't wait to listen to any more because when Esther bent to try to put a halt to the fight, a fist almost struck her. He crossed the yard and pushed past the gawking *kinder*. A blow to Esther's middle knocked her back a couple of steps. Again he caught her and steadied her, then he grasped both boys by their suspenders and tugged them apart.

The shorter boy struggled to get away, his brown eyes

snapping with fury. Flinging his fists out wildly, he almost connected with the taller boy's chin.

Shoving them away from each other, Nathaniel said, "Enough. If you can't honestly tell each other you're sorry for acting foolishly, at least shake hands."

"I'm not shaking hands with him!" The taller boy was panting, and blood dripped from the left corner of his mouth. "He'll jump me again for no reason."

The shorter boy puffed up like a snake about to strike. "You called me a—"

"Enough," Nathaniel repeated as he kept a tight hold on their suspenders. "What's been said was said. What's been done has been done. It's over. Let it go."

The glowers the boys gave him warned Nathaniel that he was wasting his breath.

"Benny," ordered Esther, "go and wash up. Jacob, wait on the porch for me. We need to talk." She gestured toward a younger woman who'd been staring wide-eyed at the battling boys. "Neva, take the other scholars inside please."

Astonished by how serene her voice was and how quickly the boys turned to obey after scowling at each other again, Nathaniel waited while the *kinder* followed Neva into the school. He knew Esther would want to get back to her job, as well. Since he'd returned to Paradise Springs, he'd heard over and over what a devoted teacher Esther Stoltzfus was. Well, his visit should be a short one because all he needed was for her to say a quick *ja*.

First, however, he had to ask, "Are you okay, Esther?"

"I'm fine." She adjusted her *kapp*, which had come loose in the melee. Her golden-brown hair glistened through the translucent white organdy of her heart-shaped *kapp*. Her dress was a charming dark pink almost the same color as her cheeks. The flush nearly absorbed her freckles. There weren't as many as the last time he'd seen her more than a decade ago.

Back then, she and her twin brothers had been his best friends. In some ways, he'd been closer to her than her brothers. Micah and Daniel were twins, and they had a special bond. He and Esther had often found themselves on one team while her brothers took the other side, whether playing ball or having races or embarking on some adventure. She hadn't been one of those girly girls who worried about getting her clothes dirty or if her hair was mussed. She played to win, though she was younger than the rest of them. He'd never met another girl like her, a girl who was, as his *daed* had described her, not afraid to be one of the boys.

"Are you sure?" he asked. "You got hit pretty hard."

"I'm fine." Her blue eyes regarded him with curiosity. "When did you return to Paradise Springs?"

"Almost a month ago. I've inherited my grandparents' farm on the other side of the village."

"I'm sorry, Nat—Nathaniel. I should have remembered that they'd passed away in the spring. You must miss them."

"Ja," he said, though the years that had gone by since the last time he'd seen them left them as little more than childhood memories. Except for one visit to Paradise Springs the first year after the move, his life had been in Elkhart County, Indiana.

From beyond the school he heard the rattle of equipment and smelled the unmistakable scent of greenery and disturbed earth. Next year at this time, God willing, he'd be chopping his own corn into silage to feed his animals over the winter. He couldn't wait. At last, he had the job he'd always wanted: farmer. He wouldn't have had the opportunity in Indiana. There it was intended, in Amish tradition, that his younger brother would inherit the family's five acres. Nathaniel had assumed he, like his *daed*, would spend his life working in an *Englisch* factory building RVs.

Those plans had changed when word came that his Zook grandparents' farm in Paradise Springs was now his. A dream come true. Along with the surprising menagerie his *grossdawdi* and his *grossmammi* had collected in their final years. He'd been astonished not to find dairy cows when he arrived. Instead, there were about thirty-five alpacas, one of the oddest looking animals he'd ever seen. They resembled a combination of a poodle and a llama, especially at this time of year when their wool was thickening. In addition, on the farm were two mules, a buggy horse and more chickens than he could count. He was familiar with horses, mules and chickens, but he had a lot to learn about alpacas, which was the reason he'd come to the school today.

He was determined to make the farm a success so he wouldn't have to sell it. For the first time in far too many years, he felt alive with possibilities.

"How can I help you?" Esther asked, as if he'd spoken aloud. "Are you here to enroll a *kind* in school?"

Years of practice kept him from revealing how her simple question drove a shaft through his heart. She couldn't guess how much that question hurt him, and he didn't have time to wallow in thoughts of how, because of a childhood illness, he most likely could never be a *daed*. He'd never enjoy the simple act of coming to a school to arrange for his son or daughter to attend.

He was alive and well. For that he was grateful, and he needed to let the feelings of failure go. Otherwise, he was dismissing God's gift of life as worthless. That he'd never do.

Instead he needed to concentrate on why he'd visited the school this afternoon. After asking around the area, he'd learned of only one person who was familiar with how to raise alpacas.

Esther Stoltzfus.

"No, I'm here for a different reason." He managed a smile. "One I think you'll find interesting."

"I'd like to talk, Nathaniel, but—" She glanced at the older boy, the one she'd called Benny. He stood by the well beyond the schoolhouse and was washing his hands and face. Jacob sat on the porch. He was trembling in the wake of the fight and rocking his feet against the latticework. It made a dull thud each time his bare heels struck it. "I'm going to have to ask you to excuse me. *Danki* for pulling the boys apart."

"The little guy doesn't look more than about six years old."

"Jacob is eight. He's small for his age, but he has the heart of a lion."

"But far less common sense if he fights boys twice his age."

"Benny is fourteen."

"Close enough."

She nodded with another sigh. "Yet you saw who ended up battered and bloody. Jacob doesn't have a mark on him."

"Quite a feat!"

"Really?" She frowned. "Think what a greater feat it would have been if Jacob had turned the other cheek and walked away from Benny. It's the lesson we need to take to heart."

"For a young boy, it's hard to remember. We have to learn things the hard way, it seems." He gave her a lopsided grin, but she wouldn't meet his eyes. She acted flustered. Why? She'd put a stop to the fight as quickly as she could. "Like the time your brothers and I got too close to a hive and got stung. I guess that's what people mean by a painful lesson."

"Most lessons are."

"Well, it was a *very* painful one." He hurried on before she could leave. "I've heard you used to raise alpacas."

"Just a pair. Are you planning to raise them on your grandparents' farm?"

"Not planning. They're already there. Apparently my *grossmammi* fell in love with the creatures and decided to buy some when she and my *grossdawdi* stopped milking. I don't know the first thing about alpacas, other than how to feed them. I was hoping you could share what you learned." He didn't add that if he couldn't figure out a way to use the animals to make money, he'd have to sell them and probably the farm itself next spring.

When she glanced at the school again, he said, "Not right now, of course."

"I'd like to help, but I don't have a lot of time."

"I won't need a lot of your time. Just enough to point me in the right direction."

She hesitated.

He could tell she didn't want to tell him no, but her mind was focused on the *kinder* now. Maybe he should leave and come back again, but he didn't have time to wait. The farm was more deeply in debt than he'd guessed before he came to Paradise Springs. He hadn't guessed his grandparents had spent so wildly on buying the animals that they had to borrow money for keeping them. Few plain folks their age took out a loan because it could become a burden on the next generation. Now it was his responsibility to repay it.

Inspiration struck when he looked from her to the naughty boys. It was a long shot, but he'd suggest anything if there was a chance to save his family's farm.

"Bring your scholars to see the alpacas," he said. "I can ask my questions, and so can they. You can answer them for all of us. It'll be fun for them. Remember how we liked a break from schoolwork? They would, too, I'm sure."

She didn't reply for a long minute, then nodded. "They probably would be really interested."

He grinned. "Why don't I drive my flatbed wagon over here? I can give the *kinder* a ride on it both ways."

"*Gut*. Let me know which day works best for you, and I'll tell the parents we're going there. Some of them may want to join us."

"We'll make an adventure out of it, like when we were *kinder*."

Color flashed up her face before vanishing, leaving her paler than before.

"*Was iss letz?*" he asked.

"Nothing is wrong," she replied so hastily he guessed she wasn't being honest. "I—"

A shout came from the porch where the bigger boy was walking past Jacob. The younger boy was on his feet, his fists clenched again.

She ran toward them, calling over her shoulder, "We'll have to talk about this later."

"I'll come over tonight. We'll talk then."

Nathaniel wondered if she'd heard him because she was already steering the boys into the school. Her soft voice reached him. Not the words, but the gently chiding tone. He guessed she was reminding them that they needed to settle their disputes without violence. He wondered if they'd listen and what she'd have to do if they didn't heed her.

As she closed the door, she looked at him and mouthed, *See you tonight.*

"*Gut!*" he said as he walked to where he'd left his wagon on the road. He smiled. He'd been wanting to stop by the Stoltzfus farm, so her invitation offered the perfect excuse.

It would be a fun evening, and for the first time since he'd seen the alpacas, he dared to believe that with what Esther could teach him about the odd creatures, he might be able to make a go of the farm.

Chapter Two

The Stoltzfus family farm was an easy walk from the school. Esther went across a field, along two different country roads, and then up the long lane to the only house she'd ever lived in. She'd been born there. Her *daed* had been as well, and his *daed* before him.

After *Daed* had passed away, her *mamm* had moved into the attached *dawdi haus* while Esther managed the main house. She'd hand over those duties when her older brother Ezra married, which she guessed would be before October was over, because he spent every bit of his free time with their neighbor Leah Beiler. Their wedding day was sure to be a joyous one.

Though she never would have admitted it, Esther was looking forward to giving the responsibilities of a household with five bachelor brothers to Leah. Even with one of her older brothers married, another widowed and her older sister off tending a family of her own, the housework was never-ending. Esther enjoyed cooking and keeping the house neat, but she was tired of mending a mountain of work clothes while trying to prepare lesson plans for the next day. Her brothers worked hard, whether on the farm or in construction or at the grocery store, and their clothes reflected that. She and *Mamm* never caught up.

Everything in her life had been in proper order...until Nathaniel Zook came to her school that afternoon. She was amazed she hadn't heard he was in Paradise Springs. If she'd known, maybe she'd have been better prepared. He'd grown up, but it didn't sound as if he'd changed. He still liked adventures if he intended to keep alpacas instead of the usual cows or sheep or goats on his farm. That made him a man she needed to steer clear of, so she could avoid the mistakes she'd made with Alvin Lee.

But how could she turn her back on helping him? It was the Amish way to give assistance when it was requested. She couldn't mess up Nathaniel's life because she was appalled by how she'd nearly ruined her own by chasing excitement.

His suggestion that she bring the scholars to his farm would focus attention on the *kinder*. She'd give them a fun day while they learned about something new, something that might be of use to them in the future. Who could guess now which one of them would someday have alpacas of his or her own?

That thought eased her disquiet enough that Esther could admire the trees in the front yard. They displayed their autumnal glory. Dried leaves were already skittering across the ground on the gentle breeze. Ezra's Brown Swiss cows grazed near the white barn. The sun was heading for the horizon, a sure sign milking would start soon. Dinner for her hungry brothers needed to be on the table by the time chores were done and the barn tidied up for the night.

When she entered the comfortable kitchen with its pale blue walls and dark wood cabinets, Esther was surprised to see her twin brothers there. They were almost five years older than she was, and they'd teased her, when they were *kinder*, of being an afterthought. She'd fired back with jests of her own, and they'd spent their childhoods laughing. No one took offense while they'd been climbing trees, fishing in the creek and doing tasks to help keep the farm and the house running.

Her twin brothers weren't identical. Daniel had a cleft in his chin and Micah didn't. There were other differences in the way they talked and how they used their hands to emphasize words. Micah asserted he was a half inch taller than his twin, but Esther couldn't see it. They were unusual in one important way—they didn't share a birthday. Micah had been born ten minutes before midnight, and Daniel a half hour later, a fact Micah never allowed his "baby" brother to forget.

Both twins had a glass of milk in one hand and a stack of snickerdoodles in the other. Their bare feet stuck out from where they sat at the large table in the middle of the kitchen.

"You're home early," she said as she hung her bonnet and satchel on pegs by the back door. The twins' straw hats hung among the empty pegs, which would all be in use by the time the family sat down for dinner.

"We're finished at the project in Lititz," Daniel said. He was a carpenter, as was Micah, but the older twin specialized in building windmills and installing solar panels. However, the two men were equally skilled with a hammer. "Time to hand it over to the electricians and plumbers. Micah already went over what needed to be done to connect the roof panels to the main electrical box."

"You've been working on that house a long time," she said

as she opened the refrigerator door and took out the leftover ham she planned to reheat for dinner. "It must be a big one."

"You know how *Englischers* are." Micah chuckled. "They move out to Lancaster County to live the simple life and then decide they need lots of gadgets and rooms to store them in. This house has a real movie theater."

She began cutting the ham into thick slices. "You're joking."

"Would we do that?" Daniel asked with fake innocence before he took the final bite of his last cookie.

"*Ja.*"

"*Ja,*" echoed Micah, folding his arms on the table. "We're being honest. The house is as big as our barn."

Esther tried to imagine why anyone would need a house that size, but she couldn't. At one point, there had been eleven of them living in the Stoltzfus farmhouse along with her grandparents in the small *dawdi haus*, and there had been plenty of room.

Daniel stretched before he yawned. "Sorry. It was an early morning."

"You'll want to stay awake. An old friend of yours is stopping by tonight."

"Who?" Micah asked.

She could tell them, but it served her brothers right to let their curiosity stew a bit longer. Smiling, she said, "Someone who inherited a farm on Zook Road."

The twins exchanged a disbelieving glance before Daniel asked, "Are you talking about Nate Zook?"

"He calls himself Nathaniel now."

"He's back in Paradise Springs?" he asked.

"*Ja.*"

"It's been almost ten years since the last time we saw him." With a pensive expression, Micah rubbed his chin between his forefinger and thumb. "Remember, Daniel? He came out

from Indiana to spend the summer with his grandparents the
year after his family moved."

Daniel chuckled. "His *grossmammi* made us chocolate shoo-
fly pie the day before he left. One of the best things I've ever
tasted. Do you remember, Esther?"

"No." She was glad she had her back to them as she placed
ham slices in the cast-iron fry pan. Her face was growing
warm as she thought again of Nathaniel's visit and how she'd
made a complete fool of herself. Hurrying to the cellar doorway, she got the bag of potatoes that had been harvested a
few weeks ago. She'd make mashed potatoes tonight. Everyone liked them, and she could release some of her pent-up
emotions while smashing them.

"Oh, that's right," Daniel said. "You decided you didn't
want to play with us boys any longer. You thought it was a
big secret why, but we knew."

She looked over her shoulder before she could halt herself. "You did?" How many more surprises was she going to
have today? First, Nathaniel Zook showed up at her school,
and now her brother was telling her he'd known why she
stopped going to the Zook farm. Had Nathaniel told him
about her brash stupidity of announcing she planned to marry
him one day?

"Ja." Jabbing his brother with his elbow, Micah said, "You
had a big crush on Nate. Giggled whenever you were around
him."

She wanted to take them by the shoulders and shake them
and tell them how wrong they were. She couldn't. That
would be a lie. She'd had a big crush on Nathaniel. He was
the only boy she knew who wasn't annoyed because she could
outrun him or hit a ball as well as he did. He'd never tried
to make her feel she was different from other girls because
she preferred being outside to working beside her *mamm* in

the house. Not once had he picked on her because she did well at school, like some of the other boys had.

That had happened long ago. She needed to put it out of her head. Nathaniel must have forgotten—or at least forgiven her—since he came to ask a favor today. She'd follow his lead for once and act as if the mortifying day had never happened.

"You don't know what you're talking about," Esther said, lifting her chin as she carried the potatoes to the sink to wash them. "I was a little girl."

"Who had a big crush on Nate Zook." Her brothers laughed as if Micah had said the funniest thing ever. "We'll have to watch and see if she drools when he walks in."

"Stop teasing your sister," *Mamm* said as she came through the door from the *dawdi haus*. She'd moved in preparation for Ezra's marriage. Though neither Ezra nor Leah spoke of their plans to marry, everyone suspected they'd be among the first couples having their intentions published at the next church Sunday.

"Well, she needs to marry someone," Micah said with a broad grin. "She can't seem to make up her mind about the guys around here. Just like Danny-boy can't decide on one girl." He poked his elbow at his twin again, but Daniel moved aside.

"Why settle for one when there are plenty of pretty ones willing to let me take them home?" Daniel asked.

Esther was startled to see his smile wasn't reflected in his eyes. His jesting words were meant to hide his true feelings. The twins were popular with young people in their district and the neighboring ones. They were fun and funny. What was Daniel concealing behind his ready grin?

More questions, and she didn't need more questions. She already had enough without any answers. The marriage season for the Amish began in October. As it approached, she'd asked herself if she should try walking out with another young man. Maybe that would be the best way to put Alvin Lee and his betrayal out of her mind. But she wasn't ready to risk her heart again.

Better to be wise than to be sorry. How many times had she heard *Mamm* say those words? She'd discovered the wisdom in them by learning the truth the hard way. She'd promised herself to be extra careful with her heart from now on.

After giving her *mamm* a hug, Esther finished preparing their supper. She was grateful for *Mamm*'s assistance because she felt clumsy as she hadn't since she first began helping in the kitchen. Telling herself to focus, she avoided cutting herself as she peeled potatoes. Her brothers were too busy teasing each other to notice how her fingers shook.

Danki, *Lord, for small blessings.*

She put the reheated ham, buttered peas and a large bowl of mashed potatoes on the table. *Mamm* finished slicing the bread Esther had made before school that morning and put platters at either end along with butter and apple butter. While Esther retrieved the cabbage salad and chowchow from the refrigerator, her *mamm* filled a pitcher with water.

The door opened, and Ezra came in with a metal half-gallon milk can. In his other hand he carried a generous slab of his fragrant, homemade cheese. He called a greeting before stepping aside to let three more brothers enter. They'd been busy at the Stoltzfus Family Shops closer to the village of Paradise Springs. Amos set fresh apple cider from his grocery store in the center of the table.

As soon as they sat together at the table, Ezra, as the oldest son present, bowed his head. It was the signal for the meal's silent grace.

Esther quickly offered her thanks, then added a supplication that she'd be able to help Nathaniel without complications. To be honest, she'd enjoy teaching him how to raise alpacas and harvest the wondrously soft wool they grew.

As she raised her head when Ezra cleared his throat, she glanced around the table at her brothers and *mamm*. She had a *gut* life with her family and her scholars and her community. She didn't need adventure. Not her own or anyone else's. How she would have embarrassed her family if they'd heard of her partying with Alvin Lee and his friends! She could have lost her position as teacher, as well as shamed her family.

Learn from your failures, or you'll fail to learn. A poster saying that hung in the schoolroom. She needed to remember those words and hold them close to her heart. She vowed to do so, starting that very second.

As Nathaniel drove his buggy into the farm lane leading to the large white farmhouse where the Stoltzfus family lived, he couldn't keep from grinning. He'd looked forward to seeing them as much as he had his grandparents when he'd spent a summer in Paradise Springs years ago. Micah and Daniel had imaginations that had cooked up mischief to keep their summer days filled with adventures. Not even chores could slow down their laugh-filled hours.

Then there was Esther. She'd been brave enough to try anything and never quailed before a challenge. The twins had been less willing to accept every dare he posed. Not Esther. He remembered the buzz of excitement he'd felt the afternoon she'd agreed to jump from the second story hayloft if he did.

He knew he was going to have to be that gutsy if he hoped to save his grandparents' farm. It'd been in the family for generations, and he didn't want to be the one to sell it. Even if he couldn't have *kinder* of his own to inherit it, his two oldest sisters were already married with *bopplin*. One of them might want to take over the farm, and he didn't want to lose it because he hadn't learned quickly enough.

Esther agreeing to help him with the alpacas might be the saving grace he'd prayed for. If it wasn't, he could be defeated before he began.

No, I'm not going to think that way. I'm not going to give up before I've barely begun. He got out of the buggy. Things were going to get better. Starting now. He had to believe God's hands were upon the inheritance that gave him a chance to make his dream of running his own farm come true.

He strode toward the white house's kitchen door. Nobody used the front door except for church Sundays and funerals. The house and white outbuildings hadn't changed much in ten years. There was a third silo by the largest barn, and instead of the black-and-white cows Esther's *daed* used to milk, grayish-brown cattle stood in the pasture. The chicken coop was closer to the house than he remembered, and extra buggies and wagons were parked beneath the trees.

He paused at the door. He'd never knocked at the Stoltzfus house before, but somehow it didn't feel right to walk in. Too many years had passed since the last time he'd come to the farm.

"Why are you standing on the steps?" came a friendly female voice as the door swung open. "*Komm* in, Nate. We're about to enjoy some *snitz* pie."

Wanda Stoltzfus, Esther's *mamm*, looked smaller than he remembered. He knew she hadn't shrunk; he'd grown. Her hair had strands of gray woven through it, but her smile was as warm as ever.

"Did you make the pie?" he asked, delighted to see the welcome in eyes almost the same shade as her daughter's.

"Do you think I'd trust anyone, even my own *kinder*, with my super secret recipe for dried-apple pie while there's breath in these old bones?" She stepped aside and motioned for him to come in.

"You aren't old, Wanda," he replied.

"And you haven't lost an ounce of the charm you used as a boy to try to wheedle extra treats from me."

He heard a snicker and looked past her. Esther was at the stove, pouring freshly brewed *kaffi* into one cup after the other. The sound hadn't come from her, but his gaze had riveted on her. She looked pretty and somehow younger and more vulnerable now that she was barefoot and had traded her starched *kapp* for a dark kerchief over her golden hair. He could see the little girl she'd been transposed over the woman she had become, and his heart gave a peculiar little stutter.

What was that? He hadn't felt its like before, and he wasn't sure what was causing it now. Esther was his childhood friend. Why was he nervous?

Hearing another laugh, Nathaniel pulled his gaze from her and looked at the table where six of the seven Stoltzfus brothers were gathered. Joshua, whom he'd recently heard had married again after the death of his first wife, and Ruth, the oldest, who had been wed long enough to have given her husband a houseful of *kinder*, were missing. A pulse of sorrow pinched at him because he noticed Ezra was sitting where Paul, the family's late patriarch, had sat. Paul had welcomed him into the family as if Nathaniel were one of his own sons.

Nathaniel stared at the men rising from the table. It was startling to see his onetime childhood playmates grown up. He'd known time hadn't stood still for them. Yet the change was greater than he'd guessed. Isaiah wore a beard that was patchy and sparse. He must be married, though Nathaniel hadn't heard about it. All the Stoltzfus brothers were tall, well-muscled from hard work and wore friendly smiles.

Then the twins opened their mouths and asked him how

he liked running what they called the Paradise Springs Municipal Zoo. Nothing important had changed, he realized. They enjoyed teasing each other and everyone around them, and he was their chosen target tonight. Nothing they said was cruel. They poked fun as much at themselves as anyone else. Their eyes hadn't lost the mischievous glint that warned another prank was about to begin.

For the first time since he'd returned to Paradise Springs, he didn't feel like a stranger. He was among friends.

Nathaniel sat at the large table. When Esther put a slice of pie and a steaming cup of *kaffi* in front of him, he thanked her. She murmured something before hurrying away to bring more cups to the table. He had no chance to talk to her because her brothers kept him busy with questions. He was amazed to learn that Jeremiah, who'd been all thumbs as a boy, now was a master woodworker, and Isaiah was a blacksmith as well as one of the district's ministers. Amos leaned over to whisper that Isaiah's young bride had died a few months earlier, soon after Isaiah had been chosen by lot to be the new minister.

Saddened by the family's loss, he knew he should wait until he had a chance to talk to Isaiah alone before he expressed his condolences. He sensed how hard Isaiah was trying to join in the *gut* humor around the table.

Nathaniel answered their questions about discovering the alpacas on the farm and explained how he planned to plant the fields in the spring. "Right now, the fields are rented to neighbors, so I can't cut a single blade of grass to feed those silly creatures this winter."

"You're staying in Paradise Springs?" Wanda asked.

"That's my plan." His parents weren't pleased he'd left Indiana, though they'd pulled up roots in Lancaster County ten years ago. He'd already received half a dozen letters from his *mamm* pleading for him to come home. She acted as if he'd left the Amish to join the *Englisch* world.

"*Wunderbaar*, Nate… I mean, Nathaniel." Wanda smiled.

"Call me whichever you wish. It doesn't matter."

"I know your family must be pleased to have you take over the farm that has been in Zook hands for generations. It is *gut* to know it'll continue in the family."

"*Ja.*" He sounded as uncertain as he felt. The generations to come might be a huge problem. He reminded himself to be optimistic and focus on the here and now. Once he made the farm a success, his nephews and nieces would be eager to take it over.

His gaze locked with Esther's. He hadn't meant to let it happen, but he couldn't look away. There was much more to her now than the little girl she'd been. He had a difficult time imagining her at the teacher's desk instead of among the scholars, sending him and her brothers notes filled with plans for after school.

Esther the Pester was what they'd called her then, but he'd been eager to join in with the fun she proposed. He wondered if she were as avid to entertain her scholars. No wonder everyone praised her teaching.

Ezra said his name in a tone suggesting he'd been trying to get Nathaniel's attention. Breaking free of his memories was easier than cutting the link between his eyes and Esther's. He wasn't sure he could have managed it if she hadn't looked away.

Recalling what Ezra had asked, Nathaniel said, "I've got a lot to learn to be a proper farmer. Esther agreed to help me with the alpacas."

"Don't let her tell you Daniel and I tried roping hers," Micah said with a laugh. "It was an innocent misunderstanding."

"Misunderstanding? Yes," Esther retorted. "Innocent? I don't think so. Poor Pepe and Delfina were traumatized for weeks."

"The same amount of time it took to get the reek of their spit off me." Micah wrinkled his nose. "Watch out, Nathaniel. They're docile most of the time but they have a secret weapon. Their spit can leave you gagging for days."

Nathaniel grinned. "I'm glad you two learned that disgusting lesson instead of me." He noticed Esther was smiling broadly. "I hope, Ezra, you don't mind me asking you about a thousand questions about working the fields."

"Of course not, though it'd be better to wait to ask until after the first of the year." He reached for another piece of pie.

Nathaniel started to ask why, then saw the family's abruptly bland faces. Ezra must be getting married. His *mamm* and brothers and Esther were keeping the secret until the wedding was announced. They must like his future bride and looked forward to her becoming a part of their family along with any *kinder* she and Ezra might have.

He kept his sigh silent. Assuming he ever found a woman who would consider marrying him, having a single *kind* of his own might be impossible. He'd been thirteen when he was diagnosed with leukemia. That had been after the last summer he'd spent in Paradise Springs with his grandparents. For the next year, he'd undergone treatments and fought to recover. Chemo and radiation had defeated the cancer, but he'd been warned the chemo that had saved his life made it unlikely he'd ever be a *daed*. He thought he'd accepted it as God's will, but, seeing the quiet joy in Ezra Stoltzfus's eyes was a painful reminder of what he would never have. He couldn't imagine a woman agreeing to marry him once she knew the truth.

When the last of the pie was gone, the table cleared and thanks given once more, Nathaniel knew it was time to leave. Everyone had to be up before the sun in the morning.

As he stood, he asked as casually as he could, "Esther, will you walk to my buggy with me?"

Her brothers and *mamm* regarded him with as much astonishment as if he'd announced he wanted to discuss a trip to the moon. Did they think he was planning to court her? He couldn't, not when he couldn't give Esther *kinder*. She loved them. He'd seen that at the school.

"I've got a few questions about your scholars visiting the farm," he hurried to add.

"All right." Esther came to her feet with the grace she hadn't had as a little girl. Walking around the table, she went to the door. She pulled on her black sneakers and bent to tie them.

The night, when they stepped outside, was cool, but crisp in the way fall nights were. The stars seemed closer than during the summer, and the moon was beginning to rise over the horizon. It was a brilliant orange. Huge, it took up most of the eastern sky.

Under his boots, the grass was slippery with dew. It wouldn't be long before the dampness became frost. The seasons were gentler and slower here than in northern Indiana. He needed to become attuned to their pace again.

Esther's steps were soft as she walked beside him while they made arrangements for the scholars' trip. He smiled when she asked if it would be okay for the *kinder* to have their midday meal at the farm.

"That way, we can have time for desk work when we return," she said.

"I'll make sure I have drinks for the *kinder*, so they don't have to bring those."

"That's kind of you, Nathaniel." She offered him another warm smile. "I want to say *danki* again for helping me stop the fight this afternoon."

"Do you have many of them?"

"*Ja*, and Jacob seems to be involved in each one."

He frowned. "Is there something wrong with the boy that he can't settle disagreements other than with his fists?" The wrong question to ask, he realized when she bristled.

"Nothing is *wrong* with him." She took a steadying breath, then said more calmly, "Forgive me. You can't know how it is. Jacob has had a harder time than most kids. He lives with his *onkel*, actually his *daed's onkel*. The man is too old to be taking care of a *kind*, but apparently he's the boy's sole relative. At least Jacob has him. The poor boy has seen things no *kind* should see."

"What do you mean?" He stopped beneath the great maple tree at the edge of the yard.

She explained how Jacob's parents had been killed and the boy badly hurt, physically and emotionally. Nathaniel's heart contracted with the thought of a *kind* suffering such grief.

"After the accident," she said, "we checked everywhere for other family, even putting a letter in *The Budget*."

He knew the newspaper aimed at and written by correspondents in plain communities was read throughout the world. "Nobody came forward?"

"Nobody." Her voice fell to a whisper. "Maybe that's why Jacob is angry. He believes everyone, including God, has abandoned him. He blames God for taking his *mamm* and *daed* right in front of his eyes. Why should he obey Jesus's request that we turn the other cheek and forgive those who treat us badly when, in Jacob's opinion, God has treated him worse than anyone on Earth could?"

"Anger at God eats at your soul. He has time to wait for your fury to run its course and still He forgives you."

"That sounds like the voice of experience."

"It is." He hesitated, wondering if he should tell her about the chemo. It was too personal a subject to share, even with Esther.

She said nothing, clearly expecting him to continue. When he didn't, she bid him good-night and started to turn away.

He put his hand on her arm as he'd done many times when they were kids. She looked at him, and the moonlight washed across her face. Who would have guessed a freckle-faced imp would mature into such a pretty woman? That odd sensation uncurled in his stomach again when she gazed at him, waiting for him to speak. Another change, because the Esther he'd known years ago wouldn't have waited on anything before she plunged headlong into her next adventure.

"*Danki* for agreeing to teach me about alpacas."

He watched her smile return and brighten her face. "I know how busy you are, but without your help I might have to sell the flock."

"Herd," she said with a laugh. "Sheep are a flock. Alpacas are a herd."

"See? I'm learning already."

"You've got much more to learn."

He grinned. "You used to like when I had to listen to you."

"Still do. I'll let you know when I've contacted the scholars' parents, and we'll arrange a day for them to visit." She patted his arm and ran into the house, her skirts fluttering behind her.

With a chuckle, he climbed into his buggy. He might not know a lot about alpacas, but he knew the lessons to come wouldn't be boring as long as Esther was involved.

Chapter Three

Nathaniel stepped down from his wagon and past the pair of mules hooked to it. There would be about twenty-two *kinder* along with, he guessed, at least one or two *mamms* to help oversee the scholars. Add in Esther and her assistant teacher. It was a small load, so it would give the mules, Sal and Gal, some gentle exercise. Tomorrow, he needed them to fetch a large load of hay. He'd store it in the barn to feed the animals during the winter.

The scholars were milling about in front of the school, their excited voices like a flock of blue jays. He was glad he'd left his *mutze* coat, the black wool coat plain men wore to church services, home on the warm morning and had his black vest on over his white shirt. His black felt hat was too hot, and he'd trade it for his straw one as soon as he got to the farm.

A boy ran over to be the first on the wagon. He halted, and Nathaniel recognized him from the scab on the corner of his mouth. It was the legacy of the punch Benny had taken from Jacob Fisher last week.

"*Gute mariye,*" Nathaniel said with a smile.

The boy watched him with suspicion, saying nothing.

"How's the lip?" Nathaniel asked. "It looks sore."

"It is," Benny replied grudgingly.

"Have your *mamm* put a dab of hand lotion on it to keep the skin soft, so it can heal. Try to limit your talking. You don't want to keep breaking it open."

The boy started to answer, then raised his eyebrows in a question.

"A day or two will allow it to heal. If you've got to say something, think it over first and make sure it's worth the pain that follows."

Benny nodded, then his eyes widened when he understood the true message in Nathaniel's suggestion. Keeping his mouth closed would help prevent him from saying something that could lead to a fight. The boy looked at the ground, then claimed his spot at the very back of the wagon bed where the ride would be the bumpiest.

Hoping what he said would help Esther by preventing another fight, Nathaniel walked toward the school. He was almost there when she stepped out and closed the door behind her. Today she wore a dark blue dress beneath her black apron. The color was the perfect foil for her eyes and her hair, which was the color of spun caramel.

"Right on time, Nathaniel," she said as she came down the steps. He tried to connect the prim woman she was now with the enthusiastic *kind* she'd been. It was almost impossible, and he couldn't help wondering what had quashed her once high spirits.

"I know you don't like to wait," he said instead of asking the questions he wanted to.

"Neither does anyone else." She put her arms around two of the *kinder* closest to her, and they looked at her with wide grins.

He helped her get the smaller ones on the wagon where they'd be watched by the older scholars. He wasn't surprised when Jacob found a place close to the front. The boy sat as stiffly as a cornstalk, making it clear he didn't want anyone near him.

Esther glanced at Nathaniel. He could tell she was frustrated at not being able to reach the *kind*. He'd added Jacob to his prayers and hoped God would bring the boy comfort. As He'd helped Nathaniel during the horrific rounds of chemo and the wait afterward to discover if the cancer had been vanquished.

"I'll keep an eye on him," he whispered.

"Me, too." She smiled again, but it wasn't as bright. After she made sure nobody had forgotten his or her lunch box, she sat on the seat with him.

He'd hoped to get time to chat with Esther during the fifteen minute drive to his farm, but she spent most of the ride looking over her shoulder to remind the scholars not to move close to the edges or to suggest a song for them to sing. Her assistant and the two *mamms* who'd joined them were kept busy with making sure the lunch boxes didn't bounce off. As they passed farmhouses, neighbors waved to them, and the *kinder* shouted they were going to see the alpacas.

"Nobody has any secrets with them around, do they?" Nathaniel grinned as the scholars began singing again.

"None whatsoever." Esther laughed. "It's one of the first lessons I learned. I love my job so I don't mind having everything I do and say at school repeated to parents each night."

"It sounds, from what I've heard, as if the parents are pleased."

A flush climbed her cheeks. "The *kinder* are important to all of us."

He looked past the mules' ears so she couldn't see his smile. Esther was embarrassed by his compliment. If the scholars hadn't been in earshot, he would have teased her about blushing.

Telling the *kinder* to hold on tight, he turned the wagon in at the lane leading to his grandparents' farm. To *his* farm. This morning, he'd received another letter from his *mamm*, begging him to return to Indiana instead of following his dreams in Paradise Springs. He must find a gentle way to let her know, once and for all, that he wanted to remain in Lancaster County. And he'd suggest she find the best words to let Vernita Miller know, as well. He didn't intend to marry Vernita, no matter how often the young woman had hinted he should. She'd find someone else. Perhaps his *gut* friend Dwayne Kempf who was sweet on her.

He shook thoughts of his *mamm*, Indiana and Vernita out of his head as he drew in the reins and stopped the wagon near the barn. Like the house, it needed a new coat of white paint. He'd started on the big project of fixing all the buildings when he could steal time from taking care of the animals, but, so far, only half of one side of the house was done.

"There they are!" came a shout from the back.

Jumping down, Nathaniel smiled when he saw the excited *kinder* pointing at the alpacas near the pasture fence. He heard a girl describe them as "adorable." Their long legs and neck were tufted with wool. Around their faces, more wool puffed like an aura.

The alpacas raced away when the scholars poured off the wagon.

"Where are they going?" a little girl asked him as he lifted her down.

"To get the others," he replied, though he knew the skittish creatures wanted to flee as far as possible from the noisy *kinder.*

Esther put her finger to her lips. "You must be quiet. Be like little mice sneaking around a sleeping cat."

The youngest scholars giggled. She asked each little one to take the hand of an older child. A few of the boys, including Jacob, which was no surprise, refused to hold anyone else's hand. Esther told them to remain close to the others and not to speak loudly.

"Where do you want us, Nathaniel?" she asked. "By the fence is probably best. What do you think?"

"You're the expert."

She led the *kinder* to the wooden fence backed by chicken wire, making sure the littler ones could see. "Can you name some of the alpacas' cousins?"

"Llamas!" called a boy.

She nodded, but motioned for him to lower his voice as the alpacas shifted nervously. "Llamas are one of their cousins. Can you tell me another?"

"Horses?" asked a girl.

"No."

"Cows?"

"No." She pointed at the herd after letting the scholars make a few more guesses. "Alpacas are actually cousins of camels."

"Like the ones the Wise Men rode?" asked Jacob.

Nathaniel saw Esther's amazement, though it was quickly masked. She was shocked the boy was participating, but he heard no sign of it in her voice when she assured Jacob he was right. That set off a buzz of more questions from the scholars.

The boy turned to look at the pasture, again separating himself from the others though he stood among them. The single breakthrough was a small victory. He could tell by the lilt in Esther's voice how delighted she'd been with Jacob's question.

The scholars' eager whispers followed Nathaniel as he entered the pasture through the barn. He'd try to herd the alpacas closer so the *kinder* could get a better look at them. His hopes were dashed when the alpacas evaded him as they always did. They resisted any attempt to move them closer to the scholars. If he jogged to the right, they went left. If he moved forward, they trotted away and edged around him. He could almost hear alpaca laughter.

"Let me," Esther called. She bunched up her dress and climbed over the fence as if she were one of the *kinder*. She brought a pair of thin branches, each about a yard long. As she crossed the pasture, she motioned for him to stand by the barn.

"Watch the *kinder*," she said. "I'll get an alpaca haltered, so we can bring it closer for them to see."

Curious about how she was going to do that, he watched her walk toward the herd with slow, even steps. She spoke softly, nonsense words from what he could discern.

She held the branches out to either side of her. He realized she was using them like a shepherd's crook to move the alpacas into the small shed at the rear of the pasture. He edged forward to see what she'd do once they were inside. He'd wondered what the shed with its single large pen was for. He hadn't guessed it was to corner the alpacas to make it easier to handle them.

She lifted a halter off a peg once the alpacas were in the pen. She chose a white-and-brown one who was almost as tall as she was. Moving to the animal's left, she gently slid the halter over its nose and behind its ears. The animal stood as docile as a well-trained dog, nodding its head when Esther checked to make sure the buckled halter was high enough on the nose that it wouldn't prevent the animal from breathing.

Latching a rope to the halter, Esther walked the alpaca from the shed. The other animals trotted behind her, watching her. Esther stayed on the alpaca's left side and an arm's length away. The alpaca followed her easily, but shied as she neared the fence where the *kinder* stood.

One *kind* pushed closer to the fence. Jacob! The boy's gaze was riveted on the alpaca. His usual anger was fading into something that wasn't a smile, but close.

Nathaniel wondered if Esther had noticed, but couldn't tell because her back was to him. Again she warned the scholars to be silent. Their eyes were curious but none of them stuck their fingers past the fence.

Esther looked over her shoulder at him. "You can come closer. Stay to her left side."

"You made it look easy," Nathaniel replied with admiration.

"Any task is easy when you know what you're doing." She winked at the scholars. "Like multiplication tables, ain't so?"

The younger ones giggled.

"Be careful it doesn't spit at you," Nathaniel warned the *kinder.*

"It won't." Esther patted the alpaca's head as the scholars edged back.

"Don't be sure. When I put them out this morning, this one started spitting at the others. She hasn't acted like that before."

"Were the males in there, too?"

He nodded. Before he'd gone to the school, he'd spent a long hour separating the males out because he feared they'd be aggressive near the *kinder.*

"Then," Esther said with a smile, "my guess is she's going to have a cria."

"A what?"

She laughed and nudged his shoulder with hers. "A *boppli*, Nathaniel."

The ordinary motion had anything but an ordinary effect on his insides. A ripple of awareness rushed through him like a powerful train. Had she felt it, too? He couldn't be sure because the scholars clapped their hands in delight. She was suddenly busy keeping the alpaca from pulling away in fear at the noise, but she calmed the animal.

"I'm going to need you to tell me what to do," Nathaniel said, glad his voice sounded calmer than he felt as he struggled to regain his equilibrium.

"There's no hurry. An alpaca is pregnant for at least eleven months, but she'll need to be examined by the vet to try to determine how far along she is."

As she continued to talk about the alpacas to her scholars, he sent a grateful prayer to God for Esther's help. His chances of making the farm a success were much greater than they'd been. He wasn't going to waste a bit of the time or the information she shared with him.

No, he assured himself as he watched her. He wasn't going to waste a single second.

Esther walked to the farmhouse, enjoying the sunshine. The trees along the farm lane were aflame with color against the bright blue sky. Not a single cloud blemished it. Closer to the ground, mums in shades of gold, orange and dark red along the house's foundation bobbed on a breeze that barely teased her nape.

She'd left the scholars with Nathaniel while she checked the alpacas. Though he didn't know much about them, he'd made sure they were eating well. She'd seen no sores on their legs. They hadn't been trying to get out of the pasture, so they must be content with what he provided.

Hearing shouts from the far side of the house, she walked in that direction. She hadn't planned to take so long with the alpacas, but it'd been fun to be with the silly creatures again. Their fleece was exceptionally soft, and their winter coats were growing in well. By the time they were sheared in the spring, Nathaniel would have plenty of wool to sell.

She came around the house and halted. On the sloping yard, Nathaniel was surrounded by the scholars. Jay, the oldest, was helping keep the *kinder* in a line. What were they doing?

Curious, she walked closer. She was amazed to see cardboard boxes torn apart and placed end to end on the grass. Two boxes were intact. As she watched, Nathaniel picked up a little girl and set her in one box. She giggled and gripped the front of it.

"All set?" he asked.

"Ja!" the *kind* shouted.

Nathaniel glanced at Jay and gave the box a slight shove. It sailed down the cardboard "slide" like a toboggan on snow. He kept pace with it on one side while Jay did on the other. They caught the box at the end of the slide before it could tip over and spill the *kind* out.

Picking her up again, Nathaniel swung her around. Giggling, she ran up the hill as a bigger boy jumped into the other box. His legs hung out the front, but he pushed with his hands to send himself down the slide. Nathaniel swung the other box out of the way just in time.

Everyone laughed and motioned for the boxes to be

brought back for the next ride. As the older boy climbed out, Esther saw it was Benny. He beamed as he gathered the boxes to carry them to the top. Nathaniel clapped him on the shoulder and grinned.

She went to stand by the porch where she could watch the *kinder* play. She couldn't take her eyes off Nathaniel. He looked as happy as he had when they were *kinder* themselves. He clearly loved being with the youngsters. He'd be a *wunderbaar daed*. Seeing him with her scholars, she could imagine him acting like her own *daed*.

Her most precious memories of *Daed* were when he'd come into the house at midday and pick her up. They'd bounce around the kitchen table singing a silly song until *Mamm* pretended to be irritated about how they were in the way. Then they'd laugh together, and *Daed* would set her in her chair before chasing her brothers around the living room. If he caught them, he'd tickle them until they squealed or *Mamm* called everyone to the table. As they bent their heads in silent grace, their shared joy had been like a glow around them.

Watching Nathaniel with the *kinder*, she wanted that for him. Too bad she and he were just friends. Otherwise—

Where had *that* thought come from? He was her buddy, her partner in crime, her competitor to see who could run the fastest or climb the highest. She *had* told him she'd marry him when they were little kids, something that made her blush when she thought of how outrageously she'd acted, but they weren't *kinder* any longer.

When Nathaniel called a halt to the game, saying it was time for lunch, the youngsters tried not to show their disappointment. They cheered when he said he had fresh cider waiting for them on a picnic table by the kitchen door.

They raced past Esther to get their lunch boxes. She smiled as she went to help Nathaniel collect the pieces of cardboard.

"Quite a game you have here," she said. "Did you make it up?"

As he folded the long cardboard strips and set them upright in one of the boxes, he shook his head. "Not me alone. It's one we played in Indiana. We invented it the summer after I couldn't go sledding all winter."

"Why? Were you sick?"

"*Ja.*"

"All winter?"

"You know how *mamms* can be. Always worrying." He gathered the last bits of cardboard and dropped them into the other box. Brushing dirt off himself, he grimaced as he tapped his left knee. "Grass stains on my *gut* church clothes. *Mamm* wouldn't be happy to see that."

He looked very handsome in his black vest and trousers, which gave his dark hair a ruddy sheen. The white shirt emphasized his strong arms and shoulders. She'd noticed his shoulders when she tumbled against him at school.

"If you want," she said when she realized she was staring. "I'll clean them."

"I can't ask you to do that." He carried the boxes to the porch. "You've got enough to do keeping up with your brothers."

"One more pair of trousers won't make any difference." She smiled as she walked with him toward the kitchen door. "Trust me."

"I do, and my alpacas do, too. It was amazing how you calmed them."

"I'll teach you."

"I don't know if I can convince them to trust me as they do you. It might be impossible. Though obviously not for Esther Stoltzfus, the alpaca whisperer."

She laughed, then halted when she saw a buggy driving at top speed along the farm lane. Even from a distance, she recognized her brother Isaiah driving it. She glanced at Nathaniel, then ran to where the buggy was stopping. Only something extremely important would cause Isaiah to leave his blacksmith shop in the middle of the day.

He climbed out, his face lined with dismay. "Esther, where are the *kinder*?"

"Behind the house having lunch."

"*Gut.*" He looked from her to Nathaniel. "There's no way to soften this news. Titus Fisher has had a massive stroke and is on his way to the hospital."

Esther gasped and pressed her hands to her mouth.

"Are you here to get the boy?" asked Nathaniel.

"I'm not sure he should go to the hospital until Titus is stable." Isaiah turned to her. "What do you think, Esther?"

"I think he needs to be told his *onkel* is sick, but nothing more now. No need to scare him. Taking him to the hospital can wait until we know more."

"That's what I thought, but you know him better than I do." He sighed. "The poor *kind*. He's already suffered enough. Tonight—"

"He can stay here," Nathaniel said quietly.

"Are you sure?" her brother asked, surprised.

"I've got plenty of room," Nathaniel said, "and the boy seems fascinated by my alpacas."

Isaiah looked at her for confirmation.

She nodded, knowing it was the best solution under the circumstances.

"I'll let Reuben know." He sighed again. "Just in case."

"Tell the bishop that Jacob can stay here as long as he needs to," Nathaniel said.

"That should work out...unless his *onkel* dies. Then the

Bureau of Children and Family Services will have to get involved."

Nathaniel frowned, standing as resolute as one of the martyrs of old.

Before he could retort, Esther said, "Let's deal with one problem at a time." She prayed it wouldn't get to that point. And if it did, there must be some plan to give Jacob the family he needed without *Englisch* interference. She had no idea what, but they needed to figure it out fast.

Chapter Four

Esther looked around for Jacob as soon as her brother left. Isaiah was bound for their bishop's house. He and Reuben planned to hire an *Englisch* driver to take them to the hospital where they would check on Titus Fisher.

She wasn't surprised Jacob had left the other scholars and gone to watch the alpacas. The boy stood by the fence, his fingers stuck through the chicken wire in an offer for the shy beasts to come over and sniff them. The alpacas were ignoring him from the far end of the pasture.

The sight almost broke her heart. Jacob, who was small for his age and outwardly fragile, stood alone as he reached out to connect with another creature.

"Are you okay?" asked Nathaniel as he walked beside her toward the pasture.

"Not really." She squared her shoulders, knowing she must not show the *kind* how sorry she felt for him. Jacob reacted as badly to pity as he did to teasing. He'd endured too much during his short life.

Suddenly she stopped and put out her arm to halt Nathaniel. He frowned at her, but, putting her fingers to her lips, she whispered, "Shhh..."

In the pasture, one of the younger alpacas inched away from the others, clearly curious about the boy who had been standing by the fence for so long. The light brown female stretched out her neck and sniffed the air as if trying to determine what sort of animal Jacob was. Glancing at the rest of the herd, she took one step, then another toward him.

The boy didn't move, but Esther guessed his heart was trying to beat its way out of his chest. A smile tipped his lips, the first one she'd ever seen on his face.

In the distance, the voices of the other scholars fluttered on the air, but Nathaniel and Esther remained as silent as Jacob. The alpaca's curiosity overcame her shyness, and she continued toward the boy. His smile broadened on every step, but he kept his outstretched fingers steady.

The alpaca paused an arm's length away, then took another step. She extended her head toward his fingertips, sniffing and curious.

Beside her, Esther heard Nathaniel whisper, "Keep going, girl. He needs you now."

Her heart was touched by his empathy for the *kind*. Nathaniel's generous spirit hadn't changed. He'd always been someone she could depend on, the very definition of a *gut* friend. He still was, offering kindness to a lonely boy. Her fingers reached out to his arm, wanting to squeeze it gently to let him know how much she appreciated his understanding of what Jacob needed.

Her fingers halted midway between them as a squeal came from near the house where the other scholars must be playing a game. At the sound, the alpaca whirled and loped back to the rest of the herd.

"Almost," Jacob muttered under his breath.

Walking to the boy, Esther fought her instinct to put her hand on his shoulder. That would send him skittering away like the curious alpaca. "It'll take them time to trust you, Jacob, but you've made a *gut* beginning."

When he glanced at her, for once his face wasn't taut with determination to hide his pain. She saw something she'd never seen there before.

Hope.

"Do you think so?" he asked.

She nodded. She must be as cautious with him as she was with the alpacas. "It'll take time and patience on your part, but eventually they learn to trust."

"Eventually?" His face hardened into an expression no *kind* should ever wear. "I guess that's that, then. We'll be leaving for school soon, ain't so?"

He'd given her the opening to tell him the bad news Isaiah had brought. She must tell him the truth now, but she must be careful how she told him until they were sure about Titus Fisher's prognosis.

"Jacob, I need to tell you about something that's happened," she began.

"If Jay said it was my fault, he's lying!" Jacob clenched his hands at his sides. "Benny tipped over Jay's glass, but said I did it. I didn't! I always tell the truth!"

Tears welled in the boy's eyes, and she saw his desperate need for her to believe him. And she did. Unlike some *kinder*, Jacob always admitted what he'd done wrong...if he were caught.

She squatted in front of him, so her eyes were even with his. Aware of Nathaniel behind her, she said quietly, "Nobody has said anything about a glass. This has nothing to do with the other *kinder*."

"Then what?" He was growing more wary by the second.

"I wanted to let you know your *onkel* isn't feeling well, so he went to see some *doktors* who will try to help him."

"Is it his heart?" Jacob's hands loosened, and he folded his arms over his narrow chest. Was he trying to protect himself?

When she glanced at Nathaniel, he looked as shocked as she felt at the forthright question. Clearly the boy was aware of his *onkel's* deteriorating health. Jacob Fisher was a smart *kind*. She mustn't forget that, as the other scholars did far too often, underestimating his intelligence as well as how brittle his patience was.

"*Ja,*" she answered. "The *doktors* want to observe him. That means—"

"They want to watch what his heart does so they can find out why it's giving him trouble." He gave a careless shrug, but he couldn't hide the fear burning in his eyes. "*Onkel* Titus explained to me the last time he went to the clinic."

She wanted to let him know it was okay to show his distress, but she wouldn't push. *Ja,* he was scared, but Titus had prepared the boy. She reminded herself that Jacob didn't know the full extent of what had happened. For now, it would be better not to frighten him further. She didn't want to think of what would happen if his *onkel* didn't recover. If she did, she wouldn't be able to hold back the tears prickling her eyes.

And that would scare Jacob more.

Nathaniel saw Esther struggling to hold on to her composure. He should have urged her to let him talk to Jacob alone. Unlike him, she knew Titus Fisher, and she must be distressed by the old man's stroke.

He drew her to her feet. He tried to ignore the soft buzz where his palms were spread across her arms. Releasing her because he needed to focus on the boy, he was amazed when the sensation still coursed along his hands.

Trying to ignore it, he said, "Jacob, under the circumstances, I think Esther would agree with me when I say you don't need to go back to school today."

"I don't?" Glee brightened his face for a moment, then it vanished. "Then I'll have to go to my *onkel's* house by myself."

Nathaniel tried not to imagine what the boy was thinking. The idea of returning to an empty house where he'd be more alone than ever must be horrifying to Jacob. Knowing he must pick his words with care, he said, "I thought you might want to stay here."

"With the alpacas?" Jacob's eyes filled with anticipation.

Nathaniel struggled to keep his smile in place as he wondered if that expression would have been visible on Jacob's face more often if he hadn't watched his parents die and been sent to live with an elderly *onkel*. Titus Fisher had provided him with a *gut* home, or as *gut* as he could. The old man had protected his great-nephew from the realities of his failing health by telling him enough to make this moment easier for the boy.

What would Jacob—or Esther—say if he revealed how his own childhood had been filled with *doktors* and fear? His *mamm* had overreacted any time he got a cold, and his *daed* had withdrawn. If it hadn't been for their *Englisch* neighbor, Reggie O'Donnell, who'd welcomed Nathaniel at his greenhouses whenever he needed an escape, there would have been no break from the drama at home. The retired engineer had let Nathaniel assist and never made him talk or wash his hands endlessly or avoid playing with other *kinder* because he might get some germ that would bring on another bout of what they called "the scourge."

Though the *Englisch doktors* had assured his parents that, upon the completion of the treatments, Nathaniel had no more chance than any other person of contracting cancer again, they never could let go of their fear. He suspected that was one of the reasons his *mamm* insisted he return to Indiana. She wanted to keep an eye on him every second to make sure the scourge didn't return.

Was Titus Fisher a sanctuary for Jacob as Reggie had been for Nathaniel? Someone who didn't talk about the past or what might await in the future? Had he, like Reggie, been someone with a heart big enough to offer a haven for a lonely, lost *kind*?

Grief for the old man and the boy hammered Nathaniel. "*Ja*," he said, "you can stay here with me and the alpacas, if you'd like."

"And if I don't like?" Jacob asked cautiously.

Esther looked away, and he knew she was having difficulty keeping her feelings from showing. As he was. No *kind* Jacob's age should have to ask such a question. The boy had learned life could change in the blink of an eye. He probably hadn't had any say in where he would go after his parents' funeral.

"Then other arrangements will be made for you, and you can come and visit the alpacas."

Jacob shook his head. "No, I want to stay here. I think I can get one of them to come to me if I've got enough time."

"Then it's settled." Nathaniel tried to curb the sudden disquiet rising in him at the thought of being responsible for the boy. *Dear Lord, help me know the right things to do and say while he's here.* He forced a smile. "We'll work together to convince the alpacas to trust us. It'll be fun."

"It will!" The boy turned to look at the herd again. "Let's start now."

"I have to take everyone back to school."

The boy's shoulders slumped. "Can I stay here? *Onkel* Titus let me stay by myself."

Unsure if Jacob was being truthful or not, in spite of his assertion that he always was honest, Nathaniel hesitated.

Esther didn't. "If it's okay with you, Nathaniel, I can drive everyone to school. I'll take your wagon to our farm tonight. You can come and get it when it's convenient."

Again he hesitated. He'd planned to leave early tomorrow to get the hay for winter feedings, but those plans must change.

"All right," he said. "I'll help you hook Sal and Gal to the wagon. Do you know how to handle mules?"

"*Ja.* A little, but my brothers will know because *Daed* had a team to plow the fields. Ezra will make sure they're taken care of tonight."

He had no choice but to agree or upset Jacob further. He couldn't blame the boy for not wanting to spend more time with his classmates, especially now.

"I'll be right back," Nathaniel said.

"Can I go into the pasture?" asked Jacob.

"Maybe later tonight when I feed them. Let's see how they're behaving then."

He thought the boy would argue, but Jacob nodded. "I'll wait here for you."

For a moment, Nathaniel wished the boy had protested like a regular kid. He remembered times, especially when he was going through chemo, when he'd found himself trying to be *gut* so he didn't upset the adults around him more. It hadn't been easy to swallow his honest reactions. His respect for Jacob grew, but the boy's maturity also concerned him. A *kind* needed to be a *kind*, not some sort of miniature adult.

When he said as much to Esther as they walked into the barn to get the mules, she sighed and stole a glance at where the boy was gazing at the alpacas once more. "I worry about him when he's cooperative and when he's fighting. It's as if he can't find a middle path."

"He probably can't. When everything inside you is in a turmoil, it's hard to trust your own feelings. Most especially when you've let them loose in the past and people haven't reacted well. Instead they've told you how you should feel so many times you begin to wonder if they're right and you're wrong."

She paused as he kept walking toward where he kept the harnesses for the mules. When he turned to see why she'd stopped, she said, "I hadn't thought about it like that."

Emotions he couldn't decipher scuttled across her face. He wanted to ask what she was thinking, but satisfying his curiosity would have to wait. She hurried past him, murmuring how she'd told the scholars' *mamms* she'd have everyone back by now. They'd spent more than an hour longer at the farm than she'd planned.

As he put Sal and Gal into place and hooked them to the wagon, Nathaniel glanced at Jacob standing by the alpacas' pasture, and then to the other *kinder* racing about by the house. The difference was unsettling, and he wondered if it was possible for Jacob to become carefree again. He had to believe so.

He looked across the mules at Esther, who was checking the reins. "Do you think we should let him continue to believe his *onkel*'s heart is why Titus was taken to the hospital?"

"I don't know." Her expression matched her unsteady words. "Let me talk to Isaiah when he gets back."

"A *gut* idea."

"Are you sure you want Jacob to stay with you? Is that why you asked?"

"No. I'm sure staying here is best for him now. The boy needs something to do to get his mind off the situation, and the alpacas can help."

She nodded. When she called to the other *kinder* to pack their things and prepare to leave, there were the protests Nathaniel had expected to hear. She handled each one with humor and serenity. She was a stark contrast to his *mamm* and his older sisters who saw everything as a potential tragedy.

He smiled as the scholars clambered onto the flatbed. When they passed him, each of them said, *"Danki."* Telling them to have a *gut* ride to school, he held his hand out to assist Esther onto the seat.

She regarded him with surprise, and he had to fight not to smile. Now *that* reaction reminded him of Esther the Pester, who'd always asserted she could do anything the older boys did...and all by herself.

Despite that, she accepted his help. The scent of her shampoo lingered in his senses. He was tempted to hold on to her soft fingers, but he released them as soon as she was sitting. He was too aware of the *kinder* and other women gathered behind her.

She picked up the reins and leaned toward him. "If it becomes too difficult for you, bring him to our house."

"We'll be fine." At that moment, he meant it. When her bright blue eyes were close to his, he couldn't imagine being anything but fine.

Then she looked away, and the moment was over. She slapped the reins and drove the wagon toward the road. He watched it go. A sudden shiver ran along him. The breeze was damp and chilly, something he hadn't noticed while gazing into Esther's pretty eyes.

The sound of the rattling wagon vanished in the distance, and he turned to see Jacob standing by the fence, his fingers through the chicken wire again in the hope an alpaca would come to him. The *kind* had no idea of what could lie ahead for him.

Take him into Your hands, Lord. He's going to need Your comfort in the days to come. Make him strong to face what the future brings, but let him be weak enough to accept help from us.

Taking a deep breath, Nathaniel walked toward the boy. He'd agreed to take care of Jacob and offer him a haven at the farm. Now he had to prove he could.

Chapter Five

As Jacob helped with the afternoon chores, which included cleaning up after the alpacas and refilling their water troughs, Nathaniel watched closely. He knew Esther would want to know how the boy did in the wake of the news about his *onkel*. She worried about him as if he were her own *kind*. Nathaniel suspected she was that way with each of her scholars.

Jacob didn't say much, but he was comfortable doing hard work. Nathaniel wondered how many of the chores at Titus Fisher's house had become Jacob's responsibility as the old man's health declined. He seemed happy to remain behind, which was no surprise. A chance to skip school was something any kid would enjoy, but Nathaniel couldn't help wondering what the boy was thinking.

One thing he knew from his own childhood. Growing boys were always hungry.

Flashing Jacob a smile and a wink, he asked, "How about grabbing a snack before we feed the alpacas?"

"Whatcha got?"

Nathaniel chuckled as he motioned for the boy to follow him toward the house. Jacob seemed to walk a fine line between being a *kind* and being a wraith who floated through each day, not connecting with anyone else.

"I know there's church spread in the fridge," he answered.

Jacob grinned, and Nathaniel was glad he'd guessed what the boy would like. There weren't too many people who didn't enjoy the combination of peanut butter and marshmallow creme. Keeping it around allowed him to slap together a quick sandwich when he had scant time for dinner or was too tired to cook anything for supper.

"What else do you have to eat with it?" Jacob asked.

"We'll look through the kitchen. A treasure hunt without a map. Who knows what we might find?"

"As long as it's not growing green stuff." Excitement blossomed in Jacob's eyes.

Nathaniel laughed and ruffled the boy's hair. Jacob stiffened for a second, then relaxed with a smile.

The poor kid! Did anyone treat him as a *kind* or did others think of him solely as his sad experiences? The boy needed a chance to be a boy. Nathaniel knew that with every inch of his being. After having his own parents, with their *gut* intentions, nearly deny him his own chance to be a kid, he didn't want to see the same happen to another *kind*.

He wasn't going to let that occur. God had brought Jacob into his life for a reason, and it might be as simple as Nathaniel being able to offer him an escape, temporary though it might be, into a normal childhood. Reggie had given that to him. Now Nathaniel could do the same for Jacob.

With a laugh, he said, "You've got to be tired after tidying up."

"A bit."

"*Gut*. Then you won't be able to beat me to the kitchen door." With no more warning, Nathaniel loped away.

A moment passed, and he wondered if his attempt to get Jacob to play had failed. Then, with a whoop, the boy sped past him. Nathaniel lengthened his stride, but the *kind* reached the door before he could. Whirling to face him, Jacob pumped his arms in a victory dance.

Nathaniel let him cheer for a few moments and didn't remind him it wasn't the Amish way to celebrate beating someone else. There was time enough for those lessons later. For now, Jacob needed to feel like a kid.

"Well done." He clapped the boy on the shoulder. "Next time, I'll beat you."

"Don't be so sure." As Jacob smiled, his brown eyes were filled with humor instead of his usual lost expression.

Nathaniel laughed, thinking how pleased Esther would be when he shared this moment with her tomorrow. He opened the door and ushered the boy into a kitchen that looked the same as it had the day he'd arrived from Indiana for his summer visit so many years ago. The kitchen was a large room, but filled to capacity with furniture, as the living room was. There were enough chairs of all shapes and sizes to host a Sunday church service. His grandparents had been fond of auctions, but he'd been astounded when he arrived to discover the house chock-full of furnishings.

Nathaniel had stored many chairs and two dressers from the living room in an outbuilding, which was now full. He had to find other places to put the rest until there was a charity auction to which he could donate them. Until then he had to wend his way through an obstacle course of chairs every morning and night to reach the stairs.

Jacob walked in and sniffed. "This place smells like *Onkel* Titus's house."

"In what way?" He hoped something familiar would make the boy feel more at home.

"Full of old stuff and dust." He looked at Nathaniel. "Don't grown-ups ever throw anything out?"

He grinned. "Not my grandparents. My *grossmammi* saved the tabs from plastic bags. She always said, 'Use it up, wear it out—'"

"'...make it do or do without,'" finished Jacob with an abrupt grin. "*Onkel* Titus says the same thing. A lot." He glanced around. "Don't you think they could get by with a lot less stuff?"

"I know I could. If you can find an empty chair, bring it to the table while I make some sandwiches."

That brought a snort of something that might have been rusty laughter from the boy, but could have been disgust with the state of the house. Nathaniel didn't look at Jacob to determine which. Getting the boy to smile was *wunderbaar*. As they had an impromptu supper, with Nathaniel eating two sandwiches and Jacob three, he let the boy take the lead in deciding the topics of conversation.

There was only one. The alpacas. Jacob had more questions than Nathaniel could answer. Time after time, he had to reply that Jacob needed to ask Esther. The boy would nod, then ask another question. That continued while they got the alpacas ready for the night.

Nathaniel hid his smile when he heard Jacob chatter like a regular kid. He thanked God for putting a love for alpacas in his *grossmammi*'s heart, so the creatures could touch a lonely boy's. God's methods were splendid, and Nathaniel sent up a grateful prayer as he walked with Jacob back to the house when their chores were done.

Leading the boy upstairs—where there were yet more chairs—he smiled when Jacob yawned broadly. He opened a door across the hall from his own bedroom. It was a room he'd had some success in clearing out. In the closet were stairs leading to the attic, where he'd hoped there might be room to store furniture. However, like the rest of the house, it was already full.

"Here's where you'll sleep." Nathaniel was glad he'd kept the bed made so the room looked welcoming. He'd slept on the bed with its black and white and blue quilt the time he came to stay with his grandparents. Pegs on the wall waited for clothes, and a small table held the storybooks Nathaniel had read years ago. The single window gave a view of the pasture beyond the main barn.

"I can see them!" crowed Jacob, rushing around the iron bed to peer out the window. "The alpacas! They're right out there."

"They'll be there until I move them to another pasture in a couple of weeks."

The boy whirled. "Why do you have to move them?" His tone suggested Nathaniel was doing that to be cruel to him and the animals.

"If I don't move them, they'll be hungry." He tried to keep his voice calm. The boy needed to learn that not everything was an attack on him, but how did you teach that to a *kind* who'd seen his parents cut down and killed by a car? "Once the alpacas eat the grass in that field, I must put them in another field so they can graze."

"Oh." Jacob lowered his eyes.

"But they'll be right there in the morning. Why don't you get ready for bed? I'll put an extra toothbrush in the bathroom for you."

The boy nodded, his eyelids drooping. "Can we pray for my *onkel* first?"

"*Ja.*" Nathaniel was actually relieved to hear him speak

of Titus. The boy had said very little about his *onkel* since Esther left.

Kneeling by the side of the bed along with Jacob, Nathaniel bowed his head over his folded hands. He listened as Jacob prayed for his *onkel*'s health and thanked God for letting him meet the alpacas. Nathaniel couldn't help grinning when the boy finished his prayers with, "Make the alpacas like me, God, cuz I sure like them."

Nathaniel echoed Jacob's amen and came to his feet. Telling the boy he'd be sleeping on the other side of the hall, he added that Jacob should call if he needed anything.

An hour later, after he'd washed the few supper dishes and put them away, Nathaniel closed his Bible and placed it on a small table in the living room. The words had begun to swim in front of his eyes. He went upstairs and peeked into Jacob's room. The boy was sprawled across the bed in a shaft of moonlight. He'd removed his shoes and socks but not his suspenders. One drooped around his right shoulder, and the other hung loose by his left hip. His shirt had pulled out of his trousers, revealing what looked like a long scar. A legacy of the accident that had taken his parents? He mumbled something in his sleep and turned over to bury his head in the pillow once more. Nathaniel wondered if the boy had nightmares while he slept or if that was the one time he could escape from the blows life had dealt him.

Nathaniel slowly closed the door almost all the way. The evening had gone better than he'd dared to hope. He went into his own room. He left his door open a crack, too, so he'd hear if the boy got up or if someone came to the kitchen door.

He went to the bedroom window and gazed out at the stars overhead. Was Esther looking at the same stars now? Was her heart heavy, as his was, with worries for Jacob and his *onkel*? Was she thinking of Nathaniel as he was of her? Since she'd fallen into his arms at the ball game he'd found it impossible to push her out of his thoughts. Not that he minded. Not a lot, anyhow, because it was fun to think of her sparkling eyes. It was delightful to recall how perfectly she'd fit against him.

He shook the thought from his head. Remembering her softness and the sweet scent of her hair was foolish. No need to torment himself when holding her again would be wrong. He couldn't ignore how much she loved being with *kinder* and how impossible it could be for him to give her *kinder* of her own. He needed to put an end to such thoughts now and concentrate on the one dream he had a chance of making come true: being a success on the farm so it didn't have to be sold.

Esther had just arrived home from school when she heard the rattle of buggy wheels. She looked out the kitchen window in time to see Nathaniel drive into the yard. She went to greet him and Jacob. She hoped letting him skip school had been a *gut* idea.

The afternoon breeze was strengthening, and her apron undulated on top of her dress. Goose bumps rose along her bare arms. She hugged them to her as she rushed to the buggy.

From it, she heard Jacob ask, "Isn't this where Esther lives?"

"*Ja*" came Nathaniel's reply.

"Why are we coming here? I thought we were going to *Onkel* Titus's house?"

"We are."

Esther kept her smile in place as a wave of sorrow flooded

her. Never had she heard Jacob describe Titus's house as his home. Did he see it as another temporary residence?

Calling out a greeting, she pretended not to have heard the exchange. She gave Nathaniel and Jacob a quick appraisal. Both appeared fine, so she guessed their first day together had gone well. That was a great relief, because last night she'd felt guilty for letting Nathaniel take on the obligation of the boy. More than once, she'd considered driving over to his farm and bringing Jacob to her family's house. She was glad to see it hadn't been necessary. At least, not yet.

"Any news about Titus's tests?" Nathaniel asked.

She shook her head, glad he'd selected those words that suggested the elderly man's condition wasn't too serious. "Nothing, and you know what they say."

"No news is good news?"

"Exactly." She motioned toward the bank barn. "Ezra put Gal and Sal on the upper floor. He wasn't sure how they'd be around his cows."

"Is it all right if they stay here a little while longer? We're on our way to Titus's house to get some of Jacob's clothes and other things."

Glancing at Jacob, who hadn't said a word, she replied, "I'll go with you, if you don't mind."

"No, of course we don't mind."

"Jacob?" she asked.

The boy nodded with obvious reluctance.

"Let me get my bonnet." She hurried into the house. After letting *Mamm* know where she was going, she grabbed her black bonnet and her knitted shawl. She threw the shawl over her shoulders and went outside to discover Nathaniel had already turned the buggy toward the road.

Jacob slid over, leaving her room by the door. As soon as she was seated and the buggy was moving, he began asking her questions about the alpacas. She was kept so busy answering his question that the trip, less than two miles long, was over before she realized it.

The buggy rolled to a stop by a house whose weathered boards were a mosaic of peeling paint. The front porch had a definite tilt to the right, and Esther wondered if it remained connected to the house. Cardboard was set into one windowpane where the glass was missing. However, the yard was neat, and the remnants of a large garden out back had at least half a dozen pumpkins peeking from under large leaves.

As they stepped from the buggy, Jacob ran ahead. Nathaniel motioned for Esther to wait for him to come around to her side.

He chuckled quietly. "Blame those questions on me. Yesterday, Jacob asked me a lot of things I didn't know about. I kept telling him to ask you the next time he saw you. I didn't think he'd ask you *all* the questions at once."

"I'm glad to answer what I can, and I'm glad you're here to hear as well, so I don't need to explain them again to you."

He pressed his hand over his heart and struck the pose of a wounded man. "Oh, no! I didn't realize I was supposed to be listening, too."

"You should know anytime you're around a teacher there may be a test at the end."

He laughed again, harder this time, as they walked to the door where Jacob was waiting impatiently. When the boy motioned for them to follow him inside, Nathaniel's laughter vanished along with Esther's smile.

The interior of the house was almost impassable. Boxes and bags were piled haphazardly from floor to ceiling. Esther stared at broken pieces of scooters, parts from *Englisch* cars and farming equipment mixed in with clothing and books and things she couldn't identify. If there was any furniture beneath the heaps it was impossible to see.

She guessed they were in the kitchen, but there were no signs of appliances or a sink. Odors that suggested food was rotting somewhere in the depths of the piles turned her stomach. She pushed the door open again, knowing she couldn't reach a window, even if she knew where one was, to air out the house.

"My room is this way." Jacob gestured again for them to follow him as he threaded a path through the piles with the ease of much practice.

Esther looked around in disbelief. Softly, so her words wouldn't reach Jacob, she said, "I had no idea Titus Fisher was living this way."

"I don't think anyone did other than his nephew." Nathaniel's mouth was a straight line as he walked after the boy.

She hesitated, not wanting to be buried if a mountain of debris cascaded onto her. How could this house have become filled with garbage and useless items? Surely someone came to call on the old man once in a while. She needed to alert the bishop, because other elderly people who were alone might also be living in such deplorable conditions.

Titus couldn't come home to this. Isaiah had said the stroke was a bad one, and if the elderly man survived he would be in a wheelchair. The path from the kitchen was too narrow for one.

Taking a deep breath, Esther plunged into the house. Her shawl brushed the sides of the stacks as she inched forward. How was Nathaniel managing? His shoulders were wider than her own. When she saw him ahead, sidling like a crab, she realized it was the only way he could move through the narrow space.

"Having fun?" he asked as he waited for her to catch up with him.

"Fun? Why would you say that?"

He grinned. "It's like being an explorer in another world. Who knows what lurks in these piles?"

"Mice and squirrels, most likely. Maybe a rat or two. Cockroaches. Do I need to go on?"

"Where's your sense of adventure?"

"Gone."

"I noticed." His face was abruptly serious. Tilting his head and eyeing her as if trying to look within her heart, he said, "You used to see an adventure in everything around us. What happened?"

She didn't want to have this discussion with him, especially not now when Jacob should be their focus. She tried to push aside some of the stacked items so she could move past him. It was as useless as if she were shoving on a concrete wall.

"Esther, tell me why you've changed." His voice had dropped to a husky whisper that seemed to reach deep inside her and uncurl slowly as it peeled away her pretense.

No! She wouldn't reveal the humiliating truth of how she'd been so eager for adventure that she'd gotten involved with Alvin Lee. How could she explain she was supposed to be a respectable daughter and teacher, but she'd ridden in his buggy while he was racing it? What would Nathaniel think of her if he learned how she'd tossed aside common sense in the hope Alvin Lee would develop feelings for her?

Because he reminded me of Nathaniel, who, I believed, was gone forever from my life.

Astonishment froze her. Could that be true? No, she had to be *ferhoodled*. If she wasn't mixed-up, it had to be because she was distressed by the state of Titus's house and knowing

Jacob had been living here. That was why she wasn't thinking straight. It had to be!

Nathaniel was regarding her with curiosity because she
hadn't answered his question. She raised her chin slightly so
she could meet his steady gaze.

"What happened? I grew up," she said before turning
and shoving harder on the junk. Items fell on others, and it
sounded as if several pieces of glass or china shattered. The
path widened enough so she could squeeze past him without
touching him. She kept going and didn't look back.

Chapter Six

Esther followed Jacob up the stairs, which were stacked with boxes. She heard Nathaniel's footsteps behind her but didn't turn. She shouldn't have spoken to him like that. It had been rude, and her reply was sure to create more questions. She didn't need those.

The upper hallway was as clogged with rubbish as the first floor. Each room they passed looked exactly like the rest of the house until Jacob opened a door and led them into a neat room.

How often *Mamm* had chided her and her siblings throughout their childhoods to keep their rooms orderly! *Mamm* would have been delighted to see how well Jacob kept his room.

Was it something he'd learned from his own *mamm*, or did he keep the clutter out of his room to have a refuge from his *onkel*'s overpowering collection? She blinked back tears. Either way, it was another sign of a *kind* who'd lost too much and was trying not to let his true feelings show.

Speaking around the clog in her throat, she said, "The first things we're going to need are some bags or a *gut*-sized box."

"I think I know where I can find a box." Nathaniel grinned.

Jacob stepped in front of him to keep him from leaving the room. The boy's eyes were wide with horror. "No! You can't use one of *Onkel* Titus's boxes. Nobody touches anything in *Onkel* Titus's house but *Onkel* Titus."

"Not even you?" asked Esther gently.

The boy shook his head, his expression grim. "I did once, and I got the switch out behind the well house. I learned when *Onkel* Titus says something he means it."

Nathaniel glanced at her over the boy's head, and she saw his closely reined-in anger. A *kind* must learn to heed his elders, but that could be done gently. The idea of Titus striking Jacob for simply moving one of dozens of cardboard boxes set her teeth on edge, as well.

"Wait here." Jacob rushed from the room.

"No *kind* should live as he has here," Nathaniel said.

She squared her shoulders and took a deep breath. "We need to contact Reuben."

"The bishop—" He halted himself as Jacob sprinted into the room.

The boy tossed some cloth grocery bags on the bed. "We can use these. *Onkel* Titus says they're worthless. He'll be glad to get them out of his house."

"*Gut.*" Esther kept her voice light. "Are your clothes in this dresser?"

"*Ja.*"

"Pick out things other than clothes you want to bring and put them on the bed. Nathaniel and you can take them to the buggy." She counted. There were ten bags. "These should be enough to hold your things."

The boy faltered. "How long is *Onkel* Titus going to be in the hospital?"

Esther knew she must not hesitate. She didn't want to cause the boy more worry. "He has to stay there until the *doktors* tell him he can come home. I know you want him home right away, but it's better that the *doktors* are thorough so they know everything about your *onkel*'s health."

Jacob pondered that for several minutes, then nodded. "That makes sense."

"Don't forget your school supplies," she added.

"School?" He looked at Nathaniel. "I thought I didn't have to go to school while I was at your house."

"All *kinder* must go to school." Nathaniel grinned. "Nice try, though."

"When do I have to go back?"

"Monday will be early enough," Esther answered.

Jacob frowned, then began to gather his belongings. For the next ten minutes they worked in silent unison. Jacob set a few books, a baseball and his church Sunday black hat on the bed. Nathaniel put them into bags, making sure nothing was crushed. Esther packed Jacob's work boots and his best pair of shoes into another bag before turning to the dresser.

Like everything else in the room, the drawers were neat. Too neat for an eight-year-old boy.

When she mentioned that to Nathaniel while Jacob was carrying the first bags of clothing downstairs, he said, "Maybe it's his defense against the mess in the rest of the house. I'm glad we're getting him out of here." He picked up the last two cloth bags.

"Has he said anything about going to visit his *onkel*?"

"No."

"You'll let me know if he says something about going to the hospital, won't you?"

"*Ja*." He gave her a faint smile. "I'm sure he'll ask once he's less fascinated with the alpacas." Before she could add anything else, he asked, "Don't you think it's odd Titus wants to get rid of perfectly *gut* bags when he's stockpiling ripped and torn plastic ones?"

"Everything about him seems to be odder than anyone knows." She walked toward the door. "If I had to guess, I'd say Titus doesn't like cloth bags because you can't see through them. The plastic ones let him keep an eye on his possessions."

"How can he—or anyone else—see into the bags at the bottom of a pile?"

"You're being logical, Nathaniel. I don't think logic visits this house very often."

He led the way down the cramped stairs. When a board creaked threateningly beneath her foot, he turned and grasped her by the waist. He swung her down onto the step beside him. Her skirt brushed against the junk on the stairs. An avalanche tumbled loudly down the stairs and ricocheted off stacks on the ground floor. Things cascaded in every direction.

The noise couldn't conceal the sharp snap of the tread where she'd been standing. It broke and fell into the open space under the stairs.

Nathaniel's arm curved around her, pulling her away from the gap. Her breath burst out of her, and she had trouble drawing another one while she stood so near to him. When she did, it was flavored with the enticing scents of soap and sunshine from his shirt. With her head on his chest, she could hear the rapid beat of his heart. She put her hand on his arm to make sure her wobbly knees didn't collapse beneath her like the boxes and bags. His pulse jumped at her touch, and his arm around her waist tightened, keeping her close, exactly where her heart wanted her to be.

"Are you okay?" he whispered, his breath swirling along her neck in a gentle caress.

More than okay. She bit back the words before they could seep past her lips. At the same time, she eased away from him. Glancing at the hole in the staircase, she rushed the rest of the way down the stairs, past half-open bags spilling their reeking contents onto the steps.

She couldn't stay there with him. She'd been a fool to linger and let her heart overrule her head. Hadn't she learned that was stupid? Every time she gave in to her heart's yearnings for something it wanted—whether it was to let a much younger Nathaniel know how much he meant to her or to chase adventure with Alvin Lee—she'd ended up humiliated and hurt.

Esther hurried through the barely passable room, not slowing when Nathaniel called after her to make sure she wasn't hurt. She was, but not in the way he meant. It hurt to realize she still couldn't trust her heart.

Nitwit! Nitwit! Nitwit!

The accusation followed her, sounding on every step, as she found her way out of the horrible house. Fresh air struck her, and she drew in a deep, satisfying breath. Maybe it would clear her mind as well as her lungs.

Seeing Jacob trying to close the rear of the buggy, Esther went to help him. It took the two of them shoving down the panel to shut it after he'd squeezed the bags in there.

"All set," she said with a strained smile.

"If you say so…" His voice was taut, and she shoved her problems aside. "I don't think I need all that."

"If you're worried about Nathaniel making room for your things at his house, don't be."

Jacob surprised her by giving her a saucy grin. "I guess you've never been inside the house."

"I was years ago when I was about your age."

"That's a *long* time ago."

She smiled when she realized she was talking about a time before he was born. "Quite a long time ago. His *grossmammi* liked to quilt, so there were always partially finished projects in the living room."

"Not any longer. There wouldn't be room for a quilt!" He started to add more, then halted when Nathaniel pushed his way out of the house and gave the pair of bags to Jacob.

"These are the last of your clothes," he said. "You may have to hold them on your lap because I'm sure the storage area behind the seat is full."

"Let me check to see. I think I can fit these in there."

"Make sure the rear door closes. I don't want a trail of your things from here to Esther's house."

The boy smiled and opened the back. Bags started to spill out, but he shoved them back inside. Tossing the other two on top, he managed to close the door again.

Jacob chattered steadily on the way to the Stoltzfus farm. That allowed Esther to avoid saying anything. Nathaniel was, she noticed, as quiet, though he replied when Jacob posed a question to him. Unlike the swift ride to Titus Fisher's house, the one back seemed too long.

As soon as the buggy stopped in front of the white barn, Esther jumped out. She was surprised when Nathaniel did, too. He told Jacob to wait while he hooked up the mules before Jacob drove the buggy to his farm. She'd assumed Nathaniel would tie the horse and buggy to the rear of his wagon.

"He'll be fine," Nathaniel said, and she knew her thoughts were on her face. "I've had him show me how he drives, and he's better than kids twice his age. From what he's told me, he's been driving his *onkel* to appointments with *doktors* and on other errands for the past six months or more."

She hesitated, then went with him into the barn. "Are you sure? I could drive him."

"Then we'll need to get you back here, and chores won't wait." He smiled. "I'll be right behind him, so he won't get any idea about racing my buggy. Not that he's foolish! The boy has a *gut* head on his shoulders."

His words silenced her. She'd thought she had a *gut* head on her shoulders, too, but she'd let herself get caught up in racing buggies on deserted roads late at night.

Nathaniel must have taken her silence for agreement because he went to the stall where the mules watched them.

As he led Gal out to the wagon, Esther asked, "Have you noticed Jacob never calls Titus's house his home? Only his *onkel*'s?"

"Now that you mention it, I have noticed that. I wonder why."

"He lost one home and one family." She watched Nathaniel put the patient mule into place, checking each strap and buckle to make sure it was right.

Straightening, he said, "Maybe he's afraid of losing another."

"That's sad. No *kind* should have to worry about such things."

"No *kind* should, but many don't have the happy and comfortable childhood you did, Esther." His mouth grew taut, and she got the feeling he'd said something he hadn't intended to.

"But he seems happier and less weighted down since you've taken him under your wing."

"Jacob has had too much sorrow and responsibility." Picking up the reins, he put his hand on the wagon's seat. "*Danki* for your help today, Esther. Let me know what Reuben says."

"I will." She drew in a deep breath, then said something she needed to say. Something that would be for the best for Nathaniel and for her. Something to prevent any misunderstandings between them. The words were bitter on her tongue, but she hurried to say, "I'm glad you're my friend. You've been my friend since we were *kinder*, and I hope you'll be my friend for the rest of our lives." She put her hand out and clasped his. Giving it a squeeze, she started to release it and turn away.

His fingers closed over hers, keeping her where she stood. She looked at him, astonished. Her shock became uncertainty when she saw the intensity in his gaze. Slowly, he brought her one step, then another toward him until they stood no more than a hand's breadth apart. She couldn't look away from his eyes. She longed to discover what he was thinking.

Suddenly she stiffened. What was *she* thinking? Hadn't she decided she needed to make sure he knew friendship was all they should share? She drew her arm away, and after a moment's hesitation he lifted his fingers from hers. At the same moment his eyes shuttered.

"*Ja,*" he said, his voice sounding as if he were waking from a dream. Or maybe her ears made it sound that way because the moment when they'd stood face-to-face had been like something out of time.

"*Ja?*" Had she missed something else he'd said?

"I mean, I'm glad, too. We're always going to be friends." Now he was avoiding her eyes. "It's for the best."

"For us and for Jacob."

"Of course, for Jacob, too." A cool smile settled on his lips. "That's what I meant."

"I know." She took another step away. She couldn't remember ever being less than honest with Nathaniel before.

But it was for his own *gut*.

Right?

That's right, God, isn't it? She had to believe that, but she hadn't guessed facing the truth would be so painful.

"What a sad way for a *kind* to live!" *Mamm* clicked her tongue in dismay as she set her cup of tea on a section of the kitchen table where Esther wasn't working. "I don't know why none of us wondered about the state of the house before. An old bachelor and a young boy. Neither of them knows a lick about keeping a house."

Esther raised her eyes from where she was kneading dough for cinnamon rolls for tomorrow's breakfast. She'd added a cup of raisins to the treat she hadn't made for the family since spring. Now she chased the raisins across the table when they popped out as she folded the dough over and pressed it down. Dusting her hands with more flour so they didn't get stickier, she continued working the dough.

"Jacob never gave us any reason to think his *onkel* wasn't taking *gut* care of him." She beat the dough harder. "He comes to school in clean clothes, and he never smells as if he's skipped a bath."

"Don't take out your frustration on that poor dough." *Mamm* chuckled. "Don't blame yourself for not knowing the truth. None of us did, but now you have the responsibility of letting Reuben know."

"I plan to speak to Reuben. I'll go over once I get the bread finished." She was certain the bishop would know a way to help Jacob and his *onkel* without making either of them feel ashamed. She was as sure the *Leit*, the members of their district, would offer their help.

But where? At Titus's house or Nathaniel's? Jacob had mentioned in passing that the Zook farmhouse was as cluttered as his *onkel*'s. She was astonished. When she'd visited Nathaniel's grandparents during her childhood, the house had been pristine. In fact, he'd joked that no dust mote ever entered because it would die of loneliness. Sometime between then and now, the condition of the house had changed.

"Going to talk to Reuben is a *gut* idea," *Mamm* said, "but I don't think that's necessary."

"What?" Esther looked up quickly and flour exploded from the table in a white cloud. Waving it away, she said, "*Mamm*, we need to do something. Nobody should be living in there." *Or at Nathaniel's if it is also in such a sorry state.*

"You don't need to visit Reuben, because he just pulled into the dooryard."

"Oh." Esther punched the dough a couple more times and then dropped it into the greased bowl she had ready. Putting a towel over it, she opened the oven she'd set to preheat at its lowest temperature. A shallow pan of water sat on the bottom rack, so the dough would stay moist in the gas oven. She put the bowl with the bread dough on the upper rack, checked the kitchen clock and closed the door. The dough needed to rise for an hour.

She began to wash the flour off her hands as her *mamm* went to the back door.

"Reuben, *komm* in," *Mamm* said. "We were talking about Esther paying you a call later today."

The bishop entered and took off the black wool hat he wore when he was on official business. He hung it on one of the empty pegs near *Mamm*'s bonnet. His gray eyebrows matched his hair and were as bushy as his long beard. He wasn't wearing the black coat he used on church Sunday. Instead he was dressed in his everyday work clothes, patched from where he'd snagged them while working on his farm.

"A cup of *kaffi*?" Esther asked as she took another cup from the cupboard. Everyone in the district knew the bishop's weakness for strong *kaffi*.

"*Ja,*" he said in his deep voice. "That sounds *gut.*"

She filled a cup for him from the pot on top of the stove. She set it in front of where he sat at the kitchen table where the top was clean. Taking her *mamm*'s cup, she poured more hot water into it before placing it on the table, as well. She arranged a selection of cookies on a plate for Reuben, who had a sweet tooth.

"Pull up a chair, Esther," Reuben said with a smile. When she did, he said, "Tell me how the boy is doing."

"He seems as happy as he can be under the circumstances." She was amazed she could add with a genuine smile, "Jacob has fallen in love with the alpacas at Nathaniel Zook's farm, and they're pretty much all he thinks about."

"He needs to return to school."

"*Ja.* He'll be back on Monday. I wanted to give him a bit of time to become accustomed to the changes in his life. That also gives me time to work with the other scholars so they understand they need to treat him with extra kindness."

The bishop nodded. "An excellent plan. So tell me what you want to talk to me about."

"When we took Jacob to his *onkel*'s house, Nathaniel and I were disturbed by what we saw there." Esther quickly explained the piles of papers and boxes and everything anyone could collect. She told him about the narrow walkways through the rooms, even the bathroom. "The only place not filled to overflowing is Jacob's bedroom."

Reuben sighed and clasped his fingers around his cup. Letting the steam wash his face, he said, "I shouldn't be surprised. Titus is a *gut* man, but he's never been able to part with a single thing. I understand his *daed* was much the same, so the hoarding is not all his doing. *Danki*, Esther, for caring enough about the Fishers to want to help them. However, I'm not sure if we should do anything until we know what's going to happen with Titus. If it's God's will that he comes home, having his house cleaned out will upset him too much."

"How is he?" *Mamm* asked.

The bishop's face seemed to grow longer. "The *doktors* aren't optimistic. At this point, they can't be sure what his condition will be if he comes out of his coma. One told me he hadn't expected Titus to last through the first night, but he's breathing on his own and his heart remains strong. Is there anything of the man himself left? Nobody can know unless he awakens."

"Jacob will want to know how his *onkel* is doing," Esther said.

"Having the boy visit the hospital now might not be a *gut* idea. I'd rather wait until there's some change in Titus's condition before we inflict the sight of his *onkel*, small and ill in a hospital bed, on the boy."

"Can I tell him nothing's changed?"

"*Ja.*" He took a deep sip of his *kaffi*. "I don't like not telling Jacob the whole truth, but having him worry won't help."

Mamm stared down into her cup. "While we're waiting, we'll pray."

Reuben smiled and patted *Mamm*'s arm. "Putting Titus in God's hands is the best place for him."

"And Jacob, too," Esther said softly around the tears welling in her throat.

"And Jacob, too," repeated the bishop. "We'll need God's guidance in helping him as he faces the days to come."

Chapter Seven

Nathaniel ignored the chilly rain coursing down the kitchen windows as he tapped his pencil against the table. In front of him were columns of numbers he'd written. No matter how he added them, his expenses almost matched his income. The money from the rents on the fields was supposed to tide him over until he could bring in his own harvest next fall.

He wasn't going to have enough. He didn't want to start selling fields to keep from losing everything. If he sold more than one or two, he wouldn't have enough land to keep the farm going.

He could look for someone to loan him enough to get through the winter, spring and summer. Someone in Paradise Springs. He wouldn't ask his parents. They had money put away, but he knew they'd pinched pennies for years hoping his *daed* could retire from the factory in a few years.

There was another reason he couldn't ask his family for help. An unopened envelope sat on the table beside his account book. He didn't need to read it, because he knew his *mamm* was pleading with him again to return to Indiana where *doktors* would be able to help him if "the scourge" returned. He'd told her so many times that he hadn't needed to see an oncologist in six years. She refused to listen to the facts, still too shaken by what he'd gone through to believe the battle against his cancer had been won.

He pushed back his chair, something he was able to do now that he and Jacob had moved more of them into the barn. Leaning on the chair's two rear legs, he raked his fingers through his hair. There must be some way to keep the farm going until the fields produced enough that he didn't have to keep buying feed for the animals.

His *grossmammi* had bought the alpacas. Her mind had not been as muddled at the end of her life as his *grossdawdi*'s apparently had been. She'd intended the herd to be more than pets.

Hadn't she?

Looking across the kitchen, he stood. He paused when he heard footsteps upstairs. He was still getting accustomed to having someone else in the house, but he was glad Jacob was settling in well. Today would be the last school day he was skipping. On Monday, Nathaniel would have him there before Esther rang the bell.

Esther...everything led to her. When he'd held her close as the stair splintered, any thought of Esther the Pester disappeared as he savored the warmth of the woman she'd become. If she hadn't pulled away then—and again at her house—he wasn't sure if he could have resisted the temptation to kiss her. Just once. To see what it would be like. He should be grateful she'd stepped away, because when he was honest with himself, he doubted a single kiss would have been enough.

He couldn't kiss her when he couldn't offer to marry her. Assuming she'd be willing to be his wife, he couldn't ask her. He'd first have to tell her the truth about his inability to give her *kinder*, and he didn't want to see pity in her expressive eyes.

Hochmut. Pride was what it was, and he wasn't ready to admit he wasn't the man he'd hoped to be: a man with dreams—no, expectations—of a home filled with *kinder*.

You could tell her the truth. His conscience spoke with his *grossmammi*'s voice. When he was young, she'd been the one to sit and talk to him about why things were right or wrong. Everyone else laid down the rules and expected him to obey them. Because of that, he shouldn't be surprised her voice was in his head, telling him that he was trying to fool himself.

Nathaniel grumbled under his breath. God had given him this path to walk. *Forgive me, Lord. You have blessed me with life, and I'm grateful.*

He went into the living room and to the bookcase next to his *grossmammi*'s quilting frame. Scanning the lower of the two shelves, he smiled as he drew out a thin black book. It was the accounts book his *grossmammi* had kept until she became ill. When he'd first arrived, he'd scanned its pages and seen something about income from the alpacas in it.

Returning to the kitchen table, he began to flip through it. His eyes narrowed when he noticed a listing for income from the alpacas' wool. He'd assumed they were sheared in the spring, and the dates of the entries in the account book confirmed that.

How did someone shear an alpaca? He'd seen demonstrations of sheepshearing at fairs, but had never seen anyone shear an alpaca. The beasts were bigger and stronger—and more intelligent—than sheep. Three factors that warned it'd be more difficult to shear them.

Jacob came into the kitchen and went to the refrigerator.

He pulled out the jar of church spread and reached for the loaf of bread.

"Hungry already?" Nathaniel asked.

"It's noon."

"Really?" Nathaniel glanced at the clock, startled to see the morning had ended while he was poring over his accounts...and thinking of Esther.

Closing the account book, he stuck his mother's letter in *Grossmammi*'s book to mark the page with the entry about the alpacas' wool. He'd deal with writing back to *Mamm* later, and he'd ask Esther about shearing the alpacas when he and Jacob attended services in her district on Sunday.

"Do you want a sandwich?" asked Jacob as he slathered a generous portion of the sticky, sweet spread on two slices of bread.

Before Nathaniel could reply, a knock came at the kitchen door. Who was out on such a nasty day? Dread sank through him like a boulder in a pool. Was it Reuben or Isaiah with news about Jacob's *onkel*?

Please, God, hold Jacob close to You.

His feet felt as if they had drying concrete clinging to them as he went to the door. He couldn't keep from glancing at the boy. Jacob was moving his knife back and forth on the bread, making patterns in the church spread. The boy tried to look nonchalant, but Nathaniel knew Jacob's thoughts were identical to his own.

Be with him, Lord. He needs You more than ever right now.

Hoping no sign of his thoughts was visible, Nathaniel opened the door. So sure was he that a messenger with bad news would be there that he could only stare at Esther. Her blue eyes sparkled with amusement, and it was as if the clouds had been swept from the sky. A warmth like bright summer sunshine draped over him, easing the bands around his heart, a tautness that had become so familiar he'd forgotten it was there until it loosened. Suddenly he felt as if he could draw a deep breath for the first time in more years than he wanted to count.

"Hi." Esther smiled. "We're here for a sister day."

"You want to have a sister day *here*?" Nathaniel's voice came out in a startled squeak as he looked past Esther, noticing for the first time that she wasn't alone. Behind her were two other women.

They crowded under the small overhang as they tried to get out of the rain. Each carried cleaning supplies, and he heard rain falling into at least one of the plastic buckets. Looking more closely, he realized one of the other women was Esther's older sister Ruth. She hadn't changed much because she'd been pretty much grown when he left Paradise Springs. She was more than a decade older than Esther and very pregnant.

He didn't recognize the younger blonde who was also several years older than Esther. When the woman smiled and introduced herself as Leah Beiler, he wondered why she was involved in a sister day with Esther and Ruth. He didn't want to embarrass her by asking.

"It's a school day," he managed to blurt out.

"Neva is teaching today. I decided I was needed here more than there."

"I don't understand."

"May we come in?" Esther asked, her smile never wavering. "I'll explain once we're out of the rain."

"Of course." He stepped aside so she and the other two women could enter. Hearing footsteps rushing into the front room, he knew Jacob was making himself and his sandwich scarce. Did the boy think his teacher was there to bring the schoolwork he'd missed?

"Do you remember Ruth?" Esther motioned for her sister to come forward. "She offered to help when she heard what I planned to do."

"Danki," he said, not sure why. It seemed the right thing to say.

Ruth, who resembled their *mamm* more than any of the other Stoltzfus *kinder,* nodded as she walked through the kitchen into the even more cluttered living room.

"Leah's already told you her name." Esther put her arm around the blonde's shoulders. "I don't know if you two ever met. The Beilers live on the farm next to ours." Without a pause, she went on, "We thought you could use a little help getting settled in here, Nathaniel."

Her sister grumbled, "It'll take more than a little help."

Esther ignored her and lowered her voice. "Jacob mentioned when we were at Titus's house that yours didn't look much better. I'm glad to see he was exaggerating."

"Not much." He put his hands on the backs of two chairs he'd pushed to one side. "My grandparents accumulated lots of things. I don't remember so many chairs when I came to visit."

"That, as Jacob reminded me the last time we talked, was a very long time ago. How were you to know what was going on while you were far away?"

Was she accusing him of staying away on purpose? When he saw her gentle smile, he knew he was allowing his own guilt at not returning to Paradise Springs while his grandparents were alive trick him into hearing a rebuke where there wasn't one. Except from within himself. For so long his parents had insisted he do nothing to jeopardize his health. He'd begun to feel as if he lived in a cage. The chance to try to make his dream come true had thrown a door open for him, and he'd left for Pennsylvania as soon as he could purchase a ticket.

"Where would you like us to start?" Esther's question yanked him out of his uncomfortable thoughts.

"You really don't need to do this. The boy and I are doing okay."

"I know we don't need to, but we'd like to."

"Really—"

He was halted when Leah smiled and said, "I've known Esther most of her life, and I can tell you that you're not going to change her mind."

"True." He laughed, wondering why he was making such a big deal out of a kindness. "I've noticed that about her, too."

"I'm sure you have." Leah chuckled before taking off her black bonnet and putting it on a chair. Instead of a *kapp*, she wore a dark kerchief over her pale hair.

Esther and her sister had work kerchiefs on, as well. He wasn't surprised when Esther toed off her shoes and stuffed her socks into them. She left them by the door when she picked up her bucket and a mop.

"You need a wife, Nathaniel Zook!" announced Ruth from the living room in her no-nonsense voice. "If you cook as poorly as you keep house, you and the boy will starve."

"I'm an adequate cook. Jacob is fond of church spread sandwiches."

Ruth rolled her eyes. "You can't feed a boy only peanut butter and marshmallow sandwiches."

"I know. Sometimes we have apple butter sandwiches, instead."

When her sister drew in a deep breath to retort, Esther interjected, "He's teasing you." She and Leah laughed, but Ruth frowned at them before she began pushing chairs toward the walls so she could sweep the floor.

Esther went to the sink. Sticking the bucket under the faucet, she started to fill it.

"You'll have to let it run a bit to get hot," he called over the splash of water in the bucket.

She tilted the bucket to let the water flow out. Holding her fingers under the faucet to gauge the temperature, she gave him a cheeky grin. "You need to have Micah come over and put a solar panel or two on your roof. You'll have hot water whenever you want it."

"Are you trying to drum up business for your brother?"

"You know how we Stoltzfuses stick together." She laughed lightly.

He did know that. It had been one of the things he'd first noticed about the family when he was young. Esther and her brothers might spat with each other, but they were a united front if anyone else confronted them. That they'd included him in their bond had been a precious part of his childhood in Paradise Springs.

Esther shooed him out of the kitchen so she and the others could get to work. He paused long enough to collect the sandwich Jacob must have made for him. Not wanting to leave the boy alone in the house with women determined to chase every speck of dirt from it, he called up the stairs. Jacob came running, and they made a hasty retreat to the barn.

"I hope they leave my things alone," the boy said when they walked into the barn and out of the rain.

"Don't worry." Nathaniel winked. "Your bedroom and mine should pass their inspection without them doing any work."

Jacob looked dubious, and Nathaniel swallowed his laugh. After he set the boy to work breaking a bale of hay to feed the horses and the mules, he went to get water for the animals. He stood under the barn's overhang and used the hand pump to fill a pair of buckets.

Hearing feminine laughter through a window opened enough to let air in but not the rain, he easily picked out Esther's lyrical laugh. He couldn't help imagining how it would be to hear such a sound coming from the house day after day. Listening to it would certainly make any work in the barn a lighter task.

"Hey, stop pumping!" cried Jacob from the doorway.

Nathaniel looked down to see water running from the bucket under the spout and washing over his work boots. He quickly released the pump's handle. Pulling the bucket aside, he sloshed more water out.

"Are you okay?" Jacob asked.

"Fine. Just daydreaming."

"About what?"

"Nothing important," he replied, knowing it wasn't a lie because what he'd been imagining wasn't ever going to come true. He needed to work on the dream he could make a reality—saving the farm from being sold. Otherwise, he'd have no choice but to return to Indiana and a life of working at the RV plant. He couldn't envision a much worse fate. He'd be stuck inside and never have the chance to bring plants out of nourishing soil.

And he wouldn't see Esther again.

He tried to pay no attention to the pulse of pain throbbing through him. Picking up the bucket, he walked into the barn. The boy followed, chattering about the alpacas, but Nathaniel didn't hear a single word other than the ones playing through his head. *You've got to make this farm a success.*

Esther wasn't surprised that the attic with its sharply slanting roof was filled with more chairs. What about them had fascinated Nathaniel's grandparents so much?

She wasn't sitting on one. Instead, she perched on a small

stool so she could go through the boxes stacked beside her. Ruth and Leah had gone home an hour ago after leaving the house's two main floors sparkling and clean. Esther had remained behind, because she'd suspected the attic would be overflowing with forgotten things.

She'd found two baseball bats and a well-used glove that needed to be oiled because the leather was cracking. Jacob might put the items to *gut* use. In addition, she'd set a nice propane light to one side for Nathaniel to take downstairs, because it was too heavy for her to carry. If he put it by the small table in the living room, Jacob would have light to do one of the puzzles she'd stacked by the top of the attic stairs. As the weather grew colder and the days shorter, the boy would be confined more and more to the house.

Opening the next box, she peered into it with the help of a small flashlight. She wanted to make sure, before she plunged her hands into it that no spiders had taken up residence inside.

"Finding anything interesting?"

Esther glanced over her shoulder and smiled when she saw Nathaniel on the stairs. His hair was drying unevenly, strands springing out in every direction. He looked as rumpled and dusty as she felt, but she had to admit that looked *gut* on him. And she liked looking.

The thought startled her. Nathaniel was a handsome man, as he'd been a *gut*-looking boy. But she wanted his friendship now. Nothing more. She didn't want to make another mistake with her heart. It hadn't seemed wrong at the time when she discovered that Alvin Lee had loved racing. She'd been seeking an adventure. Exactly as Nathaniel was with his all-or-nothing attitude toward the farm.

She never again wanted the insecurity of wondering if the next dare to race a buggy or have a drink would lead to more trouble than she could get out of. Or of suspecting Alvin Lee might not be honest about being in love with her, despite his glib comments about how she was the one and only girl for him. Or of realizing, almost too late, how much her sense of her self-worth was in jeopardy.

No, she must not be foolish and risk her heart again.

She and Nathaniel must remain just friends.

Right?

She tightened her clasped fingers until she heard her knuckles creak. Why did she have to keep convincing herself?

Making sure she had an innocuous smile in place, she raised her eyes to meet Nathaniel's. "I've found a couple of useful things. I'm not sure I'd describe them as interesting."

"Useful is *gut*." He stepped into the attic but had to bend so he didn't bump his head on the low ceiling. Glancing around, he said, "I've been meaning to come up here to sort things out since I moved back, but somehow the day flies past and I haven't gotten around to it."

"Where's Jacob?"

"In the barn. He's hoping to coax an alpaca to come to him. He's determined. I'll give him that."

"He's patient. One of these days, he'll succeed."

"If anyone can, it'll be him." Nathaniel looked into the box in front of her and grinned. Reaching in, he pulled out a pair of roller skates. He set the pairs of wheels spinning. "I remember these. *Grossdawdi* bought them for me when my parents refused to let us have roller skates. *Mamm* feared we'd break our necks—or get used to going fast so we'd never be content driving a buggy instead of a fast *Englisch* car."

"She thought you'd get what the *kinder* call the need for speed."

He laughed. "*Ja*. My grandparents kept the skates here

and never told my folks about them, though I suspect *Mamm* grew suspicious when I returned home from visits too often with the knees on my trousers ripped. She never asked how I'd torn them, so the skates remained a secret."

"I remember you bringing them to our farm. You and my brothers used to have a great time skating in the barn."

"The only place smooth enough for the wheels other than the road, and your *mamm* wisely wouldn't allow us to play there." He set the skates on the floor beside the box. "Did you ever get a pair of your own?"

"I did. Hand-me-downs from one of my brothers, but I was thrilled to have them so I didn't have to walk to school in the fall and spring." She picked up one skate and appraised it. The black leather shoe wasn't in much better shape than the baseball glove, but with some saddle soap and attention it could be made useful again. "These look close to Jacob's size."

"I'll give them to him if you'll skate with us next Saturday."

"What?"

His eyes twinkled. "Don't pretend you didn't hear me promise your brother—our preacher—I'd make sure Jacob was kept safe. If I'm going to give him these skates, then we should make sure the boy has a place to enjoy them and someone to watch over him so he doesn't get hurt." He grinned. "I'll need someone to show me how to patch his trousers when he tears the knees out of them, too."

"You don't have any skates, do you?"

"I can get a pair. Does your brother sell them at his store?"

She shook her head. "Amos mostly sells food and household goods."

"There must be a shop nearby that sells them. I've seen

quite a few boys and at least three or four men using Roll-erblades to get around."

"Why don't you ask Amos? He usually knows where to send his customers for items he doesn't carry." She set the wheels on the skate spinning and grinned. "I used to love roller skating."

"Do you still have your skates?"

"Not the ones from back then. They were about the same size as these." She laughed as she held one against her foot. "My feet have grown since then. Besides, I don't skate any longer."

"Too grown-up?" he asked with a teasing smile, but she heard an undertone of serious curiosity in the question.

"Too busy to stay in practice."

He took the skate from her and set it next to the baseball bat. When he looked at her, his smile was gone. "I should have said this first thing. *Danki* for having your sister day here. I'm amazed at what you did downstairs in a few hours. Everything is clean, and many of the chairs are gone. Where did you put them?"

"Leah and I took most down to the cellar. We stacked the ones that would stack. The rest are out of the way behind the racks where your *grossmammi* stored her canned goods."

"*Danki*. That's a *gut* place for them until I can start donating them to mud sales in the spring."

"You may be able to get rid of them before then. Isaiah mentioned at supper last night that plans are being made for a community fund-raiser to help pay for Titus's hospital bills."

"I'd be glad to give the chairs to such a *gut* cause."

"I'll let him know."

He studied the attic again. "I should have known you'd be up here. You always liked poking around here when you and your brothers came over to play."

"Your *grossmammi* enjoyed having someone who'd listen to her stories about your ancestors who lived here long before she was born."

He squatted beside her. "Do you remember those stories?"

"A few."

"Would you share them with me?"

"Now?"

"No." His voice softened, drawing her eyes toward him. "Sometime when I can write down what you remember."

"You don't remember her stories?"

"I didn't listen." His mouth twisted in a wry grin. "I was too busy thinking of the mischief I could get into next to worry about long-dead relatives." His gaze swept the attic before meeting hers. "Now I'd give almost anything to hear her tell those stories again."

Her hand reached out to his damp cheek. He leaned against it, but his eyes continued to search hers. What did he hope to see? The answers to his questions? She doubted she recalled enough of his *grossmammi*'s stories to ease his curiosity.

"We learn too late to value what we have," he whispered. "By then, it may be lost to us forever."

Were they still talking about his *grossmammi*'s stories? She wasn't sure, and when he ran a single fingertip along her cheek, she quivered beneath his questioning touch. His finger slid down her neck, setting her skin trembling in anticipation of his caress. When his hand curved around her nape, he tilted her lips toward his.

A warning voice in her mind shouted for her to pull back, stand, leave, anything but move closer to him. She heard it as if from a great distance. All that existed were his dark eyes and warm breath enticing her nearer.

"Nathaniel, *komm* now!" Jacob exploded into the attic. He

bounced from one foot to the other in his anxiety. Water pooled on the floor beneath him.

Esther drew away, blinking as if waking from a *wunderbaar* dream. She came to her feet when Nathaniel did. He glanced at her, but she looked away. She wasn't sure if she was more distressed because she'd almost succumbed to his touch or because they'd been interrupted.

Jacob's face was as gray as the storm clouds. What was wrong? She peered out the attic window. Through the thick curtain of rain, no other buggies were in sight, so Jacob couldn't have received any news about his *onkel*.

Nathaniel asked what was wrong in a voice far calmer than she could have managed, and the boy began to talk so quickly his words tumbled over one another, making his answer unintelligible. She thought she picked out a few phrases, but they didn't make sense.

...in the side of the barn...

...just missed...

Hurry!

The last he repeated over and over as they followed him downstairs and outside.

What had happened?

Chapter Eight

Wind-driven rain struck her face like dozens of icy needles, but Esther didn't return to the house for her bonnet or shawl. She ran to keep up with Jacob and Nathaniel. The boy didn't slow as he reached the barn. Throwing open the door, he vanished inside.

The interior of the barn was darker than the rainy day. Scents of hay and animals were thick, but not unpleasant. She blinked to get her eyes to adjust to the dimness, glad the roof didn't leak. Seeing Jacob rush through the door leading outside toward the pasture where the alpacas were kept, she swallowed a groan, ducked her head and followed.

The rain seemed chillier and the wind more ferocious. It tugged at her bandanna, and she put a hand on it to keep the square from flying off.

Looking over his shoulder, Jacob motioned for them to hurry. He ran toward the alpacas, for the first time not being cautious with them. The frightened creatures scattered like a group of marbles struck at the beginning of a game. At the far end of the field, they gathered together so closely they looked like a single multiheaded creature. Something must be horribly wrong for Jacob to act like this.

Her foot slipped on the wet grass, and she slowed to get her balance. Ahead of her, Nathaniel had caught up with the boy.

"Here! See it?" Jacob pointed at the side of the alpacas' shed.

She heard Nathaniel gasp. She ran faster and slid to a stop when she saw what the boy was pointing to.

An arrow! An arrow was protruding from the side of the small building. She choked on a gasp of her own.

Whirling, she ran into the shed. The steel point of the arrowhead protruded from the wall. She didn't touch it, knowing the point would be as sharp as a freshly honed razor.

She came back outside to see Nathaniel pulling the arrow out of the shed. He held it carefully and scanned the fields around the house and barn. She did, too, squinting through the rain trying to blind her.

"Where did it come from?" Nathaniel mused aloud.

"Probably a deer hunter," she said.

"They shouldn't be firing close to the alpacas."

She scowled. "I doubt it was *close* to the alpacas. More likely, someone was aiming *at* your herd. The light brown ones are fairly close to the color of a deer."

When Jacob cried out in horror, she regretted her words. Why hadn't she thought before she'd spoken?

"They don't have antlers, and they're not the same shape or size as a deer." Jacob looked at Nathaniel for him to back up his assertion.

She selected her words carefully, not wanting to upset the boy—or Nathaniel—more. "At this time of year, archers can shoot does as well as bucks. Irresponsible, over-eager hunters have been known to shoot at anything that moves. Ezra always has his Brown Swiss cows in a pasture next to the barn during archery season. Once the hunters can use guns, he brings the whole herd inside for the winter."

"You're joking." Nathaniel put his arm around Jacob's shoulders, and she noticed how the boy was shaking.

With fear or fury? Maybe both.

"No," she replied with a sad smile. "Some hunters shouldn't be allowed to hunt because they don't take the proper precautions when they're in the woods or traipsing across the fields. They ignore farmland posted No Trespassing. They're a danger to themselves and everyone else. Don't you remember how it was when you lived here years ago? Every fall someone loses a dog or some other animal because of clueless hunters."

"I remember."

"To be honest, we count ourselves blessed when no *person* is hurt or killed." With a sigh, she wiped rain out of her hair. "Right now, we need to check the herd and make sure none of them was hit. As frightened as they are, clumped together, it's impossible to tell if one is bleeding."

"Bleeding?" cried Jacob. "No!"

Nathaniel put his hand on the boy's shoulder. "Let's pray they're fine. But we need to check them. Do you remember how Esther got the alpacas into the shed?"

Jacob nodded.

"*Gut.* I'll need your help and Esther's, so we can examine them. They'll have to stay in until…" He looked at her.

"Until mid-December," she said. "I'm not exactly sure when hunting season is over, but I can check with Ezra. He'll know."

"That's a long time," Jacob grumbled. "The alpacas like being outside."

"When they can come out again, it'll be nice and cool." Nathaniel smiled. "With their wool getting thicker, they'll be more comfortable then."

Jacob jumped to another subject with the innocence of a *kind*. He pointed to the arrow Nathaniel still held. "Can I have that?"

Nathaniel didn't wait for Esther to reply. Though she'd be cautious with the boy—after all, she seemed to be cautious with everything now—he didn't want to delay getting the alpacas into the barn. Not just the herd, but Esther and Jacob, too. The hunter might still be nearby and decide to try another shot at the "deer."

With a smile, he said, "I'll give you its feathers, Jacob. How's that?"

"Great!" His grin reappeared as if nothing out of the ordinary had happened.

"Let's get the alpacas inside first."

"Okay." He ran to get the two branches Nathaniel used to move the alpacas.

"Well done," Esther said quietly, and he knew she didn't want Jacob to overhear. "He can't hurt himself with feathers. If he had the arrow, he'd be sure to nick himself."

"I'll make sure it gets disposed of where no *kinder* can find it."

"*Gut.* There can't be any chance Jacob will decide to see if he can make it fly."

"As we would have?"

She scowled. "We were foolish *kinder* back then. I've learned it's better to err on the side of caution."

"You?" He began to laugh, then halted when she didn't join in.

"*Ja.* I don't know why you find it hard to believe."

He could have given her a dozen reasons, but she walked away before he could speak. Pushing his wet hair out of his eyes, he watched as she took the branches from Jacob and sent the boy running to open the barn door.

What had changed Esther so much? It was more than the fact that she'd grown up. He had, too, especially after facing cancer, but he hadn't lost his love of the occasional adventure. Yet whenever he hinted at fun, she acted as if he'd suggested something scandalous. What had happened to her, and why was she keeping it a secret?

Her shout for him to get inside with Jacob so the alpacas didn't see them spurred him to action. As he went into the barn, making sure the door was propped open, he saw the alpacas milling about, frightened and more uncooperative than they'd been since he'd arrived at the farm.

More quickly than he'd have guessed she could, she moved the herd into the pen at one side of the barn. He closed the door and dropped the bar, locking it into place so the alpacas couldn't push against the door and escape.

Esther moved among them, talking softly. She might be perturbed with him, but she was gentle with the terrified beasts. While she checked the alpacas in the center of the herd, he and Jacob walked around the outside, keeping the creatures from fleeing to the corners of the pen before she could look at them.

Nearly a half hour later, she edged out of the herd and motioned for him and Jacob to step back. The alpacas turned as one. They rushed toward the door, halting when they realized the opening was gone. Moving along the wall, they searched for it.

"They'll calm down soon." Esther wiped her apron. It was covered with bits of wool and debris that had been twisted into the alpacas' coats. "Are you going to let the police know what happened?"

Nathaniel couldn't hide his shock because the Amish didn't involve outsiders unless it was a true emergency. "Why? Nobody was hurt."

"This time."

He shook his head. "I won't go to the police without alerting Reuben and my district's preachers first."

"Talk to them. No one was hurt this time, but someone fired off an arrow without thinking of where it could fly." She glanced at Jacob, who was watching the alpacas intently, but didn't speak his name.

There was no need. He understood what she hadn't said. Jacob was near the alpacas whenever he could be. A careless shot could strike him. Nathaniel needed to protect the boy who was his responsibility while his *onkel* was in the hospital.

As if the boy had guessed the course of his thoughts, Jacob asked, "Can I take the feathers and show them to *Onkel* Titus?"

This time, Nathaniel didn't have a swift answer. He thanked God that Esther spoke in a tone suggesting it was a question she'd expected, "As soon as the *doktors* say we can visit the hospital, you can take the feathers and tell your *onkel* about today."

"He'll be proud of me for not pulling out the arrow myself." The boy grinned.

"*Ja*, he will."

"He says no one should handle any weapon until they've learned how to use it the right way."

"Your *onkel* is a wise man." She returned his smile, and Nathaniel tried to do the same, though the expression felt like a gruesome mask.

"Because he's old." Jacob spoke with the certainty of his

eight years. "He's had lots of time to learn." He pulled his gaze from the alpacas, which were already less frantic, and glanced over his shoulder. "That's what he tells me when I make a mistake or touch his stuff when I know I shouldn't."

Esther's smile grew taut, and Nathaniel gave up any attempt at one. Every time the boy mentioned his *onkel*'s obsession with those piles of junk, Nathaniel was torn between hugging the boy and wishing he could remind Titus that Jacob was more important than any metal or broken wood.

Jacob began to croon to the animals, but they wouldn't come closer to him. He whirled in frustration, his fists tight by his sides, and stomped his foot. At the sound, the alpacas turned and fled to the farthest corner of the barn. The boy's face fell from annoyance to dismay.

"Why don't they like me?" he asked.

Esther gave him a gentle smile. "They don't know you yet."

"I come out here every day. I help Nathaniel feed them. I make sure they have plenty of water. Why can't they see I won't hurt them?"

"Alpacas take a long time to trust someone. You have to be patient, Jacob."

"I have been."

"They still don't trust me completely," said Nathaniel, "and I was taking care of them for more than a month before you came here."

Crestfallen, Jacob nodded. "I wish they liked me."

"If you give them time, they may," Esther said.

"I want her to like me." He pointed to a light brown female. "I want her to like me before she has her *boppli*."

"How do you know she's pregnant?"

"She told me." He grinned. "Not with words. I'm not out of my mind, no matter what other kids say. She told me by the way she looks. Like our dog did when she was going to have puppies."

"How is that?" Nathaniel asked.

"Her belly moves, and I know it's the *boppli* waiting to be born."

Esther patted Jacob's shoulder. "You're right, but you need to know one thing. Newborn alpacas are called crias."

"Why?"

"From what I've read, it's because the little ones make a sound like a human *boppli*. The word is based on a Spanish one, which explorers used when they first visited the mountains in South America where alpacas come from."

He nodded and said the word slowly as if testing out how it felt. "Cria. I like that. She's not the only one going to have a cria, is she?"

"I'd say there are at least five pregnant females."

"Are you sure?" Nathaniel looked from the boy to her. How would he ever make the farm a success if he'd failed to see something obvious to an eight-year-old boy?

"Not completely." Esther put her hand on the wall. "You should have Doc Anstine stop by and look at them. He provided *gut* care for my alpacas, so he's familiar with their health needs."

Jacob grinned at Nathaniel. "Can I have one to raise by myself?"

"You need to see if the *mamm* alpacas are willing to let us near their crias."

"But if they will...?"

Nathaniel wanted to say *ja*, but he couldn't think of the alpacas and their offspring as pets. They might be the single way to save his grandparents' farm. On the other hand, he didn't want to crush Jacob's hopes.

Slender fingers settled on his sleeve, and he saw Esther shake her head slightly. How could what he was thinking be transparent to her, when he had no idea what secrets she was keeping from him?

You're keeping a big secret from her, too. His conscience refused to be silent, and he knew the futility of trying to ignore it. Now it was warning him of the dangers of ferreting out secrets better left alone.

"Let's talk about this later," Esther said, breaking into his thoughts. "Right now, will you watch the alpacas for Nathaniel?"

Jacob nodded, a brilliant smile on his face. "*Ja.* Maybe if they see me here, they'll know they're okay."

"You're right. What they need right now is what's familiar to them." She patted the boy's arm. "Stay with them ten or fifteen minutes, then come to the house. By the time you return later to make sure they're settled for the night, they should be fine. They may not know you kept them safe today, Jacob, but I know Nathaniel is grateful for your quick thinking."

"I am," Nathaniel said as the boy positively glowed. "The alpacas are important to me."

"Because they belonged to your *grossmammi*?" The boy hesitated, then reached into a pocket in his trousers. He pulled out a round disk. A yo-yo, Nathaniel realized. "This belonged to my *grossmammi*, and she gave it to my *daed* when he was a little boy. That's what my *mamm* told me." He stroked the wood that once had been painted a bright red. Only a few hints of paint remained. "My *onkel* owns a lot of stuff. He gave me some stuff of my own like my baseball and books. This is all I have that once belonged to my *grossmammi* and my *daed*."

The sight of the boy holding his single connection to the parents who had been taken from him by a drunk driver twisted Nathaniel's heart. Beside him, he heard Esther make a soft sound that might have been a smothered sob.

Knowing he must say something to the boy who had allowed them to see a portion of his pain, Nathaniel asked, "Do you always carry it in your pocket?"

"Not always." He shot a guilty glance at Esther. "I don't like others touching it, and I didn't know how much cleaning would be done in my room."

"Why don't you run and put it in your dresser drawer, so it doesn't get lost?"

"But the alpacas—"

"I'll stay here until you get back." He forced a grin. "I'll try not to upset them too much."

Jacob shoved the yo-yo into his pocket and bolted out of the barn.

By the pen, Esther wiped away tears she'd tried to hide from the boy. She gave Nathaniel a watery smile. "He'll be right back. I don't think he trusts you with *his* alpacas."

"I think you're right."

"He trusts you." She pushed away from the railing. Walking toward him, she said, "He showed you his most precious possession."

"And you, too."

She shook her head, and several light brown strands of her hair tumbled from beneath her kerchief. "No. If he trusted me, he wouldn't have put the toy in his pocket to make sure it was safe. Besides, I'm his teacher. You're his friend. He's learned he can depend on you."

"He'll come to see you're someone he can rely on, too." He stared at the long, damp curls along her neck. They appeared as silken as the alpacas' wool, and his fingers tingled at the thought of winding those vagrant tresses around them.

Pulling his gaze from them, he found his eyes lock with

her pretty blue ones. They glistened with residual tears for the boy, but he saw other emotions, as well. Would she ever look at him with the longing he felt whenever she was close, a longing to hold her? Suddenly he found himself wondering if her eyes would close, brushing her long lashes on her soft cheeks, as he bent to kiss her.

No! He couldn't take advantage of her. She was unsteady in the wake of Jacob's confession…as he was.

He clasped his hands behind him before he pulled her close as he'd started to do in the attic before Jacob intruded. "One thing I can rely on is you. You're a *gut* friend, Esther Stoltzfus."

She didn't look at him as she said, "*Danki*. So are you." She stuffed her hair under her kerchief and headed toward the barn's main door. She didn't add anything else before she opened the door and was gone, leaving him more confused than ever.

When Nathaniel walked into Amos Stoltzfus's store, it was busy. Amos's customers hurried to get their errands and chores done before day's end. Tomorrow would be a day of worship, and no work, other than the necessary tasks of caring for farm animals, could be done.

In the midst of all the activity, Amos moved with a purposeful calm. He lifted a box down from a high shelf for an elderly man, who'd been standing on tiptoe to try to reach it on his own, though a pair of box grippers hung from a brad at the end of the aisle. He answered a *kind*'s question as if it were the most important thing he'd do all day.

Nathaniel smiled. There was no doubt Amos was a Stoltzfus. Not only did he have the brothers' height, something they didn't share with petite Esther, but he had the same sense of humor. He left everyone he spoke with either smiling or laughing. The Stoltzfus brothers seemed to have an ability to make others feel better...as Esther did, too. Nathaniel doubted any of them realized what a special gift they'd been given. It was simply a part of them.

"Nate—Nathaniel!" Amos grinned. "I'll get it right one of these days."

"As I told your *mamm*, it doesn't matter which name you use."

"What can I help you with?" He wiped his hands on his apron that was stained with a multitude of colors.

"I'm looking for roller skates." He'd planned to buy a pair last week, but the days had hurried past, each one busier than the preceding one. Between caring for his animals, trying to keep the house in some sort of order and taking Jacob to school, he hadn't had a second to call his own. Only because Neva, Esther's assistant teacher, had come over to the house today to help Jacob with the schoolwork he'd missed had Nathaniel been able to come to the Stoltzfus Family Shops alone. "Do you sell them?"

He shook his head. "You might try the bicycle shop on Route 30. It's not far from the post office. Someone told me they had a small selection. Otherwise, the closest place I know of is an *Englisch* shop near the Rockvale Outlets in Lancaster, and that'll take you about a half hour drive with heavy traffic each way. The *Englischers* are already swarming on the outlets for Christmas shopping."

"It's only October."

"I know." Amos shrugged and then chuckled. "Apparently they want bragging rights to being the first one done. Traffic is really hectic this time of year."

"*Danki* for the warning. I think I'll check the bicycle shop." He started to turn to leave, so Amos could assist his other customers. When Amos spoke his name, Nathaniel paused.

"Esther tells me the boy has settled in well at your farm. If you ever need some time to yourself, he's welcome to stay at our house."

"I know, but right now some stability is the best thing for him."

"If you change your mind—"

"Danki." He let a smile spread across his face. "But think about it, Amos. Would you have wanted to stay at your teacher's house?"

With a roar of laughter, Amos clapped him on the shoulder. "That's putting it in perspective." He was kept chuckling as he turned to help a woman Nathaniel didn't recognize find a particular spice she needed.

Nathaniel walked out, hoping he had enough time to get to the other shop and back to the farm before Neva had to leave. His life was hectic now, but he wouldn't have it any other way. He still needed to talk to Esther about shearing the alpacas so he could have cash to keep the farm going until next fall's harvest. If the alpacas' wool wasn't the solution, he wasn't sure where he'd turn next. He knew he couldn't return defeated to Indiana. Not only would his parents again smother him in an attempt to protect him, but he'd have to say goodbye to Esther.

He didn't want to face either.

Chapter Nine

The Sunday service was almost over. Esther saw two *mamms* with new *bopplin* slip back into the room. Little ones seldom could remain quiet for the full three hours of the service. The *mamms* had to inch through to sit among the other women because the church benches were closer together than usual. It was always a tight squeeze at the Huyard house.

Marlin Wagler, the district's deacon, stood to make announcements. First, as he did each church Sunday, he announced which family would be hosting the district's next service. Then he paused and glanced around the room.

Esther held her breath as the room grew so silent breathing would have seemed loud. This time of year there was an air of suspense during announcements. Secret engagements were made public along with letting the *Leit* know the couple's wedding date and who would be invited. She glanced around the room, trying to see who, besides her brother Ezra, wasn't there. When Ezra had stuttered over an excuse not to drive them to the Huyards' this morning, she'd guessed his and Leah's wedding plans were going to be published today. That was confirmed when Esther noticed Leah was missing, as well. It was traditional that an engaged couple didn't attend the service when their wedding was announced.

Anyone else?

Her search of the room came to an abrupt halt when her gaze was caught by Nathaniel's. Dressed in his Sunday *mutze*, he looked more handsome than usual. The black frock coat made his hair appear darker, something she hadn't guessed was possible. She noticed how the coat strained across his shoulders and guessed the hard work he was doing on the farm was adding to his already sturdy muscles.

She looked hastily away, not wanting anyone to notice how she was staring at him. But she couldn't keep from peeking out from beneath her lashes to watch him. He was scanning the rows where the women sat. Was he trying to figure out who was missing, too?

Or was he considering which single woman he might choose as a bride? That thought sliced through her like a well-honed knife, but she couldn't ignore the truth. He was in Paradise Springs to rebuild the family's farm. Why would he do that unless he planned to marry in the hopes of having a son to take over the farm when he was ready to retire? He needed someone who loved adventures and challenges, because she knew every day with him would be one.

That woman wasn't Esther Stoltzfus. When she told him she no longer roller-skated, Nathaniel had seemed to get the idea her days of seeking out adventures were in the past. Warmth crawled up her face when she recalled how the conversation between them in the attic ended. She shouldn't have touched him. That was too bold for the woman she wanted to be, but was it wrong to reach out when a friend was troubled? It was when thoughts of friendship had vanished as his fingers danced along her skin, setting it to sparkling like stars in a moonless sky. Then she'd watched his mouth coming closer to hers for a kiss.

In the open area between the benches, the deacon cleared his throat. The sound cut through Esther's reverie and brought her back to reality. A reality where she and Nathaniel were friends.

"Ezra Stoltzfus and Leah Beiler have come to me with their intention to marry," Marlin boomed over a *boppli*'s cries. "They've asked to be in our prayers, so please keep them in yours today and from this day forward."

Esther watched as *Mamm* stood to announce the date of the wedding. Her eyes were bright with tears, but Esther couldn't be sure if they were happy ones or if *Mamm* was thinking that it should have been *Daed* sharing the information today.

"Everyone is invited," *Mamm* said with a broad smile as she looked around the room, "no matter their age. Please pray the weather will be fine so we don't have to hold the wedding dinner in the barn."

That brought laughter from the adults and eager grins from the *kinder*. Many weddings restricted the age of the guests because there wasn't enough room for youngsters to be served along with the adults. Then some people couldn't attend because they had to stay home with the *kinder*.

Two other weddings were published, both for two days after Ezra and Leah's. There weren't enough Tuesdays and Thursdays, the days when the ceremonies were held, during the wedding season, so there were always conflicts. Esther was delighted there wouldn't be another wedding in their district on the day of her brother's wedding.

With a final prayer, the service came to a close. She went to the kitchen with half a dozen women to help serve the cold meats and sandwiches that had been prepared for their midday meal. The men and older boys rearranged the church benches as tables and seats for lunch. They would eat first, and then the women, girls and younger *kinder* would have their turn. The girls were watching the smaller kids run around while they got rid of some of the energy that had been bottled up during the long service.

Esther grinned as her *mamm* accepted *gut* wishes on the upcoming wedding. Volunteers came forward to promise to help with cooking and serving as well as cleaning up. Everyone enjoyed playing a part in a wedding, no matter how big or small the task might be.

By the time she'd eaten and helped wash the dishes, Esther suspected she'd heard about every possible amusing story of past weddings. She wiped her hands on a damp towel and went outside for some fresh air.

The afternoon was surprisingly balmy after the chill of the previous week. Not needing her shawl, she draped it over her arm as she walked toward a picnic table beneath a pair of large maples. In the summer, their broad branches offered shade for half the yard.

She sat, leaning against the table as she stretched out her legs. Hearing childish shouts, she smiled when she saw a trio of boys running toward the barn. Two were the younger Huyard boys, and the third was Jacob. He was joining in their game as if he always played with other *kinder*. They were laughing and calling to each other as they disappeared around the far side of the barn.

She closed her eyes, sending up a grateful prayer. Today, at least for now, Jacob was being a *kind*. It was a gift from God who was bringing him healing.

Even that simple prayer was difficult to complete, though it came directly from her heart, because her mind was filled with the work needing to be done before the wedding day. Perhaps Neva could fill in for her afternoons, so Esther could help *Mamm* and Leah and Leah's *mamm* get everything prepared. She'd been much younger when her oldest siblings married, and when her brother Joshua had wed for the second time earlier in the year it had been a simpler celebration.

Would it be her turn one day? She almost laughed at the question. When she considered the single men in the district, she couldn't imagine one she'd want to marry and spend the rest of her life with. Most of them thought of her as "one of the boys," as they had when they were *kinder*. They laughed with her and talked about the mischief they'd shared, but when it came time to select a girl to walk out with, they looked at the girls who'd spent their childhoods learning a wife's skills instead of climbing trees and racing across fields.

Was that why she'd fallen hard for Alvin Lee when he asked her to ride in his buggy the first time? He'd come to Paradise Springs about five years ago, so he hadn't known her as a *kind*. She'd been flattered by his attention, but when he raced his buggy she knew she should tell him she wanted no part of such sport. Instead she'd remained silent, telling herself she didn't want to look like a coward. The truth was she hadn't wanted to lose the one boy who might be able to look past her tomboy past.

She'd learned her lesson. It'd be better to remain a *maedel* the rest of her life than to offer her heart to someone who didn't want it. If she could find someone who could love her as she was...

Nathaniel's face filled her mind, but she pushed it away. He was risking everything on making his family's farm prosperous once again. Though she admired his dream, as she'd discovered with Alvin Lee, when a man focused obsessively on a goal—whether it was a successful farm or the best racing buggy in the county—everything and everyone else was dispensable.

She wouldn't let herself be cast off like the junk in Titus Fisher's house. Not ever again.

Nathaniel walked back from helping Jacob and the other boys set up a temporary ball field behind the barn. He saw Esther sitting alone at the picnic table. During the meal, she and Wanda had been asked question after question about the upcoming wedding. Esther had answered many of them, giving her *mamm* a slight respite.

Now she was alone.

He sat on the other end of the bench. It shifted beneath him, and her eyes popped open. She looked at him in surprise, and he wondered how far away her thoughts had been.

"Hiding?" he asked with a grin.

"In plain sight?" She half turned on the bench to face him, her elbow resting on the table. "Just thinking. Mostly about the things we need to get done before the wedding."

"Nobody seemed surprised by the announcement."

She chuckled. "It's hardly unexpected. I'm happy it's finally coming to pass."

"*Gut* things come to those who wait."

"I can't believe that's coming out of *your* mouth! You never were willing to wait for anything."

"Look who's talking!" He grinned. "Esther the Pester never waited for anything, either."

"Oh!" she gasped, her blue eyes widening. "I'd forgotten that horrible name! Don't mention it in front of Micah and Daniel. They'll start using it again."

With an easy grin, he said, "I won't, but it's not such a bad nickname."

"It is when you're trying to keep up with three older boys who sometimes didn't want you around."

"Not true." His voice deepened, and his smile faded. "I liked having you around, Esther. When I went to Indiana, you were what I missed most. Not my home, not my grandparents, not the twins. You."

"I missed you, too." Her gaze shifted, and he wondered what she was trying to hide. "You're here now, and you're helping Jacob. I saw him playing with the other *kinder*."

"I may have let him assume the alpacas might get along with him better if he could get along with his schoolmates."

"You didn't!" She laughed, the disquiet fading from her eyes. "Whatever he assumed, it's *gut* to see him acting like a normal *kind*."

Nathaniel grimaced. "Wouldn't a normal *kind* be curious about how his *onkel* is doing? It's been more than two weeks since Titus was taken to the hospital, and Jacob has barely expressed interest in going there. He speaks fondly of his *onkel*, so I'm surprised he doesn't want to see him."

"Don't forget Jacob was in the hospital for almost a month in the wake of the accident."

"I hadn't considered that."

"I don't know any way you could use his determination to have the alpacas accept him ease *that* problem."

He smiled, then said, "Speaking of the alpacas, what can you tell me about shearing them?"

"Only what I've read and observed. I've got a book at home that explains how an alpaca is sheared." She gave him a wry grin and folded her fingers on her lap. "Not that I ever attempted it myself. I took mine to a neighbor's farm when their sheep were sheared, and the men handled it when they were done with the flock. I let them keep the wool in exchange for their work. They seemed to think it was a fair exchange."

"How long did it take them to shear your alpacas?"

"Not long. Maybe ten minutes each or less."

"So quickly?" His hopes that the alpacas' wool might be the way to fund the farm until the harvest deflated. "I guess the wool isn't worth much."

"I didn't have enough to make it worthwhile to try to sell it on my own. With your herd of alpacas, you should be able to do well. This past spring, the best wool was selling for over twenty dollars a pound. The next quality level down sells for around fifteen dollars a pound."

He stared at her in amazement. "How do you know that?"

"I'd been thinking of getting a small herd of my own. Ezra has pastures I can use. I'd started collecting information about income and expenses, but I had to set it aside to begin the school year."

"You've never said anything about that."

"You never asked." She grinned the slow, slightly mischievous smile that always made his heart beat quickly.

"True." He tapped his chin with his forefinger. "I never guessed their wool would be so valuable."

"Alpaca's wool doesn't contain lanolin, so people who are allergic to sheep's wool can wear it. The cleaner the wool, the better price you can get for it."

"How do I keep it clean?"

"Some people put thin blankets over their alpacas to keep the wool as clean as possible."

"Like a horse's blanket?" He tried to imagine buckling a blanket around a skittish alpaca.

"*Ja*, but smaller and lighter. The covers have to be adjusted as the wool grows, so the fibers stay straight and strong."

"I should have guessed a teacher would have done her reading on this."

She raised her hands and shrugged. With a laugh, she rested her elbow on the table again. That left her fingers only inches from him. If he put his hand over hers, how would she react?

Stop it! he ordered himself. *How many more ways can she make it clear she wants to be friends and nothing more?*

"Looking up things in books is as natural to me as breathing," she said, drawing his attention from her slender fingers to her words. "I saw a bunch of books behind the chairs at your house. Could any of them help you?"

"I never noticed them until the chairs were moved, but I didn't find anything about alpacas."

"You're welcome to borrow the few I've collected."

"*Danki.* I—"

"Nathaniel! Esther! *Komm!*" called one of the Huyard boys. He, his younger brother and Jacob raced toward them, their faces alight with excitement.

The boy who'd shouted grabbed Esther's hand, and Jacob and the other boy seized Nathaniel's. Pleading with them to join in the softball game because the *kinder* needed more players, they tugged on the two adults.

She laughed and said, "You want us to play so you can strike me out again, Clarence."

The older boy grinned. "We'll take it easy on you."

"No, we won't," asserted his younger brother. "That wouldn't be fair, and we have to be fair. That's what you always say, Esther."

"*Ja,* I do. Milo is very, very serious about playing ball," Esther said with another chuckle as she stood. "Do you want to play, too, Nathaniel?" She held out her hand to him.

For a second, he was transported to the days when the

Stoltzfus *kinder* had been his playmates. How many times had Esther stood as she was now, her hand stretched out to him as she asked him to take part in a game or an exploration in the woods or an adventure born from her imagination?

"Of course," he said as he would have then, but now it was because he wanted to see the excitement remain in her scintillating eyes.

When the two boys grabbed his hands again and pulled him to his feet, he walked with them and Esther to where other *kinder* were choosing teams. Soon the game began with Esther pitching for one side and he for the other. Nobody bothered to keep score as laughter and cheers filled the afternoon air.

One of the girls on his team hit a ball long enough for a home run. When she ran around the bases and to home plate, he held up his hand to give her a high five. Instead she threw her arms around him and hugged him in her excitement.

"This is the best day ever!" she shouted.

"*Ja,*" he replied, looking at where Esther was bouncing the ball and getting ready for the next batter. Her smile was warm as she urged her team not to get discouraged. When her gaze focused again on home plate, his eyes caught it and held it. Her expression grew softer as if it were especially for him. More to himself than the girl, he repeated, "*Ja.* It's a *gut* day. The very best day ever."

Chapter Ten

Esther had planned to go home from the Huyards' with *Mamm*, but stayed for the evening's singing when *Mamm* insisted she wanted some time to talk with Ezra and Leah about the wedding alone. They were waiting at the house.

"You'll be able to get a ride home with someone else," *Mamm* said, her eyes twinkling. "The Huyards have invited Jacob to stay with them and their *kinder* tonight, so Nathaniel doesn't have to bring him to school in the morning. Jacob is excited, and Nathaniel can have an evening without worrying about the boy. See how well that's working out?"

"*Ja.*" She didn't add anything else. Telling *Mamm* to stop her matchmaking would be rude. Her *mamm* wanted all her *kinder* to be happily married.

She didn't want to be matched with Nathaniel. Right? Why did she keep thinking about riding in his buggy without Jacob sitting between them? The quiet night with only the sound of buggy wheels and horseshoes to intrude, a blanket over their laps to ward off the cold…his arm around her. She could lean her head against his shoulder and listen to his voice echo in his chest as he spoke.

She ejected those too-enticing thoughts from her mind. It'd be better if she just thought about the singing that had already started. From across the yard she could hear voices, which didn't sing as slow as during the church service. Going to a singing was the perfect way to end a church Sunday. As the weather worsened with the coming of winter, many singings would be canceled so people could get home before dark.

The barn doors were thrown wide open. Inside, propane lights set on long tables and on the floor sent bright light in every direction. A trio of tables to one side held snacks. Most of the singers had chosen a place on either side of the long tables. Couples who were walking out together sat across from each other so they could flirt during the songs.

Esther paused outside the crescent of light by the doorway, not wanting to intrude on the song. She wrapped her arms around herself as the breeze blew a chill across her skin.

"Are you going in or not?" asked Nathaniel as he stopped next to her.

"I could ask you the same thing."

"*Ja*, you could. They don't need me croaking like a dying frog in time with the music." He rubbed his right shoulder and grinned. "I'm not sure I want to show off how throwing a ball the whole afternoon for the *kinder* has left my shoulder aching."

"Only *half* the afternoon," she replied, wagging her finger. "The other half I was throwing the ball."

"You look as fresh as if you'd gotten a *gut* night's sleep. Don't rub it in."

She closed her eyes as the voices swelled out of the barn

and surrounded them with "Amazing Grace." It was one of her favorite songs.

"You look pensive. Singings are supposed to be fun." He leaned against the wall by the door.

"Just listening," she said quietly. "A joyous noise unto the Lord."

"The hundredth psalm."

She nodded. "One of my *mamm*'s favorite verses, and whenever she reads it aloud, I imagine a grand parade entering the Lord's presence, everyone joyous and filled with music they couldn't keep inside."

"I know what you mean."

He did. He almost always had understood her without long explanations. Not once had he tried to make her into something she wasn't. When she looked at him, his face was half-lit by the lamps in the barn. His eyes burned through her, searing her with sweetness. He moved toward her.

She held her breath. His face neared hers, and she closed her eyes. Had time slowed to a crawl? What other explanation was there for his lips taking so long to reach hers? Her hands began to move toward his shoulders when someone stepped out of the barn and called to her.

Micah. If her brother discovered her about to kiss Nathaniel, she'd hear no end to the teasing.

Her eyes popped open. Nathaniel wasn't slanting toward her. Had she only imagined he intended to kiss her? Especially in such a public place with many witnesses? Perhaps she'd imagined his intentions in the attic, too.

As the song came to an end, Micah called, "Why are you loitering out here? The more the merrier." With a wave of his arm, he went inside.

Nathaniel glanced into the barn as dozens of conversations began among the singers. "Shall we go in? You can sing, and I can croak."

He must not have noticed her silly anticipation of his kiss. Doing her best to laugh at his jest, she walked in with him. The singers rose to help themselves to the cider and lemonade waiting among the snacks. In the busy crowd, she was separated from Nathaniel.

Esther thanked someone who handed her a cup of cider. She didn't notice who it was as she looked for Nathaniel. Not seeing him, she let herself get drawn into a conversation with Neva, Celeste Barkman and Katie Kay Lapp, the bishop's daughter. She realized Celeste and Katie Kay were peppering Neva with questions about Nathaniel.

"I don't know," her assistant teacher said in a tone that suggested she'd repeated the same words over and over. "Ask Esther. She's spent more time with Nathaniel and Jacob than I have."

The two young women whirled to Esther. She couldn't miss the relief on Neva's face. Katie Kay and Celeste were known as *blabbermauls*, and both of them fired a question at Esther. They exchanged a glance, then looked at her again... and both at the same time again.

Esther tried not to smile at the exasperated look they shot each other. Before they could speak a third time, someone clapped his hands and called for everyone to take a seat.

As the others rushed to the table, she drained the cup and put it beside others on a tray that would be returned to the kitchen later. She realized her mistake when she turned and saw Nathaniel at the far end with Katie Kay across from him and Celeste to his left. Katie Kay giggled as if what he'd said was the funniest thing she'd ever heard.

I doubt he's talking about alpacas with her. The ill-mannered thought burst through Esther's mind before she could halt it. Why was she acting oddly? Friendship was all she'd told

Nathaniel they should share. It *was* all she wanted. Right? Right! If she ever offered her heart again, the man would be stolid and settled with the quiet dignity her *daed* had possessed. Watching Katie Kay flirt with Nathaniel made Esther's stomach cramp, as if she'd eaten too many green apples.

She looked away and saw her brother Micah leaning against some bales of hay by the snack tables. His arms were crossed in front of his chest and his face was blank. Except for his eyes. They narrowed slightly when Katie Kay giggled again at something Nathaniel said.

Esther had suspected for several months that her brother had a crush on the bishop's daughter, though, as far as she knew, Micah had never asked Katie Kay if he could drive her home from a singing. It wasn't easy to think of her jovial, outgoing brother as shy, but he was around the tall blonde. That, as much as anything, told her how much he liked Katie Kay.

Now the girl he liked was flirting openly with Nathaniel, his *gut* friend.

Walking over to him, Esther said, "Micah, if—"

"Everything is fine," he retorted sharply. "I want to stand over here. Okay?"

"Okay." She wasn't going to argue with him when she could see how distressed he was. "Do you mind if I stand here, too?"

"*Ja.*"

His answer surprised her, but she simply nodded before she took one of the last empty seats at the table. It was on the end of a bench with nobody sitting across from her. She smiled at the people sitting near her and joined in the singing as each new song was chosen. Her eyes swiveled from Nathaniel to Micah and back. Her brother was growing more dismayed, but Nathaniel was grinning as if he were having the best night of his life.

When the last song was sung, the pitchers were empty and the last cookie was gone, the participants stood. Some, including Esther, carried empty plates and cups to the house. The men hooked their horses to their buggies and waited for the girls who'd agreed to ride home with them. Though nobody was supposed to take note of who rode with whom, Esther knew hers weren't the only eyes noticing how Katie Kay claimed a spot in Nathaniel's buggy before he gave the command to his horse to start. Certainly Celeste saw, because she pouted for a moment before setting her sights on someone else. Soon she was perched on a seat and heading down the farm lane toward the main road, as well.

Esther stood by the barn door and watched the buggies roll away. Several of the men had mentioned how much their younger sisters and brothers had enjoyed playing ball with her, but not one asked if she needed a ride home.

Even Nathaniel, it seemed. She'd thought—twice—he was about to kiss her, but now he drove away with another girl. *Don't blame him for your overactive imagination.* She sighed, knowing her conscience was right.

"It looks as if we both struck out tonight." Micah jammed his hands into his pockets and frowned in the direction of the departing buggies. "I figured you'd ride home with Nathaniel."

"He didn't ask me." The words burst out of her before she could halt them.

"Oh." Micah put his arm around her shoulders and gave them a squeeze. "Let's go home."

She nodded, not trusting her voice.

The next evening, Esther was putting a casserole in the oven when the door opened. As she straightened, Leah Beiler entered. Leah wore a kerchief over her hair, and like Esther, her feet were bare. Her dress was black because she was still in mourning for her brother who'd died earlier in the year, but her eyes glistened with happiness. That, as much as the fact that Ezra was always whistling a cheerful tune, had been signs of how they'd fallen in love again after years apart, separated by miles and misunderstandings.

Would Esther offer her heart again to Alvin Lee if she had the chance? No! Not even if he put an end to his wild life and made a commitment to live according to the rules of the *Ordnung*. He needed to care about something other than drinking and racing. He must start looking toward the future.

As Nathaniel clearly was, because he'd asked Katie Kay to ride home with him. She shouldn't be bothered, but she was. Pretending she wasn't was lying to herself.

Help me remember what's best for both of us, she prayed.

She put a smile on her face. "Perfect timing, Leah. I can't make any other preparations for supper until after the casserole has cooked for half an hour. Would you like something to drink?"

"Do you have lemonade or cider?" asked Leah. "It's too hot for anything else."

"I know." Esther opened the fridge and took out a pitcher of cool cider. Moisture immediately formed on its sides and around the bottom when she set it on the counter. "It feels more like August than October."

Leah took two glasses out of the cupboard and picked up the pitcher, then gave Esther a shy smile because she'd acted as if she already lived in the farmhouse.

With a laugh, Esther asked, "If you hold that pitcher all afternoon, the cider will get warm."

"Oh, *ja*." Leah poured two glasses before handing Esther the pitcher.

She put it in the fridge. "Let's sit on the porch. Maybe there's a breath of air out there." She gave Leah another teasing grin. "And who knows? You might catch sight of your future husband."

"I like how you think."

Esther kept her smile in place by exerting all her willpower. If Leah had any idea of the course of Esther's endless circle of thoughts about Nathaniel and Katie Kay, she'd know Esther's teasing was only an act.

They sat on the porch and sipped their drinks. Few insects could be seen in the wake of overnight frosts the previous week, so there were no distractions as the sun fell slowly toward the western horizon.

Leah put her emptied glass on the floor by her chair. "Would you be one of my *Newehockers*? Unless Ezra has already asked you."

"He hasn't, and I'd be honored." The four attendants to the bride and groom needed to be available throughout the wedding day to help with everything from emotional support to running errands.

"Gut!" Leah's smile became bashful. "I can't believe this is finally happening."

"I can. Ezra never looked at another girl until you came back."

Leah flushed. "You shouldn't say such things."

"I'm only being honest."

"Esther, will you be as honest when I ask you what I have to ask you?"

"I'm always honest."

"Except when you think you might hurt someone's feelings with the truth. Don't deny it. I've seen you skirt the truth, though I've never heard you lie." She looked steadily at Esther. "Tell me the truth. Are you going to be okay with me taking over the household chores?" Before Esther could answer, Leah hurried on, "I know you've been in charge of the household since Wanda moved into the *dawdi haus*. Your brothers tell me what a *gut* job you've been doing."

"I'll be more than okay with you taking over the house."

"I'm glad that's cleared up. I didn't want to step on your toes."

She took Leah's hand and squeezed it. "Please feel free to step on my toes. I'll be glad to hand over anything you prefer to do yourself. It'll give me more time to focus on my scholars."

"How are the lessons going?"

"What do you mean?" she asked.

Leah's twinkling eyes warned she wasn't talking about school. She laughed. "Just teasing. How's Nathaniel doing with learning to take care of his alpacas?"

"I've taught him pretty much all I know until one of the pregnant females is ready to deliver. Once one of them has its cria, he'll know everything I know about them."

"I'm sure you'll find some other reason to visit the farm and make sure he's doing things right." With a wink, Leah stood. She picked up her empty glass and went into the house.

Esther didn't move. She should have been accustomed to the matchmaking now, and Leah hadn't been at the singing to see Nathaniel drive away with Katie Kay. Why hadn't Esther given her soon-to-be sister-in-law a teasing answer in return, as she had when Leah talked about taking over the household chores?

Because, she knew too well, she didn't care who did the cooking and cleaning, but she cared far too much about Nathaniel. The worrisome part was she didn't know how to change that.

Or if she wanted to, and that troubled her the most.

★ ★ ★

Nathaniel turned his buggy onto the lane leading to the Stoltzfus farm. Beside him, Jacob was almost jumping in his excitement and anticipation. The boy held his skates, the ones Esther had found in the attic, on his lap. He'd wanted to wear them in the buggy, but Nathaniel had refused. The boy could slip and fall getting in or out.

As he drew the buggy around the back of the house, he smiled. Esther was outside hanging up laundry. The clothes flapped around her in the gentle breeze, sending the fragrance of detergent spilling through the air.

She paused and looked around the shirt she held. Her eyes widened, and he knew she was surprised to see him and Jacob. After she finished pinning the shirt, she picked up the empty laundry basket and walked toward the buggy.

Nathaniel had already climbed out, and Jacob was jumping down beside him, his roller skates thumping against its side.

"Ready?" Nathaniel called to her.

"For what?"

He heard the note of caution in her voice that never had been there when they were younger. What—or who—had stolen Esther's daring attitude? It couldn't be just growing up and becoming a teacher and wanting to be a role model for her scholars.

He lifted two pairs of Rollerblades out of the buggy. One was black and his perfect size. The other pair was a garish pink, the only ones he'd seen in what he guessed was her size. "It's past time to prove you've still got your skating skills. These should fit you."

"I've got some, too!" piped up Jacob.

Esther put the basket on the grass. Her gaze riveted on the bright pink skates. "Where did you find *those*?"

"At a sports store Amos recommended." Nathaniel

grinned. "They didn't have any black or white ones in your size on the shelves, so I got these."

When he held them out to her, she took the Rollerblades, examining them with curiosity. "I've never used these kinds of skates."

"You've been ice skating, right?"

She nodded. "Years ago. The pond seldom freezes hard enough."

"This is supposed to be like ice skating."

"Supposed to be?" Her eyes widened again. "Don't you know?"

"I haven't tried mine yet."

She pressed the pink skates into his hand. "Let me know how it goes."

"You don't want to try?"

"Even if I did, those are so—so—"

"Pink?" He chuckled. "If it makes you feel better, get some black shoe polish and cover the color. We'll wait."

Jacob frowned. "I want to skate now. You said as soon as we got here, we'd skate."

Nathaniel motioned toward the boy with the hand holding the pink skates. "You heard him. Are you going to disappoint him because of the color of a pair of skates?" He leaned toward her. "Don't you want to try them?"

He could see she was torn as she looked from where Jacob sat on the buggy's step lacing on his skates. Maybe the daring young girl hadn't vanished completely.

She grabbed the basket and said, "Have fun." She started toward the house.

"I dare you to try them," he called to her back.

He half expected her to keep walking as she ignored his soft words. Esther the Pester wouldn't have been able to, but this far more cautious woman probably could.

When she faced him, he made sure he wasn't grinning in triumph. She wagged a finger toward him. "I don't take dares any longer. I'm not a *kind*."

"I can see that, but if you don't take dares, do you still have fun?"

"In bright pink Rollerblades?"

"Don't you at least want to try them?" He raised his brows in an expression he hoped said he was daring her again.

With a mutter of something he didn't quite get and knew he'd be wise not to ask her to repeat, she dropped the basket and snatched the Rollerblades out of his hand. She sat, pulling the skates onto her bare feet.

Nathaniel yanked off his workboots and secured his skates tightly. He hadn't been ice-skating in years, but he remembered the boots needed to be secure or he was more likely to fall.

Esther stood beside him, rocking gently in every direction. She raised her arms to try to keep her balance. She almost fell when she laughed as Jacob couldn't stop before hitting the grass and dropped to his knees in it. The boy laughed, but Nathaniel's eyes were focused on her face.

It glowed with an excitement he'd seen only when she was playing ball with her scholars or working with the alpacas. This, he was convinced, was the real Esther, the one she struggled to submerge behind a cloak of utter respectability.

Why? he ached to shout. *Why can't you be yourself all the time?*

He didn't ask the question. Instead, he got to his feet. He took her hands and struggled not to wobble. The man at the shop had assured him anyone who had experience with ice-skating would have no trouble with inline skates. Nathaniel had had plenty of practice during the long, cold winters in Indiana. Now he wondered if the man had said that in hopes of making a sale.

As he drew Esther with slow, unsteady steps into the middle of the paved area between the house and the barn, he admitted to himself that the real reason he'd bought her the skates was for the opportunity to hold her hands as they had fun. She laughed when he struck the grass at the far end of the pavement and collapsed as Jacob had. Somehow she managed to remain on her feet.

Pushing himself back up, he dusted off his trousers. "You could have warned me how close I was to the edge."

"You could have found me skates that aren't bright pink." She folded her arms in front of her, but her scowl didn't match her sparkling eyes.

"I told you they were the only ones in your size."

"On the shelves. Did you ask what was stored in the back?"

He shook his head, unable to keep from grinning. "Probably should have."

"*Ja.* You probably should have." Her feigned frown fell away, and she chuckled. "Let's see if we can go a little farther."

She pushed off and was gliding across the pavement before he could grasp her hands again. With the skill she'd always had as a *kind*, she quickly mastered the Rollerblades and was spinning forward and backward.

More slowly, Nathaniel figured out how to remain on his feet. He doubted he'd ever be able to go backward, as she was, but he enjoyed skating with her and Jacob. The boy didn't seem to be bothered by his falls. He bounced up after each one, including one that left his trousers with a ripped knee.

"Someone's coming," called Jacob.

Nathaniel looped one arm around Jacob and another

around Esther as a buggy came at a fast pace up the farm lane. He saw Reuben holding the reins. When Esther tensed beside him, he knew she'd recognized the bishop, too. There could be only one reason for Reuben to be driving with such a determined expression on his face.

"Esther," he began.

She didn't let him finish. Sitting, she began to unhook the bright pink skates as she said, "Jacob, let's go inside and get some cookies and cider."

"Are there any of your *mamm*'s chocolate chip cookies?"

"Let's see." She had the skates off and was herding the boy ahead of her toward the house by the time the bishop's buggy stopped next to Nathaniel's. She glanced back, and Nathaniel saw anxiety on her face.

Reuben didn't waste time with a greeting as he stepped out of his buggy. "I don't think we can wait any longer. The *doktors* are concerned because Titus seems to be taking a turn for the worse. They told me if the boy wants to see his *onkel* alive, he should come soon."

"We'll arrange for him to go tomorrow."

The bishop nodded, his face lined with exhaustion and sorrow. "*Danki*, Nathaniel. You and Esther have been a blessing for that boy." He glanced at the pink Rollerblades she'd left in the grass and smiled. "Though I can't say I would have approved of those if I'd been asked. *Gut* neither of you asked me." He turned to his buggy. "Let me know how the visit to the hospital goes."

"If Jacob wants to go."

Reuben halted. "You don't think he'll want to go?"

"He's been reluctant when I've asked him. Esther believes it's because he was in the hospital so long himself."

The bishop considered Nathaniel's words, then nodded.

"We're blessed to have Esther as our teacher. She understands *kinder* well. Someday, she'll be a fine *mamm*."

Nathaniel must have said something sensible because the bishop continued on to his buggy. He had no idea what he'd said. Reuben's words were a cold slap of reality. *Ja*, Esther would be an excellent *mamm*. She deserved a man who could give her *kinder*. That couldn't be Nathaniel Zook.

The thought followed him into the house as he gently broke the news to Jacob, who was enjoying some cookies, that his *onkel* wasn't doing well. He didn't have details, because he realized he hadn't gotten them from Reuben.

"Do you want to go to the hospital to see your *onkel*?" he asked.

"Why can't I wait until he comes home? I hate hospitals!"

He looked over the boy's head to Esther whose face had lost all color. She comprehended, as the boy didn't, what it meant for the *doktors* to suggest he visit.

She sat beside Jacob. "I don't like hospitals either, but I think it's important you visit your *onkel*."

"Will you come with me, Esther?"

Surprise filled her eyes, and Nathaniel couldn't fault her. He hadn't expected Jacob to ask her to join them at the hospital that was on the western edge of the city of Lancaster.

She didn't hesitate. "If you want me to, I will."

Her response didn't surprise Nathaniel. Esther would always be there for her scholars or any *kind*. Another sign that he needed to spend less time with her because he was the wrong man for her.

So, why did life feel perfect when they were together?

Chapter Eleven

Esther didn't regret agreeing to go with Nathaniel and Jacob to the hospital, but that did nothing to lessen her dread about what they'd find there. In the weeks since Titus Fisher had his stroke, no *gut* news had come from the hospital. The reports she'd heard from Reuben and from Isaiah were the same—the old man showed no signs of recovery. His heart remained strong, but it was as if his mind had already departed.

She made arrangements for an *Englisch* driver, Gerry, to take them to the hospital the next morning in his white van. Also, she alerted her assistant teacher that Neva would be the sole teacher today.

When Gerry's van pulled into the farm lane, Esther hurried outside. The day promised to be another unseasonably warm one, so she didn't bring a coat or a shawl. She wore her cranberry dress and her best black apron. Beneath her black bonnet, her *kapp* was crisply pressed, and she wore un-snagged black stockings and her sneakers.

She watched while Gerry turned his van around so it was headed toward the road. The white van with a dent in its rear left bumper beside a Phillies bumper sticker was a familiar sight in Paradise Springs. The retired *Englischer*, who always wore a baseball cap, no matter the season, provided a vital service to the plain communities. He was available to drive anyone to places too far to travel to in a buggy. Also he'd drop passengers off and pick them up at the train station and the bus station in Lancaster. *Englischers* could leave their cars in the parking lot, but that wouldn't work with a horse and buggy. Though he claimed not to understand *Deitsch*, Esther suspected Gerry knew quite a few basic phrases after spending so much time with Amish and Mennonites.

"Good morning, Esther," he said when he opened the door to let her climb in. "It's good to see you again."

"How are you, Gerry?" She sat on the middle bench.

"Good enough for an old coot." He winked and closed the door as she pulled the seat belt over her shoulder. As she locked it in place, he slid behind the wheel. "Did your students like those colored pencils you bought for them before school started?"

"Ja." The *Englisch* driver had a sharp memory, another sign he cared about his passengers.

While Gerry chattered about baseball, his favorite topic even when the Philadelphia team wasn't in the playoffs, Esther sat with her purse on her lap and stared straight ahead. If she looked out the side windows at the landscape racing past at a speed no buggy could ever obtain, her stomach would rebel. She was already distressed enough about how Jacob would handle the upcoming visit. She didn't need to add nausea to the situation.

Gerry flipped the turn signal and pulled into the lane to Nathaniel's farm more quickly than she'd expected. She took a steadying breath when the van slowed to a stop between the house and the barn. Glancing at the empty field where the alpacas had been, she wondered how they were faring inside. They'd be as eager to return outdoors as she was to have the visit to the hospital over.

As if he were bound for the circus rather than the hospital, Jacob bounced out of the house. He would have examined every inch of the van if Nathaniel hadn't told him that they needed to get in because Gerry might have other people waiting for a ride. As he climbed in, the boy noticed Gerry's Phillies cap. He edged past Esther and perched behind their driver. Nathaniel sat on the back bench and reminded Jacob to latch his seat belt. When she realized he didn't know how, Esther helped him.

Jacob peppered Gerry with questions about post-season baseball games as they drove to the hospital. Soon they were talking as if they were the best of friends, arguing the strengths and weaknesses of the various teams.

"How are you doing?" Nathaniel whispered from the seat behind her.

She turned to see him leaning forward. Their faces were only inches from each other. She backed away. Or tried to, because her seat belt caught, holding her in place. When he grinned, she did, as well. It would be silly to try to hide her reaction when it must have been obvious on her face.

"I'll be glad when this is over," she murmured, though she needn't have worried about Jacob. He was too enthralled with Gerry's opinion of the upcoming World Series to notice anything else.

"Me, too." His eyes shifted toward the boy. "He hasn't asked a single question."

She nodded, knowing he was worried about Jacob. She was, too. Jacob was holding so much inside himself. He must release some of it, or…she wasn't sure what would happen, but it couldn't be *gut* for the boy.

Neither she nor Nathaniel said anything else while the van headed along Route 30 toward Lancaster. When Gerry pulled into a parking lot in front of a four-story white building, she saw a sign pointing ambulances to the emergency room. She looked at the rows of windows that reflected a metallic blue shine, and she wondered if Jacob's *onkel* was behind one of them.

Gerry stopped in a parking spot that would have been shaded by some spindly trees in the summer. Now sunlight pushed past empty branches to spill onto the asphalt. He shut off the engine.

"When will you want to return?" Gerry asked, reaching to turn on the radio. The sounds of voices discussing the upcoming baseball games filled the van.

"We shouldn't be more than an hour," Nathaniel said.

"Take all the time you need. I don't have anywhere else to be the rest of the afternoon."

"Danki," he said, then quickly added, "Thank you."

"Anytime." Gerry folded his arms on the wheel and looked at where Jacob was staring at the hospital. "Like I said, take all the time you and the boy need."

Nathaniel got out first. Esther was glad for his help, and she had to force herself to relinquish his hand before they walked through the automatic doors. Jacob was delighted with how they worked with a soft whoosh, and she guessed he would have liked to go in and out a few more times. Instead, Nathaniel herded him toward a reception desk.

Esther followed. She was uneasy in hospitals, but found them fascinating at the same time. People who came to them were often sick to the point of dying, and she despised how they must be suffering. On the other hand, she was impressed and intrigued by the easy efficiency and skill the staff showed as they handled emergencies and wielded the machinery that saved lives.

The receptionist looked over her dark-rimmed glasses as they approached. "May I help you?"

"We're here to visit Titus Fisher," Esther said quietly. "Can you tell us which room he's in?"

"Are you family?"

"Jacob is." She glanced at the boy who was watching people go in and out the doors.

"Let me see which room Mr. Fisher is in." She typed on the keyboard in front of her, then said, "Mr. Fisher is in the ICU."

Jacob, who clearly had been listening, frowned. "I see you, too, but what about my *onkel*?"

"ICU means the intensive care unit," Esther explained.

"Oh." The boy tapped his toe against the floor, embarrassed at his mistake.

"Don't worry, young man," the receptionist said with a compassionate smile. "We've got lots of strange names for things here. It takes a doctor almost ten years to learn them, and they keep inventing new ones."

That brought up Jacob's head. "*Doktors* are really smart, ain't so?"

"Very, so the rest of us can't be expected to know the words they use right away." Turning to Nathaniel and Esther, she said, "The ICU is on the third floor." She pointed to her right. "The elevator is that way. When you reach the third floor, follow the signs marked ICU."

"*Danki*," Esther said, and hoped the receptionist understood she was more grateful for her kindness than for the directions.

Nathaniel led the way toward where three elevators were set on either side of the hallway. He told Jacob which button to push, and the boy did, his eyes glowing with excitement as the elevator went smoothly to the third floor.

Jacob faltered when it came time to step out. Esther looked at him and saw his face was ashen. The full impact of where they were was hitting him. Did he remember similar hallways and equipment from his long stay in the hospital? She wanted to take him in her arms and assure him everything would be all right. She couldn't.

"Let's go," Nathaniel said, his arm draped around Jacob's shoulders.

When Jacob reached out and gripped her hand, Esther matched her steps to the boy's. She glanced at Nathaniel. His jaw was tight, and he stared straight ahead.

The ICU didn't have rooms with doors like the other ones they'd passed. Instead, one side of each room was completely open, so anyone at the nurses' desk could see into it. Some had curtains drawn partway, but the curtains on most were shoved to one side. Monitors beeped in a variety of rhythms and pitches. Outside each room, a television monitor displayed rows of numbers as well as the ragged line she knew was a person's heartbeat. Everything smelled of disinfectant, but it couldn't hide the odors of illness.

A nurse dressed in scrubs almost the exact same shade as the pink Rollerblades came toward them. "May I help you?"

"This is Jacob. He's Titus Fisher's great-nephew," Nathaniel explained.

Sadness rippled swiftly across the woman's face before her professional mask fell into place. "Follow me," she said. As she walked past the nurses' station, she explained to the other staff members the visitors were for Titus Fisher. When she continued toward the far end of the ICU, she added over her shoulder, "Usually we allow only two visitors at a time in here, but when children visit, we like having both parents here."

Esther opened her mouth to reply, then shut it. If the nurse discovered they weren't Jacob's parents, they might not be able to stay with him. She glanced at the boy. He was intently watching the monitors, his face scrunched as he tried to figure out what each line of information meant.

"Here you go," said the nurse as she pulled aside a curtain.

Stepping into the shadowed room, because there was no window, Esther looked at the bed. She'd rarely seen Titus as he seldom attended a church Sunday, but she hadn't expected to see him appearing withered on the pristine sheets. Tubes and other equipment connected him to bags of various colored solutions as well as the monitors.

Jacob's hold tightened on her hand. She winced but didn't pull away. He needed her now. When his lower lip began to quiver, Nathaniel put his arm around the boy's shoulders again. They stood on either side of him, and she guessed Nathaniel's thoughts matched hers. They wished they could protect Jacob from pain and grief and fear.

"Your *onkel* is asleep," she said in not much more than a whisper. If she spoke more loudly, she feared her voice would break. She didn't want to frighten the *kind* more.

"He sleeps a lot," the boy said.

"This is a special kind of sleep where you can talk to him, if you want."

Jacob's brow furrowed. "What kind of sleep is that?"

Before she could answer, Nathaniel asked, "You know how you talk to the alpacas and they understand you, though they can't talk to you?"

The boy nodded, his eyes beginning to glisten as they did whenever the conversation turned to the alpacas.

"It's like that," Nathaniel said. "Right now, your *onkel* isn't able to answer you, but he can hear you. Why don't you talk to him?"

"What should I say?"

"You could tell him how much you love him," Esther suggested.

"That's mushy stuff." His nose wrinkled.

Esther smiled as she hadn't expected she'd do in the ICU. "Then tell him about the alpacas. That's not mushy."

The boy inched toward the bed and grasped the very edge of it. He was careful not to jar any of the wires or tubes, and he gave the IV stands a scowl. Again she wondered what he'd endured when he'd been in the hospital after his parents were killed.

"*Onkel* Titus," he began, "I got my stuff and took it to Nathaniel's, and some things fell into the hole when a stair broke. Otherwise, nothing's been touched. All your bags and boxes—except for the ones that fell in the hole—are there just as you like them."

He glanced over his shoulder at her and Nathaniel, then went on. "I'm staying with Nathaniel Zook. Do you remember him? He used to live in Paradise Springs when he was a kid. He's back now, and he's got alpacas!" The boy's voice filled with excitement as he began to outline in excruciating detail how he was helping take care of the herd and his efforts to get them to trust him.

Esther was glad for the shadows in the room so nobody could see the tears filling her eyes as she gazed at the boy who was brave and loving and compassionate. She wished she had his courage and ability to forgive. Maybe...

She kept herself from looking at Nathaniel. If things had been different. If things *were* different.

Things weren't different. He was walking out with Katie Kay, and he was her friend…just as she'd asked him to be.

But she knew it wouldn't be enough, and she'd thrown away her chance at love by ignoring her heart.

Nathaniel said nothing as he held the curtain open for Esther and Jacob. The boy was once again holding on tightly to her hand. Esther's taut jaw was set, and he couldn't ignore the tears shimmering in her eyes. He couldn't say anything about them, either. He didn't want to bring Jacob's attention to them or embarrass her in the ICU.

What he truly wanted to do was draw her into his arms and hold her until they both stopped shaking. Until he'd stepped into that room, he'd harbored the hope Titus would recover. Now he knew it was impossible. The elderly man hadn't reacted to anything while they were there, and Nathaniel knew that while Titus's body might be alive, his mind was beyond recovery.

In the elevator going down to the main floor, he sought words to comfort Jacob and Esther. He couldn't find any. He wasn't sure there were any, so he remained silent as they walked out of the hospital and toward the white van.

Gerry must have read their faces because he got out and opened the doors without any comment. Jacob claimed the middle bench, and Esther sat with Nathaniel. As soon as they were buckled in, the van started for Paradise Springs.

They hadn't gone more than a mile before Jacob curled up on the seat. The emotions he hadn't shown in the ICU were like a shadow over him. When Esther began to talk to him, Jacob cut her off more sharply than Nathaniel had ever heard him speak to her. Shortly after, the boy fell asleep, exhausted from the visit.

Nathaniel turned to Esther whose gaze was focused on the boy. "*Danki* for coming with us," he whispered. "I wasn't sure how he'd handle seeing the old man."

As he did, she chose words that wouldn't intrude on Jacob's slumber. "He handled it better than either of us." Her voice caught. "He's too familiar with how quickly life can be snuffed out like a candle."

"Yet he knows when the old man dies, he'll have no place to go."

She faced him. "He does have a place to go. He's with you."

"He's welcome to stay at the farm for as long as he wishes, but he needs someone who knows how to be a parent. That's not me."

"You're doing a great job."

He gave a soft snort to disagree. "I depend on those witless beasts my *grossmammi* bought to keep him entertained. Otherwise, I don't know what I'd do. He's becoming more skilled with them than I'll probably ever be."

"You'd have managed to help without the herd."

"You've got a lot of faith in me."

"I do, but I also have a lot of faith God arranged for him to be at the best possible place when his *on*—the old man was taken to be monitored." She corrected herself with a glance at the boy. "God's plans for us are only *gut*."

This time, he managed to silence his disagreement. If God's plans for His *kinder* were only *gut*, then why had Nathaniel lost his hope of being a *daed*? He appreciated every day he'd been given, and he enjoyed having Jacob living with him in that big farmhouse. He was grateful the boy had found happiness as well as frustration with the alpacas. However, the boy was also a reminder of everything Nathaniel wouldn't have in the future.

Chapter Twelve

The day of Ezra and Leah's wedding dawned with the threat of clouds on the horizon, but by the time the service was over shortly before noon, the sun was shining on the bride and groom. Almost everyone in the district had come to the farm for the wedding, as *Mamm* had hoped.

After the service, Esther sat with her brother and new sister-in-law at a corner table among those set in front of the house. Everyone was excited to celebrate the first wedding of the season, especially one so long in the making. She smiled as she watched Ezra and Leah together. They were in love, and her brother had waited for ten years for Leah to return from the *Englisch* world. They deserved every ounce of happiness they could find together.

It was delightful to sit with them as food was served. Stories ran up and down the tables as the guests shared fond and fun memories of the newlyweds. Leah's niece Mandy and Esther's niece Debbie could barely sit still in their excitement, and more than one glass of milk was tipped over among the younger guests.

Mamm was just as happy. She'd had a broken arm and couldn't do much when Joshua, Esther's oldest brother, had married for the second time earlier in the year. She was trying to make up for that with Ezra's wedding as she talked to the many guests and made sure everyone had plenty to eat.

The day sped past, and Esther saw Nathaniel and Jacob in the distance several times. When she noticed Jacob joining other *kinder* for games in the meadow beyond the barn, she was relieved. She hadn't seen him since they went to the hospital. She'd agreed with Nathaniel that a few more days skipping school might help the boy. Now she was glad to discover he hadn't become traumatized and withdrawn again.

Jacob wasn't the only subject she wanted to discuss with Nathaniel, but she never had a chance to talk to him. During the afternoon singing, she'd been in the kitchen with *Mamm*, her sister and other volunteers while they washed plates from the midday meal and readied leftover food for dinner. The married or widowed women had urged her to join the singles for the singing, but she'd demurred after seeing Nathaniel walk into the barn with Katie Kay and Celeste. She didn't want to watch him flirting with them while they flirted with him.

Now the guests were leaving, and she hadn't even said hello to him. She stepped out of the kitchen and huddled into her shawl as the breeze struck her face. It was going to be cold tonight. Looking around the yard, she spotted several men standing near the barn where the buggies were parked.

Through the darkness, she could pick out Nathaniel. Her gaze riveted on him as if a beam of light shone upon his head. There was something about how he stood, straight and sure of himself, that always caught her eyes. Her heart danced at the thought of having a few minutes with him. Just the two of them. She waited for her conscience to remind her that friendship should be all she longed for from him.

It was silent, and her heart rejoiced as if it'd won a great battle.

Esther hesitated. Maybe she should stay away from him while her brain was being overruled by her heart. She might say the wrong thing or suggest she'd changed her mind.

But you have!

Ignoring that small voice of reason, she came down off the steps, but had to jump aside as a trio of young women burst out of the night. They were giggling and talking about the men who were taking them home. When she recognized them as Katie Kay, Celeste and her own cousin Virginia, she greeted them.

They waved with quick smiles, but were intent on their own conversation. Esther flinched when she heard Nathaniel's name, but she couldn't tell which one spoke it because they'd opened the door and the multitude of voices from the kitchen drowned out their words. She assumed it was Katie Kay. She squared her shoulders and crossed the yard. Clearly, if she wanted to speak with Nathaniel she needed to do so before he drove away with the bishop's daughter.

Again she faltered. Should she skip talking with him? No, she needed to know how Jacob was doing because he would be returning to school tomorrow. Because she was racked with jealousy—and she couldn't pretend it was anything else—didn't mean she could relinquish her obligations to her scholars.

The thought added strength to her steps as she left the house lights behind and strode toward the barn. She'd reached the edge of the yard when she heard a voice.

"Guten owed," said someone from the shadows.

Esther peered through the dark, wondering who'd called a "good evening" to her. Her eyes widened when Alvin Lee stepped out into the light flowing from the barn door in front of her. He hadn't attended church services or any other community function since the last time she'd spoken with him, the night she refused to be part of his reckless racing any longer.

There was no mistaking his bright red hair and his sneer. He used that expression most of the time. He had on the simple clothes every Amish man wore, but everything was slightly off. His suspenders had shiny clips peeking out from where he'd loosened his shirt over them. His hair was very short in the style *Englischers* found stylish and the faint lettering of a T-shirt was visible beneath his light blue shirt. She couldn't read the words, but the picture showed men wearing odd makeup and sticking out their tongues. She guessed they belonged to some *Englisch* rock-and-roll band.

She waited for her heart to give a leap as it used to whenever he appeared. Nothing happened. Her heart maintained its steady beat. She murmured a quick prayer of praise that God had helped it heal after Alvin Lee had turned his back on her because she didn't want to go along with his idea of fun and games.

"Heading toward the singing?" He leaned one elbow nonchalantly against the tree. He thought such poses made him look cool.

Cool was the best compliment he could give anyone or anything. In retrospect, she realized he'd never used it while describing her. Not that she needed compliments, then or now. They led to *hochmut*, something Alvin Lee had too much of. He was inordinately proud of his fancy buggy and his unbeaten record in buggy races. Though he'd never admitted it, she'd heard he'd begun wagering money with friends, Amish and *Englisch*, on his driving skills and his horse's speed. That would explain how he could afford to decorate his buggy so wildly.

"The singing was earlier today," Esther said, selecting her words with care. What did he want?

"Glad I missed it. Singings are boring, and nobody ever wants to sing music I like." He flexed his arm, and she saw the unmistakable outline of a package of cigarettes beneath his shirt. Smoking wasn't forbidden by the *Ordnung*, and some older farmers in the area grew tobacco, but it wasn't looked upon favorably, either. "I'm sure it was boring as death." He pushed away from the tree. "Attending singings is for the kids, anyhow. Why don't you come with me, and we'll have some real excitement?"

At last, she realized why he'd shown up after dark. He was looking for people to race with and drink with, and she didn't want to think what else he had in mind. She didn't want any part of it. Not any longer.

"I'm not interested." She turned to walk away.

He stepped in front of her again, blocking her way. "Hey, Essie, are you mad at me?"

"No." She didn't feel anger at him any longer. Nor did she feel special, as she used to when he called her by that nickname. She didn't feel anything but dismay at how he was risking his life for a few minutes of excitement.

"Are you sure? You act like you're mad." His ruddy brows dropped in a frown. "Is it because I asked Luella to ride with me one time?"

"No," she answered, glad she could be honest when he wasn't. New reports of him and Luella riding together in his garish buggy were whispered almost every weekend. Esther had to be grateful that Alvin Lee hadn't decked out his buggy when *she* was riding with him. Otherwise, rumors would have flown about her and him, as well. "I'm not interested tonight."

"Sure you are, Essie. You've always been interested in fun."

"Not your kind of fun. Not anymore."

His eyes narrowed. "You're serious, aren't you?"

"How many different ways do I have to tell you I'm not interested?"

"They got to you, didn't they? Broke your spirit and made you a Goody Two-shoes."

She wasn't quite sure who "Goody Two-shoes" was, but the insult was blatant. "Nobody's broken my spirit. I've simply grown up." She flinched when she remembered uttering those same words to Nathaniel after they'd gone to Titus Fisher's house.

She hurried away, leaving Alvin Lee to grumble behind her. Relief flooded her. She'd spoken with him for the first time since he'd crushed her heart, and she hadn't broken down into tears or been drawn into being a participant in his dangerous races. Maybe she was, as she'd told him and Nathaniel, finally putting her childish ways behind her.

Esther heard him stomp away in the opposite direction. He hadn't pulled his buggy into the barnyard as the others had. With a shudder of dismay, she realized he'd cut himself off from the community as surely as Jacob once had. Would Alvin Lee see the error of his ways and reach out to others again as the boy was doing? Or was he too much a victim of *hochmut* to admit he was wrong?

She continued toward the barn. She wanted to talk to Nathaniel more than ever. She needed to listen to him. He didn't focus completely on himself. Even his idea of adventure was doing something important for his family, not something to give him a few moments of triumph over someone else.

As she neared the men, they were laughing together. She

started to call out, but paused when she heard Nathaniel say, "Ah, I understand you now, Daniel. Playing the field is *gut* in more than baseball."

Her twin brothers roared in appreciative laughter before Micah replied, "Now there will be two of you leaving a trail of broken hearts in your wake."

"No, I wouldn't do that," Daniel said with a chuckle.

"No?" challenged Micah.

"No, and nobody seems to wonder if *I've* got a broken heart."

His twin snorted. "Because nobody's seen any sign of it."

"I like to enjoy the company of lots of girls, and they enjoy my company."

"Because they think you're serious about them." Micah's voice lost all humor. "I got a truly ferocious look this afternoon from Celeste Barkman until she realized I wasn't you, baby brother."

Nathaniel laughed along with Daniel before changing the subject to the upcoming World Series.

Esther knew she should leave. None of them had noticed her yet, and she shouldn't stand there eavesdropping. Yet, if she moved away, they would see her and realize she'd been listening.

The quandary was resolved when Nathaniel and her brothers walked toward the parked buggies. They didn't glance in her direction.

She turned and hurried toward the house. She was a short distance from the kitchen door when it opened, and Celeste and Katie Kay rushed out. They were giggling together as they told her *gut nacht.*

Thin arms were flung around her waist, and she smiled as Jacob hugged her.

"Are you leaving now?" she asked.

"*Ja.* Will you be coming to visit the alpacas soon?"

"I hope to."

"You could drive me home after school tomorrow, and you could see them then." He looked at her with expectation.

She hid her astonishment when he called Nathaniel's farm "home." Not once had he described Titus's place as anything other than his *onkel*'s house. It was a tribute to Nathaniel that the boy had changed. She was grateful to him for helping Jacob, but she shouldn't be surprised. Nathaniel had welcomed the boy as if he were a member of his own family from the very first. Though she was disturbed by how contemptuous Nathaniel had sounded about courting, she had to admit he'd done a *wunderbaar* job with Jacob.

Why had Nathaniel talked about playing the field as her brother Daniel did? She'd heard what sounded like admiration and perhaps envy in his voice at her brother's easy way with the girls.

"Esther?"

Jacob's voice broke into her thoughts, and Esther smiled at the boy. "*Ja.* I'd like to check on the alpacas." She refused to admit she'd accepted the invitation so she could see Nathaniel without everyone else around to distract him.

"I'll tell Nathaniel!" With a wave, he ran toward where the buggies were beginning to leave.

Esther didn't follow. She stayed in the shadows beneath a tree as buggy after buggy drove past. Some contained families or married couples. Others were courting buggies, some with one passenger but most with two. Only one held three crowded in it: Nathaniel's.

She turned to watched Nathaniel's courting buggy head down the farm lane. From where she stood, she could hear Celeste's laugh drifting on the night air. That Jacob was riding with them, acting as a pint-size chaperone, didn't lessen the tightness in her chest or the burning in her eyes.

Nathaniel couldn't ask to drive Esther when she was already home, but why did he have to ask flirtatious Celeste, who hadn't made any secret of her interest in him? Why hadn't he spoken a single word to Esther all day?

Because you avoided him. Oh, how she despised the small voice of honesty in her mind! *Ja,* she'd found ways to stay away from him, but what would it have mattered if she'd shadowed him as Katie Kay and Celeste had? He was enjoying playing the field, an *Englisch* term for enjoying the company of many single girls. *And you told him you weren't interested.*

She'd been sincere when she said that, but was beginning to see her attempts to protect her heart by not risking it had been futile. Her heart ached now more than it had when Alvin Lee pushed her out of his life. God had led her away from that dangerous life, and she should be grateful He'd been wiser than she was. She was, but that did nothing to ease her heart's grief.

God, help me know what to feel. She longed to pray for God to give her insight into why Nathaniel had gazed at her with such strong emotions while they rode from the hospital… and days later blithely drove past her with another woman by his side.

Abruptly the night had become far colder—and lonelier—than she'd guessed it ever could.

Nathaniel turned his buggy onto a shortcut between the Barkman farm and his own. He hadn't planned to go so far out of his way when Jacob needed to be at school tomorrow. However, at this time of night, the winding, hilly road was deserted and the drive was pleasant. As the moonlight shone down on the shorn fields, he was alone save for his thoughts because Jacob was asleep.

He'd enjoyed the wedding more than he'd expected he would. Seeing friends whom he'd known as a *kind* had been fun, and he was glad they hadn't jumped the fence and gone to live among the *Englischers*. Several had married someone he never would have guessed they would. Time had changed them, and he knew they'd faced challenges, too, because they spoke easily of what life had thrown at them since the last time Nathaniel had visited his grandparents. Among the conversations that were often interrupted when someone else recognized him, nobody seemed to notice he said very little about his own youth.

He'd deflected the few questions with answers like, "Things aren't different in Indiana from here," or "Ancient history now. My brain is full of what I need to do at the farm. There isn't room for anything else." Both answers were received with laughter and commiserating nods, which made it easy to change the conversation to anyone other than himself.

However, he hadn't had a chance to spend any time with Esther. He'd known she'd be busy in her role as a *Newehocker*, but he'd hoped to have some time with her. She hadn't come to the singing, though he wouldn't have had much time to talk with her. The singing had gone almost like the one after church. Katie Kay Lapp had monopolized his time that day, not giving him a chance to speak to anyone else. At this afternoon's singing, she'd been flirting with a young man who was a distant cousin of the Stoltzfus family.

He'd been greatly relieved, until Celeste Barkman had pushed past several other people and lamented to him that her brother was going home with someone else and she didn't have a ride. As the Barkman farm wasn't too far out of his way, Nathaniel had felt duty-bound to give her a ride. He hadn't thought much about it until he happened to glance at the Stoltzfuses' house and saw Esther standing alone beneath one of the big trees.

She'd looked upset, though the shadows playing across her face could have masked her true expression. If she'd been disconcerted, was it because he was giving Celeste a ride? An unsettling thought, especially when Esther had stressed over and over she wanted his friendship and nothing more. Why wasn't she being honest with him?

Shouts came behind him, and Nathaniel tightened his hold on the reins. He'd been letting the horse find its own way, but the raucous voices were mixed with loud music coming toward him at a high speed. As Jacob stirred, Nathaniel glanced in his rearview mirror. He was surprised not to see an *Englischer*'s car or truck.

Instead, it was a buggy decked out with more lights and decals than any district's *Ordnung* would have sanctioned. What looked like *Englisch* Christmas lights were strung around the top of the buggy, draped as if on the branches of a pine tree. He wondered how either the driver or the horse could see past the large beacons hooked to the front of the buggy. Twin beams cut through the darkness more brilliantly than an automobile's headlights. The whole configuration reminded him of decked-out tractor-trailers he'd seen on the journey from Indiana to Paradise Springs.

Who was driving such a rig? He couldn't see into the vehicle as it sped past him on the other side of the road, though they were approaching a rise and a sharp corner. Large, too-bright lights were set next to the turn signals at the back, blinding him. When he could see again, it was gone.

He continued to blink, trying to get his eyes accustomed to the darkness again. What a fool that driver was! He prayed God would infuse the driver with some caution.

"What was that?" asked Jacob in a sleepy tone.

"Nothing important. We'll be home soon."

"*Gut.* I want to make sure the alpacas' pen is clean before Esther comes tomorrow."

Nathaniel's hands tightened on the reins, but he loosened his grip before he frightened Bumper. The horse was responsive to the lightest touch.

Trying to keep his voice even, Nathaniel asked, "Esther said she was coming over tomorrow?"

"I asked her. She needs to check the alpacas."

"The veterinarian did."

Jacob yawned. "She knows more about them than Doc Anstine does."

Nathaniel had to admit that was true. She had a rare gift for convincing the shy creatures to trust her as she had with Jacob...and with him. He'd trusted her to tell him the truth, but he wasn't sure she had.

But you haven't been exactly honest with her, ain't so? Again his conscience spoke to him in his *grossmammi*'s voice.

He pushed those thoughts aside as his buggy crested the hill. He frowned. The flashy vehicle was stopped on the shoulder of the road. Slowing, he drew alongside it.

"Is there a problem?" he asked, bringing Bumper to a halt.

"Not with us." Laughter followed the raucous reply.

For the first time, Nathaniel realized that, in addition to the driver, there were a woman and two men in the buggy that had been built to hold two people. He wondered how they managed to stay inside when the buggy hit a bump. Two men were dressed in *Englisch* clothes, but he couldn't tell if they were *Englischer* or young Amish exploiting their *rumspringa* by wearing such styles.

"Nice buggy," the driver said. In the bright light, his red

hair glowed like a fire. "It looks as if it were made by Joshua Stoltzfus."

"I guess so." He really hadn't given the matter any thought. It had been in the barn when he arrived at his grandparents' farm.

"He builds a *gut* buggy."

"I can't imagine any Stoltzfus not doing a *gut* job with anything one of them sets his or her mind to."

"Prove it."

Nathaniel frowned. "Pardon me?"

"Prove it's *gut*. We'll have a race."

He shook his head, aware Jacob was listening. "I don't want to race you."

"Scared I'll beat you?"

The driver's companions began making clucking sounds, something Nathaniel had heard young *Englischers* do when they called someone a coward.

"It doesn't matter why I don't want to race," he said, giving Bumper the command to start again. "I don't want to."

The outrageous buggy matched his pace. "But we do."

"Then you're going to have to find someone else." He kept his horse at a walk.

"We will." The driver leaned out of the buggy and snarled, "One other thing. Stay away from my girl."

He frowned. The red-haired man was trying to pick a fight, futile because Nathaniel wouldn't quarrel with him.

When Nathaniel didn't answer, the driver hissed, "Stay away from Esther Stoltzfus. She's my girl."

"Does she know that?" he retorted before he could halt himself.

The other men in the buggy crowed with laughter, and the driver threw them a furious glare.

"*Komm* on, Alvin Lee," grumbled one of the men. "He's not worth it. Let's go find someone else who's not afraid."

The buggy sped away, and Nathaniel wasn't sorry to see its silly lights vanish over another hill. Beside him, Jacob muttered under his breath.

When Nathaniel asked him what was wrong, Jacob stated, "Racing could hurt Bumper. That would be wrong."

"Very wrong."

"So why do they do it?"

He shrugged. "I don't know. Boredom? Pride? Whatever the reason is, it isn't enough to risk a horse and passengers."

"Would you have raced him if I hadn't been here?"

"No. I'm not bored, and I know *hochmut* is wrong." He grinned at the boy. "I know Bumper is a *gut* horse. I know I don't need to prove it to anyone."

Jacob's eyes grew round, and Nathaniel realized the boy was startled by his words. He waited for the boy to ask another question, but Jacob seemed lost in thought. The boy didn't speak again until they came over the top of another hill only a few miles from home and saw bright lights in front of them.

"What's that?" Jacob pointed along the road.

Nathaniel was about to reply that it must be the redhead's buggy, then realized the bright lights weren't on the road. They looked as if they'd fallen off it.

"Hold on!" he called to Jacob. "Go!" He slapped the reins on Bumper.

As they got closer, he could see the buggy was lying on its side in the ditch. The sound of a horse thrashing and crying out in pain was louder than Bumper's iron shoes on the asphalt. He couldn't hear any other sounds.

After pulling his buggy to the side of the road, taking care not to steer into the ditch, he jumped out.

"Stay here, Jacob."

"The horse—"

"No, stay here. There's nothing you can do for the horse now."

The boy nodded, and Nathaniel ran to the broken buggy. He had to leap over a wheel that had fallen off. Pulling some of the lights forward, he aimed them within the vehicle. One look was enough to show him the two passengers inside were unconscious. Where were the others?

Running to his own buggy, he pulled out a flashlight. He sprayed its light across the ground and saw one crumpled form, then another. He took a step toward them, then paused at the sound of metal wheels in the distance.

Nathaniel looked past the covered bridge on a road intersecting this one. He saw another buggy rushing away into the night. Had it been racing this one? How could the other buggy flee when these people were hurt?

No time for answers now. He scanned the area and breathed a prayer of gratitude when he saw lights from an *Englisch* home less than a quarter mile up the road. He'd send Jacob to have the *Englischers* call 911.

He halted in midstep. He couldn't do that. The boy had seen his parents killed along a country road like this one.

Knowing his rudimentary first aid skills might not be enough to help now, he moved his own buggy far off the road. He told Jacob to remain where he was. Sure the frightened boy would obey, he ran toward the house. He hoped help wouldn't come too late.

Chapter Thirteen

Esther was on time for school the next morning, but several of her scholars were late. She guessed they'd stayed in bed later, as she'd longed to do. It hadn't been easy to face the day…and the fact Nathaniel had left with Celeste from the wedding. He seemed to be doing as he'd discussed with her brothers: playing the field.

She should be pleased he didn't include her in his fun and adventures, but it hurt. A lot. Alvin Lee had dumped her without a backward glance when she urged him to stop his racing. He'd called her a stick-in-the-mud, though he'd tried to convince her to join him again.

Telling herself to concentrate on her job, she looked around her classroom. Jacob wasn't at his desk. She wondered why he hadn't come to school. The other scholars were toiling on worksheets, and the schoolroom was unusually quiet.

Maybe that was why she heard the clatter of buggy wheels

in the school's driveway. So did the scholars, because their heads popped up like rows of woodchucks in a field.

She rose and was about to urge the *kinder* to finish their work when the door opened. In astonishment, she met her brother Joshua's brown eyes. Whatever had brought him to the schoolhouse must be very important because he hadn't taken time to change the greasy shirt and trousers he wore at his buggy shop.

Her niece and nephew jumped to their feet and cried as one, *"Daed!"*

He gave them a quick smile and said, "Everything is fine at home and at the shop. I need to speak to Esther for a moment."

"Once you're done with your numbers," Esther said to the scholars, pleased her voice sounded calm, "start reading the next chapter in your textbooks. Neva and I'll have questions for you on those chapters later." She gave her assistant teacher a tight smile as a couple of the boys groaned.

Neva nodded, and Esther was relieved she could leave the *kinder* with her. Next year she wouldn't have that luxury, because Neva would have a school of her own.

As she walked to the door, Esther saw the scholars exchange worried glances. Apparently neither she nor Joshua had concealed their uneasiness as well as she'd hoped.

Her brother waited until she stepped out of the schoolroom and closed the door. She motioned for him to remain silent as she led him down the steps. He followed her to the swing set.

"Was iss letz, Joshua?" She could imagine too many answers, but pushed those thoughts aside.

"Alvin Lee is in the hospital."

She sank to one of the swings because her knees were

about to buckle. Holding it steady, she whispered, "The hospital?"

"*Ja.* I thought you'd want to know." Joshua didn't meet her eyes, and she wondered how much about Alvin Lee courting her the family had guessed.

"What happened?" she asked, though her twisting gut already warned her the answer would be bad.

"He crashed his buggy last night while racing."

"How is he?" A stupid question. Alvin Lee would only be in the hospital if he was badly hurt. Otherwise, he'd be recovering at home.

"It's not *gut,* Esther. I don't know the details."

"What do you know? Was he alone?" The questions were coming from her automatically, because every sense she had was numb. Alvin Lee had wounded her deeply, but she'd believed she loved him.

"I know Alvin Lee is in the hospital because Isaiah was alerted and came to tell me before he left for the hospital. Luella Hartz was one of the passengers with Alvin Lee. She was treated in the emergency room and released to her parents. From what Isaiah heard, she's pretty badly scraped, and she has a broken leg and some cracked ribs. Two *Englisch* men were in the buggy, too, and they were banged up but nothing is broken." His mouth drew into a straight line. "The buggy was too small for four adults. No wonder it rolled when Alvin Lee couldn't make the corner. If a car had come along..." He shook his head.

Sickness ate through her. Alvin Lee had asked her to ride with him last night. If she had, she'd be the one with broken bones and humiliation. Or it could have been worse. She might be in the hospital, as Alvin Lee was.

God, danki *for putting enough sense in my head to save me from my own foolishness.* She added a prayer that all involved would recover as swiftly as possible.

"I hate to think of what might have happened if help hadn't arrived quickly," Joshua continued when she didn't reply. "They should be grateful Nathaniel went to a nearby *Englisch* house and called 911."

Her stomach dropped more. "Nathaniel? He was there?"

"*Ja.*"

Esther wasn't able to answer. She felt as if someone had struck her. She couldn't catch her breath. Nathaniel? He'd been racing last night? With Alvin Lee? She was rocked by the realization she must have misjudged Nathaniel as she had Alvin Lee. Many times, Nathaniel had spoken of having a *gut* time. Was he—what did *Englischers* call it?—an adrenaline junkie like Alvin Lee?

Jacob had been with him. She asked her brother about the boy, but Joshua couldn't tell her anything. How could Nathaniel have been so careless? Blinding anger rose through her as she jumped to her feet.

"I want to go to the hospital and find out how Alvin Lee is doing," she said.

"They may not tell you." Joshua rubbed his hands together. "*Englisch* hospitals have a lot of rules about protecting a patient's privacy. When Tildie was in the hospital toward the end of her life, I had to argue with the nurses to let some of our friends come there to pray for her."

Esther blinked on searing tears. Though her brother was happy with his new wife and their melded family, the grief of those difficult months when his first wife had been dying of cancer would never leave him completely.

"I know they may not tell me anything, but I should go," she said.

"You know what you need to do, Esther." He gave her a

faint grin. "I know better than to try to stand in your way. From what Isaiah told me, Nathaniel is still at the hospital."

She glanced at the schoolhouse. "What about Jacob?"

"I don't know. Isaiah didn't say anything about him." He put his hand on her shoulder. "What can I do to help, Esther?"

"Call Gerry and tell him I need him to take me to the hospital as soon as he can. He can pick me up here."

"I'll call from the shop." He squeezed her shoulder gently, then strode away to his buggy.

Esther hurried into the school. She had a lot of things to go over with Neva before she left. If Gerry wasn't busy, his white van would be pulling up in front of the school shortly. She needed to be ready.

What a joke! How could she ever be ready to go to the hospital where Alvin Lee was badly injured? As well, she'd see Nathaniel to whom her heart desperately longed to belong...and who clearly wasn't the man she'd believed him to be. One fact remained clear—she had to be there for Jacob because she couldn't trust Nathaniel with him any longer.

Gerry's white van arrived in fewer than fifteen minutes. Esther knew she must have spoken to him on the trip to the same hospital where Jacob's *onkel* was. She must have made arrangements for him to take her home. She must have crossed the parking lot and entered the hospital and gotten directions to Alvin Lee's room. She must have taken the elevator to the proper floor and walked past other rooms and hospital staff.

All of it was a blur as she stood in the doorway of the room where Alvin Lee was. She resisted the urge to run away and looked into the room. Her breath caught as the beeping machines created a strange cacophony in the small room where the curtains were pulled over the window.

For a moment, she wasn't sure if the unmoving patient on the bed was Alvin Lee. She hadn't imagined how many tubes could be used on a single person. One leg was raised in a sling, and she saw metal bolts sticking out of either side. Each was connected to lines and pulleys. Bandages covered his ashen face except where a breathing tube kept raising and lowering his chest. Sprigs of bright red hair sprouted out between layers of gauze. That, as much as his name on the chart in the holder outside his room, told her the man who looked more like a mummy than a living being was Alvin Lee Peachy.

"Oh, Alvin Lee," she murmured, her fingers against her lips. "Why couldn't you be sensible?"

She received no answer as she walked to his bedside. She didn't expect one. A nurse, she wasn't sure which one because everything between her stepping into Gerry's van and this moment seemed like a half-remembered nightmare, had told her Alvin Lee was in what was called a medically induced coma. It had something to do with letting his brain heal from its trauma while keeping his heart beating. Everything else was being done for him by a machine or drugs.

She bowed her head and whispered a prayer. She'd have put her hand on his, except his had an IV taped to it.

Footsteps paused by the door, and she looked over her shoulder, expecting to see a doctor or nurse. Instead Nathaniel stood there. He was almost as haggard as Alvin Lee. A low mat of whiskers darkened his jaw and cheeks, and his eyes looked haunted by what he'd seen.

Suddenly she whirled and flung herself against him. His arms enfolded her, and his hand on her head gently held it to his chest. Her *kapp* crinkled beneath her bonnet as he leaned his cheek against it.

The tears she'd held in flooded down her cheeks and dampened the black vest he'd worn to the wedding. Safe in his arms—and she knew she'd always be safe there—she could surrender to fear and sorrow. She remained in his arms until her weeping faded to hiccupping sobs.

"I'm done," she whispered, raising her head. "Where's Jacob?" She was caught by his wounded gaze, and she wished he'd free his pain as she had. She'd gladly hold him while he wept.

Esther stiffened and pulled away as she recalled what Joshua had told her. Nathaniel had been the one to call an ambulance last night. He'd been there when Alvin Lee was racing. Had they been competing against each other?

Nathaniel put his arm around her shoulders and drew her out of the room. The beeping sound of the machines followed them down the hall to a waiting area. After she'd entered, he followed, closing the door. She looked at Jacob who stood up from where he'd been sitting on what looked like an uncomfortable chair. He appeared as exhausted as Nathaniel, and she realized the boy had been at the hospital since last night.

Jacob threw his arms around her as he had after the wedding last night. Just last night? It seemed more like a decade ago now.

She hugged the boy and kissed his hair, which needed to be brushed. As she looked over his head toward Nathaniel, she had to bite her tongue to halt her furious words. How could he endanger this boy?

Nathaniel's brows lowered, but his voice remained steady as he said, "It was nice of you to come and see him, Esther."

"He didn't know I was there."

"According to his parents, the *doktors* say he can hear us, but he can't speak to us right now."

"Like my *onkel*," Jacob said as he rocked from one foot to the other. "*Onkel* Titus can't talk to us because he's listening to God now. God knows what he needs more than any of us, including the *doktors*. He can't talk to us because it's not easy to listen to God and to us at the same time."

Her eyes burned with new tears. What a simple and beautiful faith he had! Nathaniel's eyes glistened, too, and she knew he was as touched by Jacob's words as she was.

Not looking away from her, Nathaniel said, "Jacob, you remember where the cafeteria is, don't you?"

"*Ja.*"

"Go and get yourself a soda." He pulled several bills out of his pocket. "There should be enough here for some chips, as well."

The boy grinned at the unexpected treat. When Nathaniel told him he'd stay in the waiting room with Esther, Jacob left.

"Go ahead," Nathaniel said. "Tell me what's got you so upset you're practically spitting."

"You."

"Me?" He seemed genuinely puzzled. "Why?"

"I thought you were smarter than this, Nathaniel. I thought you meant it when you said making the farm a success was the great adventure you wanted. And Jacob...how could you risk him?"

Anger honed his voice. "What are you talking about?"

"Racing! How could you race Alvin Lee when a *kind* was in your buggy? Was Celeste in there, too? Were you trying to show off for her?"

"I wouldn't ever do anything that might hurt Jacob or anyone else." His gaze drilled into her. "I thought you knew me better."

"I thought I did, too." Her shoulders sagged. "But when I heard how you were racing Alvin Lee—"

"I didn't race him! He tried to get me to, but I refused."

"I was told—"

"I was the one who went to find a phone to call 911? *Ja*, that's true, but it was because I was the first one to come upon the accident." He dropped to sit on a blue plastic sofa. "After I told him I wouldn't race him, he took off. He must have found someone else to race because we came upon the buggy on its side only a little farther ahead. I don't know whom he was racing because the other buggy was more than a mile away on the far side of the covered bridge out by Lambrights' farm."

She sank to another sofa, facing him as she untied her bonnet and set it beside her on the cushion. "The other driver just left?"

"I told the police I saw a buggy driving away beyond the covered bridge, and they're going to investigate. Of course, it could be someone who wasn't involved. Maybe Alvin Lee was simply driving too fast."

"No. He's too skilled a driver to make such a mistake."

His brows lowered. "How do you know?"

"We all know each other in our district, Nathaniel."

"Be honest with me. You seem to have more knowledge of racing buggies than I'd thought you would."

Esther gnawed on her bottom lip. Why hadn't she kept quiet? She should have pretended she didn't know anything about the young fools who challenged one another.

He reached across the space separating them and took her hand. He clasped it between his. "I'm your friend, Esther. Tell me the truth about how you know so much about Alvin Lee's racing. Did you watch him?"

"Okay, if you want the truth, here it is." She doubted he'd

think the same of her once she divulged what she'd hidden from everyone. "I know about racing. Not because I watched it, but because I was in buggies during races."

He pulled back, releasing her hands. "You could have been killed!"

"I wasn't. By God's *gut* grace, I know now, but at the time it was only meant to be a fun competition." She put up her hands when he opened his mouth to argue. "I learned it's dangerous. When I realized that, I didn't take part in any more races."

"Why did you start?"

Heat rose up her face, and she prayed she wasn't blushing. "Alvin Lee asked me to ride with him in one race. I didn't want to look like a coward."

"Oh."

Esther watched Nathaniel stand and walk toward the hallway. Was he looking for Jacob, or was he eager to get away from a woman who'd been silly?

"Is this why you're cautious about everything now?" he asked without facing her.

"I'm sure that's part of it. When we're young, we can't imagine anything truly terrible happening."

"Some do."

She waited for him to explain his cryptic comment. Silence stretched between them until the faint sounds from beyond the door seemed to grow louder and louder with each breath she took.

Slowly she stood. "Nathaniel, I was foolish, but please don't shut me out."

"I'm not shutting you out." He turned to look at her, his face as blank as the door behind him.

"No? I don't have any idea what you're thinking."

"You don't?" A faint smile tickled the corners of his

mouth. "That's a change. You almost always have known what I'm thinking."

"I don't now. I wish I did."

He closed the distance between them with a pair of steps. Gently he framed her face between his work-roughened hands and tilted it as he whispered, "You're curious what I'm thinking? Do you really want to know?"

"Nathaniel—"

He silenced her as his mouth found hers. She froze, fearing she'd forgotten how to breathe. Then she softened against his broad chest as he deepened the kiss. She slid her arms up his back, wanting to hold on to him and this *wunderbaar* moment. All thoughts of being only his friend were banished from her mind as well as her heart.

He raised his head far enough so his lips could form the words, "*That* was what I was thinking. How much fun it would be to kiss you."

Fun? Was that all their kiss was to him? Fun? Another adventure? She didn't want to think of his jesting words with her brothers, but they rang through her mind.

Playing the field is gut *in more than baseball.*

"Esther…" he began.

The door opened, and Jacob came in. His grin was ringed with chocolate from the candy he'd been eating. He held a half-finished cup of soda in one hand and a crinkled bag of chips in the other.

"I should go," she said, grateful for the interruption.

She picked up her bonnet. If Nathaniel noticed how her hands trembled, he didn't mention it. Somehow, she managed to tell him and Jacob goodbye without stumbling over her words. She didn't wait to hear their replies.

★ ★ ★

What a mess he'd made of everything!

Nathaniel took off his straw hat and hung it by the kitchen door. The alpacas and the other animals were fed and watered and settled for the night. He checked the door out of the barn and the gate to the alpacas' pen to make sure they were locked. They constantly tested every possible spot to find a way out.

As Esther had at the hospital after he'd kissed her.

He couldn't guess why she'd retreated quickly, but he should be relieved she had. What had he been thinking to give in to his yearning to kiss her? A woman considered a man's kiss a prelude to a proposal, and he wouldn't ask her to be his wife. He cared about her too much—he *loved* her too much—to ask her to marry him when he couldn't give her *kinder*. The memory of one perfect kiss would have to be enough for him for the rest of his days.

God, You know I want her in my life. To watch her wed another man, knowing her husband will savor her kisses that set my soul alight, would be the greatest torment I can imagine.

He made himself a glass of warm milk and went into the living room, glad Jacob was upstairs. Sitting in the chair that had been his *grossdawdi*'s, he didn't light a lamp. Instead he stared out into the deepening darkness. It was silent save for the distant yapping of a dog. Not even the sound of a car intruded.

How could he stay in Paradise Springs where he'd see Esther and her husband and their *kinder*? He was realizing now that becoming a farmer and making his grandparents' farm a success had been in large part a cover for his desire to return to Lancaster County and to her. Something he hadn't realized himself until he understood he could have lost her forever in a buggy accident.

Should he give in to his *mamm*'s frequent requests and return home? He could sell the farm and the animals. Ironically, Esther would be his best chance of finding a home for the alpacas. She wanted a herd of her own. He couldn't imagine a better home for his animals—or for himself—than with her.

Stop it! Feeling sorry for himself was a waste of time and energy. The facts were unalterable.

Another thought burst into his head. *All you have to do is tell her the truth.* He needed to, because kissing her had changed everything. She might think he wanted to court her.

He did.

But he couldn't. Not without telling her the truth. He wasn't the man for her.

He needed to think of something else. He'd been shocked when she told him she'd taken part in buggy races. He wondered how many of those friends living a fast life she'd estranged when she came to her senses. Some important ones, he'd guess, by how dim her eyes had become as she spoke.

Abruptly he understood what she was *not* saying. One of those people who'd turned away from her must have been a suitor. It would explain why she'd lost much of her daring, turning into a shadow of the girl he'd known. She needed someone special to bring forth her high spirits again. Someone who understood Esther the Pester resided somewhere deep within her.

Someone like Nathaniel Zook.

He growled a wordless argument with his own thoughts, but halted when Jacob came down the stairs.

"Why are you sitting in the dark?" Jacob asked.

He held out his glass of lukewarm milk to the boy. "Sometimes a man likes to have some quiet time to think."

"*Onkel* Titus used to say that." Taking the glass, Jacob sat on the sofa. He swallowed half the milk in a big gulp.

"Your *onkel* sounds as if he's a very wise man."

"You'll see for yourself when he comes home from the hospital." Sipping more slowly, Jacob grinned. "I'm going to ask *Onkel* Titus if we can get some alpacas to raise on our farm. He's going to like them as much as we do, ain't so?"

Nathaniel let him continue to outline his plans for fixing his *onkel*'s outbuildings for alpacas and how he'd teach Titus what Esther had helped him and Nathaniel learn. There was no reason to dash the boy's dreams tonight, simply because his own had been decimated.

At last, Nathaniel said, "Time for you to get to bed, Jacob. You didn't sleep much last night, and you don't want to fall asleep while they're making cider tomorrow, do you?" Before the wedding, Jacob had told him about a trip the scholars were taking to a neighboring farm to watch windfall apples being squeezed into cider.

"No!" He jumped to his feet, ran out to the sink, rinsed out the glass and put it near the others to be washed after breakfast. With a cheerful wave, Jacob rushed up the stairs. His bedroom door closed with a distant click.

Nathaniel was left in the dark to try to figure out what he'd do and say the next time he saw Esther. As long as he was in Paradise Springs, he couldn't avoid her forever.

Chapter Fourteen

Nathaniel stepped out of his buggy and let the reins drop to the ground. Bumper would stay put until he returned. If the horse thought it was strange they'd returned to the place they'd left ten minutes before, he kept his thoughts to himself as he chomped on dried grass.

Hearing excited voices and a heavy metallic clunk, Nathaniel walked toward an outbuilding at the rear of the Gingerichs' farm where he'd been told the cider press was kept. The aroma of apples reached him long before he stood in the doorway.

Sunlight burst between the planks in the walls and seemed to focus on the large cider press in the middle of the barn. It was a simple contraption. Tall, thick wooden beams stood upright on either side. Stacked on a metal table with narrow gutters across it were planks with apples sandwiched between them. Heavier beams had been set on top of the uppermost plank and a heavy metal weight had been lowered onto them.

From between the planks and running down the gutters to a hole in the side of the table were steady streams of the juice being squeezed out slowly by the weight.

Nathaniel noticed that in a single glance as his eyes adjusted to the dim interior of the barn. His gaze went to where Esther stood with her hands on the shoulders of two smaller scholars. She was making sure they could see the great press and the juice.

It'd been two weeks since he'd said more than hello or goodbye to her when he dropped off Jacob at school or picked him up at the end of the day. He'd known he would see her at services on Sunday if he attended in her district, but he hadn't made up his mind about going or not.

During that time, Alvin Lee Peachy had been released from the hospital into a rehab facility. The community was planning several fund-raising events to help pay for his care, which likely would continue for months, if not years. Nathaniel had seen flyers for a supper to be held next week as well as an auction after the first of the year. He planned to donate the extra furniture his grandparents had collected. If he did decide to sell the farm, the new owners wouldn't have to deal with the chairs.

But that wasn't the reason he'd returned to the Gingerichs' farm shortly after he'd brought Jacob to join the other scholars. He'd met the bishop on way home, and Reuben had shared news with him that he needed to deliver to Esther and the boy immediately.

He took a step into the barn, and Esther's head snapped up as if he'd pulled a string. Her smile evaporated. She bent to whisper to the two scholars beside her. Walking toward him, she caught her assistant's eye and pointed toward him and the door. Neva glanced at him and nodded.

Nathaniel went outside to wait for Esther. As she emerged

from the barn, three apples in her hands, he saw wisps of cobwebs clinging to her dark blue dress. It was the same one she'd worn to her brother's wedding, and its color was a perfect complement to her eyes. His heart did somersaults, but he tried to ignore it.

"I thought you'd already left," Esther said in the cool, polite voice she'd used since the night he'd kissed her.

Not now, he ordered those memories that were both *wunderbaar* and sad. Squaring his shoulders, he said, "I did, but I have some news I didn't want you to hear from anyone else."

His face must have displayed the truth, because she clutched the apples close to her as she whispered, "Jacob's *onkel*?"

"He died this morning."

Tears rushed into her eyes, and he had to fight his hands that immediately wanted to pull her to him so he could offer her what sparse comfort there was. When she glanced at the barn, she asked, "What will happen to Jacob now?"

"I don't know." He swallowed hard. "I need to tell him."

"*We* will tell him. After school." A single tear fell down her cheek. "He's having such a *gut* time, and there's nothing he can do now, anyhow."

"I agree. Let him enjoy the day. I can stay here until…"

She shook her head. "No. We must make this seem like a normal day until we tell him what's happened. If you'd like to help—"

"You know I do."

"Bring Reuben with you," she finished as if he hadn't interrupted.

"*Gut* idea. I'll talk to him." He hesitated, wanting to add that he needed to talk with Esther as well, to clear the air between them. He missed their friendship. How could a single kiss—a single splendid kiss meant to show her how much he cared for her—drive such a wedge between them? He hoped she wanted to recover their friendship as much as he did.

"*Danki.*" She took a step back and wiped away her tears with the back of her hand. "I'll see you and Reuben after school."

He didn't have a chance to reply as she rushed into the barn. No sign of her dismay would be visible on her face when she was among the *kinder*. She'd make sure each of the scholars enjoyed the day. What strength she possessed! Exactly as she had when she was a little girl and kept up with and then surpassed him and her brothers. He'd loved her then, and his childish love had grown into what he wanted to offer her now.

Turning away, he went to his buggy. He'd drive to Reuben's farm and talk to the bishop before going to his own farm to tend to the animals. It was going to be a long, difficult day.

Esther didn't pretend to do work at her desk when the other *kinder* left after school. Jacob stood by a window and watched for Nathaniel's buggy.

"I'm sorry he's late," the boy said for the fourth time in as many minutes. "He's usually on time. Do you think the alpacas are okay?"

"I'm sure they're fine." It wasn't easy to speak past the lump filling her throat.

"What if one is having her cria?"

"Nathaniel knows you don't want to miss that."

"But—" He halted himself, then laughed. "Here he comes now. He won't be able to tease me about being slow in the morning!"

She smiled, but her heart was breaking at the sight of his easy grin. Jacob had become a cheerful *kind* during his time with Nathaniel. Everything was about to change for the boy again, and she wished she could spare him the sorrow.

God, give us the right words and let him know we are here for him, though everyone in his family has gone away.

"Someone's with him," Jacob called from by the window. "It's Reuben. What's he doing here?"

"I'm sure he'll tell us."

"I haven't been fighting again. I'm being honest." His face flushed. "Most of the time, and always when it matters."

She put her arm around his shoulders. Was he trembling hard or was she? "Jacob, you know the bishop doesn't discipline members of our community. You don't need to worry, anyhow." She forced another smile. "You've been a very *gut* boy lately."

His shoulders drooped beneath her arm, and she realized how tense he'd been. She couldn't help recall how he'd mentioned his *onkel* punishing him harshly for the slightest transgression.

The door opened, bringing chilly air into the classroom. Reuben entered first, taking off his straw hat and hanging it where the scholars usually did. Nathaniel followed. As he set his hat on the shelf above the pegs, he looked everywhere but at her and Jacob. His face was drawn and looked years older than it had that morning. The day had been as painful for him as it had for her. Such news shouldn't ever be held as a secret within a heart because it burned like a wildfire, without thought or compassion.

She fought her feet that wanted to speed her across the room so she could draw his arms around her. She stayed where she was.

"Are the alpacas okay?" asked the boy before anyone else could speak.

"They're fine." Nathaniel gave him a gentle smile. "You can see for yourself as soon as we get there."

"Gut!" Jacob shrugged off Esther's arm and sprinted toward the door. "I'm ready. Let's go home now."

She saw the glance the two men exchanged, and she wondered if it was the first time they'd heard Jacob describe Nathaniel's farm as home.

Reuben cleared his throat. "Jacob, can we talk for a minute?"

"Ja," the boy answered, though it was clear from his expression he wished he had any excuse to say no.

The bishop motioned toward the nearest desk. "Why don't you sit down?"

"What's happened?" Jacob's eyes grew wild with fear, and his face became a sickish shade of gray. "They told me to sit down when they told me *Mamm* and *Daed* were dead. Is it *Onkel* Titus? Is he dead?"

Esther knew she should leave the answer to the bishop, but she couldn't bear the pain in the *kind*'s voice. Putting her arms around Jacob, she drew him close to her. He resisted for a moment, then clung to her as if she were a lifesaver in a turbulent sea.

"I'm sorry," she whispered against his hair.

"Danki." His voice was steadier than hers. As he stepped away and looked at Reuben and Nathaniel, he asked in his normal tone, "Can we go home now?"

"Go on out and turn the buggy around, so it'll be ready when we leave," Nathaniel said quietly.

The boy grabbed his hat, coat and lunch box before racing out of the schoolroom. Esther went to the window to watch him scurry to the buggy. He patted Bumper and spoke to him before climbing in and picking up the reins. Except for a brief moment when he'd held on to her, he acted as if nothing had occurred.

"We grieve in different ways," Reuben murmured, as if she'd spoken aloud. Turning to Nathaniel, he added, "You must watch for his moods to change abruptly. He understands more than most *kinder* his age about death and loss, but he's still only eight years old."

Walking away from the window, Esther asked, "What will happen to him now? Titus Fisher was, as far as we could find out, his only living relative."

"He's welcome to stay with me," Nathaniel replied quietly. "For as long as he needs to."

The tears that had scorched her eyes all day threatened to fall when she heard the genuine emotion in his words. Not only had Nathaniel made a positive change in Jacob, but the boy had done the same for him. Nathaniel had become more confident in handling the animals at the farm and had a clear vision of how he could make the farm a success.

If only he wasn't playing the field like Daniel, I could...

She silenced the thoughts. This was neither the time nor the place for them. She should be grateful she knew his intentions.

"That is *gut* of you, Nathaniel," Reuben said. "However, the choice isn't ours. With his *onkel*'s death, Jacob is now a ward of the Commonwealth of Pennsylvania. I received a call earlier today. An *Englisch* social worker named Chloe Lambert will be visiting you at your farm once the funeral is over."

"Is it just a formality?" Esther asked.

The bishop raked his fingers through his beard as he did often when he was distressed. "I wish I could say it was, but Nathaniel isn't related to Jacob, so there will need to be supervision by a social worker."

"What can we do?" Nathaniel asked.

"I'll be talking to the *Leit* about making a plan for taking care of the boy. I suggest you do the same. He has done well at your farm, Nathaniel." Reuben sighed and looked at Esther. "The two of you need to think about the ways you have helped the boy and ways you can in the future."

"We will," Esther said at the same time Nathaniel did. "Will that be enough to convince an *Englisch* social worker Jacob's place is here among us?"

The bishop looked steadily from her to Nathaniel. "We must heed the lesson in the Book of Proverbs. 'Trust in the Lord with all thine heart; and lean not unto thine own understanding. In all thy ways acknowledge Him, and He shall direct thy paths.' He knows what lies ahead and is here to guide us."

"What else can we do?"

She expected Reuben to answer, but instead Nathaniel did. "We must believe our combined efforts and prayer are enough to touch an *Englisch* woman's heart and open her eyes to the truth that Jacob's home is with us."

Chapter Fifteen

Esther closed the teacher's edition of the fifth graders' text-book. She rubbed her tired eyes and looked out at the star-strewn sky. It wasn't late, just after supper, but sunset was so early this time of year. As the weather grew colder, the stars became brighter and somehow felt closer to her window. She leaned back in her chair and turned out the propane light hissing on her bedroom table.

Instantly the sky seemed a richer black, and the stars burned more fiercely. She sat straighter when a shooting star raced across the sky. *Englischers* made wishes on them, but that was a *kind*'s game.

What would she wish if she believed in such silliness? For hearts to be healed, most especially Jacob's. The boy had been stoic during his *onkel*'s funeral, but she'd seen the anger in his eyes when he didn't think anyone was looking at him. He'd started getting into fights at school again and seemed to think everyone was against him. Nothing Esther said made a difference.

You should discuss this with Nathaniel. The thought had nagged her every day for the past week. She'd spoken with him a few times during the funeral, but otherwise she'd avoided him. It was cowardly, she knew, but allowing herself to be drawn to him again would be foolish. He wanted to play the field.

She heard her name shouted up the stairs. "Esther, a call came at the barn for you."

"For me?" She had no idea who'd use the phone to contact her.

Micah answered, "*Ja.* Jacob Fisher called. A cria is coming, and they could use your help."

Esther didn't hesitate. Jumping to her feet, she grabbed a thick wool shawl from the chest by her bed and picked up the bag of supplies she'd packed. She ran down the stairs, barely missing Micah who stood at the bottom.

"Jeremiah is getting your buggy ready," he said.

"*Danki.*" She didn't add anything else as she raced into the kitchen, snatched her bonnet and set it on her head with one hand while opening the door with the other.

The ride to Nathaniel's farm seemed longer in the darkness. There wasn't much traffic, but she slowed at the crest of each hill in case a vehicle was coming. She wasn't worried solely about *Englisch* cars. Despite Alvin Lee's accident, others might foolishly be racing their buggies tonight.

She breathed a sigh of relief when she pulled into Nathaniel's farm lane. The house was dark, but light shone from the barn. She jumped from her buggy, collected her bag and ran in. She started to call out to Nathaniel and Jacob, but clamped her lips closed when she saw the astounding sight in front of her.

In the glow of several lanterns arranged around the barn, Nathaniel stood inside the alpacas' pen, his back to her. He was staring at Jacob. The boy was surrounded by the herd, which seemed to be seeking his attention. He stroked one, then another. None of them shied from his touch. His face was glowing with happiness.

She wanted to praise him for his patience in letting the alpacas come to him. She stayed silent because the sound of her voice might send the excitable creatures fleeing, and that could be dangerous for the one in labor.

Crossing the barn, she opened the gate so she could stand beside Nathaniel. He glanced at her with a wide grin before looking at the boy.

Jacob pushed his way through the herd and loped over to the gate. "Did you see that?"

"You're a *wunderbaar* friend to the alpacas," Esther said, then laughed when one of the braver ones trotted after him, clearly hoping he had something for her to eat. "They've discovered that."

"*Ja.* I like them, and they like me." His eyes glowed with joy.

"Well done," Nathaniel said, clapping his hand on the boy's shoulder with the respect one man showed another.

Esther looked at one corner of the pen where a young alpaca was lying on her side. Nathaniel started to give her a report on the alpaca's labor. She waved him to silence.

"Let the *mamm* alpaca do what she needs to," she said as she knelt in the hay by the gate.

"Shouldn't we do something?" asked Jacob.

"She should do well by herself. If she needs help, we'll be here to offer it. Otherwise, we'll watch and cheer when her cria comes."

"That's it?" asked Nathaniel.

"Alpacas have been giving birth on their own in the wild forever. She'll do fine."

Though Esther saw doubt on their faces, the alpaca proved her right when, about ten minutes later, the cria made its entrance, nose and front legs first. Within moments of its head's appearance, the cria was born. It sniffed the world, trying to find out more about it. The alpaca stretched to nose her newborn. A couple of the other alpacas came over to do the same, but she stood and got between them and her cria.

"Wait here," Esther whispered as she carried her bag closer to the *boppli*.

The *mamm* shied away, but not too far, her eyes remaining on the cria. Speaking in a low, steady voice, Esther opened the bag and withdrew a sling hooked to a handheld scale. She carefully lifted the unsteady cria into the sling and held it up.

"She's sixteen pounds," Esther said with a smile. "A *gut* size for a female cria." Lowering the *boppli* to the hay, she crooked a finger at Jacob. "Come over and see her."

"The *mamm* won't care?"

"They trust you now. Move slowly and don't get between her and the cria."

The boy crept closer. "She's cute."

"Would you like to pick out a name for her?" Nathaniel asked.

"Me?" His grin stretched his cheeks. "You want me to name the cria?"

"If you want to. Take a few days and think it over."

"Ja," Esther said. "Right now, the cria isn't going to do much other than eat and sleep. Her *mamm* will take care of her, but in a few days, the cria will be running about and playing."

Jacob considered that, then asked, "What if something happens to her *mamm*?"

Esther wiped her hands on the towel Nathaniel held out to her. "She's healthy, and she should live a long time. Some live until they're twenty years old."

"My *mamm* wasn't much older when she died."

Esther couldn't move as she stared at the *kind* who was regarding her and Nathaniel with an acceptance beyond his years. Yet she saw the pain he was again trying to hide. Jacob seldom spoke of his parents and never this directly.

"We'll watch over the cria," she replied, "and we won't be the only ones. God keeps a loving eye on all of us."

"Not me."

Nathaniel started to say, "Of course He—"

Esther halted him. One thing she'd learned as a teacher and as an *aenti*, trying to tell *kinder* their feelings were wrong got her nowhere.

"Why do you think God doesn't look out for you?" she asked.

"Why would He? He knows how furious I am with Him. He let my *mamm* and *daed* die, and He let me live so I can't be with them."

Squatting in front of the *kind*, she put her hands on his shoulders. "We have to believe, no matter what happens, God loves us."

"But if He loved me, why...?" His voice cracked as tears filled his eyes that had been joyous moments before.

"Why did He take your parents? I can't give you an answer, Jacob. There are things we can't know now. That's what faith is. Believing in God's *gut* and loving ways when our own hearts are broken."

"I miss them." He leaned into her, reforming his body to fit against hers.

"I know. I miss my *daed*, too."

Jacob raised his head. "You have your *mamm*."

"For which I'm grateful, but that doesn't lessen my sorrow when I think of my *daed* and how he used to make me laugh when I was a little girl." She wiped one of his tears away with the crook of her finger. "If he were here, he'd be in great pain, and I don't want him to suffer."

"My parents would have suffered, too. Really bad. *Onkel* Titus told me I shouldn't want them to stay here."

"It's okay to miss them and want to be with them."

"It is?"

"*Ja*, but we have to believe God has His reasons for healing some of us and for releasing others from their pain by bringing them home to Him. We have to see His grace either way and realize mere humans can't understand what He chooses. But we know God grieves along with us because He loves us."

"Does God cry, too?"

"When we turn away from Him," Nathaniel said. Pointing to the alpaca that had given birth, he added, "Look at her. She's glad because her *boppli* is alive. She wants to keep her cria close to her, to protect and nourish it. That's what makes her happy. Just as God is happy when we are close to Him."

"Oh." Jacob didn't say more as he watched the alpaca and the cria.

"When the cria is old enough to go off on her own," Esther whispered, "the alpaca won't be angry. She knows that is how life is intended to be, and to be angry at her daughter would be as useless as being angry at a piece of hay. That's how parents think, and God is our heavenly Father. He knows sometimes we have to make mistakes, but His love for us never falters. Even if you're angry with Him, He isn't angry with you."

The boy searched their faces, then looked at the alpacas. "He loves me like I love the alpacas." The tension slowly slid from his shoulders. Without another word, he went to the rest of the herd and let them surround him as he petted them.

Nathaniel smiled at Esther, and she saw the same pure happiness in his eyes as the boy's. It was a perfect moment.

And a moment was all it lasted. One moment, because before she could say anything, gravel crunched beneath rubber tires in the driveway. Someone was coming. Someone who wasn't driving in on metal wheels.

Her stomach cramped as the late model *Englisch* car stopped by the house and the driver turned off the engine. Through the windshield in the lights from the dashboard, she could see it was a young woman.

"The social worker." Esther didn't make it a question.

She heard the same uncertainty and dismay in his voice when he said, "We knew the state would be sending someone."

"But why now?"

Nathaniel glanced over his shoulder to where Jacob was relishing his chance to pet the alpacas and feed them by hand. Esther did the same. He knew what she was thinking. It'd been such a *wunderbaar* moment, and it was sad to have it interrupted by the outside world. But the outside world was there, and they must deal with it.

Putting his arm around Esther's shoulders and picking up a lantern, he told Jacob they'd be back in a few minutes. He wasn't sure if the boy heard them because he was enthralled by the alpacas nuzzling him.

The *Englisch* woman was stepping out of the car as they emerged from the barn. Chloe Lambert was nothing like he'd expected. Nothing like he'd feared. Instead of wearing a fancy business suit, the young woman had on khaki pants and a simple blouse. She wore sneakers like Esther's, and her dark hair was short and flattered her round face. One thing was as he'd anticipated. Chloe Lambert carried a briefcase with a long strap to allow it to hang from her shoulder.

"I'm Nathaniel Zook," he said.

She nodded and looked at Esther. "Where's Jacob Fisher?"

"He's feeding the alpacas. I'm Esther, by the way."

"Very nice to meet you, Esther. Is Jacob safe with those animals?"

Esther laughed, but the sound was laced with anxiety. "He's very safe. He's been trying to convince the herd for almost a month to let him get close to them. Tonight that happened just before a new one was born."

She glanced down at Esther's feet. "Is he wearing sneakers, too? Does he need to wear boots?"

"He's fine," Nathaniel said. "Why don't you come in and see for yourself?"

"Thank you. I'd like that." Chloe took a step, then looked steadily at them. "Please understand we want the same thing. What's best for the boy. I'm not your enemy or his."

Nathaniel nodded. "I'm sorry if we gave you that impression."

Miss Lambert smiled kindly. "You haven't. I wanted to make that clear. Now please show me where the boy is."

Esther began talking with the social worker as if they were longtime friends and with an ease Nathaniel couldn't have managed. He remembered the social workers who'd spoken with his parents at the hospital, outlining programs available to him and them. Some had sounded interesting and probably would have been approved by their bishop, but his parents wanted nothing more to do with *Englischers* and hospitals and *doktors* and tests.

Had they been right to distrust the *Englisch* system, or had it been only the unrelenting fear and guilt driving them? He hadn't known then, and he didn't know now. At last he understood how intrusive it was to have someone examining every aspect of his life and how little control he had over the situation.

I can hand control over to You, Lord, and trust You'll direct our paths in a direction where we can travel toward You together.

The prayer eased the initial panic he hadn't been able to submerge. No wonder Miss Lambert thought he saw her as an enemy. As he watched Esther introducing Miss Lambert to Jacob and listened while the social worker spoke to the boy about the alpacas as if they were the most important thing in the world, he relaxed further. He doubted the social worker was as interested in the herd as she acted, but she was allowing Jacob to tell her every detail about the cria's birth. She oohed and aahed over the adorable *boppli*. It was a *gut* way for her to get insight into the boy's life.

A half hour later, they were sitting in Nathaniel's living room. Miss Lambert got out her computer and put it on a chair she'd drawn near where she sat.

"Do you mind?" she asked as she opened her laptop. "I'd like to take notes while we're talking. It'll make it easier for me later to transfer the information to the department's forms."

"Of course not," Nathaniel replied. What else could he say? He hated everything about this situation where each word he spoke could be the wrong one. *Lord, be with us today and guide our words and actions so Miss Lambert sees Jacob belongs here with this community. Here with me!* The last came directly from his heart.

"Let me say again how much I appreciate you being willing to let me come and visit like this, Mr. Zook."

"Please call me Nathaniel."

"Thank you. I appreciate that, and I think it'll be simpler if you call me Chloe."

"*Danki.* I mean, thank you."

She smiled, obviously trying to put them at ease. "I understand enough of the language of the plain folk to know what *danki* means. I've worked with other plain families, which is why I was assigned as Jacob's social worker. If you say something I don't understand, I'll ask you to explain. Please do the same if I say something you don't understand."

Nathaniel nodded and watched Esther do the same. Jacob was hunched on his chair, trying to make himself as small as possible. Did he have any idea why the social worker was there? Probably not. It was more likely he wanted to return to the alpacas.

Chloe looked at Esther. "I understand you are Jacob's teacher."

"I am."

She typed a few keys on her computer, then said, "I know it'll be an imposition, but I'll need to see Jacob at school. I can't let you know before I arrive." She gave Esther a wry smile. "We're supposed to drop in so we see what's really going on. I hope that won't be a problem."

"The scholars—our students are accustomed to having parents come to the school to help. You're welcome to come anytime you need to, but I must ask you not to talk to the *kinder* without their parents' permission."

"That is fair. Will you arrange for me to obtain the permission if I need it?"

"It will be for the best if our bishop does."

"That's Reuben Lapp, right?"

"*Ja.*"

Chloe smiled as she continued typing. "I've already spoken with Bishop Lapp. He expressed his concerns about the situation, and I told him—as I'm telling you—those concerns will be taken into consideration before any decision will be made."

"*Gut.*" Relief was evident in Esther's voice.

When she looked at him, Nathaniel gave her what he hoped she'd see as a bolstering smile. The situation between them might be tenuous now, but she was his greatest ally...as she'd always been. It wasn't a *kind*'s game they were caught up in now, but he knew he could trust she'd be there for him and for Jacob. Her heart was steadfast, and in spite of her trepidation now, he knew she had the courage of the Old Testament woman whose name she shared. That Esther had done all she could to save her people, and Esther Stoltzfus would do no less for an orphaned boy.

His attention was pulled back to the social worker when Chloe said, "Now, Nathaniel, I've got a few questions for you."

When she saw Nathaniel's shoulders stiffen, Esther wanted to put her hand out to him as she had in the schoolroom on the day they'd told Jacob of his *onkel*'s passing. She wasn't sure how Chloe would react, so she clasped her fingers together on her lap.

She listened to questions about Jacob's schedule, what he ate, and where he slept. The boy began to squirm with boredom, and she asked if he could be excused. Her respect for the *Englisch* woman rose when Chloe gave him a warm smile and told him to enjoy his time with the alpacas, but not to spend so much time with them he didn't get his homework done.

"I don't give the *kinder* homework," Esther said when Jacob regarded the social worker with bafflement. "They've got chores, so the scholars complete their work at school. Besides, they need some time to play and be *kinder.*"

Chloe's smile broadened as Jacob made his escape. "I wish more people felt that way. Children need to be children, but too many find themselves in situations where that's impossible." She looked at Nathaniel. "Just a few more questions. I know this must seem like the whole world poking its nose into your business, but we must be certain being here is the best place for Jacob."

"It is." Not a hint of doubt was in his voice or on his face.

"I hope you're right." Glancing at the screen, she asked, "Do you have family in the area, Nathaniel?"

"Not any longer. This farm belonged to my grandparents, and when they died, it became mine."

"So your parents are deceased, too?"

"No. They're in Indiana with my four sisters and younger brother. Two of my sisters are married, and I have several nephews and nieces. They live near my parents."

"So there's nobody here to help you with Jacob?"

"Our community is here to help if we need it." His smile was so tight it looked painful. "So far, we haven't. Jacob and I have gotten along well."

As she'd promised, the social worker had only a few more questions. Esther listened as Nathaniel answered thoughtfully and without hesitation or evasion. When Chloe asked to see the boy's room, Esther didn't follow them upstairs. She remained in the living room, listening to the hiss of the propane lamp and staring at the computer. If she peeked at the screen, would she be able to see what Chloe had written?

She couldn't do that. If the social worker found her snooping, it might be a mark against Nathaniel. What did Chloe think about Jacob's situation? Would she recommend he stay with Nathaniel?

The social worker and Nathaniel returned to the lower

floor. They spoke easily before Nathaniel said he'd go and get Jacob to have a few words with the social worker.

As he went outside, Chloe closed her computer and put it in her bag. "Thank you for taking time to speak with me." She straightened. "I appreciate you being forthcoming. Some people aren't, but you and your husband—"

"Nathaniel isn't my husband."

The social worker stared at her, astonished. "I'm sorry. When I saw you together, I assumed you were married. I know I shouldn't assume anything about anyone, but you two seem like a perfectly matched set..." She turned away, embarrassed.

"Would it make a difference in your recommendation for where Jacob will live?" Esther asked before she could halt herself.

"What?" Chloe faced her.

"If Nathaniel and I were married?"

"Maybe. Maybe not. I can't give you a definite answer. Without any blood relationship between either of you and the boy, it's far more complicated."

"Jacob having a *mamm* and a *daed*..." She halted and amended, "Having a mother and a father would make a difference, wouldn't it?"

"It could." The social worker put the bag's strap over her shoulder. "Don't worry that my mistake will have any impact on this case, Esther. I can see both of you care deeply about the boy. However, sometimes the best thing for a child isn't what the adults around him want. We have to think first and foremost of what will give him the stable home he's never had. We prefer that to be with two parents."

Esther felt her insides turn to ice. She couldn't doubt Chloe's earnestness, but were her words a warning the state would take Jacob away? Somehow she managed to choke out a goodbye as the social worker left to speak to Jacob once more.

Groping for a chair, she sat and stared at the spot where Jacob had been curled up. She didn't move and couldn't think of anything other than watching the boy being taken away from his community and his heritage.

She wasn't sure how long she sat there before Nathaniel returned. He strode into the living room. When she turned her gaze toward him, his face grew grayer.

"What is it?" he asked. "Did she say something to you?"

She explained the short conversation before saying, "Chloe suggested her superiors would prefer Jacob being in a family with two parents who can help him try to overcome the pain he has suffered. We can't offer him that now unless…"

"It sounds as if you want me to ask you to be my wife."

"I don't know what I'm saying, Nathaniel." She surged to her feet. "All I know for sure is Jacob needs to stay here. He's begun to heal, and if he's taken away, he'll lose any progress he's made."

"Did you tell her that?"

"No." Her eyes swam in tears. "I don't think I needed to. She looked dismayed when she found out we aren't married."

"Esther, you're probably the best friend I've ever had. Now and when we were kids, but—"

"That's all we'll ever be." Why did the words taste bitter? She'd told him many times friendship was what she wanted from him. She'd been lying. Not just to him, but to herself. Maybe not at the beginning when she first learned he'd come back to Paradise Springs, but as the days went on and she spent time with him and Jacob. Sometime, during those weeks in spite of her assertions, she'd begun to believe she and Nathaniel might be able to build a life together.

Then he'd kissed her…and her old fears of taking a risk had returned.

His broad hands framed her face and tilted it toward him so his gaze met hers. She saw his sorrow. Did he regret their agreement to be friends, too? Or was his grief focused on Jacob?

"I can't marry you, Esther. Not now." His voice broke. "Not ever."

She pulled away before her tears fell and betrayed her. "*Danki* for telling me that. You've made yourself really clear."

"Esther, wait!" he called as she started to walk away. "I've got a *gut* reason for saying that. I should have told you this right from the beginning, but I was ashamed."

"Of what? Most young men like to play the field, as you put it so tersely."

"What?"

"I heard you and Micah and Daniel laughing at the wedding about how you weren't going to settle down."

"Esther, look at me."

She slowly faced him. "Don't tell me you didn't say that, because I heard you."

"I'm sure you did. What you didn't hear were the words before those. Micah and I were teasing Daniel about his habits of bringing a different girl home from every event. I was repeating his words to him in jest."

"If that's not the reason—"

"The truth is I may never be able to be a *daed*." The resignation in his voice was vivid on his face. It was the expression of a man who had fought long and hard for a goal, but it was still beyond his reach, and it might be forever.

"I don't understand," she whispered.

"After we left Paradise Springs, I came back the next summer."

"I remember." She did. That year she'd been too bold

and told him she planned to marry him. How ironic that sounded now!

"I didn't return the next summer because I was ill." He took a deep breath and said, "I had leukemia."

"Cancer?" she choked out. "I never knew."

"I know. My parents wanted to keep it quiet, even from our neighbors in Indiana. They sold off most of their farmland to pay the bills for my treatment." He rubbed his hands together as if he didn't know what else to do with them. "They were horrified one of their children was weak enough to succumb to such a disease."

"Weakness or strength has nothing to do with it." She pulled his hands apart, folding one between hers. "You know that, don't you?"

"*I* do, but I don't think they've ever accepted the truth. They always believed they or I had done something wrong. Something to call the scourge down on me." His mouth tightened into a straight line. "That's what they call it. The scourge."

"I'm sorry." She was beginning to understand his compassion for Jacob and why it went beyond the simple kindness of helping a *kind* who was alone in the world. He knew too well how it was to be different.

"I appreciate that, Esther."

"You are all right now?"

"As *gut* as if I'd never had cancer. With chemotherapy and radiation, the *Englisch doktors* saved my life from the disease. That's how they saw it. A disease that strikes indiscriminately, not a scourge sent to punish my family." He sighed. "However, the *Englisch doktors* warned me that the treatments probably had made it impossible for me ever to father a *boppli*."

Tears flooding her eyes blurred his face, but she doubted she'd ever be able to erase his desolate expression from her memory.

"Oh, Nathaniel, I'm sorry. I know how you love *kinder*."
She pressed her hands over her heart. "Now you have to worry
about losing Jacob. If you think it'll make a difference—"

"Don't say it, Esther. I won't do that to you. I won't ask
you to take the risk. How many times have you told me
you aren't the same person you were when we were little?
That you like to consider all aspects of an issue before you
make a decision, that you no longer leap before you look
around you."

"Nathaniel—"

"No, Esther, I'm sure of this. I've seen you with your
scholars. You love *kinder*. You light up when they're around,
whether at school or at home with your nieces and nephews.
Or with Jacob who, despite his grumbling, appreciates the
time you spend with him."

"So I have nothing to say about this?"

"What do you mean?"

She stood on tiptoe and pressed her lips against his. When
his arms came around her, they didn't enfold her. They drew
her away but not before she saw the regret in his eyes.

"Stop it, Esther. My *daed* warned me I must be stronger
than I was when I contracted cancer." He groaned. "I never
imagined I'd have to be this strong and push you away."

"Your *daed* is wrong." She took his hand again and folded
it between her fingers as if in prayer. "I was wrong, Nathaniel, when I let myself believe it's a *gut* idea to hide from my
adult pain by putting aside my childhood love of adventure.
Remember what it was like then? We never questioned if
something was worth the risk. We simply went with our
hearts."

"And ended up bruised and battered."

"And happy." She hesitated, then realized if she hoped for
him to open his heart to her, she must be willing to do the

same to him. With a tentative smile, she said, "Well, except for one time I've never forgotten."

"Which time?"

"You don't remember?" She was astonished.

"I'm not sure what you're referring to. We got into a lot of scrapes together, so you'll need to be more specific."

She looked down at their hands. "I'm talking about the day when you were visiting from Indiana and I came over to your grandparents' farm, and I took your hand...like this."

He smiled as he put one finger under her chin and tipped it so her gaze met his. "I do remember. I thought you were the most *wunderbaar* girl I'd ever known." He chuckled. "That hasn't changed."

"I told you I was going to marry you as soon as we were old enough. Remember that?"

"*Ja.* I thought you were joking."

"*I* thought I was going to die of embarrassment."

He put his hands on her shoulders and smiled. "Never be embarrassed, Esther, to tell someone how you feel. You were brave enough to be honest. If more of us were like that, the world would be a better place."

"It didn't feel like that at the time." She took a deep breath, knowing if she backed away from risking her heart now, she'd never be able to risk it again. "I'm not going to be embarrassed now when I tell you I love you. I always have, and I always will. Get that through your thick head, Nathaniel Zook. I love you. Not some *kinder* we might be blessed with some day. You. I'm not saying this because of Jacob. I'm saying this because I can't keep the truth to myself any longer. If you don't love me, tell me, but don't push me away because you're trying to protect me from what God has planned for the future."

She held her breath as he stared at her. Had she been too blunt? Had she pushed too hard?

"That was quite a speech," he said with a grin.

"Don't ask me to repeat it."

"Not even the part when you said you love me?" His arm around her waist drew her to him. As he bent toward her, he whispered, "I want to hear you repeat that every day of our lives, and I'll tell you how much I've always loved you, Esther Stoltzfus. I don't need to be like your brother and play the field." He chuckled. "Actually I was in the outfield when you tumbled into my arms. From that moment, I knew it was where I wanted you always to be. But—"

She put her finger to his lips. "Let's leave our future in God's hands."

"As long as you're in mine." He captured her lips, and she softened against him.

Savoring his kiss and combing her fingers through his thick hair, letting its silk sift between her fingers, she wondered why she'd resisted telling him the truth until now. Some things were worth any amount of risk.

Epilogue

"Hurry, hurry!" called Chloe as she motioned for them to enter a small room beside one of the fancy courtrooms. "You should have been here ten minutes ago so we could review everything before we go before the judge."

"We're sorry. We were delayed." Nathaniel, dressed in his church Sunday *mutze* and white shirt, smiled at Esther. In fact, he hadn't stopped smiling the whole time they rode in Gerry's van from Paradise Springs into the city of Lancaster.

She put her hand on his arm, still a bit unsteady after her bout of sickness that morning. When it first had afflicted her last week, she'd thought she'd contracted some bug. However, the illness came only in the first couple of hours of each morning before easing to a general queasiness the rest of the day. It had continued day after day for nearly ten days now.

This morning, she'd told Nathaniel she believed she was pregnant. His shock had been endearing. She'd warned him that she must go to the midwife and have a test to confirm her pregnancy tomorrow, but she was certain what the test would show. They'd been married only three months, taking their vows barely a month after Ezra and Leah had, and already God had blessed them with a *boppli*.

"As long as you're here now." Chloe smiled at them. "Any questions before we go in?"

Jacob tugged on Nathaniel's sleeve. When Nathaniel bent down, the boy whispered frantically in his ear.

The social worker smiled and answered before Nathaniel spoke. "Down the hall on your right. Don't forget to wash your hands, Jacob. The judge will want to shake your hand when she finalizes your adoption."

As the boy scurried away, Nathaniel put his arm around Esther. They listened while Chloe explained again what would happen when they went into the courtroom. Official paperwork and recommendations from social services would be presented to the judge, who'd already reviewed copies of them. The judge might ask Jacob a few questions, but the procedure was simple and quick.

Jacob rushed into the room as another door opened, and a woman invited them into the courtroom. As they walked in, Jacob took Nathaniel's hand and then Esther's. They went together to a table where they sat facing a lady judge on her high seat behind a sign that read Judge Eloise Probert.

The paperwork was placed in front of the judge who barely glanced at it. She smiled at Jacob and asked him if he understood what was going on.

"*Ja*... I mean, yes, your honor," he replied as he'd been instructed. "Once you say so, I won't be Jacob Fisher any longer. I'll be Jacob Zook, and Nathaniel and Esther will be my new *daed* and *mamm*." He gulped. "I mean, dad and mom."

"That's right, Jacob." Judge Probert had a nice smile and

a gentle voice. "So this is what you want? To be Nathaniel and Esther's son?"

Jacob nodded so hard Esther had to bite her lip not to laugh. She heard a smothered sound from either side of her and saw Nathaniel and Chloe trying not to laugh, too.

"More than anything else in the whole world," Jacob answered. "Except maybe a couple more alpacas for our herd."

This time, nobody restrained their laughter, including the judge. "Well, I'll leave that decision to your new parents. Congratulations, Zook family. From this day forward, you *are* a forever family. All three of you."

Esther hugged Jacob and Nathaniel at the same time. She felt so happy and blessed.

After the paperwork was checked and they signed a few more papers and shook the judge's hand as well as Chloe's, Esther walked out of the courtroom with her husband and their son. They smiled at other families awaiting their turn to go before the judge. Congratulations were called to them, and her face hurt from smiling so widely.

They stepped through the doors and walked toward the tall columns edging the front of the courthouse, Nathaniel said, "You know, the judge got almost everything right."

"Almost?" she asked.

"She said the three of us are a forever family. It's the *four* of us."

Tapping his nose, she said, "So far. Who knows how often God will bless us?"

With a laugh, he spun her into his arms and kissed her soundly. Then, each of them grabbing one of Jacob's hands, they walked toward where the white van was parked. The van that would take their family home.

★ ★ ★ ★ ★

"Get back!"

Definitely a female voice, from the other side of the barn. He walked around the barn. If someone had asked him to guess what he might find there, he wouldn't in a hundred years have guessed correctly.

A young Amish woman—Plain dress, apron, *kapp*—was holding a feed bucket in one hand and a rake in the other, attempting to fend off a rooster. At the moment, the bird was trying to peck the woman's feet.

"What did you do to him?" Daniel asked.

Her eyes widened. The rooster made a swipe at her left foot. The woman once again thrust the feed bucket toward the rooster. "Don't just stand there. This beast won't let me pass."

Daniel knew better than to laugh. He'd been raised with four sisters and a strong-willed mother. So he snatched the rooster up from behind, pinning its wings down with his right arm.

"Where do you want him?"

"His name is Carl, and I want him in the oven if you must know the truth." She dropped the feed bucket and swiped at the golden-blond hair that was spilling out of her *kapp*. "Over there. In the pen."

Daniel dropped the rooster inside and turned to face the woman. She was probably five and a half feet tall and looked to be around twenty years old. Blue eyes the color of forget-me-nots assessed him.

She was also beautiful in the way of Plain women. The sight of her reminded him of yet another reason why he'd left Pennsylvania. Why couldn't his neighbors have been an old couple in their nineties?

"You must be the new neighbor. I'm Becca Schwartz—not Rebecca, just Becca, because my *mamm* decided to do things alphabetically. We thought you might introduce yourself, but I guess you've been busy. *Mamm* would want me to invite you to dinner, but I warn you, I have seven younger siblings, so it's usually a somewhat chaotic affair."

Becca not Rebecca stepped closer.

"Didn't catch your name."

"Daniel…Daniel Glick."

"We didn't even know the place had sold until last week. Most people are leery of farms where the fields are covered with rocks and the house is falling down. I see you haven't done anything to remedy either of those situations."

"I only moved in yesterday."

"Had time to get a horse, though. Get it from Old Tim?"

Before he could answer, a dinner bell rang. "Sounds like dinner's ready. Care to meet the folks?"

"Another time. I have some…um…unpacking to do."

Becca shrugged her shoulders. "Guess I'll be seeing you, then."

"Yeah, I guess."

He'd hoped for peace and solitude.

Instead, he had half a barn, a cantankerous rooster and a pretty neighbor who was a little nosy.

He'd come to Indiana to forget women and to lose himself in making something good from something that was broken.

He'd moved to Indiana because he wanted to be left alone.

Don't miss
The Amish Christmas Secret *by Vannetta Chapman,*
available October 2020 wherever
Love Inspired books and ebooks are sold.

LoveInspired.com

LOVE INSPIRED
INSPIRATIONAL ROMANCE

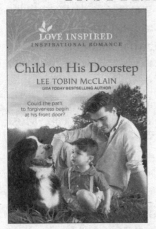

Save $1.00
on the purchase of ANY Love Inspired or Love Inspired Suspense book.

Available wherever books are sold, including most bookstores, supermarkets, drugstores and discount stores.

Save $1.00
on the purchase of any Love Inspired or Love Inspired Suspense book.

Coupon valid until August 31, 2021.
Redeemable at participating outlets in the U.S. and Canada only.
Limit one coupon per customer.

52616916

Canadian Retailers: Harlequin Enterprises ULC will pay the face value of this coupon plus 10.25¢ if submitted by customer for this product only. Any other use constitutes fraud. Coupon is nonassignable. Void if taxed, prohibited or restricted by law. Consumer must pay any government taxes. Void if copied. Inmar Promotional Services ("IPS") customers submit coupons and proof of sales to Harlequin Enterprises ULC, P.O. Box 31000, Scarborough, ON M1R 0E7, Canada. Non-IPS retailer—for reimbursement submit coupons and proof of sales directly to Harlequin Enterprises ULC, Retail Marketing Department, Bay Adelaide Centre, East Tower, 22 Adelaide Street West, 40th Floor, Toronto, Ontario M5H 4E3, Canada.

U.S. Retailers: Harlequin Enterprises ULC will pay the face value of this coupon plus 8¢ if submitted by customer for this product only. Any other use constitutes fraud. Coupon is nonassignable. Void if taxed, prohibited or restricted by law. Consumer must pay any government taxes. Void if copied. For reimbursement submit coupons and proof of sales directly to Harlequin Enterprises ULC 482, NCH Marketing Services, P.O. Box 880001, El Paso, TX 88588-0001, U.S.A. Cash value 1/100 cents.

5 65373 00076 2   (8100)0 12478

LICOUP0820TRADE

LOVE INSPIRED
INSPIRATIONAL ROMANCE

UPLIFTING STORIES OF FAITH, FORGIVENESS AND HOPE.

Join our social communities to connect
with other readers who share your love!

Sign up for the Love Inspired newsletter
at **LoveInspired.com** to be the first
to find out about upcoming titles,
special promotions and exclusive content.

CONNECT WITH US AT:

 Facebook.com/LoveInspiredBooks

 Twitter.com/LoveInspiredBks

Facebook.com/groups/HarlequinConnection